More Praise for the Novels of Emma Wildes

"A luxurious and sensual read. Both deliciously wicked and tenderly romantic. . . . I didn't want it to end!"
—*New York Times* bestselling author Celeste Bradley

"Regency fans will thrill to this superbly sensual tale of an icy widow and two decadent rakes. . . . Balancing deliciously erotic encounters with compelling romantic tension, and populating a convincing historical setting with a strong cast of well-developed characters, prolific romance author Wildes provides a spectacular and skillfully handled story that stands head and shoulders above the average historical romance."
—*Publishers Weekly* (starred review)

"Wickedly delicious and daring, Wildes's tale tantalizes with an erotic fantasy that is also a well-crafted Regency romance. She delivers a page-turner that captures the era, the mores, and the scandalous behavior that lurks beneath the surface."
—*Romantic Times* (4½ stars, top pick)

"Emma Wildes has thoroughly enchanted e-book readers with her emotionally charged story lines. . . . [A] gem of an author . . . Ms. Wildes tells this story with plenty of compassion, humor, and even a bit of suspense to keep readers riveted to each scandalous scene—and everything in between."
—*Romance Junkies*

continued . . .

EMMA WILDES

My Lord Scandal

NOTORIOUS BACHELORS

A SIGNET ECLIPSE BOOK

SIGNET ECLIPSE
Published by New American Library, a division of
Penguin Group (USA) Inc., 375 Hudson Street,
New York, New York 10014, USA
Penguin Group (Canada), 90 Eglinton Avenue East, Suite 700, Toronto,
Ontario M4P 2Y3, Canada (a division of Pearson Penguin Canada Inc.)
Penguin Books Ltd., 80 Strand, London WC2R 0RL, England
Penguin Ireland, 25 St. Stephen's Green, Dublin 2,
Ireland (a division of Penguin Books Ltd.)
Penguin Group (Australia), 250 Camberwell Road, Camberwell, Victoria 3124,
Australia (a division of Pearson Australia Group Pty. Ltd.)
Penguin Books India Pvt. Ltd., 11 Community Centre, Panchsheel Park,
New Delhi - 110 017, India
Penguin Group (NZ), 67 Apollo Drive, Rosedale, North Shore 0632,
New Zealand (a division of Pearson New Zealand Ltd.)
Penguin Books (South Africa) (Pty.) Ltd., 24 Sturdee Avenue,
Rosebank, Johannesburg 2196, South Africa
Penguin Books Ltd., Registered Offices:
80 Strand, London WC2R 0RL, England

First published by Signet Eclipse, an imprint of New American Library,
a division of Penguin Group (USA) Inc.

First Printing, September 2010
10 9 8 7 6 5 4 3 2 1

To my lovely nieces
Megan, Amy, Haley, and Sara

ACKNOWLEDGMENTS

I am lucky to have a wonderful agent in Barbara Po-elle, and a talented editor in Laura Cifelli. As always, my thanks for all you do. I also wish to acknowledge the support of fellow authors Lara Santiago, Morgan Ashbury, and Raina James. You fabulous ladies both challenge and encourage me every single day. The Indiana Chapter of RWA is an example of what the organization wishes to represent in my humble opinion. Whether published or not yet published, they are sisters who share cheers over triumphs and tears when disappointment happens. What a lovely group.

Prologue

It took courage, especially considering the hour.

Yet, she reminded herself, drawing her cloak close around her, for someone with nothing to lose, what did it matter if it was very late, or that the filtered moonlight bathed the stone building in a wash of pale illumination and cast eerie oblongs of shadow from the surrounding headstones?

She carried a covered lantern and lifted it, the tug of the breeze blowing a teasing tendril of loosened hair across her lips. The witching hour, she thought, feeling in her pocket for the key to unlock the ornate door, and a secret....

Perhaps one day she would pen a gothic novel, but now was stark reality, and the protest of the old hinges as she unlocked the door and opened it interrupted the night, making her start.

Nothing whispered past but the breeze, though the air held a stale odor of dust and decay.

Ashes to ashes ...

She shivered, halted at the edge of the doorway, the interior black, silent, waiting.

Lifting the lantern high, she stepped inside.

Chapter One

The alley below was filthy and smelled rank, and if he fell off the ledge, Lord Alexander St. James was fairly certain he would land on a good-sized rat. Since squashing scurrying rodents was not on his list of favorite pastimes, he tightened his grip and gauged the distance to the next roof. It looked to be roughly the distance between London and Edinburgh, but in reality was probably only a few feet.

"What the devil is the matter with you?" a voice hissed out of the darkness. "Hop on over here. This was your idea."

"I do not *hop*," he shot back, unwilling to confess that heights bothered him. They had since the night he'd breached the towering wall of the citadel at Badajoz with the forlorn hope. He still remembered the pounding rain, the ladders swarming with men, and that great, black drop below. . . .

"I know perfectly well this was my idea," he muttered.

"Then I'm sure, unless you have an inclination for a personal tour of Newgate Prison, which, by the by, I do not, you'll agree we need to proceed. It gets closer to dawn by the minute."

Newgate Prison. Alex didn't like confined spaces any more than he liked heights. The story his grandmother had told him just a few days ago made him wish his imagination was a little less vivid. Incarceration in a squalid cell was the last thing he wanted. But for the ones you love, he thought philosophically as he eyed the gap, and he had to admit that he adored his grandmother, risks have to be taken.

That thought proved inspiration enough for him to leap the distance, landing with a dull thud but, thankfully, keeping his balance on the sooty shingles. His companion beckoned with a wave of his hand and in a crouched position began to make a slow pilgrimage toward the next house.

The moon was a wafer obscured by clouds. Good for stealth, but not quite so wonderful for visibility. Two more alleys and harrowing jumps and they were there, easing down onto a balcony that overlooked a small walled garden.

Michael Hepburn, Marquess of Longhaven, dropped down first, light on his feet, balanced like a dancer. Alex wondered, not for the first time, just what his friend did for the War Office. He landed next to him, and said, "What did your operative tell you about the layout of the town house?"

Michael peered through the glass of the French doors into the darkened room. "I could be at our club at this very moment, enjoying a stiff brandy."

"Stop grumbling," Alex muttered. "You live for this kind of intrigue. Lucky for us, the lock is simple. I'll have this open in no time."

True to his word, a moment later one of the doors creaked open, the sound loud to Alex's ears. He led the way, slipping into the darkened bedroom, taking in with a quick glance the shrouded forms of a large canopied bed and armoire. Something white was laid out on the bed, and on closer inspection he saw that it was a night-dress edged with delicate lace, and that the coverlet was already turned back. The virginal gown made him feel very much an interloper—which, bloody hell, he was. But all for a good cause, he told himself firmly.

Michael spoke succinctly. "This is Lord Hathaway's daughter's bedroom. We'll need to search his study and his suite across the hall. Since his lordship's rooms face the street and his study is downstairs, this is a much more discreet method of entry. It is likely enough they'll be gone for several more hours, giving us time to search for your precious item. At this hour, the servants should all be abed."

"I'll take the study. It's more likely to be there."

"Alex, you do realize you are going to have to finally tell me just what we are looking for if I am going to ransack his lordship's bedroom on your behalf."

"I hope you plan on being more subtle than that."

"He'll never know I was there," Michael said with convincing confidence. "But what the devil am I looking for?"

"A key. Ornate, made of silver, so it'll be tarnished to black, I suspect. About so long." Alex spread open his hand, indicating the distance between the tip of his smallest finger and his thumb. "It'll be in a small case, also silver. There should be an engraved *S* on the cover."

"A key to *what*, dare I ask, since I am risking my neck to find it?"

Alex paused, reluctant to reveal more. But Michael had a point, and moreover, could keep a secret better than anyone of Alex's acquaintance. "I'm not sure," he admitted, quietly.

Michael's hazel eyes gleamed with interest even in the dim light. "Yet here we are, breaking into a man's house?"

"It's . . . complicated."

"Things with you usually are."

"I'm not at liberty to explain to anyone, even you, my

reasons for being here. Therefore my request for your assistance. In the past you have proven not only to think fast on your feet and stay cool under fire, but you also have the unique ability to keep your mouth firmly shut, which is a very valuable trait in a friend. In short, I trust you."

Michael gave a noncommittal grunt. "All right, fine."

"If it makes you feel better, I'm not going to steal anything," Alex informed him in a whisper, as he cracked open the bedroom door and peered down the hall. "What I want doesn't belong to Lord Hathaway, if he has it. Where's his study?"

"Second hallway past the bottom of the stairs. Third door on the right."

The house smelled vaguely of beeswax and smoke from the fires that kept the place warm in the late-spring weather. Alex crept—there was no other word for it—down the hall, sending a silent prayer upward to enlist heavenly aid for their little adventure to be both successful and undetected. Though he wasn't sure, with his somewhat dissolute past—or Michael's, for that matter—if he was at all in a position to ask for benevolence.

The hallway was deserted but damned dark. Michael clearly knew the exact location of Hathaway's personal set of rooms, for he went directly to the left door and cracked it open, and disappeared inside.

Alex stood at a vantage point where he could see the top of the staircase rising from the main floor, feeling an amused disbelief that he was a deliberate intruder in someone else's house, and had enlisted Michael's aid to help him with the infiltration. He'd known Michael since Eton, and when it came down to it, no one was more reliable or loyal. He'd go with him to hell and back, and quite frankly, they *had* accompanied each other to hell in Spain.

They'd survived the fires of Hades, but had not come back to England unscathed.

Time passed in silence, and Alex relaxed a little as he

made his way down the stairs into the darkened hallway, barking his shin only once on a piece of furniture that seemed to materialize out of nowhere. He stifled a very colorful curse and moved on, making a mental note not to take up burglary as a profession.

The study was redolent of old tobacco and the ghosts of a thousand glasses of brandy. Alex moved slowly, pulling the borrowed set of picklocks again from his pocket, rummaging through the drawers he could open first, and then setting to work on the two locked ones.

Nothing. No silver case. No blasted key.

Damn.

The first sound of trouble was a low, sharp, excited bark. Then he heard a woman speaking in modulated tones—audible in the silent house—and alarm flooded through him. The voice sounded close, but that might be a trick of the acoustics of the town house. At least it didn't sound like a big dog, he told himself, feeling in a drawer for a false back before replacing the contents and quietly sliding it shut.

A servant? Perhaps, but it was unlikely, for it was truly the dead of night, with dawn a few good hours away. As early as most of the staff rose, he doubted one of them would be up and about unless summoned by her employer.

The voice spoke again, a low murmur, and the lack of a reply probably meant she was talking to the dog. He eased into the hallway to peer out and saw that at the foot of the stairs a female figure was bent over, scratching the ears of what appeared to be a small bundle of active fur, just a puppy, hence the lack of alarm over their presence in the house.

She was blond, slender, and, more significantly, clad in a fashionable gown of a light color. . . .

Several more hours, my arse. One of Lord Hathaway's family had returned early.

It was a stroke of luck when she set down her lamp and lifted the squirming bundle of fur in her arms, and instead of heading upstairs, carried her delighted burden through a door on the opposite side of the main hall, probably back toward the kitchen.

Alex stole across the room, and went quickly up the stairs to where Michael had disappeared, trying to be as light-footed as possible. He opened the door a crack and whispered, "Someone just came home. A young woman, though I couldn't see her clearly."

"Damnation." Michael could move quietly as a cat, and he was there instantly. "I'm only half done. We might need to leave and come back a second time."

Alex pictured launching himself again across more questionable, stinking, yawning crevasses of London's rooftop landscape. "I'd rather we finished it now."

"If Lady Amelia has returned alone, it should be fine," Michael murmured. "She's unlikely to come into her father's bedroom, and I just need a few more minutes. I'd ask you to help me, but you don't know where I've already searched, and the two of us whispering to each other and moving about is more of a risk. Go out the way we came in. Wait for her to go to bed, and keep an eye on her. If she looks to leave her room because she might have heard something, you're going to have to come up with a distraction. Otherwise, I'll take my chances going out this way and meet you on the roof."

With that, he was gone again and the door closed softly.

Alex uttered a stifled curse. He'd fought battles, crawled through ditches, endured soaking rains and freezing nights, marched for miles on end with his battalion, but he wasn't a damned spy. But a moment of indecision could be disastrous with Miss Patton no doubt heading for her bedroom. And what if she also woke her maid?

As a soldier, he'd learned to make swift judgments, and in this case, he trusted Michael knew what the hell he was doing and quickly slipped back into the lady's bedroom and headed for the balcony. They'd chosen that entry into the house for the discreet venue of the quiet, private garden, and the assurance that no one on the street would see them and possibly recognize them in this fashionable neighborhood.

No more had Alex managed to close the French doors behind him than the door to the bedroom opened. He froze, hoping the shadows hid his presence, worried movement might attract the attention of the young woman who had entered the room. If she raised an alarm, Michael could be in a bad spot, even if Alex got away. She carried the small lamp, which she set on the polished table by the bed. He assumed his presence on the dark balcony would be hard to detect.

It was at that moment he realized how very beautiful she was.

Lord Hathaway's daughter. Had he met her? No, he hadn't, but when he thought about it, he'd heard her name mentioned quite often lately. Now he knew why.

Hair a shimmering gold caught the light as she reached up and loosened the pins, dropping them one by one by the lamp and letting the cascade of curls tumble down her back. In profile her face was defined and feminine, with a dainty nose and delicate chin. And though he couldn't see the color of her eyes, they were framed by lashes long enough they cast slight shadows across her elegant cheekbones as she bent over to lift her skirts, kick off her slippers, and begin to unfasten her garters. He caught the pale gleam of slender calves and smooth thighs, and the graceful curve of her bottom.

There was something innately sensual about watching a woman undress, though usually when it was done in his presence it was as a prelude to one of his favorite pastimes. Slim fingers worked the fastenings of her gown and in a whisper of silk, it slid off her pale shoulders. She stepped free of the pooled fabric, wearing only a thin, lacy chemise, all gold and ivory in the flickering illumination.

As a gentleman, he reminded himself, *I should look away.*

The ball had been more nightmare than entertainment, and Lady Amelia Patton had ducked out as soon as possible, using her usual—and not deceptive—excuse. She picked up her silk gown, shook it out, and draped it over a carved chair by the fireplace. When her carriage had dropped her home, she'd declined to wake her maid, instead enjoying a few rare moments of privacy before bed. No one would think it amiss, as she had done the same before.

It was a crime, was it not, to kill one's father?

Not that she *really* wanted to strangle him in any way but a metaphorical one, but this evening, when he had thrust her almost literally into the arms of the Earl of Westhope, she had nearly done the unthinkable and refused to dance with his lordship in public, thereby humiliating the man and defying her father in front of all of society.

Instead, she had gritted her teeth and waltzed with the most handsome, rich, incredibly *boring* eligible bachelor of the *haut ton*.

It had encouraged him, and that was the last thing she wanted to happen.

The earl had even had the nerve—or maybe it was just stupidity—to misquote Rabelais when he brought her a glass of champagne, saying with a flourish as he handed over the flute, "Thirst comes with eating . . . but the appetite goes away with drinking."

It had really been all she could do not to correct him, since he'd got it completely backward. She had a sinking feeling that he didn't mean to be boorish; he just wasn't very bright. Still, there was nothing on earth that could have prevented her from asking him, in her most proper voice, if that meant he was bringing her champagne because he felt, perhaps, she was too plump. Her response had so flustered him that he'd excused himself hurriedly—so perhaps the entire evening hadn't been a loss after all.

Clad only in her chemise, she went to the balcony doors and opened them, glad of the fresh air, even if it was a bit cool. Loosening the ribbon on her shift, she let the material drift partway down her shoulders, her nipples tightening against the chill. The ballroom had been unbearably close and she'd had some problems breathing, an affliction that had plagued her since childhood. Being able to fill her lungs felt like heaven, and she stood there, letting her eyes close. The light wheezing had stopped, and the anxiety that came with it had lessened, as well, but she was still a little dizzy. Her father was insistent that she kept this particular flaw a secret. He seemed convinced no man would wish to marry a female who might now and again become inexplicably out of breath.

Slowly she inhaled and then let it out. Yes, it was passing. . . .

It wasn't a movement or noise that sent a flicker of unease through her, but a sudden, instinctive sense of being watched. Then a strong, masculine hand cupped her elbow. "Are you quite all right?"

Her eyes flew open and she saw a tall figure looming over her. With a gasp she jerked her chemise back up to cover her partially bared breasts. To her surprise, the shadowy figure spoke again in a cultured, modulated voice. "I'm sorry to startle you, my lady. I beg a thousand pardons, but I thought you might faint."

Amelia stared upward, as taken aback by his polite speech and appearance as she was by finding a man lurking on her balcony. The stranger had ebony hair, glossy even in the inadequate moonlight, and his face was shadowed into hollows and fine planes, eyes dark as midnight staring down at her. "I . . . I . . ." she stammered. *You should scream*, an inner voice suggested, but she was so paralyzed by alarm and surprise, she wasn't sure she was capable of it.

"You swayed," her mysterious visitor pointed out, as if that explained everything, a small frown drawing dark, arched brows together. "Are you ill?"

Finally, she found her voice, albeit not at all her regular one, but a high, thin whisper. "No, just a bit dizzy. Sir, what are you doing here?"

"Maybe you should lie down."

To her utter shock, he lifted her into his arms as easily as if she were a child, and actually carried her inside to deposit her carefully on the bed.

Perhaps this is a bizarre dream....

"What are you doing here? Who are you?" she demanded. It wasn't very effective, since she still couldn't manage more than a half mumble, though fright was rapidly being replaced by outraged curiosity. Even in the insubstantial light she could tell he was well dressed, and before he straightened, she caught the subtle drift of expensive cologne. Though he wore no cravat, his dark coat was fashionably cut, and his fitted breeches and Hessians not something she imagined an ordinary footpad would wear. His face was classically handsome, with a nice, straight nose and lean jaw, and she'd never seen eyes so dark.

Was he really that tall, or did he just seem so because she was sprawled on the bed and he was standing?

"I mean you no harm. Do not worry."

Easy for him to say. For heaven's sake, he was in her bedroom, no less. "You are trespassing."

"Indeed," he agreed, inclining his head.

Was he a thief? He didn't look like one. Confused, Amelia sat up, feeling very vulnerable lying there in dishabille with her tumbled hair. "My father keeps very little money in his strongbox here in the house."

"A wise man. I follow that same rule myself. If it puts your mind at ease, I do not need his money." The stranger's teeth flashed white in a quick smile.

She recognized him, she realized suddenly, the situation taking on an even greater sense of the surreal. Not a close acquaintance, no. Not one of the many gentlemen she'd danced with since the beginning of her season, but she'd seen him, nevertheless.

And he certainly had seen *her*. She was sitting there gawping at him in only her thin, lacy chemise with the bodice held together in her trembling hand. The flush of embarrassment swept upward, making her neck and cheeks hot. She could feel the rush of blood warm her knuckles when they pressed against her chest. "I . . . I'm undressed," she said unnecessarily.

"Most delightfully so," he responded with an unmistakable note of sophisticated amusement in his soft tone. "But I am not here to ravish you any more than to rob you. Though," he added with a truly wicked smile, "perhaps, in the spirit of being an effective burglar, I should steal *something*. A kiss comes to mind, for at least then I would not leave empty-handed."

A kiss? Was the man insane?

"You . . . wouldn't," she managed to object in disbelief. He still stood by the side of the bed, so close that if she reached out a hand she could touch him.

"I might." His dark brows lifted a fraction, and his gaze flickered over her inadequately clad body before returning to her face. He added softly, "I have a weakness for lovely, half-dressed ladies, I'm afraid."

And no doubt they had the same weakness for him, for he exuded a flagrant masculinity and confidence that was even more compelling than his good looks.

Her breath fluttered in her throat and it had nothing to do with her affliction. She might be an ingenue, but she understood in an instant the power of that devastating, entirely masculine, husky tone. Like a bird stunned by smoke, she didn't move, even when he leaned down and his long fingers caught her chin, tipping her face up just a fraction. He lowered his head, brushed his mouth against hers for a moment, a mere tantalizing touch of his lips. Then, instead of kissing her, his hand slid into her hair and he gently licked the hollow of her throat.

Through her dazed astonishment at his audacity, the feel of his warm lips and the teasing caress caused an odd sensation in the pit of her stomach.

This was where she should imperiously order him to stop, or at least push him away.

But she didn't. She'd never been kissed, and though, admittedly, her girlish fantasies about this moment in her life hadn't included a mysterious stranger stealing uninvited into her bedroom, she *was* curious.

The trail of his breath made her quiver, moving upward along her jaw, the curve of her cheek, until he finally claimed her mouth, shocking her to her very core as he brushed his tongue against hers in small, sinful strokes.

She trembled, and though it wasn't a conscious act, somehow one of her hands settled on his shoulder.

It was intimate.

It was beguiling.

Then it was over.

God help her, to her *disappointment* it was over.

He straightened and looked more amused than ever at whatever expression had appeared on her face. "A virgin kiss. A coup indeed."

He obviously knew that had been her first. It wasn't so surprising, for like most unmarried young ladies, she was constantly chaperoned. She summoned some affront, though, strangely, she really wasn't affronted. "You, sir, are no gentleman."

"Oh, I am, if a somewhat jaded one. If I wasn't, I wouldn't be taking my leave lest your reputation be tarnished by our meeting, because it would be, believe me. My advice is to keep my presence here this evening to yourself."

True to his word, in a moment he was through the balcony doors, climbing up on the balustrade, and bracing himself for balance on the side of the house. Then he caught the edge of the roof, swung up in one graceful athletic motion, and was gone into the darkness.

Chapter Two

Parliament was in session, so the voices were a little louder, as politics was the subject of the day. It was fine, because it actually created privacy. Alex handed over his dripping greatcoat to the steward, the weather having turned into the typical spring drizzle, and saw that both Luke and Michael were there before him at their favorite spot in the corner, a bottle of fine whiskey on the table and a spare glass waiting.

He lost no time in pouring a good measure in the tumbler before he dropped into his chair. A lazy grin tipped the corner of his mouth upward. "I'm a bit late, but for a good reason."

"What's her name?" Luke Daudet, Viscount Altea, asked in a dry tone. "Or need I ask? Word has it one very sultry Italian opera singer is more than willing to perform a private aria for your enjoyment at the crook of your finger."

So *that* rumor was still circulating. It was an annoyance to have an older brother with John's reputation sometimes. Not that Alex was a saint by any means, but he was more infamous by association than by deed. Society seemed to expect him to follow in his brother's licentious footsteps, and especially more now that John was a married man and had retired from the game of seduction and scandal. Alex might not be the ducal heir, but he had inherited his brother's notoriety. It didn't help they looked so very much alike.

"No, I'm not referring to Maria." Alex lifted the glass to his mouth, sipped the smooth, fragrant beverage, and regarded his friends over the rim with an amused gaze. "It seems I am an uncle."

"Ah." Michael elevated his brows.

"My brother's pretty wife was delivered of a healthy baby in the wee hours while you and I were frolicking across slippery rooftops, and I am happy to say both mother and child are doing quite well, though for whatever reason, my brother looked like hell. I don't see why, when his wife did the difficult part, but it's all the pacing and brandy, he claims. Serves him right, most probably, for all his past sins. But, truthfully, I've never seen him so happy. I received the summons to go to Berkeley House early this morning."

"I take it the child is a boy."

"The child will be christened Marcus, after my father. This event means I have just sunk in the ranks of the eligible bachelors, unlike the two of you, who remain solid prospects despite your less than pristine reputations. I'm now a not very promising fourth in line for a dukedom after my brother Joel, while you, Michael, are already a marquess and will be duke one day if your nefarious duties don't spell your doom first. And as for Luke, he's inherited his title and the grandiose Daudet fortune already."

"I believe I object to the term nefarious." Michael, casual in buff breeches and a dark blue coat, his cravat knotted simply, feigned affront, settling lower in his chair, his long legs extended, booted feet crossed at the ankle. But a slight smile curved his mouth. His sun-streaked chestnut hair and bronzed skin were indicative of his recent return from Spain, and his eyes, a vivid hazel color, held amusement.

"And don't look so damned smug, Alex," Luke said with a cynical lift of a brow. "Your family name still will attract the eager mamas on the hunt with their vapid daughters in tow. Plus, for reasons unfathomable to me, females seem to like your pretty face."

Alex laughed. "Perhaps, but with two older brothers and now a direct heir, I will never have a title besides an honorary one. There is quite a difference in being a decent match and being a prestigious one. You two, unfortunately, are the latter."

"There's a gloomy thought," Luke murmured, picking up his drink. "But, while I hate to deflate your effervescent mood, may I point out it is no secret you have a very respectable fortune of your own? I don't think you are immune yet."

That was probably true, but Alex was so relieved the birth had gone well that nothing could tamper his current good cheer. His sister-in-law hadn't had the easiest confinement, and though it was unspoken, Alex had known John was afraid for both her and the child. Luckily, a difficult pregnancy had resulted in an easy delivery. When his brother had finally fallen in love and abandoned the profligate tenor of his bachelor life, he had fallen hard. He adored his wife.

"Speaking of marriageable young ladies, just what explanation are you going to offer Lord Hathaway if his beauteous daughter tells him she caught you lurking on her balcony?" Michael asked, the question deceptively casual, but as usual, his eyes held sharp interest that was anything but nonchalant. "The man would have every reason to be furious. At the least, since it was impossible for you to relock the drawers to his desk, he is going to know someone was in his study. If she says nothing, there is a possibility he might think he forgot to lock them, especially with no actual theft. But if she reveals you were in her room, he will easily put two and two together."

Which would be damned unfortunate for many reasons, Alex had to acknowledge. He knew it would be disastrous to be caught before he asked Michael to check into the layout of the Hathaway town house and accompany him on the ill-fated venture. There was no love lost between his family and the Pattons. He'd never fully understood why until his grandmother's recent shocking confidence, but his entire life he'd known the enmity existed. If Hathaway knew the story—if the man knew *half* the story—he'd be a great deal more than furious to know Alex had touched his daughter. Murderous was probably a better word.

That kiss. What the hell had he been thinking?

His cock had taken charge; he could not come up with any other explanation. The moment he touched her, felt her soft, warm body in his arms, inhaled the delectable scent of attar of roses drifting from her smooth skin, he'd behaved like a damned fool.

Yes, she was beautiful, but there was no shortage of beautiful women. The incident was entirely out of character.

He hadn't been able to stop thinking about the taste of her mouth all morning. Or that golden hair and perfect skin. Her beguiling eyes had been an unusual shade of crystalline blue. . . .

"What's this?" Luke demanded, glancing from one to the other of them. "Hathaway's daughter *caught* you? Back in Spain I saw you get past French sentries without so much as cracking a twig."

"Our friend Alex caught *her*, actually. In a literal sense, no less." Michael refilled his glass, the splash of the liquid drowned out by a loud guffaw from a portly gentleman at a nearby table having an animated conversation about crop importation. "He claims she opened the balcony doors and looked perhaps like she might swoon. Obviously trying to get some fresh air. Being an avid rescuer of fair maidens—which, might I remind him, almost cost him his life at Badajoz—he materialized from the shadows and swept her into his arms."

"Oh, bloody hell. No one materialized from anywhere. It's not a large balcony, and I was standing only a few feet away," Alex muttered. "She would have seen me anyway. What was I supposed to do—let her fall at my feet? She closed her eyes and swayed. Either of you would have done the same. It turns out she was perfectly fine, but I didn't know that at the time."

"But now she knows you were there." Luke gave him a skeptical look. "Looking for some mysterious key, no less. That's intriguing—admit it. You must know both Michael and I are curious."

Truth be told, he didn't have a lot of information himself. "The key is a family heirloom."

"Then why does Hathaway have it?" Michael had his characteristic bland expression, his chestnut brows lifted slightly in question. "And more importantly, why aren't you confiding the story to us?"

"That's quite a valid point," Luke agreed.

"The two of you have your secrets," Alex said irritably, though he was more annoyed with himself than the interrogation. Not only hadn't he found the key, but he had been discovered. Then he'd yielded to an impulse—and he was never impulsive—and actually kissed the almost-undressed Lady Amelia, who was not only virginal, but also the last female in London he should touch. There was long-standing enmity between their fathers that Alex always assumed stemmed from some sort of quarrel in their youth, but now appeared to be more involved than he thought with this damned key business. It was obvious Lady Amelia had no idea who he was, but when she did discover his identity—and she would, for they were bound to see each other at social events—what she did next could spark a new eruption of ill will. It would also backfire on him, for it would raise the question to Hathaway of what Alex might have been seeking.

Still, she'd looked so fragile there, pale in the moonlight, with her shoulders bare, the upper swells of her breasts exposed, her eyes drifting shut. . . .

Well, damn all, perhaps he *did* have a weakness for beautiful damsels in distress. He also liked children, solitude, and astronomy, because he had a fascination for the stars and the vastness of the night sky. And, because he had never really known his mother, he adored his grandmother, which was how he'd gotten into this situation in the first place. The gossips wouldn't believe any of that except that he had a weakness for damsels of all kinds, no distress needed.

"I'd appreciate all discretion, because this is important to my grandmother. All I know is that years ago—decades ago, in fact—my grandfather's sister had an illicit affair with Lord Hathaway's father. She was unmarried and young. He was very much married and acted dishonorably. She died in an accident, and he died at the end of my grandfather's dueling pistol. What this key has to do with it," he added in quiet explanation, "isn't clear to me either."

"Interesting," Michael murmured.

"I agree." Luke nodded after a moment. "Well, then, consider the subject dropped. When and if you can expound, I look forward to it."

Privacy was something all three of them understood very well, and they talked about Lord Liverpool's new policies for a while, mostly in agreement, but in companionable discord when they didn't see eye to eye. When, a second empty bottle later, Alex left the club, he had forgotten the Earl of Hathaway's tempting daughter.

Or so he assured himself.

There must be something wrong with her, because dressing for the ball held little to no excitement. Weren't young women seeking the frivolity and glitter of ballrooms and the endless round of parties supposed to plot for hours over which gown would make them look so dazzling, all the gentlemen would fall at their feet? Instead Amelia considered her gowns with disinterest.

She decided on the blue silk to please Aunt Sophie, for she had rhapsodized over the color of the material when the dressmaker had brought it out amid bolts of fabric and spools of lace, with hovering assistants taking measurements for what seemed like an eternity.

Though she knew her father had spent a small fortune on her wardrobe, Amelia had the sinking feeling his motivation in such extravagance was a desire to expedite a suitable marriage rather than any fatherly generosity.

Perfectly acceptable, a part of her rationalized. What every father wanted for his daughter.

Perfectly unacceptable, another part argued, for, since he'd never been a part of her life in the first place, how unfair was it of him to try to be rid of her as fast as possible now that she was old enough for her first season? Until now, she'd lived at their country estate and had seen her father only when he visited there for business purposes. Her arrival in London had changed nothing. They rarely even spoke unless it was politesse exchanged over a meal, and there were few enough of those, as he ate at his club quite often.

In other words, he tended to live his life as if she didn't exist. Was that why she hadn't told him about the man on her balcony?

Maybe. Or it might be she was still thinking about raven hair, a pair of captivating dark eyes, and the flash of a smile. And that kiss ... well, she had to admit that she wasn't sure what to expect when it happened, but the experience of her first kiss had been interesting.

No, wrong word, she thought as she crossed the room to ring for her maid. Exhilarating. Enchanting. Captivating.

No, still wrong.

Deliciously forbidden.

She had never done anything forbidden. Before *him*.

"Miss?" Her maid, Beatrice, came into the room, her dark hair drawn back in a neat bun, her uniform pressed and clean, her curtsy perfectly executed. Amelia found her father's London household much more formal than the country house in Cambridgeshire. The girl asked, "Are you ready to get dressed now?"

Whoever he was, the man who had invaded her bedroom was a member of polite society. For once Amelia felt a flicker of anticipation over the upcoming evening. "I think I'll wear the azure silk," she murmured, and to her own surprise actually took an interest in how she would arrange her hair.

When she descended the stairs a half an hour later, she found her father in the formal drawing room, his face set, a glass of sherry in his hand. He turned at her entrance, and while he was never warm and affectionate, he looked particularly grim at the moment. "Would you like a small glass before we depart for the evening, Amelia?"

His glass was half full. If they were going to sit together while he finished it, she thought it wise to have a glass of her own to sip at while they struggled through stilted conversation. She nodded and chose an elegant upholstered chair, and sat down and elaborately fussed with her skirts as he poured her a drink and brought the delicate goblet over.

"I think you should probably entrust your mother's jewelry to my strongbox," he informed her in clipped tones as he handed her the sherry. "I have every reason to believe one of the servants might be untrustworthy."

Off balance, she stopped with her glass halfway to her mouth. "What . . . why?"

"Someone was in my study and searched my desk." He didn't sit, but went over to a Chippendale table and moodily examined a small statue covered in mother-of-pearl. "There are valuable items in this house, but most are not easily portable. Jewelry is small, and can be hidden in a pocket or small purse. The diamond pendant earrings I gave you for your birthday, for instance."

He meant the diamond earrings he'd sent for her seventeenth birthday, with a note explaining he had business in London and couldn't possibly come himself to the country estate to celebrate.

The dark-haired man on my balcony . . .

It could hardly be feasible that there were two mysterious intruders. Very carefully, she asked, "Did he . . . er . . . whoever was in your study take anything?"

"Not that I can tell. I just noticed the unlocked drawers before I went up to dress for dinner. I summoned the staff, but no one admits to any culpability."

At least her intriguing, seductive visitor wasn't a thief . . . though he was an interloper, it seemed. "I doubt any of them would steal," Amelia remarked. "Robert and James are brothers, and neither one would endanger the other's position. Cook is far too comfortable ruling over the kitchen, and Perkins is quite meticulous overseeing the maids."

"Robert and James?"

"Footmen," she supplied ironically.

"You are far too familiar with the staff if you know their first names." Her father frowned.

She was far too familiar with the staff in that, at least while growing up, sequestered at the country estate, she had no one else. It had instilled in her a lack of snobbery because, quite frankly, they had all been more her family than her own father. When she'd come to London finally for her coming-out in society, even on short acquaintance it had been natural enough to treat the servants here with the same informality.

"Perhaps you forgot to lock the drawers," she suggested, and sipped the golden sherry while trying to hypothesize why an aristocratic gentleman would risk breaking into her father's house to search his study. Not for money. She'd believed him when he'd said he didn't need it. The way he was dressed, the way he carried himself . . . no, it hadn't been to steal anything for monetary gain.

"I wouldn't forget to lock both," her father said testily. He drained his glass and set it impatiently aside. "Shall we go?"

Absolutely, she thought, rising obediently. This soiree might not be the usual dead bore.

Chapter Three

Perhaps the turban with the jeweled brooch had been a bit much, but the sensation her arrival created was worth it. Sophia McCay strolled past a group of huddled matrons, ignoring their pointed stares. It felt rather good to be so shockingly original, she had to admit. It always did, and she liked to indulge her personal taste, even if it was a little on the flamboyant side. Her William had encouraged it, and often whispered in her ear that conventional women bored him to tears.

How she missed him. The pressure of his hand lay over hers, the light sound of his spontaneous laugh as she imparted some ridiculous piece of gossip, the cadence of his breathing in the dark as he fell asleep ...

Squaring her shoulders, she scanned the glittering crowd. Most people of consequence were in attendance, she saw with an expert, sweeping assessment, for it was still officially the beginning of the season.

If she were going to be a proper chaperone for her niece, she should at least know where Amelia might be. The child—well, no, she had to admit Amelia was no longer a child—had a habit of fading into the background at events like this one. Not that the attentive gentlemen of society made it easy, but Amelia had never been one to shy away from a challenge.

She was, after all, her mother's daughter, from the tip of her shining head to her toes.

Intrepid.

Such a lovely word. Sophia rather liked it and thought it applied to all the women of their family, and despite her niece's slight affliction, Amelia was as independent as she was lovely.

"Sophia, how delightful to see you this evening. You are as stylish as ever, I see."

Sophia turned to see a gray-haired gentleman, a twinkle clear in his eyes as he politely bent over her hand. He straightened, his formal evening wear immaculate as always, his hair brushed neatly back from a high forehead, the small mustache he favored perfectly groomed. On Sir Richard she'd always—secretly, of course—thought it rather dashing.

Someday, when she was so inclined, she just might marry again. Though he was considerably older than she, Richard Havers would undoubtedly make as excellent a husband as he was a friend. She muttered, "Since arriving I have wondered if perhaps the Turkish look is a bit too progressive for the tastes of some. I don't look as if I have a giant beehive on my head, do I?"

"Not at all. But in my humble opinion it is a crime to cover up your lovely hair."

He looked so bland, she couldn't help but burst out laughing. "Ever the diplomat. Very well. I thought it most daring when I left this evening, but am rethinking my choice. Not because half the people in attendance are staring at me as if I've gone mad, but because it is, quite frankly, devilishly hot. I do not see how Eastern gentlemen endure it."

"They wear them to insulate themselves from the scorching sun. You," he said succinctly, "are in a most crowded ballroom in London on a dreary spring evening. Now, then, dare I hope you will favor me with a dance at some point?"

She arched her brows and smiled with deliberate coyness, as she enjoyed flirting with him. "If you promise to not waltz too vigorously and send my headdress flying across the floor. That would be the height of poor taste. I am not certain even my considerable consequence could overcome it."

Richard chuckled.

"But first I must find my niece. Have you, by chance, seen Amelia?"

"Indeed. Just a few moments ago. She looks exquisite always, but particularly so this evening, I must say."

"Point me in the right direction, if you would, please."

"Better than that, I'll escort you." He gallantly offered his arm. "In this crush, it might take you forever, and she has chosen an inconspicuous spot."

Moments later Sophia caught a glimpse of a blue skirt, but a pillar blocked her view of the person wearing it, which didn't surprise her at all. Stifling a sigh of resignation, she murmured, "She's hiding again."

"It intrigues all the gentlemen that she refuses to dance more than a select few times in one evening and then declines all other offers. If she wished to pick a method to increase her appeal, she could not have chosen better. When a gentleman is granted a dance, everyone notices."

It was true, though Sophia knew that more than anything else, Amelia sat out more so she didn't become overtaxed. Usually she was perfectly healthy, but bouts of strenuous activity could trigger an attack, and her niece was careful to guard against it. "It isn't calculated," Sophia said with just a shade of defensiveness. "Quite frankly, she'd rather have less attention than more. I won't say she's shy, but she definitely tends toward quieter entertainments than crowded balls."

Richard patted her hand where it rested on his

sleeve. "That was not a criticism, my dear. I've always wondered if it wasn't tedious being the Incomparable of the season. All those fawning men with posies and badly written doggerel about eyes and lips and moonlit passion. There is something to be said for being past the impetuous bloom of youth. If I flung myself to my knees and pledged my undying love for you now, you possibly might have to help me get back up. That's hardly romantic, and the blow to my dignity would be immense."

As he was still trim and cut a fine figure, Sophia rather doubted she would be required to haul him back to his feet. In the same light-hearted tone, she quipped back, "As I am well beyond pressing my hand to my heaving bosom and swooning over such an event, I think we can skip such theatrics anyway. Impassioned men on their knees never held much appeal, even in my younger days. I prefer an intelligent, reasonable approach to most matters, including those of the heart."

He looked into her eyes. "I am glad we are in agreement, then. When the time comes to declare our feelings, we will discuss it rationally. Please give my regards to Lady Amelia, and do not forget our sedate waltz later."

With that he turned and disappeared into the crush. Sophia watched him go, realizing her pulse had quickened. Drat the man; she had a feeling he was astute enough to know how her attraction to him had deepened lately. Good heavens, they'd been friends for years. When had everything changed?

She'd have to ponder it later. At the moment her duty to her sister's child beckoned. Amelia, standing behind the pillar, didn't notice her approach, her distracted gaze fastened on one corner of the huge, grand room. Sophia knew from experience that if Amelia didn't make herself as invisible as possible, suitors kept her hemmed in, and this evoked an understandable sense of discomfort in her niece. She'd had fewer and fewer breathing attacks as she matured, and the doctors even offered hope they might disappear completely one day, but for now the occasional occurrence still surfaced. As determined as her father was to keep it some deep dark secret, Amelia often slipped away for a few minutes.

It was unfortunate, in an ironic sort of way, she had turned out to be such a stunning beauty. Amelia had asserted jokingly that she might accept a proposal soon just to deflect all the attention and get the business over with.

And Sophia was just as determined to make sure her niece made a love match. Amelia's mother would have wanted it for her.

"Here you are, darling," she said, agreeing silently with Richard about her niece's appearance. Tonight Amelia wore her hair dressed simply, caught up in an elegant twist with a few artful tendrils framing her face and brushing her graceful neck. Though she was more slender than was fashionable, she still had curves in all the places that made men watch admiringly as she walked by, and her natural reserve gave her an air of sophisticated poise despite her age.

Amelia glanced up and her smile was warm, but then her gaze returned to the same spot, which, oddly enough, was an almost deserted corner by the entrance, away from the milling throng. "Aunt Sophie. I didn't see you arrive."

Considering that she wore a giant yellow turban—she really should have chosen a different color—that was somewhat of an odd statement. "How could you miss me?" Sophia asked bluntly.

"Hmm."

A little puzzled, Sophia studied Amelia's expression. "Is something amiss?"

"What? Oh ... no. Well, I mean ... not particularly ... that is. . . . Well, tell me, who is that man over there?"

"What man?" Sophia gazed in the same direction. "This room is full of gentlemen."

"That one." Discreetly Amelia used her fan to indicate the person in question. "The tall, handsome one."

Sophia, distracted by plucking a glass of champagne from a passing footman with a tray, didn't quite realize who she meant until she focused on the quiet corner where three men stood apart from the melee, also drinking champagne and conversing. Yet the word handsome rang an alarm bell. The flute froze halfway to her mouth. She did indeed know the identity of all three of them, and, unfortunately, all three of them were very handsome indeed.

Dangerously so. And she wouldn't let a single one of them within yards of her niece.

The Marquess of Longhaven, well dressed and inscrutable as always with his chestnut hair and remarkable hazel eyes. Luke Daudet, Viscount Altea, urbane and impossibly good-looking. And of course, the youngest son of the Duke of Berkeley, Lord Alexander St. James, who, despite being a war hero, had a most scandalous reputation for disdaining convention and being inconstant when it came to women. Society referred to them collectively as the Notorious Bachelors, and the epithet fit well enough.

"I'm sorry. I should have been clearer. The one with the dark curly hair," Amelia explained, obviously misreading Sophia's consternation and silence. When she still didn't respond, a frown furrowed Amelia's smooth brow and she added, "The one leaning so negligently with his shoulder against the wall."

So rarely had Amelia seen her aunt flustered, she wasn't sure what to do. She waited for an answer to what seemed to be an innocent enough question, and noticed under the brilliant saffron of Aunt Sophia's turban—which actually made her look regal, but, unfortunately, hid her thick brunet hair—her face had taken on a peculiar expression. She was lovely this evening; in fact, in a scarlet gown that contrasted with the eccentric wrap around her hair, and among the insipid whites of the ingenues and discreet browns and darker colors of the other matrons, her aunt stood out like a beautiful jeweled bird. A glittering sapphire necklace completed the ensemble, and somehow it all looked good together. Amelia had gotten well used to her aunt's flamboyant style, but occasionally she was still amused.

The gilded ballroom, the fluid dancers, the stilted laughter, and more prominent whispers—all faded away, though, at Aunt Sophie's suddenly closed expression.

Had she said something wrong?

Obviously.

After a moment Sophia rallied and took a deliberate sip of champagne. Then she asked, in a most careful voice, "May I ask why you wish to know about a gentleman I am certain has never been introduced to you?"

That was an interesting nonanswer. Obviously if he had been introduced, she wouldn't have to ask his identity. Amelia countered, "Why are you certain he hasn't been introduced to me?"

"For several reasons: the first being the man in question is not interested in being introduced to marriageable young ladies, the second being if he *had* asked, I would have been informed immediately by the gossip mill, and the third . . . well, we won't even talk about the third."

"Why not?"

"Not for your innocent ears, my dear."

This became more interesting by the moment. Amelia narrowed her gaze on the man in question. "He's notorious?"

She had, actually, already guessed it by his parting remark when he exited her bedroom.

"Absolutely." Sophia's voice was dry. "And now it is my turn. Why are you asking about Lord Alexander St. James?"

Alexander. That was his name. It suited him. He had the look of an infamous conqueror, a slight arrogance in his stance. His movements were assured, aristocratic, his ease and elegance in his dark, tailored clothing unmistakable. She'd stood there watching him for the better part of an hour.

But ... St. James? Amelia searched her memory. For whatever reason, that name meant something to her, but she wasn't sure why.

One of his friends said something, and he laughed. A gleam of straight white teeth, the smile his alone, confirming his identity. There was also the way he held himself, as distinct as any feature on his face. Even if she hadn't easily recognized him, that mesmerizing curve of his lips would give him away.

But it would hardly do to tell her aunt the man had been lurking on her balcony, not to mention the scandalous state of undress she'd been in when she'd discovered him there.

Or that he'd carried her into her bedroom and kissed her. Even a female as emancipated as Aunt Sophie might swoon if given that information.

She opted for the truth in a roundabout way. "As I said before, he's very handsome. I noticed him and could not help but wonder why we had not yet met. I feel like I've been introduced to half of London. Is he married?"

"Good heavens, child, no." Sophia popped open her fan and used it vigorously. "He has a legendary aversion to anything but fleeting liaisons of a scandalous nature."

"Impoverished?"

"The son of the Duke of Berkeley? I'd say not. Quite the opposite, even though he's the youngest of three sons. But you needn't concern yourself with his wealth or looks. He has a rakish reputation, and that is that. Let's dismiss the subject. You could have your pick of an abundance of *respectable* gentlemen who wish to offer for you and would make admirable husbands."

It was unfortunate that at that moment, Lord Alexander, perhaps due to the same sixth sense that alerted her she was being watched last night on the balcony, glanced over and caught her looking at him. As Sophia was also gazing directly at him, there was probably no doubt he was the topic of their conversation.

Though it was her first impulse to look hastily away, Amelia managed to quell it. After all, why shouldn't she be curious—and outraged, for that matter—as to why an aristocratic gentleman was loitering on her balcony in the dead of night? And to compound the crime, he'd taken quite an unforgivable liberty. He'd told the truth and robbery wasn't his goal, and apparently Lord Alexander *was* rich.

I am not here to ravish you. . . .

He hadn't either, but he had stolen that unforgettable kiss.

Next to her, Aunt Sophia made an inarticulate sound of dismay as they stared at each other, and it turned to an outright gasp as he straightened away from the wall and impudently raised his glass in a small, irreverent toast in their direction.

Chapter Four

Gabriella missed a step, and usually she was a flawless dance partner. "Let me make sure I understand your request. *You* are inquiring about Hathaway's young, naive, virginal, pure, virtuous, untouched—"

"Enough. No need for any more adjectives describing her innocence," Alex interrupted as he balanced her and they swept into a turn. "All I want is to learn what you know about her, and it goes without saying that I'd appreciate you keeping my request to yourself."

He was only asking for the sake of trying to come up with a new way to find that damned key.

Wasn't he?

"Now, that's unfair, darling." She fluttered her lashes. Tall, with thick dark hair, large doelike eyes, and a pouty, full mouth, Gabriella Fontaine was considered one of the *ton*'s leading beauties, even in her early thirties. "Do you know how the gossipmongers would leap upon this delectable little tidbit? The infinitely unsaintly St. James eyeing the most marriageable young maiden of this season's crop of debutantes . . . um, yes, *delicious* information."

"I am not eyeing her." Well, that wasn't quite true. Lady Amelia was exquisite this evening in a blue watered-silk gown that flattered the curves he had seen firsthand a few nights before, the neckline modest, the color setting off her amber hair. It showcased beautiful, lush, feminine breasts, full, firm, and high, and a slim waist, the gentle flare of her hips drawing the eye. All the usual parts of a woman, but made more perfectly than most. He shrugged and admitted neutrally, "I've noticed her, which is quite different. I'm a healthy male, and she's infinitely noticeable."

Gabriella gave him her most winsome smile and her tone dropped suggestively, her dark rose satin skirts whirling against his legs as they moved with the music. "You are quite *healthy*, my lord, if my memory serves me well. Perhaps you'd care to demonstrate your state of well-being a little later and see if I can't put the little ingenue out of your mind?"

"No," he said gently, not wanting to seem confrontational.

"You're sure?" The offer was openly there in her eyes.

While their brief affair had been satisfying, he wasn't interested in renewing it now that Gabriella had remarried. "Your husband might take issue," he said tactfully, swinging her into a turn. "And you know my stand on dallying with married women."

That reminder won him a theatrical sigh. "Yes, I do. For a rake of the first caliber, darling, you have some puritanical ideals." The music came to a flourishing end and they stopped. She said, "La, it is close in here. Let's step outside for a moment for some fresh air and I will tell you what I know. But, honestly, it isn't much. How interesting can a young virgin who is constantly chaperoned be?"

Very, he thought silently, remembering how their gazes locked earlier in the evening, not to mention the way she'd not screamed the house down in a fit of hysterics when a strange man picked her up, intruded into her bedroom, and then dared an intimate kiss.

Now that she knew his identity, he wondered if she might say something to her father, though, to his relief, somehow he doubted it. The challenge in her eyes as they looked at each other across the room earlier seemed to be from her alone.

Outside, the terrace was deserted, the flagstones wet because it had rained off and on all day, but it was much cooler than inside. A few stars were visible through the tearing clouds. Even though they were alone, Gabriella was ever the consummate actress and lowered her voice to a conspiratorial tone. "The bare facts I assume you know. She's the daughter of the Earl of Hathaway. Her mother died in childbirth with a stillborn son several years after Lady Amelia was born. Her aunt, who is an original, to be sure, is sponsoring her debut."

He actually knew very little except the identity of her father, and that was plenty enough right there. Whenever the Patton family was mentioned his father's face darkened, and Alex had seen firsthand his normally impassive parent cut the Earl of Hathaway in public. The dislike was mutual, apparently, from Hathaway's reaction. Before his grandmother's recent request, Alex hadn't thought much about it . . . political differences alone could make enemies of perfectly reasonable men. God knew aristocratic English families had quarrels dating back hundreds of years, so it wasn't so unusual. This dislike, though, seemed based not on political, but on personal events.

In truth, he wasn't comfortable asking Gabriella about the lovely Amelia, but his options were limited. His circle of friends did not pay attention to the new crop of young ladies being launched into society. If he asked someone in his family, his interest in a young, unmarried woman would be duly noted, and her identity would cause ripples of disquiet.

Yet he was curious enough to venture the questions.

He leaned one hip against the balustrade, lifted his brows, and folded his arms across his chest. "Anything else? Come now, Gabby. I know you. Surely, since she is so beautiful and her popularity with the males of *haut ton* is undisputed, your inner clique has taken an interest. Maybe even put down a wager or two on who might win the fair lady?"

"*So* beautiful?" A flare of resentment flashed in her eyes.

"You are an undisputed diamond of the first water, my dear, and have a great deal more sophistication," he said smoothly. "Come, now, admit it: there have been wagers, haven't there?"

That mollified her, and as it was true, he wasn't just soothing her either. Gabriella's set was well-known for its penchant for gambling. She gave him a feigned innocent look—as innocent as someone like Gabriella could manage anyway—and then laughed and reached up to touch his cheek lightly in a familiar gesture. Her fingers traveled downward, over his cravat, the lapel of his jacket, and lower until she cupped her hand between his legs. A coquette's smile graced her lips. "We know each other too well. I know I remember *this*. My new husband doesn't have your glorious cock, darling."

"Can we stay with the subject at hand?" he asked dryly, ignoring the sultry open invitation, and gently grasping her wrist to pull her hand away. "How much and on whom?"

With a small pout, she went on. "Five hundred, and my money is on Lord Westhope. Her father is in favor of the earl, and, truly, though he has the brain of a chicken, Westhope is charming enough, rich enough, and handsome enough. The standoffish chit could do worse, most certainly."

"Standoffish?" He remembered the slight look of melancholy on Amelia's face when she undressed the other evening, noticeable even when he was much more absorbed in admiring what she revealed bit by bit.

Gabriella shrugged. "She has a few friends, but generally, she tends to be aloof. As for Westhope, rumor has it she doesn't appear to be nearly as enchanted with him as he is with her. You know how the *ton* is, darling. They've christened her Elusive Venus because of her refusal to dance with more than a few suitors each evening, and how she seems to prefer seclusion to socializing."

"Not a very original sobriquet." Though, when he thought back on the evening, it was true he hadn't noticed Hathaway's daughter dancing but once among the glittering crowd. Most of the time, she appeared to be concealed as best as possible behind something like a pillar or a potted plant. She'd completely disappeared at least a half an hour before, though her aunt with the ridiculous turban was still in attendance. Rather interesting behavior for the beauteous toast of society. "Fame is nothing but an empty name," he said softly.

"What?" Gabriella looked at him in blank question.

"It's a quote," he said.

"A what?"

"Quote. From a book. I occasionally read," he supplied wryly.

That won him a disparaging wave of disdain for his intellectual bent. "If you want my opinion, she's odd. She doesn't flirt. I'm told she rides in the park at dawn every day, rather than go in the late morning or afternoon like is fashionable. My impression is she might even be boringly bookish, but if so, she doesn't tell anyone, like a true bluestocking would."

"Define a true bluestocking, in your estimation." He never ceased to be amazed at the shallow judgments of his peers.

"Those who flaunt their unladylike pursuits."

"Like enjoying literary works, I suppose."

"Precisely. Anyway, her distance creates a mystique because even though she's pretty enough, I suppose," Gabriella admitted grudgingly, "there is no attempt to ensnare every man in sight, like her contemporaries. It might be even said that she seems to avoid society as much as possible. Men don't know what to make of her, and therefore, they, being the peculiar creatures they are, are fascinated."

"We prefer to pursue, not be hunted down like a winded fox."

"Is that so?" Her eyes narrowed. "Are you in pursuit, then, of our elusive little miss?" It was clear that Gabriella was slightly jealous, even though she was on her second rich and tolerant husband. Alex had to wonder how long it would be before half the young ladies angling for husbands on the Marriage Mart decided to start limiting their dance cards in an effort to emulate Lady Amelia's singular allure.

"If she came without the price tag of a ceremony at a cathedral and a lifetime chained to one woman, perhaps, but in this case, the cost is too exorbitant. I was merely curious." He offered his arm politely. "Shall we go in? The hem of your lovely gown is getting wet."

He'd left, and then the blasted man had come back outside! Amelia had moved from the uncomfortable position of crouching behind a convenient but dripping yew and was debating on how to slip unobtrusively back into the ballroom when Lord Alexander reappeared through the door he'd just used to take his paramour inside. She stopped cold at the foot of the steps, horrified at his unexpected reappearance, but hopeful that maybe she wouldn't be seen if she didn't move. Then the fickle clouds shuttled away from the moon and he realized, in part due to her pale gown, that she stood there. His gaze fastened on her and he stopped short, his tall, elegant form limned by the uncertain light.

After a moment, he said, "So this is where you disappeared tonight, my lady."

She struggled to keep her composure in the face of being discovered in a position where she could have easily overheard them talking.

Which she had.

About *her*, no less. And from his remark, he'd been watching her enough to notice her absence from the ballroom, but she already knew that. She'd been watching him too.

"A damp choice, to be sure, but rather more comfortable than inside. Is there anything worse than a warm evening and a rainstorm? You can practically see the air, it is so humid." She kept her tone neutral and didn't move, glued to the stone path near the steps, her heart beating quickly.

For the second time, she found herself mortified in front of this man she didn't even know.

She had *eavesdropped*, which she usually found despicable in others. She'd listened to their entire discussion, skulking behind a gnarled tree like a parlor maid ducking behind the sofa to overhear a bit of tawdry gossip. Moreover, she'd seen Lady Fontaine intimately touch him in a most shocking place.

"My instincts must be failing me." Though his movements were leisurely, the way he strolled toward the stone steps reminded her of a stalking panther. "Back in Spain I could detect the enemy easily, no matter how well hidden. My men used to tell me I could smell the French." He came down the broad steps, which still glistened with rain. "Your perfume," he added softly, "I find much more pleasing. Tell me, why a wet garden rather than the adoring throng of admirers, Lady Amelia?"

It was a breach of etiquette for him to address her when he hadn't been formally introduced, but then again, hardly anything compared to that audacious kiss. Lord Alexander wasn't stuck on the proprieties, and that included searching her father's study.

Why he would do so had her puzzled, and to a certain extent affronted. He'd invaded the privacy of their home. Her balcony doors had been locked and so had her father's desk. Obviously he'd picked the locks somehow, which of itself seemed an unusual skill for the son of a duke to possess.

"I dislike crowds." It was the truth, but she wished the tremor in her voice hadn't been quite so audible. By now he stood only a very short distance away. Up close, he was somewhat intimidating, partly because of his height and the imposing width of his shoulders. Ebony brows arched over those striking midnight-dark eyes as they stared at each other. "Why are *you* out here, my lord?"

"I needed to have a brief conversation with Lady Fontaine." He added dryly, "Perhaps you heard us. That's fair enough, I suppose. I spied on you, and you spied on me. I believe the score is even now on both sides. I didn't notice your presence until you moved a little and I realized there was someone behind the tree."

She could deny it, but Amelia hated liars as much as she disliked eavesdroppers. "I had no intention of listening to your conversation with your . . . *friend*."

"I had no intention of kissing you either." His smile was a devilish curve of well-shaped lips. "But I can't say I regret I was there at such an opportune moment. And I suppose Gabriella is a friend, but from the inflection in your tone, you have a misconception of what kind of friend. In the past we had a somewhat different relationship, but not any longer."

At least he wasn't going to deny trespassing and invading her privacy, and the reference to the kiss, not to mention his open admission he'd had an affair with the sultry Lady Fontaine, made her blush furiously.

She should have soundly slapped him last night. Any true lady would have. . . . And why she hadn't, well, she'd tried not to think about it too much. About *him*.

But that had proved impossible.

In her coolest voice, she murmured, "It's none of my business what you do, or with whom you do it."

"True enough."

What she should do, Amelia knew, was sweep indignantly past him and go back to the ball. Thankfully it was dark enough that he probably couldn't see her flushed cheeks. "And outré of you to mention the liberty you took."

"No doubt your aunt told you that conforming to the rules isn't high on my list of priorities," he responded in a cool, mocking tone. "What else did she say when you asked about me?" His tall figure blocked her exit, the moonlight doing nice things to the chiseled planes of his fine-boned face. "I assume you received the requisite warnings about dishonorable gentlemen."

"Rather vain of you to think I asked at all."

"It was obvious you were discussing me earlier, just as I asked about you moments ago. Quite frankly, if I were you, I'd be dying of curiosity to know why I was on your balcony."

"You read my mind. I think you owe me an explanation. What *were* you doing on my balcony? Or for that matter, I assume you were the one who went through my father's desk. He was furious when he found it unlocked, for which, I am sure you agree, no one could blame him."

"I'm afraid I am not at liberty to explain."

Lips parted, she just looked at him; on such uncertain ground she had no idea what to say. It was unfair, for there was no question he was leagues more experienced in witty repartee—and God alone knew what else. She was at a severe disadvantage.

He laughed. It was a low sound, entirely male yet holding a certain musical quality that made her pulse quicken. "It sounds ridiculous, I know, but oddly enough it's true. I really can't tell you or I'd be breaking my word, and while I hold some gentlemanly strictures lightly, I always honor my promises. That said, may I compliment you on how lovely you look this evening?"

"You cannot dismiss the subject so easily."

"We have to, since I just explained I can't give you the answers at this time. But my flattery was sincere, trust me. I like that shade of blue on you."

"Thank you." She sounded composed, though she certainly didn't *feel* composed.

He thought she was beautiful. He'd said as much to his former mistress. Flowery compliments were one thing to one's face, but hearing it from someone who had no notion you were listening was somehow much more pleasing.

Dash it all. Why of all the young men she'd met so far in society did Lord Alexander have to be the most intriguing? The most *attractive*, actually, but that hardly mattered if Aunt Sophie caught her out in the dark, alone with him . . .

My husband doesn't have your glorious cock, darling. . . .

Was his . . . was *it* really glorious?

And where did *that* unladylike thought come from? His striking masculinity was unsettling.

"I need to go in," she said, looking pointedly at the glass doors, ajar just enough to let out the lilting sound of the orchestra. "I'll be missed."

"Your frequent disappearances have become accepted."

She'd heard Lady Fontaine's assessment of her motives for her reclusion and it made her hands curl into fists in the material of her skirts. "But not for the reason everyone thinks," she said evenly, looking him in the eye. "Not that I owe you, or anyone else, an explanation."

He inclined his head. "Granted. I am just curious as to why."

"I just don't care to dance all that much." A small falsehood, for she enjoyed dancing. It just wasn't wise to overexert herself. She definitely did not care for the consequences that came with too much dancing.

"I myself dance only occasionally."

Why did she get the impression he might be laughing at her? Amelia narrowed her eyes. In the flitting moonlight she tried to gauge his expression, but failed to see anything except the slight inquiring lift of his dark brows.

"Now that we have established our mutual disdain for the exercise of waltzes and other sundry whirling about to music, would you care to walk with me instead through the garden?"

"We haven't even been introduced."

"My dear, we've kissed. What better introduction could there be?" His smile was quixotic, just a small curve of those well-shaped lips, and she found herself looking at his mouth, remembering what it felt like, warm and insistent, on hers.

"You kissed *me*," she argued.

"And you kissed me back, if I recall."

"I was surprised." The defensiveness in her tone was only halfhearted, for he knew as well as she did that she hadn't reacted like an outraged young woman should have.

"Pleasantly surprised, I hope. In light of our established acquaintance, shall we?" He offered his arm.

"Are you sure you won't find me too *odd*?" She tried to make it sound flippant, like she didn't care, but Lady Fontaine's comment had stung. The men who flocked around her at these events admired her looks and knew she had a generous dowry. It was ironic that in her attempt to conceal her little problem, she had added fuel to the fire somehow. But the truth was, no one had troubled to *ask* her why she sat out so often; they just assumed she was being coy.

But Alex St. James had just asked.

He gazed at her, the corner of his mouth lifting attractively. "I don't find you the bland flavor of the usual innocent miss, to be sure. You must keep in mind, Gabriella is a simple creature. She cannot imagine not being flirtatious, or rising early for a morning ride, so she thinks it's odd. I imagine there is a good deal of jealousy leveled your way in general, which is why you don't have a great many friends yet. Do not worry. The intelligent ones will come around. And who cares about the others?"

His arm was still lifted expectantly.

She shouldn't walk with him. The notorious Duke of Berkeley's son was not a man a virtuous young woman should stroll through gardens with at any time.

But with all the suitors, all the flattery and masses of flowers crowding the parlor at her father's elegant town house in Mayfair, she still had never felt more than a sense of boredom with the entire process of finding a suitable husband.

At least Alexander St. James was *interesting*.

The trouble was not only who he was and his reputation, but that the man had stated clearly he had no interest in courting her.

But he also *had* correctly quoted Churchill's *The Ghost* earlier.

To her own amazement, Amelia heard herself say recklessly, "I suppose a short walk wouldn't hurt anything."

Chapter Five

The earl's gorgeous young daughter had a sense of adventure. She settled her slim fingers on his sleeve, her gaze demurely averted so he had a stunning view of her pure profile. She was dazzling this evening in a gown that was hardly risqué yet still managed to be seductive simply because she wore it. Her slender shoulders were bared just enough to encourage a man to imagine what it would be like to slip the garment downward, tumble her onto a convenient bed, loosen that unusual dark gold hair, and finish the lesson he had begun the other night in the art of making love. . . .

There was an innate sensuality about Lady Amelia. When he'd kissed her, even in her innocence she had responded to him, and damn it all if he wasn't interested to try it again.

He wondered if she knew what had happened between their two families, but guessed she didn't. Her father would hardly mention it to his sheltered daughter, and Alex himself had learned only recently about the scandal.

Get back to the business at hand, St. James.

"There is something about a garden after a rain," he murmured. "I'm no poet, but the mingled smell of wet soil, fragrant flowers, and a fresh breeze does evoke memories of childhood. I was rambunctious and hated being trapped inside. The moment it stopped raining, I was out the door. I had some inventive hiding places, and no doubt caused my poor, beleaguered nanny a great deal of trouble."

"No doubt," she agreed wryly, walking with him down the damp path. "And I am sure she is not the last female you have caused trouble. But perhaps you underestimate your poetic bent, Lord Alexander. I admit I like the smell after a rain as well, and now that you mention it, my childhood is probably why."

"Ah, see, you *were* asking about me. You know my name."

"My curiosity is understandable, as you yourself pointed out."

"True."

The froth of her azure skirts brushed a small rosebush, scattering petals and raindrops, but she didn't seem to notice. Instead she gazed up at him. "Since you refuse to say why, may I ask at least if you routinely scale roofs and hide on ladies' balconies?"

"No. You are unique."

Now, that was either put very poorly or very well, depending on the point of view, he thought sardonically. She *was* out of the ordinary for him, in that her status as a debutante would normally be a deterrent. It wasn't that he never wished to marry; it was just that five long years of war had left him with a taste for freedom. Finding a wife was not on his list of priorities, and with his wicked reputation, most of the marriageable young misses were kept out of his path anyway.

But the antipathy between their fathers aside, he had to admit that the unusual situation of their meeting, and, if he was honest, her physical allure, had caught his usually jaded interest.

"I don't know many gentlemen who wax eloquent over the smell of damp earth either," she said facetiously, "but you do it well, my lord."

He did do *some* things quite well, he'd been told, and he'd like to demonstrate his expertise to her, but that was so ill-advised the thought had barely registered before he pushed it aside. "Those years in Spain with Wellington gave me a new appreciation over some of the simpler things in life," he admitted. "The sons of dukes are not any more immune to hardships, or the bullets of the enemy, than the sons of blacksmiths or farmers."

"Aren't they?" Her expression was surprisingly introspective, her smooth brow furrowed. "I would imagine you would be more protected as an officer than as a foot soldier."

"Who do you think leads the men into battle?" He did his best to keep his tone neutral, well aware of society's negligent view of the atrocities of war. Here in London it seemed far away even to him, too, like a distant, haunting dream. "When it comes down to it, there is no rank in death."

Her lips—those soft, beguiling lips—twitched. "And you claim to not be a poet, my lord. Milton could not have said it better, and he is my favorite."

"You read Milton?" He had to admit to some surprise. *Paradise Lost* was hardly the fare of the usual English miss.

"Among other authors. Pope, Voltaire . . . and, yes, Charles Churchill." This time her smile definitely held a hint of mischief. "Please do not look so astounded. At the risk of sounding like a bluestocking, I admit I have a functioning brain, like yours. I suppose I am bookish."

"I'm not astounded," he replied automatically, not quite telling the truth. Her frankness was unusual in a world where flirtation was the order of the day.

"Yes, you are." She laughed. "But that is perfectly acceptable, since you don't appear to disapprove. Quite a different matter."

"It is hardly my place to approve or disapprove."

"Now that is entirely true, but few men feel that way. As much as it pains me to admit she is right about anything, Lady Fontaine has a point. Most men don't find intellect to be a necessary asset in a woman."

She was right, and it didn't say much for his gender. Alex had to laugh. "I see I'm dealing with a very liberal female."

"Are we 'dealing' with each other, my lord?" The question was very delicately asked, and more blunt than he expected, especially since he knew she'd overheard his very firm declaration to Gabriella about his opinion on being chained for life to one woman. That he'd said it to deflect Lady Fontaine's speculation more than as a reflection of his true view on marriage was a moot point. It had been said and duly overheard.

He was spared having to answer by Mother Nature. The rain that had ceased earlier began again without warning, no gentle patter but a true spring downpour that made Amelia utter a small cry of dismay. Luckily, down a path to their left was a small covered pavilion built for decorative purposes, like the follies in many English gardens.

"This way." It was much closer than going back the way they'd come, and Alex caught her arm and urged her in that direction, learning something else about the lovely Lady Amelia. She could sprint quite well. Breathless and damp, they ran up the short steps and stood beneath the small circular roof, listening to the rain come down in earnest.

"Oh, dear." She shook out her skirts and brushed back a wet golden tendril that was plastered to her slender neck. "I'm half-soaked."

Alex shrugged out of his damp jacket. "Are you cold?"

"No." Her face was a perfect pale oval, and one hand pressed her chest. "But I hope that short run doesn't . . . I mean, I need a moment to catch my breath."

"Looks like you have more than a moment, my lady." He peered out at the sheets of rain, the water sluicing off the roof in a running veil. "We can't leave here until this lets up." Turning back, he noticed she stood very still, as if concentrating, her face averted, apparently finding the view of one of the Grecian-style pillars fascinating.

Then he realized that even with the steady drum of the rain, he could *hear* her breathing. It wasn't much, just a faint whistle with each inhale, but alarm shot through him. "Are you quite all right?"

She nodded, but there was a slight jerkiness in the motion.

"Liar." All at once, her reluctance to dance made sense, as did her appearance on the balcony and the evident need for fresh air. There were several chairs for sitting and viewing the gardens on much more pleasant evenings than this one, and he draped his coat over her slim shoulders and urged her toward one of them. "Sit down. I assume it passes fairly quickly. I had a friend at Eton with the same problem. If we played cricket, he could only bowl a few times before he took a rest. Sitting out on a regular basis seemed to stave off a truly bad attack."

"I don't know what you mean," she said, but the weak protest lacked true conviction.

It took him only a split second to rethink pushing her firmly into the chair. Alex instead promptly lifted her into his arms and settled down himself, with her on his lap, ignoring her gasp of outrage. He held her lightly, her skirts draped over his legs, nothing sexual in the embrace. One of her hands rested palm forward on his gray satin waistcoat, but she didn't push away.

"Is it worse in the spring? It always was for Harry." He asked it softly, remembering how surprising it had been that someone so outwardly hale and hearty as his old friend had such an alarming problem.

After a moment, she whispered, "Yes. I was having

trouble earlier . . . the damp air, I think, and the crush of people. That's why I was outside."

She felt deliciously female, soft in all the right places, the curves nestled against him bringing a predictable physical response of tightening in his groin, which under the circumstances he ignored. "Just relax. I have you."

I have you. He'd like to have her, in a much different connotation than what he just meant, but at the moment she felt fragile in his arms—though he had to say already that he could no longer hear the telltale whistle as she inhaled.

"My father insists no one know."

"Why?" Alex frowned.

Her smile was slight, no more than a wry twist of her lips. "It is a fairly glaring imperfection. No man, apparently, would want a wife who could not dance two waltzes in a row."

What man wouldn't want you?

Blast it all, he almost said it out loud.

He substituted, "What nonsense."

What a lovely illusion, but an illusion just the same. Amelia felt secure, comfortable, the arms cradling her both protective and strong. Her head fit nicely into the muscled curve of his shoulder.

Is this how a woman feels with her lover? It was an intriguing question that had never occurred to her before. Yes, she'd known her entire life, theoretically, that men were bigger and more muscular than women, but Alexander St. James was the first one to truly demonstrate it in a way that confirmed the concept. To start with, he'd physically picked her up twice now, with what seemed like ease. Second, his scent held her captive—a mixture of brandy and sandalwood and something else . . . something new and exciting. As embarrassing as it was to not be able to entirely stave off the attack she'd been fighting most of the evening, it was rather nice to be gently held in his capable arms. Beneath her bottom, his thighs felt like iron.

"My father takes marrying me off quite seriously, I assure you," she said in an attempt to make light of things, and grateful she didn't wheeze embarrassingly. "Beware: I am supposed to not dawdle about, and ensnare some unsuspecting man as soon as possible."

In the length of their short acquaintance, she'd already learned his quicksilver smile had the ability to both charm and distract. He laughed, his dark eyes holding her gaze. "I would count that as a sincere warning, my lady, but a diamond of the first water like you could probably do much better than the youngest son of a duke with a somewhat dubious reputation. I don't think in your case I qualify as a good match."

"If we are found in this highly scandalous position, neither of us would have a choice."

That observation made his brows lift, but he seemed unperturbed. "I think with the rain we are quite safe."

He was no doubt right, but Aunt Sophie was probably having a small, discreet fit somewhere over Amelia's continued absence, and he didn't know her eccentric relative well. While her father and aunt understood that she needed to step outside now and again, she'd been gone longer than usual.

"Besides," he said conversationally, "there is always a choice if you simply ignore gossip. I should know."

"So I was told."

"It's quite true."

That remark alone should make her insist he release her at once. The blasé attitude might be fine for the notorious Lord Alexander, but *she* would not be able to walk away from a scandal unscathed. Instead, she murmured, "Maybe true for those with the luxury of defying convention. Women have infinitely less freedom, my lord."

"I will return you to the ballroom as soon as it is possible without both of us getting a good drenching, which would, by the way, draw quite a bit of attention to the fact that we were out in the rain together. How are you feeling?"

His solicitude was genuine, she realized, comfortably and *brazenly* nestled in his arms. The constriction in her chest she'd been fighting all evening was still there, but easier now. There was a certain relief in being able to just admit her breathing bothered her. "Better," Amelia said on a blessedly easy exhale.

"We'll wait this out. You can claim you were outside and had to duck in the servant's entrance."

"I suppose that will work."

His voice was quiet and effectively authoritative. "But we *will* stay here until you are more comfortable."

The trouble was, she actually was quite comfortable in a very shocking way. If her father saw her like this . . . draped all over a man in such a shameless fashion . . .

He'd be outraged. But then again, would it be for her reputation or for the fact that it might hurt her chances of being married off as soon as possible? She sat there, pondering that question, listening to the rain, longer than she needed.

"I think it is best if you release me." She sat up, decorum finally asserting itself.

He obligingly loosened his hold, but his handsome face wore a concerned expression. "Is it truly past?"

"I shouldn't have run," she acknowledged, slipping off his lap, self-consciously smoothing her skirts as she stood. "I knew I was having troubles already. It just bothered me for a moment. The affliction is sporadic. I can go months without problems at all."

That was true, fortunately. And he was right. In the spring, when certain flowers bloomed, she sneezed and had troubles, but usually she was as healthy as anyone else—healthier, actually, because she rarely became ill.

"I'm glad to hear it, though I doubt a good soaking does anyone much good. I'm afraid the rain shows little sign of letting up." Politely, he stood also. It was dark enough Amelia couldn't see his expression clearly, but the ebony gleam of his hair and those glorious eyes were all too fascinating.

Perhaps she should just go ahead and brave the elements. Surely Alexander St. James was much more dangerous than a case of lung fever. "I *have* to get back," she said firmly.

In answer to that vehement declaration, it began to rain harder.

"The powers that be seem to disagree." His tone was mild and amused. Then he added, in a devastatingly soft voice, "Don't run away from me."

"I shouldn't have agreed to walk with you in the first place." She tilted her head back. He seemed so very tall in the insufficient light. The weight and warmth of his jacket enveloped her in that intoxicating masculine scent.

"Probably not. Why did you?"

Nonplussed, she just looked at him, the heavens tossing buckets of water downward. To her chagrin a small tremble of excitement rippled through her. There was a certain gleam in those seductive dark eyes that she instinctively recognized.

"Perhaps," he suggested in a low voice, "you simply wanted another kiss?"

Chapter Six

Alex really wished he knew the rules of this new game he was compelled to play, wise or not. Amelia stood there, looking at him with an expression he interpreted as adorable confusion.

"Just a thought," he added mildly, as if her answer didn't matter, because if he'd confused her, he'd just confounded himself even more. He'd certainly never felt the urge to tutor a virgin before now. A dalliance was one thing when both parties were experienced and knew the rules of uncomplicated lust. It was something else altogether when it involved a virtuous young woman who was currently the toast of society and was from an aristocratic family.

And not just any family. A Patton, at that. Her father might have an apoplexy if he knew where his precious daughter was at the moment and who she was with. And though Alex was a grown man and made his own decisions, he knew his own father wouldn't be any happier.

She had such a lovely mouth, those lips petal soft and a delicate rose, and he was half-aroused already just from holding her. Without his jacket on, the growing bulge in his breeches was probably visible, but luckily she was staring at his face, not his crotch.

"You aren't serious." Her tone was hushed.

"Most certainly I am serious. Could there be a more romantic spot than this?" He indicated the interior of the little summerhouse. "Seclusion, a rainstorm, a man and a woman. It seems to me a kiss would be a natural event in this setting."

"I meant that you aren't serious about *me*, my lord." Dwarfed by his jacket, she looked quite young, her soft golden hair worn in a simple, elegant twist that pleased him. Enormous blue eyes regarded him with unsettling directness. "Please keep in mind I heard you state quite plainly to Lady Fontaine you are not interested in ... how did you put it? Ah yes, being 'chained for life to one woman.' Why the flirtation? I admit I do not know you well enough to be sure, but I am fairly certain you would not seek to ruin me and then walk away. If all you want is a diversion, you should have accepted Lady Fontaine's shameless offer."

Her insight was a little unsettling. He should be trying to coax information from Lady Amelia about where her father might keep his valuables instead of seducing another kiss from her.

"Gabriella is married," he said quietly. "On principle, I do not touch other men's wives."

Her lips twitched, unfortunately drawing his attention to her tempting mouth again. "Be careful, Lord Alexander, for I now understand you always keep your word and have principles when it comes to love affairs. You are beginning to sound rather like a respectable gentleman after all, despite your reputation."

"Please call me Alex," he suggested, reaching out to touch her cheek and gazing into her eyes. "And do not assume for a minute I am a gentleman. For instance, I am going to point out at this moment that a kiss is not a lifetime commitment, but merely an enjoyable moment between two people who are attracted to each other. That observation is entirely to my own purpose."

"What makes you think I am attracted to you?"

At least he'd distracted her from asking why he was pursuing her, and the answer to her question was a simple one. He smiled. "I don't pretend to a vast amount of knowledge on any subject usually, but there is one area of expertise I can modestly claim."

"Women," she supplied for him, her eyes luminous in the darkness.

"The rumor is I am an avid student of the subject of their desires." The truth was, he wasn't inexperienced, but neither was he as nefarious as the whispers painted him. But when he did take a lover, he was always concerned for her pleasure and not just his own.

And he was astute enough to know Lady Amelia was not immune to the pull between them.

She laughed lightly, and while it sounded breathless, it was in an entirely different way than her earlier moment of distress. "I am sure you are, but—"

He interrupted her by lowering his head until her breath fluttered against his lips. One arm went around her waist and he urged her closer. "Remember, it's just a kiss," he whispered. "May I?"

In his lifetime, he could not ever remember having to ask for permission before he kissed someone. That singular sway of a woman's body toward a man was usually enough to signal capitulation. He'd have to think about that later. But for the moment, she was in his arms and apparently willing. . . .

Her lashes drifted downward and her head tilted back just a little.

Definitely willing. Perfect.

Alex molded his mouth to hers with tantalizing gentleness, mindful of her earlier difficulties. This was not the time for a hot, devouring embrace, although his now rock-hard erection wished to argue the sentiment. He kissed her slowly, lightly stroking his tongue into her mouth, finding himself mesmerized by the sensuality of the moment, especially when her slim arm rose to circle his neck and she pressed more closely against him.

She tasted divine, sweet and warm, and he could picture only too clearly in his mind's eye a different setting of cool, crisp sheets, the two of them naked, bare breasts to chest, his hands tangled in her silken hair. . . .

His cock strained against the fabric of his breeches almost painfully and he adjusted their embrace in an effort to hide his arousal. She would have none of it, molding herself to his body with an instinctive shift of pelvis to pelvis that undoubtedly left her no longer in the dark as to his escalating need.

This was *not* just a kiss.

Awakening a woman to her first sexual desire held a spellbinding allure he'd never considered before. Or was it just awakening this particular woman? His brain rejected the notion even as he brushed his jacket off her shoulders so he could gather her closer, with less material separating them. His hand found the curve of her spine and rested at the small of her back, urging her even more against him.

"Amelia!"

Experienced enough to understand strident objection, even if it was just in the way a name was said, Alex jerked back and lifted his mouth away. He heard Amelia make a small sound, of dismay or disappointment, he wasn't sure. It was still raining fairly hard, but there stood her aunt at the foot of the steps, an incredulous expression on her face, the ridiculous turban quite soaked.

All that time in Spain confounding the French, and he'd been caught flat-out in a bad position for the second time within a day, and by women, no less, Alex thought with cynical amusement. It was a good thing his luck hadn't run this way during the war, or he wouldn't still be alive.

"Madam, perhaps you should join us out of the rain."

He let go of Lady Sophia McCay's niece and executed a slight formal bow. "We took refuge here earlier when the downpour started."

A bedraggled Lady McCay stormed up the steps and said icily, "Refuge doesn't seem to be all you've taken."

"It isn't entirely his fault." Amelia was admirably collected, her beautiful face maybe a little flushed, but her expression composed. "I left earlier because ... well, you understand why, and Alex helped me."

"Alex?" Her aunt's expression went from disconcerted to downright horrified. "I find that familiarity unsettling when just a few hours ago you asked me who he was, Amelia. Not to mention what I just saw. What is happening here?"

If he didn't take charge of this situation, it might be headed for catastrophe. Alex said smoothly, "Lady Amelia and I have met before, just never been introduced. I realize what you saw might be construed in a certain way, but—"

"Forgive me, my lord, but what I saw can be construed in one way and one way only. Amelia, please go out the back gate. The carriage is waiting. When you were gone so long, I anticipated you were having troubles and summoned it before becoming truly alarmed and looking for you. We will leave directly, but first I'd like a word with Lord Alexander."

It was difficult to pull off the regal, outraged chaperone when raindrops were dripping off her nose, but Sophia fought for the right expression anyway. The sense that something was awry had become stronger and stronger with each passing moment of Amelia's absence, and never had her instincts been so on target.

"I don't think—" Amelia began to say, managing to look very lovely even with her shining fair hair disheveled and her dress spotted with dampness. She had a just-kissed look too, her lashes slightly lowered and her mouth parted.

"Evidently you *don't* think," Sophia snapped out, adopting her best censorial tone, though she had never really scolded Amelia before. "Please go, child, and you and I will discuss this on the ride home."

"I'll get soaked." Amelia stood stubbornly in place, and the rain had nothing to do with it.

"It's a warm night, and as I am dripping wet already myself, we can ride home together in our mutual dishevelment."

Though her niece was usually more than capable of holding her ground, there must have been enough steel in Sophia's voice. Amelia capitulated with surprising meekness, though she did throw a last telling glance at the tall young man who stood with such nonchalant elegance in the middle of the pavilion, a hard-to-read expression on his all-too-handsome face. Then she went down the steps.

"Are you mad?" Sophia asked without preamble. "What are you thinking, my lord? My brother-in-law has very little love for anyone with the last name St. James. Had it been he, not I, who just discovered you in such a compromising situation with his daughter, you would find yourself summoning your seconds and rising at dawn, I promise you."

Alexander St. James merely lifted a dark brow and bent to retrieve his tailored jacket from the floor. "How long has your niece had difficulties with her breathing and how serious is it?"

She should just tell him it was none of his affair, but the faint frown of concern he wore looked surprisingly genuine.

And besides, she'd witnessed that rather extraordinary kiss. He, with his tousled dark hair and starkly masculine good looks, and Amelia, so slender and fair, together in what looked like a very tender embrace. It had been a beautiful moment, and Sophia had almost turned around and retreated quietly until she reminded herself sharply just who he was. Even if there wasn't well-known dislike between their two families, he had a rakish reputation that was undoubtedly well deserved. There were whispers that his current mistress was an Italian opera singer named Maria Greco, known both for her beauty and her volatile temperament.

Still, she found herself saying, "It was much worse when she was a child. This is the only time of year she truly has troubles now."

"So she said. Is it worse in London or when she is in the country?"

"Here in London. I suspect it has something to do with all the soot. As the weather warms and there is less smoke spewing from the chimneys all over town, she won't have nearly as much difficulty."

"Then why the devil isn't she still in Cambridgeshire if it affects her health to be here?"

Sophia adjusted her turban, which had begun to list hopelessly to the side due to its sodden state. "I did suggest we delay our arrival, but her father was adamant she not miss the beginning of the season."

He muttered something under his breath that might have been "damn fool." Sophia had to privately agree with the sentiment, though, as Amelia had been managing her affliction since childhood, she had done rather well. As far as Sophia knew, no one in society knew it was even an issue.

"That subject aside, my lord," Sophia said firmly, "I must ask you to stay away from my niece. While I appreciate your concern for her health this evening, it obviously isn't your only interest in her."

"She's quite beautiful." He looked remarkably unrepentant, perhaps even a little amused.

Exactly what one would expect from a true rake.

"Yes," Sophia agreed. "Other men have noticed as well. *Respectable* suitors who have much to offer her, starting with marriage and stability. And while I understand you have behind you a solid record as a war hero—"

"Forgive the interruption, madam, but quite frankly,

every soldier who manages to stay alive is a war hero." His voice had taken on a curious flatness. "So, let me correct you. I do not even have that much to offer your niece. I am cognizant of your objections. You needn't list them for me. I'm a libertine with a reputation for enjoying women. I have wealth, but no title. My father is a duke, but I will never inherit, which is fine with me, but makes me much less desirable as a husband. Since I am not looking for a wife anyway, I find that to be an asset, not a liability, but I'm sure you see it differently. Normally the St. James ducal connection would be a feather in my cap, but not to the Patton family, since there is enmity between us because of that ill-fated affair years ago. I understand that completely. Do not worry. I am not interested in courting Lady Amelia."

Nonplussed at that frank recital of his undesirability as a suitor, Sophia was silent a moment. Then she asked simply, "Then . . . why?"

His smile was so charming, so wickedly attractive that even at her age, she felt a small flush of feminine reaction under its compelling power. "If you are asking about the kiss, I am sorry, but I cannot quite explain it away. Occasionally I admit to yielding to a reckless impulse. Pretty females seem to be a catalyst to such moments."

"So I've heard."

"Don't believe everything, my lady." His lashes lowered slightly over those devilishly dark eyes.

Yes, he was a very beautiful young man. If he wouldn't see her do it, she would have snapped open her fan and waved it vigorously to cool her flushed face. She summoned her most severe chaperone's expression. "As long as you are not reckless again with Amelia, I will say nothing to my brother-in-law about this."

"For his sake, I advise you not to," he said with equanimity, his expression smoothing to impassivity. "I may not be a hero, my lady, but I am an excellent shot, should he choose to play the outraged father and challenge me. Now, shall I escort you to the back gate?"

Chapter Seven

Though it pained her to admit it, the aria, sung in a remarkable contralto, was superb. Amelia sat in her seat in her father's private box, her gaze fastened on the stage, and fought to ignore the disconsolate thoughts running through her mind.

She's lain beneath him, naked and eager, and he's kissed her the same way he has me, touched her intimately, and then they . . .

She wasn't entirely sure what they might have done after that, which might be more infuriating than the knowledge that Alex St. James had supposedly made love to the woman who was singing. Since no one had yet really explained exactly what men and women did together in bed, Amelia had only a fair idea what happened, but she did know if it was half as pleasurable as an intimate kiss, she was, quite frankly, jealous of the woman on the stage. It was irrational, but it just . . . was.

According to the latest gossip, Maria Greco was his mistress.

How dare he kiss me, Amelia pondered darkly, while

he was involved with another woman in what was reputed to be a long-term affair?

To her chagrin, she and the singer couldn't be more different. The opera star who held the audience spellbound at the moment was voluptuous, raven-haired, and olive-skinned. Sumptuously dressed in her costume, she walked across the stage and boldly flaunted her beauty and her talent, her movements dramatic and self-assured. The audience was mesmerized.

And the diva's lover? Was he in attendance? Amelia incessantly scoured the audience for a familiar head of glossy dark hair and a tall, well-muscled body, but didn't find him.

It wasn't until her father left at the intermission to get them all some champagne that Aunt Sophia leaned toward her and said quietly, "I hope your silence and diligent searching of the crowd don't mean that you are looking for St. James."

Since it was precisely what she was doing, Amelia couldn't help a guilty start. During their very damp carriage ride home the other evening, she'd sat and endured the lecture about young ladies avoiding certain kinds of gentlemen. She'd managed to deflect the question of how she'd met Alex in the first place without telling an outright lie, by saying they'd run into each other just outside their town house. Since the balcony off her bedroom was just outside, in a literal sense it wasn't a falsehood, was it?

"I did wonder if he was here," she admitted honestly, smoothing the silk skirt of her cream-colored gown. She gestured with studied casualness at the stage where Maria had just exited in a whirl of scarlet satin. "I mean, after all, she's supposed to be his latest paramour."

Aunt Sophie's brows snapped together. "Good heavens. How would you even know such a thing?"

"Your friends, Aunt Sophie." Amelia had to mirthlessly laugh. "You must admit their favorite topic is who is being indiscreet with whom. I cannot help but over-hear some interesting gossip."

At first it looked as if Sophie might deny it, but then she gave a rueful little smile and sank back in her velvet-upholstered chair. "People are interesting, and I suppose it is natural to talk about what they do. Alexander St. James is a little too interesting, if you ask me. I shudder to think what would be said if anyone knew about the interlude I stumbled upon the other evening. His name is enough to ruin you, Amelia, so please keep that in mind. You have always been a level-headed girl."

The din of hundreds of voices rose, the gilt boxes packed full of the fashionable crowd, the women glit-tering with jewels, the men finely dressed in the latest trend. It was too warm for her tastes, but at least Amelia was perfectly comfortable. The past few days had been clear and summerlike and she'd had no difficulties.

She affected a shrug. "It was a kiss, no more. I admit I found him charming."

"He is that," her aunt muttered.

Conscious of her father's impending return, though she was sure that getting refreshment when the theater was so packed for the closing night of Don Giovanni would not be a swift event, Amelia gazed at her aunt and remarked, "You said in the carriage the other night that even without his reputation, Father would find St. James particularly objectionable because of his last name. Since you were intent on scolding me without pause, I couldn't get a word in at the time, but I've been wondering about it. Can you tell me why?"

This evening Aunt Sophie was splendid in an inter-esting ensemble that involved yards of dark purple bro-cade and a square-cut bodice that had been in a fashion popular two centuries before. There was no turban in sight, but instead her dark brown hair was piled up in an elaborate period style to match the gown that show-cased her long, elegant neck. The eccentricity was a nat-

ural part of her personality, and Amelia was never quite
sure how her aunt might be dressed for a given event. To
his credit, her father endured it with pained silence, but
it was clear he disapproved.

It was usually a nice note of levity to each evening
to see his reaction when Aunt Sophie joined them, and
not everyone disparaged her unique sense of style. Most
gentleman turned to look when Sophia passed by, but
Amelia had heard her aunt say more than once that after being married to her William, as she always called
her deceased husband, she wasn't sure she ever wanted
to try again, for fear of disappointment. Every woman
deserved one good marriage, she'd declared time and
again, but asking for two was pressing your luck.

"I shouldn't have mentioned it, I suppose," her aunt
murmured after a moment. "I was distraught after finding the two of you in such a compromising situation."

"I'm hardly compromised by one kiss, and may I
point out that whether you should have said it or not,
you did say it." The chastening tone of her voice made
her feel guilty.

Sophia hesitated, and then said simply, "I know part
of what happened, but I am not at all sure your father
wishes for me to repeat it to you. It involves an old scandal . . . well, old but not quite forgotten, as I understand
it. Recent enough emotions still run high between the
duke and your father, so they avoid each other. Trust
me when I say that though your father wouldn't be
pleased for you to commit an indiscretion like the other
evening's with any man, finding you with Lord Alexander in particular would make him livid. Your reputation
would suffer from a duel, and, quite frankly, the duke's
son fought with Wellington for five long years. I believe
him when he claims to be an excellent marksman."

The notion of a duel hadn't occurred to her, perhaps
because it wasn't like she'd been meeting him clandes-
tinely on purpose. Both encounters had been driven by
chance. Amelia sat in shocked silence for a moment.

Her father's arrival, a glistening bottle in hand, precluded any sort of reply.

Her father was decades older than Alex St. James and he was her only parent. He wasn't warm and caring, but he wasn't cruel or neglectful. Amelia would like the chance to know him better, but she was getting the impression he deliberately kept her at a distance, at first physically by leaving her in the country her entire childhood when he obviously preferred London, and now emotionally by putting the responsibility for the season in Aunt Sophie's hands as much as possible. Intellectually she knew it couldn't be because of a distaste for her personally—he didn't know her well enough to dislike her. It could be he was disappointed she hadn't been a son. But since she'd arrived in London, she was coming to the conclusion that he simply didn't wish for her to become too involved in his life. It rankled, but just the same, the idea of being the cause of possible harm, even indirectly, to her own father was disturbing.

"That was a blasted nuisance," he announced irritably as he swept back the curtain and entered the box. "Every person in London appears to be here. Luckily I ran into Westhope and together we managed to shoulder our way through and actually obtain something to drink. Naturally, I invited him to sit with us."

Naturally. Otherwise, her father would be forced to converse politely with her and Aunt Sophie. Amelia watched dismally as the earl beamed at her, choosing the closest chair. His attire was the elegant height of fashion, and his fair hair perfectly groomed. As he handed her a glass of champagne, he made a very polite compliment about her ivory tulle gown. He looked handsome, urbane, and, as usual, when she looked into his blue eyes, she felt nothing.

Unfortunately, a moment later she finally spotted Alex.

He had entered one of the opposite gilded boxes, dressed in black and white, evidently disdaining the affection of ruffles or lace at his collar and cuffs. There were no glittering stickpins, nor did he do anything but wear his dark hair in its usual silky disarray. His height set him apart, as did the unmistakable brilliance of his signature smile as an elderly lady wearing a vivid emerald gown said something to amuse him and motioned him to take a seat next to her.

Amelia remembered the brush of that ebony hair against her fingers as his mouth moved gently but possessively against hers. . . .

She remembered something else also. The hard, long feel of him, intriguingly male—shocking, but also stirring something within her that might mean she was wanton, for she'd been little better than Lady Fontaine, pressing shamelessly against him as she kissed him back without restraint. He'd been aroused, had wanted her, and she'd found it both exhilarating and . . . fascinating.

". . . performance, isn't it?"

She jerked back into the moment. Lord Westhope looked at her expectantly over the rim of his glass. "Um, yes," she mumbled, having not the slightest notion what he'd just said and fighting a blush over her less than maidenly recollections. "It is. I agree completely, my lord."

"I am partial to the arts, of course. All of it. Literature, sculpture, music, and, of course, operatic compositions."

Since his knowledge of literature, in her experience, was dubious at best but she couldn't speak for the rest, Amelia merely lifted her opera glasses and studied the stage, though currently the curtain was down. "All noble interests, my lord."

"I don't know if you have heard, but there is going to be a display of Simeon's work at a private gallery very soon. I would be honored to escort you to the exhibition."

Actually, she hadn't ever heard of the artist. Honesty compelled her to admit it. "I'm not familiar with the name."

Lord Westhope looked triumphant, obviously pleased to relieve her of her ignorance. "He's English, but lived abroad at times. Died several years ago, and it has been discovered he had some paintings he never displayed. His grandson, who is also a rising talent, has invited a select crowd of only the most fashionable to attend a showing. As such a patron of the arts, of course I received one."

"Of course," she echoed.

He didn't notice the irony in her tone. "As the artist always selected the most unusual subjects, the younger Simeon has reputedly had repeated offers for his grandfather's work but has declined. It should be an interesting event."

As interesting as the rakish son of a duke, and a dark scandal no one wishes to discuss?

She doubted it.

Then she glanced up and saw her father staring at her, obviously listening in on their conversation. His frown deepened, and a perverse part of her wanted to just decline the invitation to thwart his obvious desire for her to accept.

Before she could speak, she heard him say smoothly, "Simeon? I've seen his work and it is brilliant. Amelia would love to go, wouldn't you, my dear?"

She looked entrancing, even from afar, and Alex noted with unexpected irritation that perhaps Gabriella was going to win her wager after all, for there sat the Earl of Westhope next to Amelia, fawning all over her.

Forbidden fruit, he reminded himself with cynical inner reflection as he sipped tepid champagne. Delicious and ripe in all the right places, but the forbidden part must account for the fascination. Not too often in his life had he encountered a woman he wanted but couldn't have. The unique situation had him off balance; that was all.

She wore white. The symbolic nature of her attire

should put him off, because purity had never been a draw before, nor, if he intellectualized the situation, should it be now. The word angelic came to mind, with her dark gold hair and that demure white gown. There were pearls around her slender neck, but otherwise, her beauty was her only adornment and it was all she needed.

A fan lightly tapped him on the wrist. "If you continue to stare at Hathaway's box, my dear boy, it will not make the location of the key any clearer, and it might cause his lordship to wonder why you are so interested in him."

Interested in the earl? Not so. His daughter was another matter.

Alex transferred his gaze with effort to where his grandmother sat primly next to him. "I've been thinking about how small a key is. And there is his country estate, besides the town house. It could be anywhere. Not to mention how perhaps he has it in the safekeeping of his solicitor."

"Hathaway doesn't know what the key is, and it is in a distinctive case." Millicent St. James held, as always, on to her formidable poise. "If he did know its purpose, we would have heard from him long ago—mark my words. So I assume it is stuck somewhere in a drawer or a closet or . . ."

"Buried in the garden," he supplied when she trailed off. "Maybe it was tossed away as useless years ago. As an object of no value, since no one knew what it unlocked. I don't know what the key is either, precisely. I think you should enlighten me. You were distraught enough when we spoke at Berkeley House—"

"I am never distraught, Alexander." The interruption was haughty and concise. "I don't want him to have this key, which I described to you in detail. This is important to me, and I do not think you need to question me further on this matter."

"Perhaps you don't, but I am not quite as sure I don't

need more information. Forgive me, Grandmama, if I think there is more to this than what you originally told me. The scandal was years ago. Why is this blasted key important now?"

She stiffened. "I have already said I do not want to explain."

Royally said and royally meant, very much the edict of the Dowager Duchess of Berkeley. "Yes, and I honored that sentiment out of respect and affection. But maybe it would help in my task if you told me why, after several decades at least, you suddenly want that key badly enough I should risk my neck to retrieve it. For instance, I'd like to know what it unlocks."

"No."

The urge to throw his hands up in exasperation was strong, but the hundreds of witnesses made him clench his jaw instead. She would deplore it if they seemed less than in perfect accord.

The orchestra was tuning again, the intermission nearly over. Next to him, in a velvet chair, her spine rigid, she looked as if she might balk entirely, but then acquiesced enough to tell him, "I didn't realize what my sister-in-law had done. I didn't know Hathaway had the key until I received a communication recently informing me of that unpalatable fact."

"Communication from where?"

"Alexander, I believe I just answered your question. It isn't complicated. He has something that belongs to our family and I want it back. Chances are Hathaway will never even know its significance and will probably never miss it. Just in case, I want to have it in *my* possession."

That stubborn tone made him want to groan out loud. Since he would walk on glowing coals for his grandmother, Alex muttered, "Can't you be more forthcoming?"

"Can't you be less inquisitive out of deference for my wish for privacy?"

This was a losing battle.

"Just work on it," she added, as if it was a simple task. *But*, those four words implied, *work harder*.

"Of course." His smile was sardonic, but she didn't notice.

"Hathaway's daughter is a beauty." His grandmother studiously did not look in the direction of the subject of their conversation, but at the currently lowered crimson curtain over the stage. "I hope she is spared the reprehensible lack of morality of the lineage of her family."

"Grandmama," he said gently but with amusement, "I am not going to comment on the issue of morality, if you don't mind. Isn't John your grandson? I believe he was once the measure against which society weighed the standard of licentious behavior. For that matter, I think my reputation compared against that of Lady Amelia would find me severely lacking. Hers is beyond reproach; mine less than admirable. But," he added softly, availing himself of the opportunity to gaze across the theater again, "you are right: she is quite memorable."

That won him a sharp look. "Since when do you think any ingenue memorable?"

"Never," he replied with a small smile and a dismissive shrug. *Before now.* "Now, tell me, what do you think of the opera so far?"

His purported dalliance with Maria was a taboo subject. His grandmother was far too dignified to mention her grandson having a possible liaison with a lowborn singer, no matter how talented the woman might be. She sniffed and folded her hands in her lap, her aristocratic face neutral. "I think it diverting enough. Did I tell you your father wants to have a private family dinner? We do not do it often enough."

Nice change of subject. He stifled a grin. Occasionally he did like to tease her.

"No."

"I will expect you for dinner at Berkeley House the day after tomorrow."

He knew well enough when an invitation could not be refused, so Alex said with resignation, "I look forward to it."

After the performance ended, he escorted his grandmother out to her carriage and handed her in, waiting until it pulled away before going back inside. The porter recognized him and allowed him to pass through the door to backstage, where, as usual, Maria was holding court for a few privileged admirers. Brilliant bouquets of flowers scattered around were a contrast to the somewhat tawdry trappings of dressing areas and the skeletons of unused sets. The odor of greasepaint and human sweat was heavy, and he didn't care much for it.

How to do this gracefully was the question.

No, *why* might actually be more pertinent, but two soft, intimate kisses might have something to do with it.

Maria's sumptuous bosom and sleek dark hair were set off by her flowing dressing gown. He waited patiently, one shoulder against the wall as she flirted and laughed with the men thronged around her, her postperformance energy still high backstage, as it always was. Finally noticing him standing there, she excused herself, her hips swaying provocatively as she walked over, a small, sultry smile curving her full lips. "You came."

He took her hand and bowed over it. "I would not miss closing night."

"A perfect performance tonight, *si*, Alexi?"

"Tremendous," he agreed, and he was sincere.

"And now you can give *me* a magnificent performance of your own. That is why you are here, no? It will take me only a moment to change."

"I can see you home, but I don't think I'll be staying tonight, Maria." He added with as much careful courtesy as he could, "Or any other night. I need to ask a favor."

Her dark eyes narrowed. "A favor? You turn me down and ask a *favor*!"

An outraged opera singer certainly could shriek out a word. Alex winced, and several of the stagehands who were hurrying about, taking care of postperformance cleanup, stopped and stared.

"We are friends, are we not?" he said evenly. "And even if we only spent the one night together months ago, I did *you* a favor by letting all of London believe we were lovers, thus saving you from having to deal with ardent suitors every single night. Everyone thought you were unavailable, and I didn't argue the point because it seemed to be what you wanted."

She sniffed, adjusting the sash on her dressing gown. "A good performer needs to sleep and sleep well. I practice also, most days, so I am busy. Nor am I as young as I once was. I admit I found there was a freedom in not having to bother with a lover. Since," she added with a coy arch of her dark brows, "you refused to cooperate, and no one else has caught my eye."

"I think we shall both remember that one night with fondness, and it is better left that way." It was true, he'd been a bit foxed, enjoyed the performance enough that he'd wanted to meet the glorious Italian who could sing so beautifully, and then had somehow ended up in her bed. In the light of day, he'd been not precisely regretful, but well aware that the attraction between them was merely physical. There had been no desire to pursue an affair beyond that one—albeit memorable—night. He reached into his pocket and produced the jewelry case. "A parting gift. I hope it will remind you of me."

She looked at the velvet-covered case, a tiny frown creasing her brow. "Why would you? As you said, we only shared passion once."

He grinned. "I think perhaps it was more than once, *signora*."

"True enough." She tossed back her dark hair and laughed. "I meant one night, Alexi. To my regret."

"We would have tired of each other quickly."

"Perhaps." Her gaze swept boldly over him. "Perhaps not."

"Trust me. And take this, please."

Mollified, she took the case, and he heard her gasp as she viewed the ruby earrings.

Perhaps I've been a bit extravagant, he thought as she lifted the jewels and the light caught the dazzling brilliance of the stones, but it was well-known that red was her favorite color. They would suit her, and he could afford it.

"Oh, Alexi . . . I am speechless."

"You will look beautiful wearing them. And if you will, as a favor to me, tell everyone we have parted ways and this was my farewell gesture."

"That is the favor? You wish for the world to know we are no longer lovers?"

"I wish," he said with equanimity, "for the world to know we are not lovers because *I* ended the affair."

It took her a moment before realization dawned in her eyes. "I see. Who is she?"

That question hit a little close to the mark for comfort, but, truthfully, he'd found in the past few days a new discomfort with the notion all of London believed Maria was his mistress. Long ago, when he was not yet twenty, he began to realize society expected him to be exactly like John, so he was to a certain extent resigned to untrue rumors. This one, however, suddenly rankled. Perhaps the earrings were a bribe, but if it would get Maria to tell the truth, it was well worth it.

With a fingertip she touched one of the dangling gems reverently. "You needn't have done this. The company will be moving on to Vienna next week."

"Not quite the same though, is it, if everyone thinks you left and that was the cause of the end of it?"

"I see. You are trying to impress her with your devotion by giving up your mistress in a public way." She shrugged. "Very well. Lord Summerfield invited me to a small gathering at his house. I said no, but perhaps now I will go." She lifted the earrings. "And wear these. By tomorrow everyone will know I am heartbroken you abandoned me. I can act the tragic, spurned woman with more finesse than anyone. Who knows which gentleman might feel the need to console me?"

He bowed and left, relieved and amused.

So now he was entirely free.

To do what? A cautious inner voice asked.

He wasn't sure, but thought perhaps it involved a certain golden-haired young lady and a missing key.

Chapter Eight

The early-morning mist drifted waist high in places, giving the park a ghostly look. It was deserted, as it usually was at this hour, and Amelia knew the paths well enough by now that, lost in thought, she walked her horse without paying a great deal of attention to her surroundings. Behind her one of her father's grooms rode at a discreet distance. In the country she was free to ride off on her own, and at first the escort bothered her, but she was used to it now.

London was rather like being in a cage, she'd decided. Trapped by society's dictates, her father's desire for her to marry well, her aversion to crowds, her affliction ... her growing fascination with Alex St. James.

Damn him.

She'd been standing with her aunt and father in the queue, waiting for their carriage, and seen him hand his grandmother most politely into her equipage with the ducal crest prominently displayed on the side. Then she witnessed him most impolitely turn and go back into the theater for the obvious purpose of visiting his Italian paramour after her triumphant performance.

Instead of attending a late-night rout, Amelia had pleaded fatigue and gone home.

The figure loomed out of a drifting bank of fog so abruptly that she jerked on the reins, making her mare toss her head in protest. As if conjured from her imagination, she recognized him, but in some disbelief. The man who pulled up his horse was dressed for riding in a dark brown coat and fawn breeches, his polished Hessians covered in droplets of dewy mist. He was hatless, his dark hair a little unruly, as usual.

Alex.

Here. *Now*.

"Good morning." His tone held that signature underlying amusement, and he handled his restive mount, a beautiful bay, with skill. "Fancy meeting you here, Lady Amelia."

She shouldn't feel that thrill of peculiar excitement coil in her stomach, but, unfortunately, she did. "Lord Alexander." The greeting was gratifyingly cool, the image of the beauteous Maria Greco still fresh in her mind. "I would think you would still be . . . *in bed*."

No real lady would refer to a man's bed, or imply anything about his mistress, but she said it without thinking, a visceral reaction to his sudden, compelling presence. Her gloved hands involuntarily tightened on the reins.

"I'm an early riser," he responded neutrally, as if he didn't catch the insinuation—and accusation—in her tone. But surely he had. His dark gaze was direct. "I thought I might like a morning ride myself. May I join you? It won't raise eyebrows, as there is no one about at this hour to see us together and you are escorted."

That he'd come on purpose to see her was clear enough. It was his motive that had Amelia off balance.

He guided his horse around a small bush and maneuvered it into position on the path so he could ride next to her without waiting for an answer.

She rides at dawn in the park every day . . .

Amelia couldn't decide if she was happy or irritated that he'd listened to Lady Fontaine's recital of her unfashionable schedule. "I suppose it is a public park and I cannot stop you."

"Of course you could," he said quietly, sitting in the saddle with the natural athletic grace of a born horseman. "Tell me you wish for me to leave, and I will."

She should.

She didn't. Instead she said nothing, letting her horse walk on. A slight breeze ruffled his hair attractively over his brow and sent a wisp of mist past them, like a suspended ghost.

"Ah. I sense I am in disfavor." His sidelong glance was appraising, holding a masculine wariness. "I assume it is because your aunt cautioned you about my nefarious intentions after catching us together the other evening. Rest assured: all I wish to do is have a pleasant morning ride. I handle most of the business matters for my father's smaller estates. It tends to keep me busy and inside a good deal of each day, dealing with factors and managers and solicitors. I thought your habit of an early outing was an excellent idea."

It really hadn't occurred to her that he worked at all, much less was that busy. Sons from noble families with their own fortunes often led indulgent lives. It was unsettling to think of a different side to him other than the rakish charmer. Besides, it was impossible to admit she was irrationally jealous of Maria Greco, so Amelia murmured tartly, "Don't assume anything."

"Fair enough, but I recognize that air of feminine indignation."

A reminder that he was leagues more sophisticated and experienced. It didn't help her mood very much. She'd slept so poorly the night before her head ached and it was, in truth, his fault. Amelia snapped out, "I'm sure you are quite familiar with it. Tell me, does your opera diva have it when she's vexed with you?"

Oh, Lord, did she just say that? How embarrassingly

naive, but then again, she didn't have much practice with hiding her feelings.

Alex almost missed ducking a low branch, catching sight of it at the last minute with a low curse. He muttered, "Oh, now I understand."

How could he possibly, when his life was a series of casual liaisons, gauge her disquiet over how his affair with someone else took those two kisses they'd shared—two deliciously romantic, unforgettable kisses—and made them both meaningless and tawdry?

Amelia discovered she was gripping the reins so tightly her fingers ached. "What do you understand?"

"The sudden antagonism." His smile was rueful. "I often forget the insidious power of the gossip mill."

Amelia looked at him, doing her best to feign indifference, when what she felt was anything but detachment.

He made a small, unmistakably frustrated gesture with his hand. "I don't know if you will believe this, but Maria and I have never had a relationship. Since I have no idea what you've heard, I am going to assume the worst. So let me explain in a frank way I probably shouldn't to an innocent young lady. The rumors linking us are false, except for one night where I might have drunk more than I should have and she apparently had the urge to celebrate the exhilaration of a grand opening-night success in her first major role."

That would have been months ago. It was still shocking, but Amelia felt some of the tension go out of her shoulders. "Oh. Then why—"

"She used the gossip to her advantage and bought herself some peace at my expense, if you can call being envied by half the hot-blooded bucks in the *ton* 'at my expense'. The general consensus is that I just travel from bed to bed anyway, so I didn't correct the misconception. I gave up on that some time ago."

The birds twittered in the background, the air smelled surprisingly fresh for London, and the cool, damp breeze brushed her face, but it all faded into the background at the hint of bitterness in his voice. It wasn't much, just a slight inflection, but she caught it and suddenly her perception of Alex St. James adjusted to a new angle.

"The whispers bother you." She asserted the words with a hint of disbelief, for he was the same man who told her he just ignored gossip.

"No." His smile was faint but the word was definite. "People can say what they like. The *misconception* bothers me. It reflects a general view of what I am like as a man, and that there may or may not be basis in fact seems to make no difference. If I do something and people are bored enough to want to talk about it, let them. But please, I have enough sins of my own without people inventing more."

Amelia could think of no real comment, her gloved hands still now and relaxed on the pommel of her sidesaddle.

He went on. "I make no apologies for my actions, for generally I am not ashamed of them and am willing to take responsibility, but it does irk me to hear of supposed acts that do not lie at my door."

"'People are interesting,'" she quoted Aunt Sophie. "And maybe you are a little too interesting."

"What the devil does that mean?" His dark eyes were veiled, and she was reminded of a mythical warrior, seated so easily on his sleek horse as they waded through another patch of spectral mist. "I am just another ordinary man."

No, she thought, studying his clean profile intently, despite the cool morning feeling warm all over. There was nothing ordinary about Alex St. James at all.

She was extraordinary, with a hint of jeweled moisture in her tawny hair, those long tresses at the moment caught back simply at her nape with a dark blue ribbon that matched her trim riding habit. Because of the damp morning a few wisps of hair curled around Amelia's oval face, emphasizing her delicate bone structure. Somehow she managed to look both prim and inviting at the same time, but he was damned if he could put his finger on how she did it.

Whatever it was, it had rousted him before the light crested the horizon, and had him washed, shaved, and on his horse at an hour when the rest of his contemporaries were still sleeping off the excesses of the evening before, and some were just coming home after a long night of festivities. Very few of them rose before noon usually, and so meeting her in the park was actually an excellent idea. The odds of anyone seeing them were very slim. The groom might report back to her father that a gentleman had ridden with her, but she could honestly say she hadn't expected anyone if that happened. With the two of them virtually the only riders in the park, it wasn't unnatural for him to join her.

It was stretching his luck a little if someone recognized them both riding together, but, really, they weren't alone. Since no scandal could result from what could be explained away as an innocent encounter, maybe he could glean a little information. After all, he still needed that infernal key.

Innately he disliked the idea of using Amelia, but then again, he had promised his grandmother.

Besides, he enjoyed seeing her like this, in relative privacy, her flawless skin as fresh as the spring dawn, the accusing look in her eyes now faded to feminine contemplation as their horses walked side by side.

"It was something my aunt said." Her lips twitched becomingly, drawing his attention to them. "I think it was a dire warning about your licentious lifestyle."

"Perhaps I should hire one of the dour, judgmental matrons to follow me around," Alex said dryly. "To set it all straight."

Her laugh was light and musical. "If you decide to take such a course of action, my lord, please don't bring her along when you hang in the shadows on my balcony."

"Point taken. If I choose to visit you again in that fashion, I'll come alone."

A prudent promise that wasn't prudent at all. Perhaps it was better if he acted as if he hadn't said it. Certainly Amelia seemed silenced by that possibility. Not that he would ever invade her bedroom again even if invited, and he doubted she would ever so issue such an invitation. She seemed far too sensible to risk being utterly ruined. *He* was certainly too sensible to risk being the culprit.

"It's a beautiful morning despite the fog, isn't it?" She pointedly changed the subject.

Yes, definitely too practical to invite a known rake into her bedchamber. Alex studied the white frothy banks with the trees rising above, the city quiet as the blush of dawn strengthened. "I like the fog. Gives the park the look of a mystic world. I remember in particular one morning during my travels in Tuscany, a mist settled over the city of Lucca. With the mountains in the background, it was very surreal."

"You've been to Italy?"

"Indeed. I stayed with a friend in Florence for a month, prowling the countryside. Then I went on to Greece, Crete, Cyprus, any place that sounded remotely exotic." The journey had been enlightening and an adventure. "I'd been at Cambridge a year, but was restless, and my father was wise enough to not object when I said I wanted to travel. When I returned, I was able to apply myself with a little more diligence to my studies."

"How nice," she said, subdued, "that your father considered your wishes."

The poignancy in her voice spoke volumes.

"We rub along fairly well together in our own way." Alex tried to sound offhand, knowing all too often that young women in her social position were given very little choice but to make an advantageous marriage. Their wishes usually had little or nothing to do with it. "As the duke, he is caught up in some rigid strictures, but he is also surprisingly understanding. Maybe because once he was young and unconventional too."

"My father understands very little."

A more cheerful subject might be better than her obviously strained relationship with her only parent. "Tell me about Cambridgeshire. I liked my time there while at university. Do you find London exciting, or do you miss the quiet of the countryside?"

"The season is very glamorous, of course." Her voice was prim. The she sighed and relented with a soft, wistful laugh. "Yes, I do. I miss the soft breezes, the green fields, the lilies in bloom in banks by the drive, the freedom of waking when I wish and having no one notice."

"I can understand that completely."

She looked forward at the path, her lovely face thoughtful. "I won't say I find London exciting. Different, of course, but it is crowded, busy, and loud, none of which make me fond of it. Though there are the compensations of the spectacular bridges, stately buildings, music, and art, of course. My father's country estate is home, familiar and warm. I know the servants better than my family in many ways, though Aunt Sophie visited quite often. The evenings are early there. . . . I still keep those hours, I am afraid. Everyone is in bed not long after dark, and since they all rose at dawn, I'm afraid I am still in that habit, however unfashionable Lady Fontaine thinks it to be."

How personal could he be? "Were you lonely?"

"I don't think I thought of it that way," she said simply, her profile pure and clean. She frowned. "When it is all you know, how can you compare it to anything else? On the other hand, the constraints of society don't appeal to me. I guess that makes me odd."

"Not at all." He smiled at her, because she looked anything but odd in her fashionable habit. Her elegance was partly what she wore, but she also had a curious poise for one so young, and maybe what she'd just told him was why. She'd lost her mother early in life; they had that in common. On the other hand, he had two older brothers, his grandmother, and assorted aunts, uncles, and cousins. His father was forbidding sometimes, but had taken a surprisingly active part in their upbringing for someone of his exalted station.

Amelia was young, beautiful, popular, and from a background of wealth and privilege, but it was possible what others viewed as aloofness was simply a cautious self reliance.

And as disparate as their situations might be, he did feel a certain kinship, for while he did have more of a family, being the youngest son of a duke did lower you considerably in importance in the household. Perhaps that was why he had turned to books and then to travel, and finally to war. Partly because he wasn't burdened with John's responsibilities as the heir or Joel's devotion to the church, and partly because he was forced to seek his own place in the world rather than having it dictated by his birth.

Alex chose to pass over any comment about Gabriella and her less than gracious observations. "You are lucky to have your aunt, just as I am blessed to have my grandmother." He grimaced. "Though I admit at times as a child, I didn't feel so blessed. The woman has a frightening ability to look right through you if you have misbehaved."

"I imagine you still see it now and again, my lord," Amelia murmured with a twitch of a smile. "Because word has it you still misbehave."

That dry observation wrung a laugh he couldn't help. His grin was slow and deliberately suggestive. "Occasionally."

"As for Aunt Sophie, yes, she is a little eccentric, but I adore her. I don't even remember my mother."

"Nor do I mine."

They rode in silence for a few moments, the mist now beginning to thin with the rising sun, but patches of it drifted by in phantom banks, brushing the legs of their horses. Behind them, the groom rode at a respectful distance, not close enough to hear their conversation.

Alex almost asked her if he could join her again on her early outing, but decided against it. It was much better to do as he'd done this morning and just appear, so she could deny planning any kind of meeting with perfect honesty. Instead he found himself asking about her interests in music, literature, flowers, bit by bit rounding out his impression of the delectable Lady Amelia.

When he politely excused himself and rode away, he found that he was rather grateful for her unfashionable habits, for he had enjoyed their conversation. He desired her on a physical level, there was no doubt of it; even clad as she was in prim poplin, buttoned to the throat, he had visions of stripping away those layers of clothes, lying her back on the dew-kissed grass, and teaching her all the ways a man and woman could pleasure each other. But she was interesting in other ways as well.

And he'd learned that it would be safe to infiltrate her father's country estate just about any time after dark.

Chapter Nine

Sophia reached for the sherry decanter, poured a generous amount of the amber liquid in one of her favorite delicate crystal glasses, and handed it to her guest. She poured a more ladylike portion for herself before settling back down on a chintz-covered settee. They were in the informal salon, the one that had long windows that faced the garden. A bee droned at the blooming bush just outside, the sound soporific on this beautiful afternoon.

"Thank you for coming so quickly." She smoothed her skirts, as if it mattered a fig to the man sitting across from her if they were perfectly draped about her ankles. This was Richard, William's oldest friend, and hers too, when it came down to it.

"Of course I came. Now, what is the trouble you spoke of in your note?"

"Lilies," she said. "Dozens of them in various colors and varieties, as if someone had opened a flower shop. None of the bouquets came with a card."

He gazed around, as if looking for the offending flowers, and appeared understandably puzzled.

"Not given to me," she explained impatiently. "To Amelia."

"Oh." Sir Richard, dressed immaculately as always, took an appreciative sip from his glass before saying, "Having an anonymous admirer is not uncommon. And with as many lovesick swains as Amelia has gathered, it isn't a surprise to me that perhaps there is one too shy to openly declare his interest. Why the dither over it?"

She gave what was probably a very inelegant snort. "You didn't see her face when they were delivered. She gets flowers quite often, and while she is not so shallow as to not be flattered, they usually don't have quite the same effect as this time. She had one bouquet of gorgeous orange blooms taken directly up to her bedroom, whereas she usually leaves them in the drawing room. My niece knows very well who sent them, card or no card. I have the dismal feeling I know who sent them also, and the man is hardly shy, but did not send a card for a very good reason."

She pictured Alex St. James, with that gorgeous raven hair that was always just a little windswept and his quicksilver smile, not to mention those sinful dark eyes . . . bedroom eyes. She'd heard the term used before and disregarded it, but in his case, it might apply. Those eyes could seduce a nun, and Amelia had never shown any inclination to take the veil.

No, no doubt about it. She was a perfectly healthy young woman, with all of the romantic notions that came with being her age. And he was . . . *dangerous*.

"The question is what to do about it. I need your advice, Richard."

"Of course."

"This discussion is to be kept between us."

"It goes without saying that I will honor your confidence, my dearest Sophia." He crossed one elegantly clad leg over the other and looked interested. "I must say, you have captured my curiosity."

"I think there is a romance brewing between Amelia and Berkeley's youngest son, Lord Alexander St. James."

"What?" He looked properly startled. Maybe even aghast.

"You heard me correctly."

"I . . . see." One hand held his glass of sherry, and with his free hand he smoothed his mustache in a mannerism he used when he was pondering what to say next. She'd always thought it rather endearing. It took a while, but finally he said, "St. James has a certain reputation, so I understand your reservations, but I know him and have never heard of him pursuing unmarried young ladies. Quite the opposite, actually. I understand he was toasting the arrival of his new nephew, the next direct ducal heir, just a few weeks ago, delighted he was even farther removed down in line. May I ask why you think his attention has fastened on your niece?"

That romantic moment in the pouring rain in the garden pavilion, that was why. Moreover, there had been something intangible in Amelia's demeanor lately. Her reaction to the lilies was also suspicious.

"I caught them in a quite tender embrace," Sophia told him, recalling how Amelia's slim arms had been most definitely around the young man's neck as they kissed, their bodies pressed together, her eager cooperation not in question. "And I can't quite put my finger on why I think so, but I could swear they've met secretly since then, for it certainly hasn't been with my permission or her father's. How would he know, for instance, she loves lilies? They haven't ever even been formally introduced."

"Meeting secretly, eh?"

"It's a guess, but I think so."

"That would be quite a risk for a man who normally shows studied detachment when it comes to love affairs." Richard stroked his mustache again. "How interesting."

"Interesting?" Sophia shot him a leveling look. "Easy for you to say. You aren't responsible for an obviously susceptible young woman."

"I see your dilemma. What does Amelia say about this?"

"I have not directly asked her yet. That is why I am talking to you first, to try to decide how to handle this. *He* most definitely knows I disapprove, though, for I asked him to stay away from her."

"And yet he made the gesture with the flowers. Harmless enough, but a statement of some kind."

This time Sophia glared at him. "Hardly harmless, Richard. He shouldn't *encourage* her."

"Yet he couldn't resist doing so. That is interesting also."

"If you say this is interesting again—I am giving you fair warning—I am going to scream like an Irish banshee."

His chuckle was low and rich. "I am duly warned. I have never heard of St. James behaving dishonorably, if it is any consolation. Scandalously, yes, if one considers the avid gossip over his decided enjoyment of the fairer sex, but quite honestly, he is considered handsome and unquestionably rich, and probably as pursued as much as he pursues. The women he is associated with are all sophisticated enough to understand that permanence isn't part of the equation, and yet they involve themselves anyway. Who can blame him for accepting what they offer? Most red-blooded males would." Richard finished his sherry, his expression thoughtful. "He was a very apt commander in Spain from what I understand, especially for one so young. He can't now be more than twenty-eight or so, and he was there five long years. My opinion is that he will either have honorable intentions when it comes to Amelia, if he is truly interested, or he will put aside the attraction and move on to the next willing, more available, beauty."

"I wish I had your confidence." Sophia got up to refill Richard's glass, inwardly cursing her sentimental soul with a few choice words no lady should use. When she settled back down, it was with a long sigh. "I am not sure which to be more afraid of, Richard, the former or the latter. There is significant enmity between my brother-in-law and the Duke of Berkeley. I cannot see either of them happy with a courtship between their children, even if the young rogue decided he was serious enough to contemplate such a course. On the other hand, if he just walks away, I am afraid Amelia might be very disappointed, maybe even heartbroken."

"You think it is that serious?" Richard had a strange, almost contemplative expression on his face. Sophia felt the same way. Who would have foreseen this complication?

"On her part, I am afraid so. I am not so old I don't recognize that supposedly secret state of giddy happiness. She's very young, after all, and he's a romantic figure." She added gloomily, "Damn him. Ask that gaudy opera star."

Richard looked entertained over the curse, but then he sobered. "I am not sure if this is at all something I should say to a lady, or if it is even significant to our conversation, but if he was entertaining the Italian diva, he is no longer. His decision, not hers, if the gift of ruby earrings to soothe the sting of rejection is an indication. She proclaimed it all to anyone who would listen at some affair after her last performance, and there was some masculine gossip over it, naturally. They've gone their separate ways, and it was his choice. I hate to mention this, but in light of what you've told me, the timing is interesting, is it not?"

"Oh, dear." Sophia took a gulp from her glass, far too large to be genteel.

This time Richard laughed out loud. He really was a dear man.

She said, "I do not believe Amelia will lie to me if I ask her about a possible clandestine romance. She might try to be evasive, but if asked in a forthright manner, she'll tell the truth. I know her well enough to be sure of it. If the answer is yes, I have a decision to make."

"You can either help her bring St. James up to scratch,

or you will have to play the dogged chaperone, suspiciously watching her every moment," Richard said with astute understanding.

"Neither is going to be easy. I don't think you understand how vehemently opposed Stephen would be to such a match."

"I might." Richard looked unperturbed. "Keep in mind I know both the duke and Hathaway. I have seen firsthand their mutual dislike. We belong to the same club."

She hadn't thought of it before, but given his age, no doubt Richard remembered the scandal. "I am sure you know why they detest each other so thoroughly."

He nodded with a slight dip of his head. "Lady Anna St. James and Samuel Patton had an affair. It was hushed up, but one can't totally hide such a notorious tragedy."

"She drowned in the river. . . ."

"And then the duke killed *him* in a duel. Yes, that's the story."

Richard was right: it was a tragic love story. But the present, not something that happened so long ago, was her concern. Well, maybe not *that* long ago. Curious, she asked, "Did you know either of them?"

"I knew them both, my dear. Fashionable society is a small circle, after all."

"Oh." She might have asked more, but really, what else was there to know? Richard was merely an outside party, after all. "Then you understand my dilemma. I am going to have to choose for Amelia, or against her, if what she really wants is St. James. That is assuming he might even be remotely serious. This is a terrible quandary."

"My dearest, when helping set the course of someone's life, especially when you care about them, no decision is easy."

She stared toward the mantel at the beautifully etched glass vase William had given her one anniversary, and remembered what it was like to be wildly in love.

"How do I even know he would make an admirable husband?"

"I see which way you are leaning if Amelia should admit feelings for St. James." Richard rose, set aside his glass, and came over to take her hand and politely brush his mouth over the backs of her fingers. He straightened and smiled. "I am not surprised. You will follow your heart, because that is your delightful nature. I believe I can help. I will try firsthand to get a sense of the young man's intentions myself, shall I? I know him, but he's much younger, so naturally we don't have more than a passing acquaintance. I'll seek him out, but try to not draw too much attention to it. I can be subtle if need be."

She let her hand linger in his for just a moment too long for propriety. Then again, she was a widow, not a maid, and he had helped her sort things out a bit, plus his offer was a generous one. Men gossiped every bit as much as women, but not *to* women. "Thank you."

"And perhaps with all the romance in the air, when this is settled, you will think about *us*." He gave her a meaningful look. "Thank you for the sherry, my dear."

After he left, Sophia sat there sipping her drink, much more cheerful than the situation probably warranted. Alexander St. James had seemed sincerely concerned about Amelia's condition the evening she'd caught them in the gazebo, so that boded well for his character. And as Richard had pointed out, he was handsome, rich, and well connected. To the wrong family, but, really, why should an old quarrel affect the present? Yes, he'd sampled a great deal of the charms of some of the *ton*'s most famous beauties, but being hot-blooded wasn't such a bad trait. Her William wasn't a saint by any means before they married. If the exquisite St. James could be reined in by one woman, Amelia might just be the one. Her niece had more to her than golden hair and a willowy figure men admired. She had a mind and was not afraid to let it show.

Perhaps this wasn't as much of a catastrophe as Sophia first imagined.

It was a damned disaster.

A blight on his life, a nuisance extraordinaire.

The note sat in his pocket. It was simple, but it was as volatile as a case of explosives.

I will be at the Morrisons' tonight. Need to see you.
A

Amelia had taken the chance on sending him word on where she would be, delivered to his town house by a young boy who accepted a coin and gleefully took off, making Alex think he was either the child of one of the servants or a lad she spotted on the streets.

Hopefully she had been that cautious. At least she hadn't signed her full name.

What was so urgent she couldn't wait until the morning? He'd joined her twice more over the past week on her morning ride, and surely she knew if she wanted to see him, he could meet her in the park. As of yet, if anyone had seen them, or if her groom thought anything was significant enough about it to tell her father, Alex was not aware of it.

What did she want? To thank him for the flowers? No, she could have put that in the note or waited for his next appearance.

The impulse to send the lilies had been reckless, he supposed, but then again, he didn't regret it. If it pleased her . . .

By God, he was thinking about her during the fish course, only half listening to his father's stand on the current law governing tariffs. *What is she eating?* he wondered, spearing a forkful of Dover sole dotted with herbs and perfectly sautéed in butter. *Does Amelia like sweets?* It was a subject they hadn't discussed yet, though they were getting to know each other in the freedom of early-morning solitude, discussing everything from art to architecture. During the course of the latter conversation, she'd described to him in detail the configuration of Brookhaven, the seat of the earls of Hathaway. He felt like a blackguard for tricking her into such confidences, but truthfully, he needed some way to find out the layout of the house. . . .

"Alex?"

He glanced up in the act of reaching for his wine. "Yes?"

"Your grandmother just asked you a question." His father, stern and upright, frowned. He sat in his natural spot at the head of the table, elegantly clad in stark black and white even for a family dinner, his dark hair threaded with flecks of gray that only made him look more austere than he did already. But as formal and distant as his father appeared, Alex did know that he held him in real affection—as he did all his sons. A confidence Amelia seemed to lack in her own parent.

They sat in the magnificent dining room of Berkeley House, with its pedimented doorways and arched ceiling, the mural painted there a masterpiece of sixteenth-century art and reminiscent of the frescoes Alex had seen in Italy. The vast table was mahogany, candelabras were alight everywhere, the rich food was brought in on sterling salvers, and the glasses were no doubt priceless heirlooms.

He always found the formality stifling. Thanks to fate or whatever controlled such things, his place in the birth order meant there was very little chance he would ever be the duke, and he was grateful.

"I'm preoccupied this evening. I beg your pardon." Alex turned to his grandmother and affected his most apologetic and hopefully charming smile.

"Yes," she agreed, looking alarmingly shrewd, "you certainly *are* distracted. May I ask what the cause is of this absorption in your own thoughts?"

Both his grandmother and his father looked at him

expectantly. Not to mention the other guests; his cousin, Lord Snow, and his extremely boring wife, who rarely said a word, and Alex's older brother, Joel, who was five years his senior and a very respectable bishop of the Church of England. Because of his calling, Joel had escaped the assumption that he would follow in John's legendary footsteps, and instead the legacy had fallen to Alex.

Might as well tell the truth. Well, not the entire truth. "It's a she," Alex said smoothly, "and I am sure none of you are surprised."

It was the right tactic, because they weren't. Everyone went back to their fish, and then the next courses were served, and by dessert he had to admit he was more than anxious to escape. Alas, his father invited him to share the after-dinner port in his private study, and Alex had little choice but to accept. To his surprise, Joel and his cousin were not included and watched them go, curious but content apparently to have their port elsewhere. One did not argue with the Duke of Berkeley.

A moment like this usually meant a good dressing-down, though casting back over his life lately, he couldn't think of anything he'd done—that was common knowledge anyway—that could fuel a lecture from his august parent.

The inevitable beverage was offered and accepted. They settled into chairs in the paneled room, Alex in the usual position in front of the magnificent rosewood desk, seated in one of the leather chairs. His father took his seat behind the desk and folded his hands on the polished surface, his expression bland, his glass ignored. "What is bothering your grandmother?"

"Sir?" Alex attempted to look noncommittal.

His father frowned. "I have noticed her preoccupation and asked her about it. She was very vague, but admitted she was troubled. She said you were helping her clear up the 'unfortunate mess,' as she calls it. I expected you would give me the details."

Given that he'd promised to not tell anyone the specifics, the question put Alex in an awkward position. He said slowly, "She approached me to attempt to recover something she felt belonged in our family. I was told a certain story—but, quite frankly, she hasn't been all that forthcoming with me either."

"What story?"

Though he was reluctant to say so, Alex admitted, "It involves the Earl of Hathaway and Grandfather's sister."

His father's face tightened. It wasn't much, just a thinning of the mouth and clenching of the jaw, but it was there. He leaned back in his chair and clasped his hand together. "I see. *That* story. My father did his best to keep it quiet, and now apparently you know why. We have nothing to do with the Patton family, though I'd believe it without hesitation if any of them were involved in some nefarious activity."

Honey-gold hair, enormous eyes of a certain pure blue that reminded him of a cloudless summer sky, porcelain skin . . . and not just those attributes. Alex couldn't help but recall the way Amelia talked to him, her lack of artifice or conceit, her quiet intelligence. Nefarious she was not.

He'd already decided it was best if he kept his distance, but unfortunately, he wasn't. Those clandestine morning rides were just too tempting. Put quite simply, he enjoyed her company.

"I have never really heard anything against Hathaway." Alex idly swirled the liquid in his glass, but he watched his father's expression carefully. "He goes about in society enough I would surely have heard if he cheated at cards or beat his servants or the like. From what Grandmama told me, I understand your dislike, but—"

"It isn't mere dislike. He and I were at Cambridge together. I detested him then. Still do, for that matter."

Considering Alex was pondering how to leave as

quickly as possible to meet with the earl's beautiful daughter at her request, that was a bit of a problem.

Well, no, he reminded himself. Only a problem if he was serious about his father's enemy's daughter. *Am I?*

"But do you detest the man or what he represents? His father wronged our family, I agree. But the current earl had nothing to do with it, as far as I can tell. He was a child, as you must have been."

"Hathaway is cut from the same cloth as his conscienceless father."

The implacable tone told him arguing the point was useless, and for all Alex knew, his father was right. The more he learned from his conversations with Amelia, the more he drew the conclusion that Hathaway was not an exemplary parent. Instead of commenting, Alex drank his port and waited.

"What is it the blackguard supposedly stole from us, and why wasn't I informed about this earlier so I could approach a magistrate?" his father asked stiffly.

With all due pontifical affront, no doubt.

Alex explained, "Hathaway didn't steal anything. He has in his possession something Grandmama wishes for me to recover that belongs to us but was given to his father. She assumes he inherited it along with the title when the former earl passed on."

"Where, I assume, the lascivious bastard is enjoying a warmer climate." Finally, his father picked up his glass of port and took a solid drink.

"It is not," Alex said with some measure of resignation, passing over the remark, "a particularly easy task, because she really won't tell me *why* this is important, just that it is. So I am supposed to plunder an earl's house in search of this small item and hope that if *I* get dragged in front of a magistrate, perhaps you might use your influence to sway the law into not tossing me in Newgate. I was in a French prison briefly, and that was, quite frankly, one time incarcerated too many."

"I know about the capture." His father curled his

fingers around the stem of his glass and regarded him gravely. "Wellington wrote me. He indicated you were a valuable officer when in his service."

Was that approval, or disapproval for being captured in the first place? He couldn't quite tell. But then again, Alex never could. Not as a child and not now. The ducal countenance was unreadable, he thought with a cynical, inward laugh. His father had a certain presence that even in the face of criminal activity was inviolate.

"If I served him well, imagine what I would do for Grandmama. I'd lie, steal, or worse for her," Alex said conversationally, raising his glass to his lips. "Hopefully that won't be the case, but if it is, so be it. War has a way of adjusting your perceptions."

"I imagine it does. You managed to escape the first time, and I trust you learned not to get caught again. In that spirit, I am going to assume you will take care of this with the utmost discretion and speed."

A royal order if there ever was one. And a dismissal of the entire unfortunate matter.

Alex finished his glass of wine and rose. "I will do my best, sir."

Chapter Ten

It was extremely difficult to sit through the recital without fidgeting, partially because Amelia thought the pianist inept, and partially because she was agitated and surreptitiously watching the door for Alex's arrival.

Would he come? It had taken quite a lot of nerve to send the note, but then again, she had been at a loss for what to do. Maybe he would join her in the morning for one of their rides in the park, but—to her disappointment—she didn't see him every day, and the idea of waiting to talk to him about this interesting development was out of the question.

Now that she had met Alex St. James, London was not quite so dull and oppressive. Quite the opposite, in fact.

She adjusted the glove on one arm and hoped she looked serene as she folded her hands back on her lap. The weather had gone from warm and sunny back to cool and rainy, but not so cool it bothered her, and for that mercy she was grateful, since the windows in the Morrisons' formal drawing room were all open to the night air. She was just as appreciative when the music crashed to a dissonant stop and the crowd politely applauded.

At least it was over.

The whispers came first, a small rise in the volume of postperformance conversation, subtle enough that she didn't notice right away, but then growing. Amelia glanced back toward the doorway even as she rose to her feet. Next to her, Aunt Sophie flicked open her fan and murmured, "Now, this is rather unprecedented, isn't it? St. James does not usually attend such small gatherings. I wonder why he is here."

Her aunt looked at her very pointedly.

Alex, tall and urbane, strolled into the room, his gaze briefly resting on Amelia before moving on, as if he were only scanning the small crowd. He wore his usual tailored black evening clothes, and with his dark hair, he did perhaps resemble Lucifer before he was cast out of heaven—beautiful and yet with that edge that hinted he might—just might—forgo virtue for wickedness.

Delicious wickedness. The kind a woman could prefer over moral strictures.

The question was, now that he had actually come in answer to her note, how did she get a minute alone with him?

"It is unusual behavior for him, isn't it?" Amelia said it a shade too late, the delay no doubt telling. The memory of her aunt catching them in each other's arms gave her conscience a twinge. Aunt Sophie was wonderful in every way possible; perhaps she should just trust her. Honesty always appealed to her more than deception anyway.

Amelia delicately cleared her throat. "Actually, I sent a note, asking him to make an appearance."

The guests were withdrawing to the formal apartments, where the ladies would now sit and sip sherry and talk, and the gentlemen play billiards and cards. Sophia's expression didn't change, but her hand faltered as she moved her fan. "Is that so? May I ask why you would do such a thing?"

"I need to talk to him."

"I am loathe to ask what this subject might be, child."

Amelia did her best to look bland. "Do not worry. It has nothing really to do with that kiss you stumbled upon the other night."

"If not," Sophia said in a low voice as they migrated out of the room with everyone else, "then I admit I am confused."

"I will explain later, but in the meantime, can you help me get a few minutes alone with Alex?"

Sophia, regal and striking with flamboyant ostrich plumes in her hair and a pale violet gown that emphasized her mature but still alluring figure, didn't show a visible reaction, but her voice lowered even more. "You do not ask much, do you, Amelia? I am your chaperone. What kind of a caretaker would I be if I arranged for you to have time alone with a man of Lord Alexander's reputation? Not to mention that your free usage of his first name is hardly seemly."

"The kind of chaperone who trusts her charge to use her head," Amelia said pointedly. "And I only use his first name to you. Besides, I only asked for a few minutes. I may not know a lot on the subject, but still am sure that even as remarkable as his virtuosity is reputed to be, he would surely need more time than that to ruin me, wouldn't he?"

"Amelia!" Her aunt's face turned pink.

Not once during those ambling morning rides had he said anything improper or suggested an impropriety. They had simply talked, walking their horses side by side. That mesmerizing smile aside, there had been no hint of any type of seduction; instead he had encouraged her to talk about her childhood and the governesses who had essentially raised and educated her, and somehow she'd found herself talking a little about her father also. He listened well for a man supposedly intent upon only licentious excess when it came to women.

"I'm safe enough in his presence," she said with a fair amount of conviction.

"How do you know that?"

"I just know. He isn't callous enough to try and take advantage of me, and he isn't interested in marriage."

"He told you that?"

"I overheard him tell someone else with enough assurance that I believe it."

"Richard seems to share your opinion on both points." There was a sigh hidden in her aunt's response.

That was startling. "You spoke to Sir Richard about Alex?"

"I always value his opinion. What am I supposed to think about your continued interest in a man who has his reputation?"

Amelia shrugged, though she was growing concerned she wasn't indifferent to Alex's stand on the issue of permanence. "I just need to ask him a question. I am going to pretend that I need the ladies' retiring room. Maybe you could direct him out to the hallway?"

Sophia looked dubious, and it was probably justified. "What if someone should see you?"

"Talking? I hardly see the harm in that as long as it is brief. Once again, it is just for a moment or two, Aunt Sophie."

Her aunt gazed at her with a resigned expression on her face, and then she gave a brief nod, her plumes bobbing. "Since I *do* trust you, I will direct him that way. Right now he is politely conversing with Eugenia Green. I am sure that won't last long, given her proclivity for rattling on about the most inane subjects ever. Wait to leave the room until you see me actually speak to him."

It was impossible not to smile. Amelia did attempt to keep it demure, though, and merely said, "Thank you."

She drifted toward the doorway, noting with amusement that Alex did have a somewhat pained look on his handsome face as the plump and talkative Lady Eugenia enthusiastically gestured with her hands. When he gave a slight bow of withdrawal, his gaze sweeping the room, Aunt Sophie neatly cornered him and gracefully gave him her hand, and Amelia went out the arched doorway into the main hall of the mansion. The public apartments were grandly appointed and salons opened off here and there, and she headed toward the room set aside for the ladies in attendance.

The footman she passed looked impassive, and several women chatted together as they swept by on their way back into the party. She walked past her supposed destination, rounded a corner, and waited, hoping Alex would follow the same course when he saw the hallway was empty, or if he didn't, knowing she'd see him walk past.

Sure enough, a few minutes later she heard the ring of booted footsteps on the marble floor, and he came into view, catching sight of her at once where she loitered near a table with a decorative urn. He approached with faintly raised brows, his crisp white cravat a foil for his dramatic, dark coloring.

"I wasn't sure I'd see you in the park soon," Amelia said by way of greeting.

His smile was that brilliant flash of straight white teeth she found far too fascinating for her peace of mind. "I'd join you more often, but I'm trying to be discreet."

"Unique for you?" she murmured the words with a teasing smile.

His smile faded. "Not as unique as the world thinks. Now, then, tell me, how the devil did you convince your aunt to deliver your message? The last time the lady and I spoke she made it quite clear she wanted me to keep my distance."

"We have about two minutes." She smiled wryly. "I promised her a time limit impossible for a fall from grace."

Alex said softly, "Yes, I would need far, far more time than that to do justice to a seduction. Now, what is so urgent you risked sending me a note?"

The words brought a sultry image of tumbled sheets and heated kisses, and ... whatever came next. She wasn't completely ignorant, just uneducated on the details, but even in her unenlightened state, she knew if any man could make physical intimacy pleasurable, he was the one. Pushing that wayward thought aside, she opened her reticule and removed a folded piece of paper. "I received this earlier today. Quite naturally, I thought of you."

"Of me?" He took it from her extended fingers and opened it, his brow furrowed as he quickly read the letter. She knew exactly what the half page of what had obviously been a much longer communication said, for she had read it over and over since its delivery.

In your arms I have found myself complete, but only because we complete each other. Who would think there was such poetry in an act some women find distasteful? I know you did not set out on this course purposefully, but it has happened. To both of us. Tell me, because I must know. Would you change it? Trade the tender touches and exquisite pleasure for a life without me? Without us knowing each other?

I would not, for I love you.

Come to me when you can, for I am desolate in our separation.

With Fondest Regards,
Anna St. James,
Dated this day, August 17, 1769

Alex lifted his head and stared at her. "Someone sent you this?"

Biting her lip, she nodded. "It arrived in the post addressed specifically to me. There was no seal but plain wax, and the sender declined, apparently, to put his name on the envelope."

"That's curious."

"I thought so, especially when I saw the signature at the bottom. Anna St. James. It seems to me that all of a sudden you are searching my father's study, and now someone is sending me part of a letter written years ago by one of your relatives, or from the name I assume so. Is she?"

"Yes." He didn't hesitate, the yellowed letter still held in his long, elegant fingers. Dark lashes dropped a fraction over his eyes. "I wonder where they—our mysterious sender—got this. I wonder a bit more than that, actually. I very much dislike it when there is a game afoot and no one bothers to tell me I am supposed to be one of the players."

"This means something to you?" Amelia demanded. "Does it relate to why you were on my balcony the evening we first met?"

"Yes and no. Yes, to the extent I would guess it does, but no, I don't understand how."

She put her hands on her hips and narrowed her eyes. "I am not sure I can stand many more answers that are more disclaimers than actual information, my lord."

Pink tulle suited her, but then again, Alex was fairly certain most colors suited Amelia, and if she wasn't wearing a stitch, that would suit her even better. The ivory swell of flesh above her bodice brought back flashes of memory of how he'd watched her disrobe: the leisurely movements of her hands as she'd slipped the gown off her shoulders, the provocative silhouette as she bent over to unfasten her garters and roll the silk stockings off her lovely legs. . . .

Stick to the moment at hand rather than fantasize about things best left alone. Innocent misses and Alexander St. James, the scandal-prone son of the Duke of Berkeley, were not a good mix, and the clock was ticking off the minutes. "I'm starting to think the information I do have is very incomplete or maybe even not all that accurate," he muttered, debating whether or not to ask to keep the letter. "I freely admit I am not certain enough of anything to try to explain to you what is going on, but believe I can venture a guess."

"I'd appreciate it." She looked delectable when irritated. Not many females could pull that off. "It is true I found London rather tedious at first, but mysterious portions of old love letters arriving at my doorstep is not how I thought my boredom would be relieved. I am rabidly curious, I own it."

He would satisfy her curiosity on any number of levels, including any questions she might have about sexual matters between men and women. . . .

Keep your mind out of the bedroom, you lascivious fool.

He said simply, "Someone wants to embarrass both our families by dragging out something best left forgotten."

"Do you know what that 'something' is?"

He might as well tell her. She had as much a right to know as anyone—more after receiving the letter. "Your grandfather lured my grandfather's younger sister into a torrid affair. Or at least that was what I was told. But there are always two sides—let's keep that in mind, shall we? As he was a married man, and she a young debutante, neither one of our families is much given to forgiveness over the ensuing scandalous implications. She died quite young, and your grandfather not long afterward."

That was somewhat evasive, for he had omitted the drowning and the duel, but it was all shocking enough anyway, and she now knew the basic facts, if not the sordid details.

He was still missing some details himself.

Amelia's beautiful face registered some measure of shock. She paled. "My grandfather? My father's father? He was her . . ."

"Lover." he supplied ironically.

"Oh. I . . . see."

"I have it on good authority it's true. This letter, if it was written to him, rather indicates my source was right."

The distressed look in her eyes deepened.

Alex might have said more, though he really didn't know what else there was to say. But at that moment a pair of ladies laughed loudly, obviously close by, and he was aware of the time constraints, so he handed back the letter. "However, the past is the past. I see no need for all this to be dredged up. Why on earth would someone send this letter to you? My word on it, I'll find out who is doing this."

"How?"

He thought about that damned key. This was a perfect chance to aid his cause. Had his schedule handling certain business matters not forbidden it—and if he admitted it, his rides in the park with Amelia diverted him—he would already have gone off to Cambridgeshire to search the house there. "It is possible I'll need your help."

"I am not sure, considering my ignorance over all this, what I can do. But if you want anything from me, just ask." The choice of words was unfortunate and she realized it as much as he did, for she turned a becoming pink.

He could not help a slow, wicked smile. "Thank you. In the meantime, I suppose our time is up. I'll head back first and you can follow when the hall is empty. How is that?"

"Fine," she murmured faintly, still blushing. "Will I see you tomorrow?"

Sooner or later someone would spot them together, and if he appeared too often, the groom would no doubt finally report back to his employer that Lady Amelia was regularly meeting with a gentleman in the park during her morning ride. Alex nodded anyway, astonished at his own recklessness. "Enjoy the rest of your evening."

He held her gaze just a fraction too long before giving a polite bow.

He was disturbed over this new development, he realized as he strode off, passing the two ladies in the hallway with little more than an inclination of his head, hoping his face didn't show his inner unrest. The situation bothered him. His grandmother had omitted something very important from her recital of what had happened all those years ago, but that wasn't the problem. Involving Amelia was definitely de trop. She wasn't part of this quarrel except by accident of birth, and she was an innocent young lady. The portion of the letter he'd read so quickly was not meant to be seen by anyone but the recipient, much less someone like Amelia. There hadn't been anything graphically sexual about the language, but every word had been weighted with erotic emotion and innuendo. While sexual intercourse was definitely a private matter, *emotion* concerning desire should also be confined to sharing between one man and one woman. It was just his opinion, but that was just as intimate as the act itself.

Maybe he should have asked to keep the missive. Since it was written by his great-aunt presumably to Amelia's grandfather, did it belong to her family, or his?

Hard to say, but what he did know was whoever sent the letter to Amelia shouldn't have had it in the first place.

Michael and Luke seemed a natural resource for help. It had always worked for the three of them in Spain. As a team, they were a formidable force, as the French could attest.

Excusing himself to their hostess, who assured him she was flattered by his arrival—and no doubt bemused by it, for he never attended insipid recitals—he left, giving his driver Luke's address. His friend's butler informed him Viscount Altea was out, but Luke proved to be at their club, which was fortuitous, because Alex needed to talk to him, and a stiff brandy wouldn't hurt either.

Luke merely nodded as Alex dropped into a chair and ordered a drink. Without preamble he said, "You are just the person I wanted to see. The puzzle master."

"Not because of my legendary charm? I think I'm offended. Though I admit I don't waste charm on you."

Luke lazily arched a dark blond brow. "The puzzle master has retired, by the way, to be replaced by the staid viscount."

"Staid? I am not sure that applies. Believe me, society would agree with me." Alex chuckled and thanked the waiter for his brandy. After the first bracing sip, he said, "Here's your challenge: tell me why would someone revive an old quarrel between two aristocratic families? I mean, the argument is something irrevocably finished, meaning both parties originally involved have passed on under dramatic circumstances, leaving only the legacy of dislike and distrust for the next generation, who still harbor ill will, but also the generation *after* that doesn't even know the story particularly."

"Generation?"

"Mine."

"Ah. Define revive." Luke looked interested, his fingers toying with his glass.

"For instance, sending one page of an old love letter to a young woman anonymously." Alex paused, and added succinctly as possible, "Lady Amelia received a portion of a letter written by my grandfather's sister, and recognized the signature on it, but she didn't know the original story until I told her. She showed it to me this evening.

"I suspect the same thing has happened to my grandmother as well, because she said it had come recently to her attention that Hathaway had that key I skittered over rooftops and burgled a man's house to look for."

"Ah, then we are talking *your* family skeletons."

"I wish we weren't. But yes, we are."

"Tell me."

Obligingly, Alex filled him in on the tone of the letter he'd read. It seemed to him the passion had hardly been one-sided between his great-aunt and Amelia's grandfather. There was seduced, and there was *seduced*.

Hathaway had apparently done an admirable job of it.

The club was fairly full at this time of the evening, the gentlemen either escaping entertainments their wives pressed them to attend or having a late dinner and drink. The low hum of dozens of conversations filled the air, and the scent of tobacco and spirits lingered comfortably. Luke, in his evening clothes, sat silent, his expression smoothed into a mask of contemplation. Alex waited, absorbed in his own thoughts, sipping his brandy.

Luke finally broke into the moment. "How did your great-aunt die?"

A good question. "Drowning, I'm told. It was supposedly accidental, but I asked a few of the older servants, who hinted it might have been suicide. And then my grandfather killed the earl in a duel."

"I see." Luke frowned. "I don't suppose anyone could blame him, having his sister ruined and then losing her altogether. She was young, you say?"

"My grandmother was suitably vague on that point, I'm afraid. I guess only that she was about Amelia's age of nineteen." Alex edged lower in his chair, his moody gaze fastened unseeingly on his glass. "I've already come to the conclusion that since there are obviously other parties involved in this affair, because someone sent that letter, this entire thing is much more complicated than it seemed at first. Any thoughts?"

"My instincts say the person who forwarded the letter has a very obscure motive. No money has been requested, which, I admit, surprises me, unless your grandmother has been approached. If blackmail is the purpose, I am very intrigued by why Lady Amelia would be contacted. A young woman her age has maybe only a modest allowance. I can't see how our friend could profit much from threatening her with this old drama."

"Quite frankly," Alex murmured, "this is more likely to embarrass my family than hers, so I am also mystified. While it was dishonorable in the extreme for her grandfather to have acted in such a fashion, my great-aunt was the one who was ruined and then died. I can see why it bothers my grandmother, and my father wasn't pleased to have it brought up again, but all the central parties involved are dead."

"So the real questions are, who is this aimed at, and what is the purpose of it all? And why, also, is your grandmother worried that Hathaway might want to use that elusive key?"

"A question indeed." Alex thought of Amelia's disillusioned expression earlier. She'd obviously been shocked over the old scandal. Maybe he shouldn't have explained, but then again, at this point, *someone* needed to tell her what happened.

"I'll be curious," Luke said with a note of speculation in his voice, "to see if your lovely Amelia receives more communications."

"She's hardly mine." Alex signaled for another drink.

"Isn't she?" Luke looked bland. "When a lady in distress sends for a male to come to her rescue and he immediately drops his plans for the evening and responds, it does make one wonder."

"Well, stop wondering." Alex heard the sharpness of his tone and calmed it. "She's a tempting young lady, but the complications of it all aside, not *that* tempting."

"Define *that* tempting."

"The fantasies are more than enough. The reality includes a permanence I'm not sure appeals to me."

"So you admit to fantasies about the fair maiden?" Luke's grin was instant.

"You've seen her." Alex kept his expression neutral.

"Yes," his friend murmured thoughtfully. "Indeed I have seen her. And you are not sure permanence appeals. Hmm."

Indeed I have seen her. It annoyed him just as much as the idea of Lord Westhope's ogling her bosom at the opera. Which made no sense, because he knew Luke had no designs on Amelia. This possessiveness was out of character and unsettling.

"After I talk with my grandmother again, I suppose I'll know more."

Luke chuckled. "I wouldn't suppose too much. I have met your grandmother. The Dowager Duchess gives up only what she wishes to reveal. If she decides to keep the details of this half-told story to herself, she will."

"You are telling *me* that?" Alex relaxed in his chair, swirling the fragrant brandy in his glass. He thought about the unusual Sophia McCay, his upright and dignified grandmother, and Amelia's stricken expression earlier. "I think," he muttered, "I am currently dealing with a few too many emotional females."

"Even one," Luke agreed with well-bred equanimity, "is too much."

Chapter Eleven

The silence of the room was broken only by the occasional rattle of a cup being replaced in its saucer and the rustle of the paper as her father turned the page. The delicious aroma of fresh-baked scones, rich with currants and butter, filled the air, and rashers of eggs, ham, and smoked fish sat on the sideboard. A footman now and then came into the room to take away a plate or offer more coffee, but otherwise only the twittering of the birds outside provided any noise.

The routine was set. Her father liked to read his paper without interruption, but this morning Amelia was not quite so inclined to let him. Two strangers in the same house they might be, but since he was disinclined to change that, maybe it fell to her. It had never before occurred to her she had any power to alter the dynamics between them, but why not?

Usually the breakfast room, with its silk-covered walls in stripes of lemon yellow and cream, the polished floor, and garden view, charmed her, and the sunny sky outside should lift her spirits, but not today. "I've been getting love letters," she announced, stirring her chocolate, which she preferred over coffee.

Even at this hour, her father wore an intricately tied cravat, and his buff waistcoat with tiny mother-of-pearl buttons was a foil for the dark brown of his fitted coat. With a visible pause of what probably was annoyance, he finally glanced up with only mild interest displayed on his face. "Oh?"

"Three so far," Amelia informed him. "They are quite extraordinarily detailed. One might even say ... *ardent.*" That was putting it in a mild way. It felt voyeuristic to read them, but she had to admit it was a fascinating window into a young woman's first experience with true passion.

> *... occurs to me we've been remiss in not*
> *considering enshrining the spot where you first*
> *took me. I remember the warmth of the sunshine,*
> *the decadent feel of my loose hair spilled on the*
> *grass, and, of course, the feel of you as it happened.*
> *The pain, but then the pleasure ... I didn't know.*
> *My mother would have told me something, I*
> *presume, if it had been before my wedding night,*
> *but all I understood was the look in your eyes and*
> *your touch and how much I wanted you.*

The word ardent got his attention. He lowered the paper. "From whom?"

"I don't know who is sending them, actually."

"They are unsigned?" He reached for his coffee, lifting the cup to his mouth.

"No, they are signed. I just don't know who is sending them to me."

His brows snapped together in a frown. "What the dev ... er, what does that mean? If they are signed, you must know who is sending them, Amelia."

"They are signed by Anna St. James and were written years ago."

"St. James!" His cup slammed down into the saucer by his plate with enough force that she was surprised it didn't break. "*What*?"

At the sound of his raised voice, the footman came dashing into the room, but her father just waved him away. He said stiffly, "I'd prefer if you didn't mention that harlot's name in my presence."

From the tender, albeit scandalous, words written in the woman's flowing hand, Amelia didn't feel the term harlot applied, but from the look on her father's face, arguing was probably not a good idea. "I just wondered if you might have an idea why anyone would send me her letters."

"Someone's idea of a dastardly joke, I imagine." His voice was grim.

"I would like to know what happened."

His napkin dropped on the table, and he rose. "No, you don't. It is sordid and does not bear repeating." In the morning sunlight, his features were shuttered and cold.

"Many men have mistresses." Amelia held his gaze, refusing to back down. "But I understand they are not usually the daughters of dukes. She sacrificed a great deal for love."

"When said by my daughter the word mistress hardly pleases me. Besides, I sense you are taking a romantic view of this. Dismiss it."

The crisp, unemotional words irritated her. Anna was becoming a real person through her thoughts and emotions in her correspondence. "Forgive me, but I am not trying to please you or displease you either, for that matter. But since this concerns our family, it concerns me. And I am no longer a child," Amelia reminded him, involuntarily conjuring up the warmth and excitement of Alex St. James's kiss in a traitorous part of her mind. "Old enough to marry, and therefore old enough to understand how our society works. Male privilege is no mystery."

"It should be," he said under his breath, but she still caught it.

"Why?"

More audibly, he told her, "Mystery or not, there are some things a lady does not discuss."

"Like why my grandfather seduced an innocent young woman?"

Perhaps she shouldn't have gone so far. His face took on a peculiar reddish hue. With visible effort, he calmed himself. "Who told you that?"

She wasn't about to bring Alex into this, so she just shook her head. "It doesn't matter. Is it true?"

"If Sophia is responsible for repeating all this to you—"

"Of course not," she said loyally. Aunt Sophie was a little unconventional, but she was very conscious of her role as chaperone.

At least her father seemed to accept that as the truth. "Amelia, this happened decades ago. It is best forgotten, and that is my last word on the subject. Burn the letters and put it out of your mind."

She continued to absently stir her chocolate, the delicate clink sound of the spoon on the porcelain loud in the room. Carefully she said, "I could never burn them."

"Why not?"

Those yellowed brittle pages held too much emotion. Maybe she was hopelessly sentimental; maybe she was currently too attuned to what it would be like to embark on a forbidden romance, but she knew she not could destroy such poignant sentiment. "May I request you read them, and maybe you'd take a different—"

"You may request all you like, but I am not going to discuss this indelicate subject with you." He swung on his heel and left the room, his discarded paper only half-read, an unprecedented event.

Well, obviously he hasn't forgotten it, she thought morosely, and neither has another party, for the letters are coming from someone. She drank her cooling chocolate and pensively stared out at the blue sky and sunny garden. Maybe she shouldn't have said anything, but her father's reaction was telling. Decades ago the affair had caused a great deal of turmoil.

She had the unsettling feeling it was causing some turmoil now.

The fist crashed into his jaw with enough force to effectively get his attention, and Alex staggered back, uttering a curse and tasting blood.

Michael, stripped to the waist, his fists up, frowned at his inattention. "What the devil is wrong with you? You might try to at least keep your mind on the task at hand."

"My apologies. I'm a bit distracted." He regained his balance and crouched a little, the fighting stance clearing his mind. The small ring was theirs alone, the place quiet at this early time of day except for the discreet attendants.

"Well, pay attention. I don't want to ruin your pretty face." Michael feinted, threw a jab that Alex parried, and danced backward, bouncing athletically on the balls of his feet. "Is this distraction about those old love letters?"

"No." Alex, also shirtless, dodged left.

"Yes, it is." Michael countered, his smile slight, perspiration gleaming on his muscular torso. "You'll never make a spy, Alex. You are far too transparent."

"Why the devil would I want to be a spy?" He sent a lower cut toward Michael, who skipped back so it missed, barely grazing his chin.

"That's a valid point, but then again, we do have our uses. Ask Wellington or Liverpool."

"So do soldiers, but I'm not of a mind to do that again anytime soon either." Alex grunted as he moved in and took a blow to the stomach, but he did satisfactorily manage to land a solid punch to rival the one Michael had given him earlier, wringing a loud expletive from his friend.

"It seems to me you are in far more danger now than you ever were in Spain."

Alex turned, narrowly missing a jab that might have blackened his eye. "How so?"

"Lady Amelia."

"What of her?" Panting, he ducked.

"I am afraid I saw that impulsive kiss the night we infiltrated Lord Hathaway's house. I heard voices, and the door was just slightly ajar."

Recalling how Amelia's aunt had caught them the second time, Alex couldn't help but mutter, "Apparently there is no such thing as privacy any longer in the city of London."

"Do you desire privacy?"

The delicately asked question was at odds with the way they circled each other, fists up.

"What the devil are you talking about?"

"My aunt had a small cottage on the Thames, not too far out of London. When she died, I inherited it. It is quite charming, actually . . . and private. If you wish some time alone with Lady Amelia to determine, let's say, the depth of your passion for her, please feel free to use it. There's no staff, but a cleaning lady comes once a week to make sure it is aired and dusted."

"Are you insane? Are you really suggesting a clandestine meeting?" Alex stopped moving, staring at his friend.

It was a mistake, for Michael swung and connected. Suddenly Alex found himself sprawled on the ground, felled neatly by a blow that had his ears ringing. He sat up, fingering his jaw, decided it wasn't broken, accepted the extended hand, and got to his feet.

"Interesting tactic," Alex told him darkly, wiping sweat off his brow.

"I am not," Michael said serenely, "the one with a penchant for a virginal miss. Which of us is insane? I wasn't the one either who recently attended a musicale where the principal guests were unattached young ladies and their mamas. That deviation from your normal behavior was duly noted in the society section of the paper."

He'd known it would be, but Alex had found it impossible to ignore Amelia's note, and, in truth, she had a legitimate reason to send it. "She said she needed to talk to me. Naturally I was curious."

"If she needs to talk to you again, why not use the cottage instead of the risk of a public venue?"

"And provide Hathaway with a reason to cut off my ballocks?" Alex said dryly, stripping off his gloves. "Even if I didn't lay a finger on her, we both know he would have just cause if we meet in secret."

"The offer stands, nonetheless."

"You are *not* doing me a favor, Michael, by offering." It was all too easy to picture Amelia, himself, and a convenient bed. The combination sounded a bit too volatile for his tastes.

"By the testy tone of your voice, I would say that's true. Just how serious is this?"

Alex accepted a towel from one of the valets and mopped his face with it. "There is no this," he said evenly. "She is who she is, and I am who I am. It's a simple equation. If I *were* to be interested in a serious way, our families would still be a problem. Were my attitude different about marriage, the situation would *still* give me pause."

"I see you've thought about it."

That observation irritated the hell out of him, simply because it was true.

Michael went on, "If nothing else, the cottage would give you a place to discuss the mysterious letter sender if he strikes again, instead of exchanging notes, which has to be even more dangerous than a clandestine meeting. The written word has a tendency to come back to haunt you. The letters alone prove that."

That was a good point. Maybe if they met, they could have more than two minutes to try to figure out together who was behind all this. . . .

Oh, hell. Who am I fooling? Alex thought in self-disgust. He'd love to get her alone, and that was the problem. Apparently it was obvious. "Have you ever been in love?" he asked Michael, the words coming involuntarily from brain to mouth because there was something shuttered about his friend.

Love. The connotation of rose petals and solemn vows and God knew what other sort of life-altering ingredients no sane man would embrace made him wary, and yet maybe not wary enough. The earl's golden-haired daughter had too much appeal. He rarely spent a lot of time thinking about his lovers. He enjoyed women, but it was done on a casual basis.

He'd been thinking about Amelia a bit too often for comfort. A part him still was assured it was because he was very attracted to her—that was undeniable—but couldn't have her. Another part was afraid that wasn't *all* of it, however.

"Ah, so we are now contemplating love, are we?" Michael said softly, his voice amused.

"Just answer the damned question," Alex muttered.

An attendant had handed Michael a towel also and he swabbed at his torso, his face unreadable. "No. You?"

Alex waited a moment, then said simply, "I thought so once. Back in Spain. I was all of twenty-two, and she was . . . well, she was married to a fellow officer. That was that. My scruples were not such that I could ignore her vows." He smiled grimly. "I wanted to, believe me, but I couldn't. All in all, it was a fairly miserable experience. I asked to be assigned to a different company."

Michael narrowed his eyes. "You always have had a bit too much moral fiber for service to the Crown. I take it the lady would have accommodated you?"

"We will never know, will we?" Alex tossed the towel aside. "That one incident makes me truly question my ability to recognize the difference between love and lust, and please be reminded I am well acquainted with lust." He added, "I *am* currently in lust, of that I have

no doubt. As for anything else, I don't know. I am not
interested in letting it happen."

"You think you can order love?" Michael gave an incredulous laugh, shaking back the chestnut hair hanging
over his eyes. "That's like thinking you can control the
weather or align the stars into different constellations.
In other words, impossible. It doesn't necessarily hit a
man in a flash either, my friend. It can sneak up on you
like a footpad in an alley from what I have observed.
You should know that more than anything, for look
what happened to you. Even more surprising, look at
your brother. If anyone was inviolate to that insidious
emotion, surely John qualified."

It was true. No one had really expected his rakehell
older brother to succumb to a sentimental attachment,
much less to choose someone like Diana, who was
pretty but not a stunning beauty and had an unremark-
able background. The unlikely match had been fodder
for the gossip mill for months once the engagement was
announced.

If it could happen to John, it could happen to anyone.
Now not only was he a faithful, attentive husband, but
also a very proud father. Alex rubbed his sore jaw. "I
suppose that's true enough. After they transferred my
command, I did my best to get myself killed. It wasn't
necessarily a conscious decision, but looking back I
wonder now if some of the reckless acts everyone else
took as bravery stemmed more from a fatalistic conviction that the only woman I would ever love was lost to
me."

They walked together toward the back of the building, past a few other gentlemen engaged in boxing or
fencing, the occasional oath or the clash of metal on
metal ringing through the air.

"I left for the war with the assurance I was going
to meet my end on Spanish soil." Michael sounded, as
usual, quite detached, though Alex sensed his friend
wasn't detached at all. Michael sent him a glance from

hazel eyes that were veiled as usual. "But would I have embraced it? No, though on some of the more dangerous missions, it seemed inevitable. You were captured by the French once as an officer. Twice for me as a spy, and I would have gladly died under the torture of one of their more inspired interrogators that last time. It still gratifies me I lost consciousness before I could tell them what they wanted to know."

Alex well remembered the dusty, crumbling fort where the enemy had held Michael in one of the airless rooms, and the horrific condition he'd been in when the British forces under his command launched a surprise attack and taken the armory. By tacit agreement they'd never discussed what had actually happened during Michael's incarceration. In his case, Alex had been treated with a decent level of courtesy due to his rank, but spies were not accorded such deferential handling. Had they not arrived when they did, no doubt Michael would have been hanged, if he hadn't died from his injuries.

"I, for one, am glad not just on a personal level, but for England that you lived," Alex murmured.

"So am I, actually." Michael grinned. "Had I perished, I wouldn't have gotten the pleasure of knocking you on your arse earlier."

"Look out for our match next week, for it isn't just my posterior that is bruised," Alex warned with a rueful laugh. "My pride needs to be redeemed."

"The mention of the cottage worked nicely to distract you." Michael cocked a brow. "Shall I give you the address?"

Chapter Twelve

. . . last night you came to me in a dream. I could swear I woke with your scent on my skin, the taste of you on my lips, the memory of the texture of your hair laced through my fingers immediate. We held each other, your hardness moving within me, my gasps caught by your mouth on mine, your hips cradled in my thighs. The pleasure was such I wanted it to never end and yet yearned for the sublime completion at the same time. Then you shuddered in my arms and I triumphed in how I could give that to you, that my femininity assuaged your need, that your satisfaction matched my own.

My beloved Samuel . . . when can you come to me again? Shall we use our usual spot? All I await is a missive from you.

Your loving Anna

Amelia set the letter aside, her cheeks a little warm. She didn't remember him because he had died many years before she was born, but just the concept of a grandfather conjured up images of gray hair and walking sticks, not the object of some young woman's passion. She felt like an interloper and yet was fascinated by the complexity of not just human emotion, but how fate could interfere with life.

If he hadn't been already married, would he have wed Anna St. James? Was he simply indulging himself, or was he also in love, as opposed to the dynastic marriage he'd made when he'd wed her grandmother? He wasn't alive to ask, so she would probably never know.

The romantic slant of it all didn't escape her, but then again, people's lives had been ruined apparently and Anna St. James had died so very young. . . .

Women had wished, for time out of mind, for what could not be theirs, had made poor decisions in the men they chose to love, and she didn't want to join those starry-eyed ranks. Resting her chin on her palm, Amelia pondered the unattainable.

Alex St. James.

Dark hair, just a shade too unmanageable, dark eyes that managed to be mysterious and heated at the same time, strong arms capable of lifting her as if she weighed nothing, a finely modeled mouth that moved against hers with a singular persuasion she hadn't yet attempted to resist . . .

Was this just physical? He was very attractive—the legions of women he had supposedly bedded were evidence enough of that, but in her heart, she didn't think that was it alone. A lot of the men she'd met already at the balls and dinners and endless soirees were handsome and charming. For that matter, Lord Westhope was very good-looking and urbane and polite.

But she hadn't ever felt a flicker of longing for any of them, much less this ill-advised fascination. She needed to face it. She was at the least infatuated, and at the most . . . illogically in love?

"Lord, I hope not," she muttered, restive in her state of chaotic emotion, the sheer task of deciding what to wear just because she might see *him*, when she usually just picked out a gown with disinterest, taking the better part of the last hour.

A part of her understood Anna and her sentiment. Amelia was also wasting her time with her impractical dreams, and *she* wasn't even asleep.

Getting up, Amelia rang for her maid. When Beatrice arrived, bobbing a curtsy and out of breath from the stairs, Amelia smiled with a certain determination. "Could I have the green watered silk and my silver shawl, please?"

"Of course, miss." The young woman went to the wardrobe and took out the specified dress and fussed over Amelia's hair. Half an hour later, Amelia went downstairs, the case clock in the hallway just ringing eleven o'clock as her skirts skimmed across the polished floor. In the foyer her father offered his arm with a look of annoyance on his face. "We are going to be late."

She winced at the curt sound of his voice. "It's fashionable to not be first to arrive, isn't it?"

"I suppose so, but Sophia is expecting us."

In other words, he really could not wait to be rid of the responsibility. She'd always accepted his lack of involvement in her life. Now, as a woman, not a child, she wasn't quite as blasé about the distance between them. "Did Mama enjoy going out? Did she like society?" she asked, suddenly aware that since she was very little, she hadn't asked questions of him about her mother. The letters, in part, had maybe made her aware that the complexity of human relationships was not limited to younger men and women. Had her parents loved each other? She had no idea.

The footman had just opened the front door, and her father didn't answer at once, his silence pronounced. Then he said in an offhand voice, "She enjoyed it to a certain extent, of course. She was a refined lady and a countess."

A stilted answer that gave nothing away, really.

Part of this is my fault, Amelia mused as they went down the steps. She should have been more curious years ago, though, in truth, her mother had seemed a shadowy figure at best and since she so rarely saw her father, she hadn't had a lot of opportunities to discuss the subject. "Only to a certain extent?"

"Some evenings she didn't enjoy it as much as others." He extended his hand to assist her into the carriage.

A sudden suspicion invaded her mind. Incredibly, it hadn't occurred to her before. "Why?" she asked flatly, refusing to move. "Please tell me."

He hesitated and then said, "She had your infirmity."

Suspicion confirmed.

Infirmity. It sounded so awful when put that way, especially when it was something she'd never been told before. How could she not have known that? "Oh."

"I suppose I should have explained that to you. Apparently it is hereditary." Her father stood there, distinguished in his evening wear, looking uncharacteristically chastened. "Now, then, shall we?"

That was it?

Aunt Sophie had never told her either, which was even more alarming. "Did Mama really die in childbirth?"

Her father looked startled. "Of course. Do you think I would keep such a secret from you?"

Well, actually, she was getting rather tired of secrets, and there were apparently a lot of them floating around. "You never told me before that she had breathing troubles," she pointed out, right in front of the footman holding open the carriage door for them.

"For a good reason," her father muttered with a pained look on his face. "Can we please discuss this later?"

"Trust me," she said grimly as she allowed him to hand her in, "we will."

For the first time in her life she thought he gave her

an appraising look that wasn't dismissive or disinterested, but instead it seemed he really *saw* her.

That was progress anyway.

If it wasn't beneath her dignity to sputter, Sophia would have, and as it was she was still on the verge. "Really, my lord, you cannot be serious."

Her brother-in-law, Stephen Patton, Lord Hathaway, simply nodded once. "Indeed I am, madam. I want you to use your considerable influence with my daughter to force her to accept Westhope."

The word *force* in particular was grating, and Sophia wasn't at all sure Amelia could be forced into anything. She'd inherited not just her mother's blond beauty, but a great deal of her spirit also. "What is the rush? The season has barely begun," Sophia pointed out, her gaze going to the dance floor, where at the moment her niece, dazzling in a verdant gown that complimented her shimmering amber hair, waltzed in the arms of a handsome young man Sophia recognized as the son of one of her friends. "I am sure Lord Westhope is, in your eyes, a suitable match, but surely it is Amelia's opinion that matters."

In Sophia's private estimation, Westhope was as dull as unsalted broth. He'd undoubtedly make the kind of husband that talked incessantly about hunting, voted with the majority in Parliament, paid more attention to his friends than his wife once he acquired her, and perhaps worst of all, was unimaginative in bed.

Not that a good marriage was based on a man's sexual skill, but Sophia was fairly sure an inconsiderate lover would be one aspect of a man's personality that was hard to forgive, at least in her emancipated opinion. Of course, she could never say so—how very indelicate.

"What matters," Stephen said firmly, "is that she is settled and well taken care of by a man who will treat her respectfully. I have even confided in him her problem and he was not put off."

"How charitable of him," Sophia said with asperity.

"I thought so."

Was there just the slightest defensive edge to her brother-in-law's tone?

"I agree she needs someone to match her lively intellect, to share her love of literature, to admire not just her looks, but her inner beauty." Sophia listened to the lilt of the music and saw Amelia laugh at something her partner said, her movements graceful. It was really a pity she couldn't dance more often. "But not Westhope, I'm afraid."

"Why not him?" Stephen asked irritably. "Let's get this business over with. My house is overrun with flowers and callers. I spend my evenings at tedious events like this rather than at my club or in one of the gaming rooms, and—"

"She is your daughter, my lord. More importantly to me, she is *Sarah's* daughter. I want to see her happy."

That silenced him momentarily. Sophia knew he loved Amelia, but he had never been very good at expressing it. This haste to marry her off was more an indication of his discomfort at finally stepping into his role as parent than anything. She was no longer packed off to his country estate with a governess in charge of her life. Amelia was a woman, and he had to interact with her. Her resemblance to Sarah could also be part of the problem. Maybe it stirred memories of her death, which was an event Sophia suspected he had never fully faced on an emotional level. He'd lost his wife and his son together, and rarely returned to the house where it happened. It was telling, but then again, he had never been very demonstrative. Eventually he muttered, "Westhope can't accomplish that?"

"No."

"You are so sure?"

She hid a smile at his resigned tone. "I'm afraid, as inconvenient as it is for you, yes, I am sure."

He looked offended, but she knew she had just struck a chord. He said stiffly, "This isn't about me, Sophia."

"Precisely."

At least he was a man who could acknowledge defeat, albeit not gracefully. With a token word excusing himself, he stalked off.

"Now, what has you laughing?"

She glanced over to see Richard edge to her side out of the well-dressed crowd, his question barely audible above the orchestra. She answered, "I just pulverized Hathaway's plan of marrying off Amelia to Westhope. He is a bit miffed with me, but he will get over it."

"No one can set a man down like you, my dear." He reached for her hand, raised it to his lips—which, to her delight, he seemed fond of doing—and murmured, "I find that ability charming in the extreme."

"Most men wouldn't."

"I am not most men."

No, he wasn't. The music stopped and Richard released her hand. She said, "St. James isn't here."

"Isn't that a good thing? I thought you wanted to keep his rakish presence away from your niece."

"At first, yes." She thought of the other evening at the musicale. There was something compelling about how he'd entered the room and his gaze had immediately fastened on Amelia. She was starting to think there was more substance to him than she first assumed. "I am, as of now, undecided. Have you spoken with him?"

"In a way."

"Well?" She fixed Richard with a demanding look. "What does that mean?"

He merely smiled in that calm way he had that seemed to be his alone. "My dearest Sophia, I can hardly walk up and bluntly ask the man if he has evil designs on Amelia. I sought him out a few days ago when we were both playing cards in the same room and managed to sit next to him when a space vacated at his table. I like him. He plays fairly; deep, but not too deep."

"How a man plays cards—" Sophia began to say before he interrupted.

"Actually says a great deal about him," Richard informed her. "He doesn't gloat when he wins nor become surly when he loses, and his sense of humor is not bawdy, nor is it constrained either. He doesn't talk about women at all, even when others are boasting—not his past paramours or his possible current involvements, I'm afraid. It says a great about his discretion, but unfortunately does not help us much."

Us. It was a telling word, but she really wasn't ready to think about an us yet. "A discreet libertine. How annoying," she murmured, noting Amelia had chosen to sit out the next set with a small group of young women, most of whom might be relegated to the wallflower category, not necessarily because they weren't pretty, but because they were extremely shy. One of them, Lady Elizabeth Daudet, was a particular friend of her niece, and they were chatting with their heads close together in a conspiratorial manner.

"Unsporting of him to be so gentlemanly," Richard agreed with a chuckle.

"It is hardy funny. We are talking about *Amelia*."

"I know," he said gently. "And she is like a daughter to you and you adore her and want her to be happy. If St. James is the answer to that happiness, the two of them will discover it soon enough. You cannot make it happen, nor, I fear, prevent it from happening either, Sophie."

She slanted him a look. "You are annoyingly right. Not that it helps matters."

"We will do what we can. In the meantime, dance with me. The other evening you disappeared instead of giving me a chance to send your attractive turban toppling to the floor amidst scandalous gasps." He reached out a hand. "I think you owe me the promised waltz."

The proffered hand was tempting. He did dance beautifully, and when occasionally she took the lead—a personal failing of gauche implications that happened all too often—he never complained. "My turban was not at all attractive," she admitted. "Don't try to patronize me. Even I make a mistake now and again when it comes to fashion."

"You always look divine, my dearest Sophia." His eyes glimmered with humor. "Now, then, shall we dance?"

Chapter Thirteen

She had danced three times in a row.

And now, damn all, he was worried. Like he had a right to count her waltzes, like he was some guardian entrusted with her well-being. Alex took a savage gulp of tepid champagne and fixed his brooding gaze on the swirling couples on the dance floor. She *shouldn't*.

And it was none of his blasted business if she did.

Bloody hell.

Tonight Amelia's gown was a vivid green, the drapery over the provocative curves of her breasts on the bodice swaying as she moved, her shoulders creamy in the lighted ballroom. At the moment she danced with some young cub Alex didn't recognize, but he knew the type from the time he'd spent in command in Spain. Privileged, arrogant, and without the slightest notion of what danger he might be in. That fit perfectly, for Alex had the unreasonable urge to stalk over and exercise a heretofore unknown overprotective desire to slaughter the presumptive idiot on the spot.

Odd, that.

And when the music ended, the situation became

even more inexplicable. He discarded his glass on a handy table and actually walked to the edge of the dance floor, waiting politely enough—though it wasn't what he preferred—until she smilingly dismissed her partner. It was impossible to miss her look of surprise when she turned and saw him standing right there. Her blue eyes widened and her soft lips parted.

"I think you've danced enough," he said smoothly, but he stepped forward to take her arm. "Perhaps you should sit this one out."

"I feel fine. I know the signs." Despite the protest, she went willingly enough, but that could have just been a consciousness of the crowd around them. "Are you my keeper?"

His gaze raked down her slender, shapely form. "A part of me would like to be. My compliments on your gown, my dear. I like it."

"Thank you." Her voice was modulated and low. "Aunt Sophie chose the color, naturally. You know my disinterest in fashion."

Three dew-kissed mornings, careful inquires meant as casual conversation, and he knew quite a lot about her, actually. "Lucky for you, you would look fetching in old rags."

"I appreciate the compliment, but do you really think it is prudent to tow me off the floor like this in front of everyone?"

"Maybe not." His smile was a little brittle as he tried to find them a spot with even a modicum of privacy. "But then again, ask anyone: I am not always prudent."

"So I hear."

"I thought you might have. In this case, I have a good reason. What would you say if I told you I also received a letter?"

She faltered. He felt it in the light pressure of her fingers on his arm. "Someone also sent you one of her letters?"

"No," he said grimly, "one of his."

"What?"

There seemed to be a secluded corner by the unused pianoforte, the dais for the orchestra at the opposite end of the room. Alex drew her toward the instrument, hoping every person in the ballroom hadn't noticed his approach and sudden appropriation of the lovely Lady Amelia. It was crowded, so that was good, and maybe the Earl of Hathaway wouldn't hear at once Lord Alexander St. James had spirited his daughter away. Not that he'd really taken her anywhere with all the people milling around them.

"From your grandfather to Anna," he confirmed as they moved around the piano to where he hoped not all of the *ton* could see them in earnest conversation. The instrument was raised enough they were sheltered from the view of most of the ballroom. "Like the one you received, but from the other source of the problem."

"I don't think problem applies—"

He impolitely interrupted, which was out of character but seemed necessary. "Amelia, it was—is—a problem. He was *married*. The love affair was ill-fated and ill-advised, and no matter what they felt for each other, others were affected. He was wrong and she was wrong."

Such a vehement, virtuous declaration apparently left her speechless. Alex went on doggedly. "Read the letter. I brought it for you. The question for us is, why are we being targeted for this particular generosity?"

"Let me see it."

He slipped it from his pocket and handed it to her, watched her frown as she scanned the words. And then obviously read them again.

Then she said it. It was simple, it was just two words, but the low whisper made him go very still.

"Someone knows."

"Knows what?" He made a restive movement with his hand.

Amelia looked at him, her lashes lowered a little, her

mouth compressed. "Well, I suppose I mean 'knows' about us somehow."

The music had swirled up again, and to his relief he didn't notice much attention being paid to their small conference. The room was maybe too crowded, for usually their heads together would have sparked much interest. "Us?" he repeated, just to buy a little time.

"Not the night on my balcony, but maybe in the gazebo. What if Aunt Sophie wasn't the only one to see that kiss?" she asked with a frown between her fine brows, dazzling in green with her dark gold hair shining in the flickering light. "There is a certain parallel romanticism between our encounter that night and what happened years ago. Don't you think?"

Alex gazed at her, nonplussed by what seemed to be evident sincerity. After a moment, he said dryly, "I don't know that I ever looked at it that way."

"They shared a forbidden passion for each other." Amelia shrugged lightly, but she held his gaze. "We meet secretly because we both know our families would not approve, and someone is aware of it."

The word passion said by a young woman caused a small ripple of alarm, but in the course of their morning rides he'd discovered artifice wasn't one of her personality traits. She was remarkably candid, which normally appealed to him, but not in the context of discussing their growing friendship.

He liked her. Oh yes, he desired her, especially at this moment, in her becoming verdant gown, with the slight flush of exertion on her cheeks and that faint, bewitching smile curving her soft, tempting lips, but he also *liked* her. She was genuine, independent—which was maybe not by choice, since it was a product of her father's indifference, but she was just the same—and unapologetic for being a female with intellect.

"I suppose there is a certain poetic similarity, but forgive me if I hope for a better outcome. It isn't exactly a happy story." He lifted a brow. "If we may return to the subject of who might be sending us these letters, please."

"I find it odd, I admit, that someone would possess both her letters and my grandfather's as well. To imagine two different people doing this is ludicrous, so we have to assume it is just one person. Who knew them both?"

"I imagine quite a few people in society knew them." Alex had already pondered the subject at length. "My grandmother is an obvious candidate for having her sister-in-law's correspondence, but though I admire many things about the dowager duchess, she is not subtle, nor would she share with anyone those extremely personal communications. If anything, she is mortified by Anna's affair."

"In the same line of thought, I suppose my father might have *his* father's papers, but he is so unlikely the culprit I think we can dismiss it altogether. I doubt he has the imagination."

"I agree on that point." Though he didn't know the man well for obvious reasons, Alex couldn't see Hathaway ever secretly mailing anything to his daughter, much less to the son of his enemy. "So what we have is an outsider, apparently. I still fail to understand the motivation."

"Let's dance." Amelia said the words abruptly.

Alex straightened. "I beg your pardon?"

"I see Lord Westhope coming this way," she said in a low, urgent tone. "Will you waltz with me?"

Just turn him down, he thought, *as you have so many others*.

Except he found he wanted to dance with her, so why the hell not just accept this chance?

She'd blatantly used the Earl of Westhope as an excuse.

As a subterfuge it might not be that original, but if it worked, so be it. Amelia placed her hand in Alex St. James' sinewy clasp and threw caution out the door. He led her toward the dance floor, through the whispering crowd, and she couldn't tell at first if anyone was interested in the youngest son of the Duke of Berkeley dancing with her or not. It didn't matter in the great scheme of things, for she had dreamed often enough of dancing slowly in his embrace.

Among other salacious and embarrassing fantasies. Her skin prickled with heat as he set his hand at her waist and looked into her eyes. Those letters . . .

> *. . . the scattered petals over the bed linens were a very amorous touch. However did you accomplish it? I walked into the room and the scent came to me . . . roses with a hint of your spicy tobacco, so I knew you'd been there, that you'd orchestrated the setting. Darling Samuel, when we meet I allow myself to ignore all the censure of the world around us, but we both know still it exists, even when we come together in body. Why is it this way? The question constantly plagues me.*

"You're sure?" Alex stared at her with concern in his dark eyes. "You swear to me you feel up to this?"

"I'm sure." She smiled, captivated by his masculine allure, his height and scent emphasizing the difference between them, as did the lithe grace in the way he moved.

The orchestra started another tune, and her partner took her toward the floor. "You danced three times earlier."

"I already told you I was fine." It warmed her he cared, and she ascertained by the expression on his face that he truly was apprehensive.

She was more than fine. Even as they swung into the throng of dancers, she felt a sense of the surreal with the light pressure of his hand at her waist and the muscled strength of his shoulder under her fingers. . . .

Especially since Alex St. James was twirling her blithely around the floor as if he routinely danced with young, unmarried ladies. Amelia couldn't decide if she was astounded they'd both agreed to it or if she was elated. After all, it was her idea.

Her father was bound to notice.

Among others. Was it her imagination, or had the volume of whispers risen?

"We might attract a lot of attention." She managed a fairly bland smile.

"I assume you are right, my lady." Alex didn't quite laugh, but his smile twitched his mouth in that unique way, with just a hint of cynicism. "I do believe people are staring. Do you mind?"

She had dreamed about his smile. Warm, disturbing dreams that still made her face heat when she thought about them. A dark, wayward curl brushed his lean jaw, the raven curve of it emphasizing that elegant, masculine line.

It was true that it was hard to ignore the avid attention from various spectators. "I think it is just the two of us together," she said lightly, but her feelings about the matter were anything but flippant. "I wonder what they are saying. The rake and the earl's standoffish daughter. Out of character for you, out of character for me."

But so right . . .

Her grandfather's letter was still fresh in her mind. All of it, from beginning to end, but this passage took on a special poignancy: *I cannot have you. I know this. My mind absorbs this reality without pause, but yet it also rejects it. How can it be so? I was not discontent with my life. You ruin all of this. I cannot think, cannot enjoy simple pleasures, cannot face my family. . . .*

"Who cares what they are saying, Amelia." Alex just looked indifferently aristocratic, his steps effortless and smooth. "And I would never describe you as standoffish. The world misinterprets your lack of coquetry as aloofness. I disagree. You are quiet, not cold. You just don't flaunt your beauty, when everyone expects you to be vain."

The compliment made her throat tighten. She cleared her throat. "Thank you."

"Not at all. I find narcissistic young ladies a complete bore."

"I think you find young ladies a bore anyway, my lord."

"Not all of them," he said with soft inflection.

Maybe if she hadn't been so touched, maybe if she wasn't falling under the spell of the fascination of those old letters and that fateful love affair, and maybe if she wasn't waltzing finally in the arms of the man she thought about almost every waking moment of her day, she wouldn't have done it. But without thinking, she reached up and tenderly brushed back that errant curl of silky dark hair off his cheek, the slight touch of his skin making her fingertips tingle, before she dropped her hand back to rest on his shoulder.

She might as well have kissed him in front of the entire ballroom. Shock rippled through her that she'd made such a familiar gesture in public, but it was too late and she thought she could hear a collective gasp come from the crowd. Even Alex looked a little bemused.

"If you are concerned about public opinion, perhaps you shouldn't have done that."

Heat flooded into her face, so acute it made even her scalp prickle. "I'm . . . I'm sorry," she whispered in mortification. "I didn't mean to . . . oh . . ."

"Pretend it never happened." His shoulders moved in the slightest of shrugs. "We're dancing, nothing more. Perfectly acceptable."

Acceptable, yes. Except now she had the feeling that most of London society understood they knew each other much better than just one turn around the floor.

That suspicion was confirmed when the music dwindled to a halt, the dance ended, and she turned to see her father standing at the edge of the crowd, a dark, disapproving expression on his face.

"He usually barely speaks to me." Amelia gave a

small, mirthless laugh and said low enough only Alex could hear her, "Why do I get the impression he is going to speak to me now?"

"Or perhaps to me," Alex said as he released her hand. "Either way, will I see you tomorrow morning at sunrise?"

"I hope so."

And God help her, she meant it with all her heart.

She was an idiot.

She was a fool.

She was undisputedly in love with Alex St. James.

The carriage swayed, the clatter of the wheels loud, but inside there was silence.

Drat it all, Sophia thought, watching her niece's averted profile. Clearly something was going to have to be done about this matter. At least Amelia's father hadn't made a scene at the ball and allowed his daughter's evening to go on as if nothing happened, but there wasn't a person in attendance with any doubt of Lord Hathaway's reaction to the sight of his daughter in Alex St. James's arms. Sophia had offered to see her niece home, and he had gone off to his club, which might be just as well.

Oh, dear. That damning moment when Amelia reached up and brushed aside that lock of hair in front of most of fashionable society, not just the gesture but the look on her face leaving little guesswork as to her feelings . . .

Perhaps it was time to delve into the truth with a practical approach rather than hope this would all just melt away. "So," Sophia said briskly, "how often do the two of you meet?"

Amelia, a silver shawl over her shimmering green gown, glanced up almost as if she realized she wasn't alone. "What?"

"You and Lord Alexander? How often? I would love to also know where, for you are forbidden to go anywhere without a chaperone."

"What makes you think we meet?"

"That interesting waltz, for one."

"I merely touched his cheek." Amelia's face had taken on a pink hue.

"I think if you took a poll of the general way that caress was interpreted by all those interested onlookers, the term merely would not be used." Sophia looked at her niece with direct inquiry. "Now tell me: where?"

"The park. My morning ride. It is innocent enough." Amelia straightened a little, but she didn't dissemble. "And I always take a groom with me."

At least she wasn't denying it, and innocent did *not* describe Alex St. James. "He must truly be in pursuit to rise so early." Sophia did her best to sound primly disapproving, but in truth, she found it touching—and a relief—that a rake of his caliber wasn't luring Amelia to some tawdry inn or persuading her to other such scandalous behavior. Richard seemed to think St. James was a nice young man despite all the rumors, so that was in his favor anyway.

"*I* asked *him* to dance this evening, Aunt Sophie."

"After he pointedly removed you from the dance floor with what looked like quite a possessive hold. Let's face it, child: this evening neither of you were being all that discreet. The *ton* will see a developing romance in all this, and I suppose my question is, is there one? Keep in mind, I saw that kiss, and after that dance . . ."

"I hope there is a romance." Amelia looked poignantly sincere, and there was now a definite deep blush in her cheeks. "He's attracted to me. I know that, but is it enough?"

"Enough to rouse a seasoned libertine from his bed in the wee hours, apparently."

In retrospect, Sophia should have left out bed from any discussion of St. James and her niece.

"I don't think he's quite as roguish as everyone believes."

Considering Amelia was inexperienced with men,

Sophia wasn't nearly as sure, especially when she recalled that captivating smile St. James seemed to be able to summon at will. "I suppose it is possible his brother's legendary reputation rubbed off on him a bit, but let's both keep in mind that I observed him kissing you in the middle of a downpour after having lured you out of a crowded ballroom."

"I was already out of the ballroom," Amelia said defensively.

Face the truth, Sophia. The girl is lost in his spell already.

"Amelia, what do you want from this?" The question was as gentle as she could make it. "Let me put it this way: if he proposed tomorrow, what would you say?"

The clatter of the wheels as they took a turn filled the ensuing silence.

"Amelia." Sophia leaned forward, her gaze intent. "I need your answer to this question. Once I know your true feelings, we can decide together what to do next."

Amelia's chin came up and her eyes held a hint of defiance. "Yes. I would say yes."

So her niece wanted the delectable St. James.

Then and there, Sophia decided she *must* have him.

Chapter Fourteen

The fire was brisk, the lamp burning low, but she probably would not have noticed if a herd of Indian elephants stampeded into the room, trumpeting and trampling everything in sight. Four days had passed since the fateful night of the ball. Four days of careful introspection, of deliberate removal from the whirl of the *ton*, of grasping to make something of that which perhaps defied calculated logic.

Love.

If I cannot understand it, she had decided philosophically, perhaps Anna could.

Amelia set aside her teacup, wrapped her robe more tightly around her, and read on.

So we met in secret yet again. Is this sin? It doesn't seem that way when I see your face, touch your skin, taste your kiss. Shouldn't love count for something? The way you run your fingers through my hair, the whisper of your breath on my lips, the light in your eyes when our gazes meet across a crowded room . . . I should not do this, but I still want it.

Samuel, we fit together beautifully, perfectly,
like magic on this earth. I did not know it could be
that way between a man and a woman, but I am
ignorant no more ...

The moonlight poured down, casting eerie shadows. Alex's booted feet brushed ferns and other plants as he tried to move with as much stealth as possible toward the sprawling grounds. The manor house rose up sharply in the distance, a dark rectangle, quiet. The windows showed no hint of illumination.

Perfect.

The narcotic scent of last year's dead leaves rose as they crunched under his passage, and he skirted a small stone wall, found the gate, and opened it with a telltale creak of rusted hinges. There was a gardener's cottage, stone and timber, but it was unoccupied—Amelia had given him that information in her innocent ramblings about the estate and he crept past it, took one of the paths lined with lilacs and glossy rhododendrons, and found himself at the back of the house.

Somewhere a night bird called, making him jump because it was close by. Alex remembered enough nights like this in Spain to be amused at his reaction. Then he had been risking his life, creeping past enemy camps, infiltrating guarded posts, fighting on foreign soil. Tonight there were no armed sentries waiting for him, nor was he waging war.

Well, perhaps a little.

He let himself in through the door that accessed the kitchen, using the picklock with ease on the simple mechanism. He slipped inside to the smoky fragrance of the hams hanging from the low ceiling and the scent of bread baked in the evening, the cooled loaves sitting on the long, scrubbed table. He'd brought a small lantern and lit it, the scrape and flare loud to his ears, but the big house was utterly silent.

Much like the night he'd broken into Lord Hathaway's town house. But this was Cambridgeshire, with its country breezes and moonlit gardens, and he hadn't braved slick, sooty rooftops or noxious alleyways.

Praise God for some small graces in life.

Alex went down a narrow hallway and cautiously pushed open a door, grateful it didn't creak. Dining room, he registered, the long table sitting expectant with its chairs and dead candelabra. Paneled walls, doors for the footmen to bring food in and out . . .

He selected one of those doors, and moments later was in the great baronial hall. From his careful queries, he had a fair idea of the position of the rooms in the house, and he chose the hallway to his right, finding an informal parlor from the collection of settees and scattered tables, a small room that could have been for correspondence for the countess, and, two doors away, his lordship's study.

Now, if he could just find the cursed box with the key and be done with it.

Only there were two immediate problems he discovered as he eased the door open. The first trouble he noticed was that the room was warm. His gaze flew to the hearth, where, sure enough, a few embers glowed. The second was, he wasn't alone.

Amelia was asleep in the chair, which could not be comfortable. Her slender form was slumped sideways at an angle, her dark gold hair loose around her shoulders, and she wore some sort of dressing gown in a pale color over a nightdress. The lace decorating the bodice was visible because the robe was only loosely tied at her slim waist, and Alex stood there, paralyzed by the vision.

What the devil?

He didn't realize he'd muttered the words out loud until she stirred, her eyes opened slowly as she shifted in the chair by the fire, blinking awake. One hand lifted to brush back her hair and she sat up, focusing on his presence just inside the doorway. "Alex."

No surprise in her voice. She expected him?

There was no other conclusion to be drawn, for he was certain she didn't regularly sleep in her father's study. Quietly, he closed the door. "Why didn't England send women to serve Wellington in Spain? We would have thrashed Bonaparte in a far shorter time."

She gathered her robe closed across her chest, which was a damned shame, in his opinion. "You searched my father's study in London. It made sense to suppose you'd search here eventually, especially with all the questions you asked me about the house. The nights since we left London I've waited here. Can I mention how grateful I am you've finally made an appearance?" She rubbed the back of her neck.

"My lack of subtlety is sufficiently humiliating." Alex moved toward the desk, trying to ignore his reaction to her presence. In her nightclothes. Not to mention that he knew for a fact her father was still in London.

Amelia. Dressed for bed. Her father miles away and everyone else asleep.

Not a great combination. Or a perfect one, depending on how one looked at the matter.

Introspection seemed very dangerous at the moment.

"I didn't hear you coming, if that is any consolation." Amelia stretched a little, her smile beguilingly sleepy. "And I doubt if what you want is in his desk. It is full of boring papers. Letters to solicitors and such. Nothing interesting at all. I decided while I waited for you to appear, I might as well help. I think in the past three days I've pretty much searched everything."

He halted, not sure whether to laugh or swear. "Since I appreciate the effort, I can't fault you, but you have no idea what I am looking for."

"What *are* you looking for?"

At this point he knew enough about her to forsake all the secrecy. "A key in a silver box. The box has an engraving."

Her lips pursed, but then she shook her head. "I've seen no such thing, not in his desk or anywhere else."

Damn. "How did you get here?"

"Carriage."

He muffled a laugh. "I meant how did you possibly get your father to allow you to come here alone?"

"I am nearly always here without him, but I'm hardly alone. My aunt accompanied me. And I informed him, truthfully, I might add, that I needed a small respite from London. At first he argued it might look as if he was sending me away because of you, but then I think he agreed for exactly that reason. Aunt Sophie took my side. It was her suggestion, really, for us to take a little time away from the season. Besides, I am currently forbidden to see you in a variety of locations and activities, all of which are in London. My father said nothing about not seeing you here."

Her smile was all female and definitely mischievous.

Alex stifled a laugh. God help him if he ever had a beautiful, subversive daughter.

A daughter? He'd never considered children except in the abstract way that if he ever married, he would probably end up a father. Now, gazing at Amelia, he wondered what it would be like to hold his own child in his arms, John's current state of euphoria over his new son fresh in his mind.

"It was one dance. Why would anyone think he would send you away because of me?" Alex asked quietly, standing there in the gloom, watching the flicker of the firelight shadow her delicate features.

But he had a feeling he knew the answer already. *Because of how I look at you.* Pure predatory, hungry male.

Hathaway had every reason to be alarmed. Her supple legs were all too visible under the thin material of the robe and nightdress she wore. Not that Alex could actually see them, but the outline beneath the thin material was more than enough.

"Not just one dance. There are also two kisses, and those morning meetings in the park," she corrected him, her voice whisper soft. "Am I the only one counting?"

The direct question took him off guard. Candid women were a rarity in his experience, but then again, he already had learned Amelia was uniquely fresh and unspoiled. Was it one-sided? No, he had to admit to himself it wasn't. What else it was, he wasn't sure.

"I am not the one who dragged *you* off the dance floor," she said when he didn't speak. "Or initiated those kisses."

"True." He moved to rest against the edge of the cluttered desk and crossed his arms over his chest. "If we are debating points over why one dance caused a fair amount of gossip, may I point out I didn't suggest the waltz in the first place, nor would I have because you'd danced three times already."

"Apparently you do count." There was a small arch note of triumph in her voice.

Devil take it, he *had*. "I didn't want you to have difficulties."

"I appreciate the concern. And if you are going to point out next that I was the one who publically touched you in a way that caused all the comment, don't bother. I am well aware of how that simple gesture was interpreted." She sat, her hands folded in her lap, and her tone was hushed. "My father's reaction alone should make me regret it."

Then she annihilated his defenses with three understated words. "But I don't."

Aunt Sophie was absolutely right.

Once she knew the whole story—or as much as Amelia knew herself, for she'd confided everything from finding Alex on her balcony to the love letters—her aunt had agreed without equivocation that Alex would eventually search the country house near Cambridge.

So she had very wisely suggested they repair to that location.

And he had come. He was right there, dressed simply in breeches, a white shirt, and a dark coat, in her father's study, where he should certainly not be, looking uncharacteristically disconcerted. "You should regret it," he said with just a subtle hint of bitterness in his tone. "For you are now linked to the infamously inconstant libertine Alexander St. James. Even my grandmother mentioned the whispers, and she holds herself quite above all gossip."

Amelia stirred in her chair, so aware of him it was like a physical touch. One of the logs on the dying fire snapped, oozing resin. "Are you?"

"A libertine or inconstant? Some of both, probably, but not as much of either as society assumes." Even if the room wasn't so dark, she knew his expression would be hard to decipher. She'd seen that bland look before but had begun to suspect, as she got to know him better, that he adopted it whenever he wanted to hide deeper emotion. It was practiced, not innate, and she wondered how often anyone besides maybe the Marquess of Longhaven or Viscount Altea knew what he was really thinking.

For instance, they were alone, she was clad in little more than her nightdress and a robe, and the house was very quiet. What was he thinking now? "I don't see you as a man who would stray if you invested emotion in a relationship you valued."

"The moment a woman mentions emotion, I must admit I feel twinges of alarm. Especially so if I have broken into her home a second time. Amelia, I—"

"Yes?" She stood when he abruptly stopped speaking. The texture of the rug under her bare feet, the slight smell of chimney smoke, the slow tick of the clock on the mantel all faded away because of the way he looked at her. There was a rawness there, and the moment she rose from the chair he'd tensed visibly.

Imagine that. She could intimidate the experienced, suave Alex St. James. Or if intimidate was the wrong word, she could at least unsettle him. Maybe even unsettle him very much.

"I've received five letters now," she whispered, tilting back her head so she could look up at him. "Have you received any more?" Without waiting for his answer, she went on. "They are ... fascinating. I'm starting to know her, know how she feels as a woman. Even Aunt Sophie has never really described the physical intimacy between a man and a woman to me. Through Anna, I am becoming *enlightened*."

"You shouldn't read them," he said gruffly, but his arms slipped down to his sides.

Playing with fire now ...

"It has all made me so very curious." She reached out a hand and touched him through the parted material of his coat, intrigued by the warmth under her palm from his skin through the fine linen of his shirt. His chest was muscular and hard, but she knew that from being held against him that night in the gazebo. The pounding of his heart was strong and steady against her splayed fingers. "I am not sure if it is better to be more informed of what happens between men and women, or if it makes it worse."

"Makes what worse?" His voice was definitely hoarse, and he hadn't removed her hand.

"Thinking about you. About *us*."

At last he touched her, his fingers sliding along her jaw in a light caress. "Amelia, this is so ill-advised as to be pronounced downright idiocy."

The fire had died down and she could barely see his face. "We are attracted to each other. I believe *you* told *me* so."

"Half the men in London are attracted to you. The other half are too old or too young."

"Are you jealous?"

"No." The word was clipped. Then he said, spurred to evident honesty, "Or I shouldn't be."

"But?"

He said a word violently under his breath and suddenly brought his mouth down on hers in a crushing, wild kiss. It was nothing like the soft, beguiling first two they had shared, but she reveled in his impatient, undisciplined need and made no move to push him away. Instead her hands crept up around his neck and she—shamelessly—clung to him.

She'd learned rather a lot from Anna's letters.

A kiss can be reverent or carnal. You taught me this, my darling, for when you need me is much different from when you want me. . . . I revel in both circumstances.

Did Alex need her or just want her? Maybe both, from the way his hands skimmed down her sides, cupping her hips and bringing her body against his, and from the low groan that reverberated against her lips. She'd never really thought so much about the physical part of desire until that first kiss. Her impression had always been that men enjoyed what happened in the bedroom more than women, but she was starting to understand that maybe it wasn't so one-sided. The letters had merely fueled a newfound awareness.

His mouth grazed her jaw, warm and teasing. "I didn't come here for this. In fact, I've been avoiding any kind of social event where you might be present and not seeking you out on your morning rides, both to protect your reputation and to protect myself. I suppose that is why I thought you were still in London."

"I wasn't aware your reputation could sustain any more damage." Amelia shivered as his lips found the hollow under her ear.

His laugh was soft, explosive, stirring her hair. "Not my reputation. Myself. From you. From *this*. I don't trust myself and obviously with good reason."

This time when he kissed her, one hand slid forward. She realized dimly the tug she felt was from the sash at her waist. A moment later her dressing gown slid to the floor. The back of his fingers brushed the side of her breast through the thin material of her nightdress and she did her best not to gasp, but her fingers curled convulsively in his hair.

"Stop me," he murmured against her mouth.

He cupped her, the weight of her breast cradled in his palm.

She was shocked when his thumb brushed her nipple, but then again, it wasn't at all unpleasant. A strange sensation curled in her belly. "My bedroom is upstairs," she pulled away enough to whisper, "and Aunt Sophie is in the guest wing."

Chapter Fifteen

The descent into madness was at least populated by visions of luscious young ladies in nothing but almost-sheer night rails, with tumbled, dark gold tresses and alabaster skin.

Only one young lady, actually.

... bedroom upstairs ... guest wing ...

Those four words echoed in his brain.

Hadn't he come for the key?

Or had he come for this, lured by a siren's song?

Alex tried to remind himself he wasn't interested in marriage at this time of his life. That neither of their families was going to make it easy, that Amelia could do better than an untitled younger son, that ...

That at the moment, with her curvaceous body in his arms, the scent of her perfume scattering his thoughts, all those obstacles didn't seem to matter. It wasn't just lust either, because he understood lust. He just didn't understand this.

"Yes," he said tersely, as if she'd asked him a question.

Her eyes were luminous even in the meager light. Which might have been how he found himself on the stairs in a few moments, following the billowing white of her nightdress as if he were bewitched—and perhaps he was, but if so, the magic was a simple one and old as time.

As old as man and woman anyway.

It had to be sorcery, hadn't it, to make a grown man abandon his scruples and good sense?

If so, he didn't care.

Amelia led the way up the curving, elegant staircase, silent, not looking back, her hair flowing down her back, her bare feet quiet on each step. He followed, conscious of what he was doing, but also aware that maybe he'd been coming to this decision slowly over the past weeks. Back in Spain, when he'd met Maggie, it had been different. At twenty-two, he was no novice when it came to women, but he hadn't been a match for her flirtatious banter and coquetry. In retrospect he knew she'd led him on, bored with her older husband's frequent absences, and only by force of will had Alex managed to retain his honor.

This time, though, the lady wasn't at all coy or experienced. Apparently he was more willing to be seduced by innocence than by design.

His body or his soul? He wasn't sure which, but thought it was both.

The bedroom was dark, scented, cool. Amelia didn't light the lamp, so he did it for her, quietly shutting the door behind them before moving to the task. Whatever happened next, he didn't want her to remember it as groping in the dark. Neither was it completely selfless. He'd been dreaming about her naked in his arms. Why leave it to his imagination when he could see it for himself?

"I could still leave," he said, his voice low despite her claim that there was no one close by, though he wasn't sure he had the willpower to follow through with the offer. Her bed was neatly turned down, the sheets inviting, and Amelia looked the picture of feminine innocence in her simple pale gown.

"Or you could stay," she countered. "If you leave, I

think we both know it would be a postponement, not the end of it. If that is the case, why should we wait?"

In his mind, he desperately wanted to argue the illogic of that statement. She should be bedded for the first time on her wedding night, reason suggested. Of course, if there was going to be a wedding anyway, she had a point.

Michael had been correct in his dry observation: Alex had been thinking about her in terms of permanence. Maybe not consciously, but the idea had been there. Amelia was bright, undeniably beautiful, and he enjoyed her company on a different level than any other woman he had ever known.

Why not marriage?

He was hard, his cock throbbing uncomfortably against the confinement of his breeches, and he had the feeling it was warping his normal conceptions of how to act when in the bedchamber of a virginal miss.

Run.

No, stay.

He didn't even realize he'd taken off his coat until it hit the floor. Next went his boots, one by one, dropped carelessly, while he assessed her reaction to the fact that he was undressing. If she was apprehensive, it didn't show, though her eyes widened slightly when he stood and his fingers went to the buttons on his shirt.

"Naked is better," he told her with a slow, deliberately suggestive smile.

"Spoken like a true rake." Her smile was tremulous, but her gaze fixed on his moving fingers as he unfastened his shirt.

"I hope this doesn't disappoint you, but I'm not much of a rake." He tugged the hem from his breeches.

"I've already come to that conclusion."

Had she? He wasn't exactly surprised. They seemed to understand each other very well.

His grin was deliberately wicked. "Make no mistake. I'm not a saint either."

Her laugh was throaty. "I've come to that conclusion too. I distinctly remember Lady Fontaine and an extremely personal remark that night on the terrace."

"I was asking her about you, remember?"

"I remember."

His mouth went dry as she tugged the ribbon free on the bodice of her gown and let the garment slip to the floor.

Amelia. Naked. His imagination, he discovered in this definitive moment, had not done her justice. Though her breasts were not overly large, the natural slenderness of her frame made them seem voluptuous, her contours willowy, the dainty triangle between her slim thighs a darker shade than her hair. Though virgins were not his usual bedmates, he could imagine it took some resolve to stand there nude, her chin slightly raised, before him.

She walked slowly toward him, shy and yet bold, her unbound hair brushing her waist. "How did I discern you aren't nearly as nefarious as you are perceived to be? I already know you do not break promises. You do not touch married women. And since it appears you do not seduce unmarried young ladies, they must seduce you. Society would be so disappointed to learn the truth."

"I don't care about society." He shrugged out of his shirt like it was on fire and it flew across the room in a careless toss. "I do care what you think of me."

Was that love? It very well might be. He had an undeniable passion for her, and he valued her regard.

"I don't think my opinion of your true character is in question, or you would not be here."

He might have replied, but he was beyond it. Alex scooped her up in his arms, carried her to the bed, deposited her on the mattress, and followed her down, covering her luscious body. His kiss was searing, hot, possessive.

Mine.

All mine. Damn Lord Westhope and his quest for a beautiful, aristocratic wife. . . . Amelia belongs to me.

Her hand explored his back, the light touch even more arousing. Their mouths mated, and he knew she could feel his rigid cock even though he hadn't yet removed his breeches. "You're so beautiful," he told her, nuzzling the slender column of her neck.

"Alex."

Was there anything more arousing than the way she breathed his name? If so, he couldn't fathom what it would be. "But that isn't all of it." He nipped a path along her collarbone. "I've known beautiful women. . . . John's reputation alone gave me access to anyone in the *ton*. They all expected the next profligate son of the Duke of Berkeley."

Her slender fingers sifted through his hair as he grazed the upper curve of her breast. "And what did they get?"

"Not what I wish to give you," he said reverently, and took one perfect rosy nipple in his mouth.

The reckless consequences of her actions might come back to haunt her, but at the moment Amelia didn't care.

Bemused, beguiled, bedazzled . . . what *was* the right word? All she knew was that the man above her licked her nipple in a slow, languid movement that tore a very unladylike sound from her throat. She arched and involuntarily pushed the crest of her breast deeper into his mouth.

Heaven. Was there any drug like love? She didn't know, but at the moment neither did she care. Maybe, if it wasn't for Anna's heartfelt letters, she would not behave with such abandon, but no one had ever told her women experienced the same level of desire as men.

Was it wrong if you loved someone?

Just the opposite. It felt oh, so right.

His hair was warm, soft in contrast to the hardness of the rest of him, like silk as she played with it, her body restless under the seeking tease of his mouth. He suckled gently—and then not so gently—and Amelia shifted, the contrast of his dark head superimposed against the paleness of her skin vivid and startling.

And the swirl of his tongue so magical she could not believe it. "Oh."

His other hand moved to the opposite breast and did something exquisite to the underside with the skilled play of his fingers.

She thought she'd melt.

"You taste delicious. Sweet and salty at the same time." His lips tantalized, taunted, and the murmur against her skin sent reverberations of sensation downward, and a peculiar warmth built between her legs.

"I want to please you too," she managed to say, though her thoughts were hardly collected.

Alex lifted his head, and his celebrated smile was slow and sinful. "You do please me. Can't you tell?"

The reference to the evidence of his desire, the hard bulge under the material of his breeches, unmistakable since he was lying on top of her, made her blush. Or maybe she just felt warm all over anyway. "Why aren't you completely undressed?"

"I am doing my best not to shock your maidenly sensibilities."

She laughed at the teasing tone of his voice, a very real wonder at the sense of intimacy, of tactile connection, making her somehow tense and languid at the same time. "Shock me. You'll have to eventually, won't you? I know *that* much."

"I don't have to take your virginity, Amelia."

What the devil did that mean? Confused, she stared at him, noting the heat in his dark eyes.

Evidently her expression was easy to read, for he explained, "I can give you pleasure—we can pleasure each other—without actual penetration."

That seemed to negate the basic concept of making love, and if he were here, in her room, in her bed, she wanted all of it.

Because she loved him, she wanted it all. "I am already naked in bed with you," she said with a firmness that surprised even her. "Don't give me a half measure of the experience."

"If I give you full measure, you are left without choices. Passion is an intoxicant, Amelia. I don't want you to wake in the morning and regret this."

"I won't."

"We'll have to marry."

An inner joy swelled. She trembled against him, bare breasts to bare chest. His eyes narrowed a fraction.

"You're surprised I just said that. What did you expect from me?" There was a touch of asperity in his voice, his face going shuttered. "Ah, I see. Not that much nobility. I guess—"

She stopped him with a touch of her fingertips to his mouth—that utterly masculine, skillful mouth—and shook her head. "Expect? I'm not that calculating."

His brows rose in minute skepticism.

How to say this correctly? Amelia swallowed and whispered, "I'd hoped you'd come to Brookhaven. Can I mention hoped enough to sit three nights, dozing in a chair in my father's study? And you did. Then you kissed me . . . and . . . well . . . I didn't plan anything. I just wanted to talk to you, but we can't seem to help it."

We can't seem to help it. . . .

And there it was. The bare truth, stated plainly.

The moment hung, rife with both desire and poignant emotion.

"No, we can't, can we? I've noticed it myself. You trust me so much, then?" His knuckles drifted across her cheek in a feather caress.

"Yes."

"Your lack of hesitation humbles me." His lashes lowered, his powerful body braced over hers so she felt only the pleasant, exciting male pressure of it.

I love you.

Even as she opened her mouth to tell him, as imprudent as it might be to cross that line, he levered himself upward and stood by the side of the bed, swiftly stripping out of his breeches. The length of his erection, high against the taut plane of his stomach, rendered her speechless. This time when he rejoined her, he didn't speak, but instead began what seemed to be a systematic assault on her senses. First slow, molten kisses, punctuated by wicked caresses, and his fingers not just exploring her breasts but everywhere. The arch of her foot, the turn of her ankle, tickling the muscles of her calves, skimming her inner thighs . . . and then, finding, seeking, invading . . .

He touched her female cleft, his long fingers persuasive, and though she instinctively clamped her legs together initially, his low laugh echoed out. "The full measure of the experience," he repeated her words in a husky, erotic instruction, "requires full cooperation. Relax and let me ready you."

She wasn't at all relaxed. She was hungry, anxious, needy, oddly tense. . . .

"You are safe with me."

The richness of his voice worked. Her limbs went limp, her breasts quivered as she took a calming breath, and her thighs parted.

Never had she made such a wise—albeit wayward—decision. There was no real comprehension of the connotation of the phrase *ready you* until his fingertips slid over the folds of her sex, parting her, finding a spot that when he touched her caused a fine ripple of pleasure so unique she couldn't control the gasp that escaped her lips.

And then he did it again, just a slow rotation of his fingers, but it was . . . indescribable.

"Oh." She didn't mean to move, but it happened anyway; the slight arch of her spine, the shift of her pelvis into that erotic touch.

"Yes?" Alex kissed her neck, and slid upward, though she wasn't sure how he could concentrate on such a hot, openmouthed kiss at the same time as he actually pushed a finger into her passage. God knew it splintered her concentration into a thousand pieces, especially when he did that sinful thing with his thumb.

It was embarrassing, but she spread her legs open even more to allow him to continue whatever he was doing, because it was just so incredibly wonderful.

She didn't understand how wonderful until the rapture built to unbearable proportions and Amelia went rigid in his arms, the spasms racking her body so blissfully that she could hardly breathe, but not for the usual reason. Then gradually, as she relaxed, she became cognizant again of his large form dwarfing hers, the press of his need, hot and long, against her thigh, and the stroke of his hand against her hair.

"The full measure?" he asked, adjusting his position.

Chapter Sixteen

Making love in the shrouded confines of a lady's bedroom was not a unique experience, but this—*this*—was so very different. Alex gazed into the eyes of the woman beneath him and began to slowly enter her body, the exquisite tightness of her vaginal passage both paradise and hell.

The last sensation he wanted her to experience was pain, but a little discomfort was inevitable, or so he'd heard. How much was the question, as was what he could do to alleviate the distress. "Tell me," he said on a low murmur, "if I hurt you."

He punctuated the request with a lingering kiss, with sheer will tamping down his sexual hunger to a manageable level so he could contain the need to thrust into her and satisfy all those glorious fantasies of finally being in this exact position. She was soft and luscious, replete and dazed from her first climax, her hands resting on the small of his back. Alex understood that familiar expression on a woman's face, vulnerable in the aftermath of orgasmic release, silkily satisfied, languorous and drifting in the moment. The tumbled gold of her hair spilled around her slender, ivory shoulders. "It doesn't hurt. It's just . . . odd."

"Odd?" He lightly licked the corner of her mouth in an effort to distract her from their slowly fusing bodies. "That is not very complimentary. But then again, you've never done this before, so I suppose it is a different sensation."

Proof of that was the resistant barrier that arrested his progress, his cock nudging the small membrane before he took a breath and pushed past in a decisive stroke that seated him completely in her body. He went still, waiting, registering her gasp as maybe more surprise than pain at the sudden invasion, when he'd been so gentle so far.

"Best over with quickly," he murmured, softly and slowly kissing her arched brows, the tip of her nose, her lips.

Quickly, he thought in a haze of carnal pleasure, could be embarrassingly applicable to this situation. Already his testicles tightened and the urge to ejaculate was strong, primal. Since he'd met the delectable Miss Patton, he hadn't been with a woman. Maybe that had been a mistake.

Or perhaps exactly the right course of action, for he really couldn't imagine wanting this with anyone else.

There seemed no question that he was a bloody, besotted fool.

"Alex . . ." She touched his cheek and shifted restlessly beneath him, her lashes half-lowered over her azure eyes and the plea undefined but clearly understood.

He didn't move yet, though he'd broken out in a sweat. The wet heat of her around his throbbing cock, her thighs smooth against his hips, made his body clamor for erotic satisfaction, but he needed control for just a few more moments. However he'd pictured this turning point in his life to be, he'd always viewed it with an abstract romanticism.

Ask the damn question.

"Lady Amelia, will you marry me?"

"I thought you said we'd *have* to marry." Her fingers trailed up his spine. The taut tips of her flawless breasts were tightly pressed against his chest.

"Not quite the same as me asking, is it?"

"I—"

"If we are betrothed, the commitment set between us, this"—he moved experimentally, withdrawing a little and surging back—"is much more acceptable as not just a deflowering, but an affirmation of our future."

"Your morals are showing again." Her fingernails lightly bit into his shoulders.

"I hope so."

"I will marry you gladly," Amelia declared, her cheeks flushed, her slender body trembling just enough he could feel each exacting quiver, "if you will just *do* something."

Her petulant tone made him grin. "Oh, I will," he promised with dark intonation, sliding back before the inward glide of sex into sex made every muscle go rigid.

She moaned, her body hot, wet, and receptive, and if he'd worried about the pain of her denouement, it seemed to have been negligible.

That permission to proceed was just what he wanted. Needed. Craved. Alex began to stroke into her slowly, but with increasing urgency. Since he'd made sure she was aroused already, Amelia's enjoyment was exactly what he wanted—and then some. She made the most delicious noises, he decided, his body on fire, and he sincerely hoped her aunt was really a wing away, snoring in blissful ignorance, for his fiancée was not quiet.

Or patient.

"Alex."

Importunate virgins—former virgins—are delightful, he decided as the enchantment washed over him. His skin was damp, his cock straining, and he tried to hold on to his resolve to put off culmination until she found the same satisfaction. His fingers went between their bodies, past the soft curve of her belly to where they joined, and to his infinite relief, it seemed all she needed. Amelia wrapped her arms around his neck and shuddered against him, a low, keening scream signaling her second release. He followed, for the first time in his life not worried about possible conception or the various ways to prevent it, and allowed himself to spill inside her with a glorious burst of pleasure that shook him from head to toe.

It shook his world, actually.

They lay together, panting, skin to skin, his face buried in her fragrant, outspread hair. The lissome feel of her gave him a special joy, and while he wasn't trying to be irreverent about their circumstances, considering the obstacles ahead, he turned his head just enough to murmur in her ear, "This bud of love, by summer's ripening breath, may prove a beauteous flower—"

"—when next we meet," Amelia finished for him.

"I adore bluestocking females." He smiled, content, lazily so in such surfeit of pleasure. Alex withdrew slowly, transferred his weight to one elbow, and twirled a lock of her long hair between his fingers.

"All of them?"

"Well, one of them in particular."

She lay, nude and lush, against the disarray of the bed, her answering smile warm but suddenly a little shy. One hand crept to the sheet, as if now, in the aftermath, she understood she was naked, he was naked, and the world had changed.

"Don't," he said, gently catching her wrist. "I like to look at you."

"The feeling is mutual." Her gaze wandered over his bare chest, then lower, and the flush in her cheeks was not just from the exertion of lovemaking. "I suppose I will get used to this, but for right now . . . I am still . . ."

When she trailed off, he supplied, "Bemused? Bewildered? Enlightened?"

Her laugh was low and rueful. "I suppose any and all of those will do, and yet still not be sufficient."

"I cannot speak for all of mankind, but if I had to guess, everyone feels that way after their first sexual experience."

"Does everyone receive a marriage proposal in the middle of things, so to speak? Since I did, I think it entitles me to be more befuddled than most."

It was hard to understand why the idea of relinquishing bachelorhood, something he'd vowed he would enjoy upon his return from those hard years in Spain, didn't bother him—or maybe it wasn't. Not with Amelia so soft and willing next to him. He wasn't yet ready to acknowledge something as profound as being in love, but he was cognizant of her fundamental appeal. He'd envisioned having a wife as a duty, but she would be a pleasure. Both in bed and out of it.

The iridescent shimmer of his semen on her thighs was tinged with blood, a reminder of her lost innocence. So was the room, now that he could focus on anything but urgent carnal need. The bed hangings were a pale, girlish pink, the carved rocking chair in the corner meant for a child, and there were ruffles on the curtains that stirred in the night breeze.

"Perhaps." He looked into her eyes and leaned forward to kiss her lightly. "But confess now: what a timely method of proposing, wasn't it? With the lady panting in my arms."

"I don't believe I panted," she said primly. But she laughed and added ingenuously, "Actually, I have no idea if I panted or not, but had you asked any other way, I would have said yes, so it doesn't matter how you did it."

His hand, which had been trailing strategically down her throat toward her breast, stilled. "I could have been more romantic, I suppose. Roses, bended knee, that sort of thing. I hadn't really thought about that. I just wanted you to know I wasn't merely taking advantage of you."

*   *   *

A reputed rake with a stricken look on his face, apologizing for despoiling a maiden, was surely a priceless sight. Alex lounged next to her, all nude male splendor, the lean length of his hard body taking over most of her bed, his raven hair more delectably disheveled than usual.

"You were extremely romantic," Amelia informed him, the memory of his delicate, skilled touch fresh in her mind, her body sated and happiness a tangible presence in her life. "I would not trade what just happened for any other scenario, believe me."

This time when she reached over to move a tangled midnight curl off his neck, the world couldn't see it. It was just the two them, safe, concealed in her favorite place on earth, the surroundings familiar, his smile enough to turn any female's head. Her eyes felt misty and her throat held a tinge of betraying tightness.

He caught her fingers and pressed a kiss to them. "I am glad you aren't having regrets already. Once the pleasure passes . . ."

His slight shrug gave her pause. He knew about the pleasure passing and interest fading. She finished for him, "The doubts set in?"

"Not in this case."

"But it has happened to you before."

"None of this has happened to me before."

And she believed him. Not the lovemaking, of course. He'd lived up to his name—whether he acknowledged it or not, he had one—but there was a certain resonance in his voice that was telling even to someone like her, who had stayed in a sheltered existence in Cambridgeshire most of her life. "Hasn't it?"

"No. You've disrupted my world."

A part of her wanted to laugh. Here she was, naked in front of a man, and not just any man but Alex St. James, with the sticky evidence of their mutual pleasure on her thighs, and she wanted to explode with mirth and with joy.

"I like you disgruntled." She smiled at him teasingly.

He did her one better, leaning forward, dark hair falling over his forehead. "I like *you*. Some women are beautiful, but it doesn't matter because there is certainly more to a person than how she looks. Some women are charming, some are witty, some are intelligent. Then there is the rare one who has all of those traits."

"What a lovely compliment." Her voice was hushed.

"Don't thank me. If I could stop thinking about you, both our lives would be much simpler, trust me."

Amelia wasn't sure she considered it as much as a problem as he did, but the issue of her father rose. "I don't want a confrontation. Let me handle my father. Aunt Sophie will know what to do."

"I don't need to hide behind your aunt." Alex's handsome face drew into a faint scowl. "Or you. And that isn't a treatise on male arrogance either. I am going to approach him honestly and openly. My first point being I don't have a personal quarrel with him. Our family issues are in the past, and though I realize they aren't so far past as to be forgotten, they are still not about *our* lives."

"Is it that simple?" Amelia caught the nape of his neck, tugging him down so their mouths touched. "If you tell me it is, I'll believe you."

There was a certain exhilaration in having power over a being so much larger and stronger. He dwarfed her in size and yet easily acquiesced to the kiss. He muttered against her lips, "No, it isn't that simple."

And kissed her. Moreover, she could feel him rise again, his sex swelling. The brush of his tongue against hers brought out a sigh, the sudden change as he adjusted her beneath him bringing a gasp. "Alex."

"Our families hate each other," he said, his lips exploring her neck, his hands busy as well.

"I know." She *did* know. She'd seen her father's face after she danced with Alex the other night. Afterward, the stinging edict for her to stay away from the Duke of Berkeley's son wasn't forgotten either, though she was currently ignoring it about as much as it could be ignored. Naked and intertwined in an intimate embrace did not translate as cooperation with her father's wishes.

"We are going to find opposition on every front." He nibbled on her earlobe.

"Yes." She arched to give him better access to the hollow of her throat. Agreement or acquiescence? It was hard to say.

"It doesn't seem to concern you." He obediently ran his tongue along a very sensitive pulse point.

"At the moment, no. Maybe in the morning I'll be more pragmatic." She ran her hand over the muscled curve of his shoulder.

"We've a few more hours of blissfully ignoring the problem, then."

Bliss was exactly the correct word, she decided as he kissed her breasts, each caress lavish in the resulting pleasure, and the word hours took on a whole new, beautiful significance. The servants rose early, true, but it had been barely midnight when Alex had slipped into her father's study. When he spread her thighs again, she let her eyes drift shut at the hard, insistent pressure of his entry, but it was easier this time, the slickness of his earlier discharge lubricating the penetration. Now that she understood what she wanted, Amelia concentrated on the sensation of each slow stroke, the tantalizing fullness and then the withdrawal, hard into soft, man into woman. The rise of anticipation was both exhilarating and glorious. She believed she now understood why some women whispered behind their hands and exchanged meaningful looks when certain men walked past.

No wonder no one saw fit to enlighten unmarried young women. The experience was not something that could be described in mere words.

"Like this." Alex cupped her bottom in his hands and lifted her into the next thrust, his eyes veiled by long, dark lashes.

Exactly like this was all she could think, white-hot

rapture within reach. Alex must have sensed her strug-
gle, or maybe he was just so experienced—something
she'd rather not dwell on—that he knew the signs, but
he obligingly changed the angle just the right amount,
and . . .

On the next inward glide she fell apart. All awareness
vanished, spiking ecstasy tore her world asunder, and
she clung to him, shaking and shaken.

With a low oath, he went rigid, and the powerful
pulse of his satisfaction mimicked the tense contractions
of her inner muscles.

Damp with perspiration, breathless, they sprawled
together across the bed until he rolled to his side and
gathered her into his arms. The sense of exhaustion was
a pleasant one, and Amelia's lassitude made her limbs
lax and her smile sleepy. Her head pillowed on his shoulder, waiting for her heart to slow to a normal pace, she
inhaled the scent of clean male sweat and felt his mouth
brush her disheveled hair.

"I'm sorry you didn't get what you came here for,"
she murmured, remembering belatedly the mysterious
item that had brought him to her. Truly, her father's desk
had revealed nothing she thought in the least would be
of interest to the St. James family, and she had searched
thoroughly.

"On the contrary, I think I found *exactly* what I was
looking for," he responded quietly. "Now go to sleep, my
sweet, because I have kept you up unforgivably late."

Had she the strength to argue, she might have, but
she didn't, and was halfway to slumber already anyway.

My sweet. She drifted off at peace.

Warm milk might do the trick, but in Sophia's experience brandy was better. Her William had suggested it
once, and it had worked marvelously. Since then she often had a wee bit before bed, or if she woke and couldn't
go back to sleep. Sophia negotiated the empty hallways
with the aid of a small candle and cursed drafty country

houses every time the flame flickered. Her brother-in-law's study was on the ground floor, and she crept down the stairs carefully, her wrapper tightly cinched, the cap on her hair probably askew from all the tossing and turning.

Surely Stephen kept some spirits in a decanter in his study. Most men of her acquaintance did, and while Lord Hathaway might be rigid and distant in some ways, he was still a typical English male. If nothing else, maybe she could keep Amelia company.

The smell of tobacco was a specter as the door creaked open, and she entered the room with her candle held high. The wavering light rippled over tall bookcases crammed with volumes, the fireplace, which still held a glow of dying embers, the cluttered desk . . . and ah-ha, the gleaming crystal of a bottle and glass in the corner by the window. Sophia made her way to the small table, poured out a generous measure, and took a sip, assuming Amelia had tired of her vigil and gone to bed.

Until she turned and saw the crumple of pale blue silk on the floor.

Lowering her glass, Sophia stared at the discarded dressing gown. It was near the desk, which was why she hadn't seen it immediately. Why on earth would Amelia take off her dressing gown on this cool night and toss it carelessly on the floor?

The turn of the door handle made a soft click. Sophia caught her breath as a tall man stepped into the room. He halted, arrested midstep by the sight of her candle on the desk, and muttered an oath she didn't quite catch. There was no mistaking Alex St. James's raven hair, even more wild than usual, or the fact that he wasn't wearing his coat or his boots, the former tossed over his shoulder as if he'd dressed hastily, both the latter held in one hand. Even his shirt was buttoned only halfway.

Suddenly the heap of material on the floor was not such a mystery. After all, Sophia had seen them in each other's arms before, and besides, she was the one who had advised they come here in case St. James decided to pay the estate a visit. She cleared her throat. "Good evening, my lord. Or is it good morning?"

"Lady McCay." He bowed, the graceful, courtly movement incongruous to his half-dressed state. "Why am I not surprised to find you here? Let me answer my own question. Errant females seem to pop up wherever I go lately, especially if I am trying to be secretive."

"I couldn't sleep." Sophia wasn't sure why she should sound defensive, except she'd been caught red-handed with a glass of brandy. After all, she had more of a right to be there than he did, though she sincerely doubted her stuffy brother-in-law would approve of her pilfering liquor from his study.

Alexander St. James smiled and said dryly, "I find a wee dram before bed does wonders."

"Where is Amelia?"

"Asleep."

Asleep. And here he was barefoot, shirt unfastened, coat off. He hadn't arrived that way at the house, of that she was certain. This was certainly a case of "be careful what you wish for," because while she'd wanted to make sure Amelia had a chance to talk to her erstwhile lover, Sophia also had the impression it had gone rather farther than that.

Oh, dear.

"Mind if I join you?" He inclined his head toward the decanter.

"I suppose under the circumstances, a stiff drink might be in order." She set down her glass and poured one for him, turning to offer it. "I take it you found Amelia here and were distracted from your original purpose?"

"She can be very distracting indeed." He accepted the snifter, took a sizable drink from his glass, and gave her a quizzical look. "You seem remarkably undaunted by my appearance or the situation, my lady."

"A man in a state of partial undress who knows my niece is sleeping does give me pause, I assure you."

"It gives *me* a bit of pause, actually," he said wryly.

"When you and I last spoke, I did not know the extent of my niece's attachment to you." Sophia realized that with her standing he couldn't sit down, not even to pull on his boots, so she chose one of the chairs by the fireplace and plopped down, unabashedly sipping her brandy. "As for your appearance, it was Amelia who came to the conclusion that some of your questions about the estate were quite pointed. I warn you, my lord, she might be young and her beauty dazzling enough few men see past it, but she is not a fool. You told her yourself her father has something you want, and if you didn't find it in London, it makes perfect sense you'd come here."

"That any of this makes sense to anyone is an amazement to me." St. James sat down in the opposite chair, placed his drink on a small, convenient table, and began to pull on his boots. "I am sent on some obscure errand, looking for an item I am assured is most important but is about as easy to find as the proverbial needle in a stack of hay. And instead of being able to actually look for this elusive object, I somehow end up engaged to be married."

Engaged? That had a promising ring to it, especially since it was easy enough to see that a swift wedding was in order. Considerably cheered up, Sophia finished her drink enthusiastically, choked a little on the large mouthful, and had to clear her throat. Her idea to come to Cambridgeshire had been a brilliant one after all. "Congratulations."

"We both know Lord Hathaway won't be pleased."

"There's always Scotland."

At that calm statement, his brows shot up. "When Amelia said you were a liberal woman, she was not exaggerating, was she? Are you suggesting we elope?"

Am I? Not necessarily, but she did know her brother-in-law was not going to welcome Alex St. James into the family with open arms. "Hathaway *is* going to be difficult."

"Not that I require his permission to marry, but my father isn't going to be happy either." St. James hesitated, but then asked bluntly, "Do you understand why they have such an antagonism for each other? I know the old earl had an affair with my great-aunt when he was married, ruining her and scandalizing everyone who knew about it, but it didn't directly involve my father or the current earl. Case in point: I certainly don't harbor a grudge against Amelia because of something her grandfather did years ago."

"That, my lord, is quite obvious," Sophia said primly.

His mouth twitched, but his expression was charmingly rueful. "I suppose it is. Rest assured, though, the events of this evening were not planned."

While he looked every inch the wicked young rogue, with his shirt partially unbuttoned, coatless, Sophia still believed him. "Amelia has always had the ability to know what she wants. I fear that trait comes from our side of the family."

"I'll take that as fair warning."

"So you should. As for your father and Hathaway, you might wish to keep in mind that whether it was provoked or not, your grandfather killed Amelia's grandfather. Swallowing that bitter dose would not be easy for anyone. Your family feels betrayed because of the affair, and the Pattons are bitter because of their loss also."

"It's a damnable problem," he admitted. "I believe I know why the duel happened after she was already dead. It is possible Anna took her own life."

That made sense. Awful sense, but sense just the same. A grieving brother who already was affronted might very well issue a challenge to the man who destroyed his sister's life. "How tragic," Sophia murmured, truly sorrowed. "Is that what you are looking for? Something to prove her suicide?"

"No, I am looking for a key. In a silver case."

She met his inquiring gaze and shook her head. "I haven't seen it, but keep in mind, though I visit, this is not my home."

"Amelia hasn't either." He rubbed his jaw in evident frustration. "But it could be hidden."

Sophia looked at the case clock in the corner. The brandy had done its work, and it was terribly late. She rose. "I'd guess you wish to search this room and that is why you returned here. When you are done, I expect you to leave as discreetly as you came, to protect her reputation."

He didn't deny it, but looked amused. "I will do my best, Lady McCay."

Chapter Seventeen

John nudged his mount with his heel and broke into a canter down the hill. Alex followed suit. Having arrived just as his brother was riding out was actually opportune, for Alex wanted a chance to talk to him alone, and a glorious, sunny afternoon provided a chance for them to choose a secluded spot for a conversation he didn't want overheard.

"By the old ruins?" John suggested, flinging the words over his shoulder. "You said 'private.' As it is still whispered it is haunted, no one ever goes there."

"Sounds fine," Alex said, his horse a new mount from the ducal stables, his own horse tired from the trip. The bay disliked a heavy hand, he'd found right away, and the frisky three-year-old pranced sideways as they reined in, and tossed his head.

The old abbey had been abandoned centuries before, the flying buttresses reduced to crumpled outcrops, the skeleton of the walls like moldering remains, lichen on the fallen rocks. "Father never has wanted to tear this down." Alex swung from the saddle.

"And upset the fey spirits supposed to gather here?

Heaven forbid." John also slid off, letting his stallion graze on the tender grass of the secluded spot. He grinned. "And I can say that I might have exploited a time or two the perceived romantic elements of this particular spot for a moonlit tryst. Fair damsels find it intriguing."

"You would have such experiences to relate," Alex observed wryly. "Do you have any notion of how many times I have been approached by one of your former conquests, curious to know if my talents in the boudoir equal your legendary prowess?"

"My amours tended to be adventurous ladies." John chuckled. "It doesn't surprise me that a few of them find the idea of a younger brother titillating."

A few? Upon his return from Spain, Alex had found himself besieged, and a great deal of it stemmed from their very close resemblance. He hesitated, and then said simply, "Actually, since you brought up the subject of fair damsels, I might have a story of my own. It is why I am here."

"Is it?"

"Yes."

"*My* stories are just memories now. The words respectable and married come to mind." John stepped over part of a wall now reduced to rubble. "Pardon me, but *you* have a story? It's not like you to discuss your private life. I admit I am now intrigued. What prompted this sudden visit?"

The vision of Amelia in delectable disarray after their lovemaking was all too immediate. "I was on my way back to London and thought I would stop and talk to you. I need some advice."

"This sounds serious." John stopped, the wind ruffling his dark hair. His eyes narrowed. "No, let me correct myself: this *is* serious. I can tell. I wondered what brought you to Berkeley Hall without notice when you rode up. What's wrong?"

In town the St. James residence was Berkeley House;

in the country, the family home Berkeley Hall. The grand manor of his youth, a symbol of his family's wealth, the burden Alex was glad to be absolved of as a younger son. But it seemed he had inherited something else from the St. James legacy: a mystery, a quest, and a scandal.

"Wrong seems an ill-fitting word," he said truthfully, propping his foot on a convenient rock. "I'm to be married."

It was rare that John was at a loss for words, but that seemed the case, at least for a few moments. His brother's face was a study in surprise. "I was unaware of a courtship, but I suppose I have been occupied here with my wife, new son, and estate matters. Who is she?"

Ah yes, the crux of the matter. "Amelia Patton."

"Patton? . . . Oh, bloody hell, Alex, *Patton*? Not a relation to Lord Hathaway?"

"His daughter."

"Oh, *fuck*."

Considering John's reaction was probably mild, that intonation was not a good sign. He spread his hands. "Hence the advice, John."

"Select another bride." The words were clipped and concise.

"Does it work that way?" he asked just as sharply. "I didn't select her in the first place. It just happened."

The question brought on a small silence with nothing but the whisper of the breeze through the decrepit ruins. "No," John finally said in a flat, resigned tone. "Had I not fallen in love with Diana, I probably would not understand. But I did and I do. It *doesn't* work that way. Do you mind telling me how it came to be Lady Amelia? Hell and blast, she must just have had her bow. I don't even know of her."

And John knew every beautiful woman in the *ton*, or at least he used to be aware, though Alex had to admit an ingenue like Amelia would not draw his brother, who before he met his wife avoided innocent debutantes. "Indeed. Just out into society. Intelligent, stunning, with eyes a man could lose himself in and a body Aphrodite would envy."

His brother sat down abruptly on stray stone. "Such eloquence indicates a real infatuation," he acknowledged.

The situation went well past infatuation. "Even without the ill feeling between our families, Hathaway would have legitimate reason to object to me for his daughter. My reputation alone would cause any father concern."

"Mine was worse. *I* married."

"You are titled already, rich, and going to be a duke, John." Alex smiled wryly. "Come, now. As worldly men, we both know it makes a difference. Amelia and her father don't have a close relationship either, so I am not sure of how much he'll take her wishes in this matter into consideration."

"An alliance with our family is a prestigious one."

"Unless you happen to have a very real distaste for any person with St. James blood flowing through his veins. How shall I handle this? As little as I look forward to petitioning Hathaway for his daughter's hand in marriage, I don't look much more forward to telling Father either."

"I see your dilemma." John, his dark eyes narrowed in thought, rubbed his jaw and watched a small bird hop through the springy grass. "He won't be happy."

Though he wasn't anxious to embarrass Amelia, John could be trusted. Alex said matter-of-factly, "I wish it, so it is hardly a hardship, but I *have* to marry her."

"I see." John crossed one booted foot over the other and gave him an ironic look. "Even I never ruined the daughter of an earl. I didn't think you had it in you, little brother."

"Yes, well, she can be very persuasive," Alex muttered.

John laughed outright. "It was her idea? That's even better and makes more sense. I am anxious to meet this daring young woman. But it really doesn't help your case, because the blame will fall your way. If I were in your position, the very last point I'd want to make to Hathaway is that an expedient marriage is necessary."

"That *has* occurred to me, thank you." The worst scenario he could imagine was an angry, maybe even murderously angry, confrontation with Amelia's father. Whatever their relationship, the man was her only parent, and God forbid Alex be the cause of more distance between them, much less find himself in a position where he had to defend himself against Hathaway.

"If you want my advice, I'd recommend a swift trip to Gretna Green. I'm trying to imagine our two families at a wedding, and the vision isn't filled with joyous tears and interchanged congratulations." Any amusement in John's expression had faded.

The Scotland theme persists, Alex noted sardonically. "I am not interested in depriving her of a proper wedding, if it is in my power to give it to her."

"Then perhaps you should have resisted that *improper* interlude. I had my vices, certainly, but I didn't initiate virgins."

Maybe it was a valid point, but Alex could see her in vivid memory, her delicious body superimposed on the linens of her bed, peaceful in sleep. The sweet rapture of her response would stay with him his entire life. "I am sure you can understand when I say the opportunity presented itself, neither of us caring about the consequences enough to stop, and what is done is done. I don't even have regrets, but I need to weigh my options."

"You really are smitten, aren't you?"

"Don't look so infernally amused at my predicament."

A pragmatic man always, John said succinctly, "Consider the elopement. I don't think you have other choices that do not include raised voices and possible bloodshed. If it is a fait accompli, both families have little choice but to accept it."

Amelia's aunt seemed to have come to the same conclusion, but Alex rose and said with resignation, "I want to give her everything. A rushed, secretive wedding certainly is an option, but I hope my last one."

"That," his older brother declared with equanimity, "is exactly what I would do."

"John, you had a magnificent wedding that people still talk about."

His brother's grimace looked sincere. "I know. I am trying to spare you that. Elope. If I had it to do over again . . . well, let's just say I would consider it with the advantage of experience."

"Most of England believes I am just like you. Pardon me for not cooperating in every way with the misconception." Alex caught the reins of his horse and swung back into the saddle.

John's grin was as impious as his reputation. "I opt to not take offense to that remark. Besides, if you end up half as happy in your marriage as I am in mine, count yourself a very lucky man for following in my rakish footsteps."

"I think," Amelia said with what she hoped was perfect poise, "we should consider returning to London. Maybe tomorrow."

Aunt Sophie poured more tea into her cup, added two lumps of sugar, and stirred the steaming liquid. "My darling child, you really are not at all good at subterfuge. You do realize that?"

It was difficult to conceal her guilty start, so maybe her aunt was right. Not that guilt was precisely what she felt about the events of the previous evening. Elation, wonder, a secret sense of empowerment as a woman, a rare and special joy . . .

Alex wished to marry her. No, it wasn't an undying admission of love, but he *had* asked and she had accepted, and the world held a special, rosy glow. "I am not sure what you mean."

"Don't you?" Sophie serenely sipped her tea.

They were in the yellow sitting room, with its chintz

curtains and comfortable sofas, all in bright floral patterns. The day was pleasant and the sun brilliant in a halcyon sky, which emphasized the cheery atmosphere. Amelia had always loved the informality of the country estate. In contrast, the stiff formality of the London town house was stifling. But if Alex had returned there, the city held a new appeal. "What are we discussing?" she asked cautiously.

"A very imprudent but attractive young man, I believe."

Imprudent? She had been the imprudent one, but if she recalled her own bold behavior she would blush, and that would never do. With great care she made quite a business of setting aside her cup on the tea cart. "I assume you mean Alex."

"He was here last night."

That calm declaration sounded a great deal more like knowledge than assumption. Amelia had awakened in bed naked, and though the scent of lovemaking lingered on her skin, Alex was not there. Not that she had expected him to stay, of course, and be discovered in her bed, but a certain sense of loss lingered through her current joyous state. Was he on his way to London to approach her father? She had agreed to marry him, but she didn't know his plans. Had she not been so languorous and pleasantly tired, she would have asked more questions about what came next before drifting to sleep in his arms. "What makes you think so?"

It was Sophie's turn to look a little uncomfortable. "We might have run into each other."

"Oh." *That would have had to be afterward. . . .*

"I understand you are engaged."

They had apparently more than just run into each other. Amelia abandoned all pretext. "I already told you I'd say yes."

"It seems you did, and I am not talking about his marriage proposal."

Now it was impossible not to blush. Amelia took a

moment, tried to ignore her burning cheeks, and then asked tartly, "Was my mother as forthright as you?"

"Worse." Aunt Sophie, pretty in a surprisingly normal deep blue day gown, her striking dark hair dressed in a braided coil, set aside her cup, a nostalgic smile on her face. "Always to the point, sometimes painfully so. Sarah didn't tolerate secrets easily. When I met my William, she knew at once I was infatuated, even though I pretended indifference at first. He was, after all, not the catch of the season. It didn't matter; she saw right through me. In some ways, she was a very irritating older sister."

"And in other ways?"

"I adored her."

"I've always wished I'd known her."

The sunlight in blocks on the floor suddenly seemed very interesting. As close as Amelia was with Sophie, they rarely spoke of her mother. Looking back, Amelia wondered if the reason she didn't ask questions was because her father so deplored discussing her mother, she'd learned a long time ago to not be overinquisitive on what was obviously, even to a child, a subject too painful to discuss. "You look remarkably like her," her aunt said softly, still staring downward as if absorbed in the pattern on the rug. "More beautiful, maybe, but almost a mirror image. She had your sense of self also, without any conceit. She approached life in a straightforward way. When she met your father, that was that."

"Truly?"

"You sound dubious."

It *was* a little hard to imagine. Her father tended to be so distant and autocratic. But then again, Anna's letters gave her a new conception of the mystery of love. "*Others may not, but I know you.*"

Aunt Sophie looked up and raised her brows in inquiry.

"A quote from one of Anna St. James's letters," she supplied, suddenly too restless to sit. She got up and paced over to the window. "Obviously she loved my grandfather."

"Obviously. She spurned the censure of her powerful family and society for nothing more than the questionable position as his lover."

"And my mother loved my father?" It wasn't an unreasonable question to ask, because society marriages were often based on different principles, like money and stature.

"Sarah never did anything she didn't wish to do, just like you."

The indulgent chuckle was reassuring. Amelia said with dry humor, "I take it that is a criticism of my behavior, but quite frankly, I am—"

She broke off as a carriage rolled up the drive, the crest quite prominent from her vantage point by the window. A little prayer of thanks went heavenward over the timing. A day earlier, and her life might be quite different. "It seems we have company."

"St. James?" Aunt Sophie asked with complacency. "I wondered how long it would take him to consider my advice."

The new arrival was not Alex, but Amelia turned in surprise. "What advice would that be?"

"A swift elopement. Keep it simple, I always say."

"You suggested we run away together?"

"I might have hinted at it."

"Aunt Sophie!"

"Don't look so outraged, darling; it is hardly an original idea. Come to think of it, your lovely young man had the same reaction as you did just now. Really, for two people who have behaved very unconventionally, you are both quite respectable when it comes down to it."

It was impossible not to laugh. "I keep accusing Alex of the very same attribute. Rather amusing, isn't it, since he is generally viewed in such a disreputable light?"

"Yes, well, after the events of last evening I won't

comment on whether or not his reputation is deserved. The question is how you both will handle your father."

"I don't know, but did you have any idea he planned on coming here?"

"Your father?" Sophia looked properly startled.

Amelia nodded. "He is the one who just arrived."

Chapter Eighteen

Though Sophia normally thought her brother-in-law was a decent, if somewhat emotionally distant man, he really was making a mistake. Yet no one could explain to him just how awkward of one.

Across the table, Amelia, fetching in a rose colored gown, her dark gold hair gathered up off her slender neck, pushed her roast beef around her plate while stealing the occasional glance at the ormolu clock on the mantel at the end of the dining room. The tension in the room was palpable.

Stephen really could be the most misguided father on English soil.

"Both Lord Howard," he said between bites of food and sips of wine, "and Sir Neville Norton meet with my approval. They have each presented themselves to me in the past few days. Naturally, Lord Howard, being a marquess, is very appealing, but Norton is in line for his father's title, and he has the advantage of being both younger and—"

"Is this why you came here?" Amelia was a touch defiant as she interrupted and set aside her fork. "Why

the haste? Aunt Sophie and I were planning on traveling back to London tomorrow. If you wished to shove
prospective bridegrooms at me, you could have saved
yourself the trip."

At the word *shove*, he looked up, his expression going cold. "I am planning your future. I thought two very
promising offers for your hand merited the journey."

"You are *deciding* my future, which is not the same."

Hathaway had never known his own daughter, and
in her newly emancipated state as an engaged woman—
even if he didn't know about the betrothal—Amelia
looked dangerously rebellious.

"Pick whichever man you wish."

"That is simple enough. Neither one."

"Sophia said she didn't think you wished for Westhope, and I took that into consideration."

"How very generous." Amelia's tone was acid and
clipped.

"My lord," Sophia interjected in the interest of keeping the conversation under control, "did you really come
all this way to just tell Amelia that Lord Howard and Sir
Neville had offered for her? As she said, we planned on
returning to London tomorrow."

"How was I supposed to know that?" Stephen said
defensively, stabbing a piece of beef and waving it in the
air. "You left with very little explanation."

"You didn't ask." Amelia gave up all pretense of eating and pushed her plate a little to the side. "When I said
we were leaving, you simply shrugged."

"I thought your breathing"—his voice lowered as
he looked at the stolid footmen in the dining room—
"might have been bothering you."

As if every servant in the house didn't know of her
problem already. The staff clearly adored Amelia and
were touchingly protective. To herself, Sophia gave a
shake of her head.

"Asking me if that was the problem is a logical alternative," Amelia murmured.

Apparently there was nothing so militant as a newly ruined young woman. This was not going in a wonderful direction. Sophia said quickly, "We all know you are busy, Stephen. But quite frankly, as we have discussed, there is no rush on this. Upon our return to London, we can surely look at this issue."

"Why not look at it now? I came all this way. Tell me, what is the point of putting off an engagement?" He imperiously motioned for more potatoes, though there were still some on his plate.

In her opinion, Sophia thought it would be a disastrous mistake under the circumstances for Amelia to blurt out anything to her father about her secret betrothal. Just how to approach this situation was a problem that required some thought and planning. Hastily, she jumped in again before Amelia could speak. "Three of the most eligible bachelors in England have already shown sincere interest. Surely there will be more offers. Lord Bellingham always requests a dance. I am surprised he hasn't come forward yet."

"He *has* sent a conservatory full of flowers," Stephen muttered, but looked thoughtful as he dabbed his napkin at his mouth. Bellingham was rumored to be one of the wealthiest men not just in Britain, but on the continent.

"He has to be at least two decades my senior." Amelia shot Sophia an accusing glance that spoke clearly of her feelings on Lord Bellingham as a possible husband.

Sorry, darling. Simply trying to distract him.

"So?" Her father was unmoved. "Older men often marry younger women, and I happen to like Bellingham. He's a good sort."

"Oh, well, if *you* like him," Amelia murmured, "that's sufficient, I suppose."

"Your sarcastic tone is unappreciated, young lady."

"I didn't mean any disrespect. I was simply pointing out the flaw in that statement. And while I think Lord Bellingham is a pleasant man, I am not going to marry him because he has an affable smile, and certainly not because he has a sizable fortune. Nor should he want me to. Since he is quite likable, I wish for him a woman who marries him for love."

Stephen leaned back as the footman, no doubt listening avidly to every word, refilled his wineglass. He said shortly, "It sounds to me like you've been reading too much romantic drivel, my dear. It is all well and good if one is fond of the person she marries, but it is hardly necessary."

"You were in love with my mother, were you not?"

"We had an affection for each other, yes." His voice took on an arctic chill. "My very point."

What a lie. Sophia was five years younger than her sister, but she clearly recalled the whispers at the time over their tempestuous romance, which reminded her more than a little of the one happening right under Stephen's nose between his beautiful daughter and St. James. He'd changed dramatically after Sarah's death.

She said in her calmest tone, "I am sure your father will never force you into a match you don't desire, Amelia."

"Not if she desires one soon." His smile was tight, the words said with implacable authority. "I am her father. I can arrange a marriage for her at my discretion, and she shouldn't forget it. Now, then, we shall consider this subject closed for the duration of our meal so we can all enjoy our food."

He did lord of the manor very well, but it was hardly the way to handle his intelligent, independent daughter, who because of his distance had learned to make her own decisions without him. Coming in with an autocratic approach now was a mistake, and Sophia knew it would break Sarah's heart if she were there to see them at odds.

It was her fervent hope St. James had *some* sort of plan.

He had no idea how to approach this quandary.

Damnation.

No, two quandaries. Both important to women Alex loved, even if he loved them in entirely different ways.

Yes, he was in love. Blast it. It was the only explanation for his recent behavior. No, recent *mis*behavior.

"You look like the very devil, you know." Michael hunched over his cup of ale, the stale, unappealing odor of the squalid taproom like a pall in the air. The floor was sticky, and the neighborhood, frankly, deplorable. "Have you slept at all lately?"

As a matter of fact, he hadn't. He'd spent his time haring back and forth between London and Cambridgeshire, interspersed with bouts of ineffectual burglary and seducing the alluring daughters of prominent earls.

"Are you my friend or my mother?" Alex asked sourly. "It doesn't take much in deductive powers to tell I'm on the tired side, which makes me wonder what the hell we are doing here anyway."

When Alex had stopped by his club for a hot meal and a drink, Michael had been just coming out and suggested they stop instead at a little tavern he knew. Since his friend was ever unpredictable, this disreputable place wasn't exactly a surprise. When Michael changed into a somewhat shabby coat in the carriage and suggested Alex remove his cravat, he'd resigned himself to an interesting evening.

Michael made a dismissive gesture with his hand. "As I told you, I'm just waiting for a small communication. It shouldn't take long."

"What kind of communication?"

His only answer was a faint smile. Michael murmured, "May I suggest a bed might do you some good?"

"A bed is part of the problem," Alex muttered.

Two burly ruffians in the corner burst into a volatile argument over a game of dice, but all Michael did was chuckle, even when one of them whipped out a wicked-looking knife and snarled obscenities at his fellow player. "I take it," the usually impeccably well-dressed

Marquess of Longhaven drawled, "the offending piece
of furniture had a young lady in it. I believe I can come
to an accurate conclusion as to her identity also. Tell me,
when is the wedding?"

"Your easy assumption that there has to be a wedding isn't exactly flattering." If the ale hadn't been so
tepid, Alex might have drunk some, but then again he
was probably a little too fatigued for it to be wise to
indulge in any kind of spirits.

"You were the one who brought up the topic of love
recently. After the kiss I witnessed and the recent mur-
murs over a somewhat memorable waltz that had the
ton agog, I don't need superior intellect to draw some
obvious conclusions. She left town, and then so did you."
Michael sprawled back in his chair, seemingly oblivious
to the murderous fight starting over the dice game. He
simply raised his voice over the din. "I know you. That
ingrained sense of honor has always been one of your
handicaps, Alex."

Trust Michael to speak so casually of honor as if it
were a flaw, when truthfully he was one of the most
honorable men Alex knew. A slightly different code of
it, perhaps, but in his line of work, the ethics were as
changeable as shifting sands. Alex blew out a breath. "I
want to marry Amelia, so the problem does not lie there.
I fear her father will refuse."

"He has to agree, as far as I can tell."

"Explain to me how to delicately impart that information in a manner that does not involve resulting
violence. Besides, I don't want to put her through that
particular confrontation. It will hardly endear me to
him, and embarrass her."

"I can see the problem," Michael admitted.

"Because of the enmity between him and my father,
I really don't know the man. From what Amelia has told
me, he isn't approachable even in her estimation. I admit I am torn between just carrying her off to Scotland
like my brother and her aunt both suggested, and the

notion that I should, in all decency, go to Lord Hathaway, hat in hand in the appropriate manner. It's a devil's own dilemma."

"What does she say?"

"When I last saw her, she was sleeping."

Michael grinned and actually drank some of the awful beverage in his glass. "Well done."

It had been all Alex could do to slip out of that bed and leave her there. "I doubt her father would agree."

"An excellent point. I do know Hathaway. Well, to the extent that he serves on a committee with several associates of mine. We've attended the same private dinners on occasion."

Michael's friends ranged anywhere from the highest officials in England to the most dubious sorts of characters. Alex merely said, "And?"

The fight that had escalated into a brawl, with several of the other patrons joining in, ended abruptly when the proprietor of the establishment roared a warning across the room, brandishing what appeared to be a well-used musket. Grumbling—and some bleeding—the combatants subsided back into their chairs.

Not exactly roast beef and an excellent glass of whiskey at my club, but more interesting on the whole, Alex thought in cynical amusement. In his salad days he'd certainly swilled blue ruin in places as seedy as this one, but it had been a while.

"As for Hathaway's character, I'd say he is, in essence, a fair man." Michael frowned. "Self-contained, maybe a little rigid, but not an opinionated ass on a usual basis. I would trust his integrity but not his open-mindedness. Would I want him for a father-in-law? I am not sure."

"I'm not sure either, but Amelia is his daughter."

"Enough said, then." Michael calmly glanced at the doorway. A new arrival had entered the taproom; a rough-looking younger man with pockmarked skin and a low hat that shaded his eyes. He lurched toward them in a drunken reel, actually bumped their table, and mumbled, "Excuse me, guv."

Even on the alert for it, the exchange was so skillfully done Alex didn't catch it, but he knew it had happened as the man stumbled away. "Former pickpocket?" he asked in amusement, his voice low.

Michael didn't dissemble. "I never inquire where certain skills come from, as long as they are useful. For that matter, you have never told me how you so adroitly can pick a lock. My service to Wellington was much different than yours. Upstanding colonels don't have the same training as spies."

"One of my men," Alex explained, remembering some of those long, hellish Spanish nights. "Before battle you do anything to distract yourself. Thinking about it too much is never a good idea. We told stories, sang songs, even, to fill the time until sunrise and the inevitable conflict. I had the usual rabble under my command, some of them questionable, some of them friends I will never forget. One of them taught me how to pick a lock during one such cold, miserable night. It passed the time."

"But still no key?"

Alex shook his head. "It is my concerted opinion that if Lord Hathaway ever had it, he might have just gotten rid of it as a bit of rubbish. I've said as much to my grandmother."

"But she hasn't absolved you from the task."

"No." Alex stared moodily at the amber liquid in his glass. "I am constrained by her remarkable stubbornness. The mystery over why she now finds this so important, after all the time passed, remains exactly that."

"I happen to love mysteries, which is a good thing, since I am often enough charged with small puzzles to decipher." Michael slipped his hand from his pocket, his face neutral.

"*This* one feels nigh onto impossible," Alex said with feeling.

His companion shook his head, his eyes gleaming.

"None of them are impossible. You just need to ask yourself one important question."

"And what is that?" Alex asked dryly, the rickety chair he sat in creaking ominously as he shifted his weight.

"What is the missing piece?"

"I just said—"

"She won't tell you. That I understand. But usually, the seemingly impossible is more obvious than you think. If something triggered her sudden need for you to retrieve this nefarious key, you have to ask yourself what it is your grandmother doesn't want Lord Hathaway to have. That's the only logical conclusion. If he's had the key all along and doesn't know what it is for, I'm going to assume something is about to happen to enlighten him."

It made sense, but only from the aspect that none of the rest of it really made sense at all. "Both Amelia and I are getting letters. Old love letters. The sender has done an admirable job of staying anonymous. I don't understand the purpose, but it connects my family with hers. It obviously has something to do with Anna's death and the resulting duel."

Michael smiled in his negligible way. "Then that is where I would start."

Chapter Nineteen

A return to London was rife with mixed emotions, quite like her initial arrival. *Different* emotions, though, Amelia philosophized as she stared out the carriage window. As a young woman about to encounter society for the first time, she'd been apprehensive, but also curious as to what her bow would bring. A husband? That was, of course, the purpose of it all; the new gowns, the glittering parties, the melee of crowds, the endless glasses of tepid champagne.

The concept of a husband had been abstract, a shadowy figure.

Now she knew. Alex with his irresistible, dark good looks and flashing, perfect smile. More than that, his sense of humor and intelligence and the delicacy of his touch were branded forever into her senses, like an addictive drug. . . . Where was he now?

"You'll enjoy the exhibition, I'm sure." Lord Westhope beamed at her. He was, as usual, just on the edge of foppish, with a light blue coat, frothy neckcloth, and diamond shoe buckles. But even though she had forgotten she'd promised—no, her *father* had promised—she'd

•

attend the art showing with him, she had, luckily, been dressed to go out when he arrived to escort her to the event.

Aunt Sophie had taken the sudden change in plans with her usual aplomb. "To be able to see Simeon's last collection is a rare treat, my lord."

"I understand his grandson is quite an eccentric character," Westhope informed them. "All artists are, as far as I can tell. Writers also, and actors. Too much imagination is never a promising characteristic."

"You don't suffer that affliction, my lord," Amelia observed innocently, sitting with her hands folded demurely in her lap.

Aunt Sophie shot her a quelling look. No, she probably shouldn't have said it, but the comment sailed right over his head. "True. I am much more inclined to practical pursuits," he said with enthusiasm. "Hunting being my favorite. Do you ride to the hounds, Lady Amelia?"

Since she could think of nothing more reprehensible than pursuing an innocent animal for the sole purpose of killing it and calling it a sport, much less thinking it was practical, she had to bite back a sharp retort. Instead she answered, "I'm afraid not, my lord."

"Oh." He looked disappointed, but only vaguely.

He was vague all too often, and Amelia wondered once again how her father could ever have imagined her in a marriage with such a vapid man.

Fortunately, at that moment the equipage began to slow. It stopped in front of a brilliantly lit mansion that she had never visited before but recognized as the home of one of society's most reclusive women, a dowager countess who had, it was rumored, retired from all social contact upon the death of her husband.

"I don't believe I knew Lady Bosworth was the benefactress of this showing," Aunt Sophie murmured as a liveried footman opened the door of the carriage with a flourish. "That makes it all the more fascinating. We are friends, but I haven't seen her in some time. I was sorry when she went into mourning and then declined to re-enter the *ton*. She's been on the continent. I thought she was still in Italy. The last letter I had from her was over a year ago."

Although there was no saffron-colored turban in sight, her aunt did look more than a little unconventional in a daring orange gown that wrapped around her remarkable figure like an Indian sari, her dark hair in a long braid, her eyes tinged with just a bit of kohl. A brilliant scarf rounded out the ensemble, draped over her shoulder in a graceful fall. The exotic attire suited her, but Amelia did wonder how it was that Sophie insisted her gowns be conservative and decorous and then managed to come up with such interesting attire for herself.

The foyer was crowned with a magnificent, shimmering chandelier, the floor gleaming marble, the black-and-white theme offset by vases of brilliant crimson roses. An impeccably dressed manservant directed them to the hallway on their left and the formal drawing room, the hum of voices low and restrained as they paused in the doorway.

"I say"—Lord Westhope sounded miffed—"there are more people here than I anticipated."

Perhaps the gathering wasn't as small and exclusive as his lordship had anticipated, but it was certainly at least in part made up of the cream of society. Even as new as she was to the *haut ton*, Amelia recognized some of the more elite. Almost more telling, there were some, plainly dressed, that she didn't recognize at all, mingling with the nobility.

On the spot she decided she liked Lady Bosworth. After all, she'd been raised with the familiarity of servants like family around her. Some of the mingling guests were not wealthy or highborn, at least from their appearance.

The paintings themselves were strategically placed about the room, but it was impossible to even get close to one, as small crowds milled around the canvases. Lord

Westhope muttered, "I will get us some refreshment. Please excuse me."

Aunt Sophie watched him start to edge his way through the throng and failed to conceal her amusement. "The poor earl. He thought to appear with you on his arm in exclusive company, with only a select few of our acquaintances admiring his good taste and even better fortune. He looks quite crestfallen."

"I never promised to even come here." Amelia looked around at the eclectic furnishings, including, incredibly, what seemed to be a full-sized statue of Neptune in the middle of the room, trident and all, sans any scrap of clothing, rising from the sea, realistic droplets of water on his marble skin. "If you remember, my father agreed to this for me."

"I remember." One brow lifted. "I realize we've only just returned, but I rather thought a message from St. James might be waiting for you."

"I thought so myself," Amelia admitted.

"He's intelligent enough to know your father will be opposed."

"Yes."

"But you don't necessarily have all the time in the world to settle this."

"I suppose not with Father wanting a swift betrothal." It was impossible to not sound at least a little bitter. Amelia kept her gaze fastened on where Lord Westhope stood at the drinks table.

"Your father is hardly perfect, but I do believe he thinks he is doing what is best for you by trying to arrange an advantageous match as quickly as possible. And," Sophie said with an odd inflection, "that isn't what I meant by saying time may or may not be an issue."

Amelia turned with an inquiring look.

"Darling, what if you are even now with child?"

The question was gently said, but it had the impact of a blow. Amelia opened her mouth to argue, but then closed it. It wasn't that she was so sheltered she didn't connect what had happened between her and Alex with how children were conceived; it just hadn't occurred to her that it might have happened already. "After one time?" she asked, her tone quite faint. "Well, I suppose it was two . . . oh . . ."

That was certainly more than she meant to say. From the feel of it, her cheeks were undoubtedly now a deep crimson.

Her aunt chuckled. "Good for him. But yes, darling, one could be quite enough."

The arrival of the earl with their drinks put an end to the disconcerting discussion, but as Amelia sipped her cool, sweet wine, she frantically tried to maintain a facade of calm interest in the first painting in the queue as they drifted toward it with the crowd.

Alex's child.

What a lovely, lovely thought. Shocking, yes, as she was still an unmarried woman, but as scandalous as it was to imagine, she might be already pregnant?

Surely, being older and a great deal more worldly, this had also occurred to him?

"Intriguing." Lord Westhope's voice seemed skeptical for such a self-proclaimed aficionado of the arts.

Brought back into the moment, Amelia blinked and looked at the picture. It actually was exquisitely well-done, if the subject matter unusual. Instead of the usual landscape or stiff portrait, it depicted an ethereal garden with flowers of a variety she'd never seen before in her life. Huge scarlet blooms with lush leaves, startling sapphire trees, and in their midst, tiny figures, so delicate with their brilliant wings . . .

"It's Mab's court. She was the queen of the fairies," Amelia said automatically. Fables were some of her favorite stories as a child. "Most unusually done, but that would be my guess."

"And it is a fine one." A young man standing next to her turned, and though he didn't smile, there was approval in his eyes. He was one of the throng dressed very plainly in a dark, somewhat threadbare coat and plain breeches and boots. His dark hair curled in wild ringlets and his brows were untidy, but yet he was attractive in an unusual fashion. "My grandfather thought the scale the best part of the work. The flowers are not actually tall; the figures are allegorical to how our perceptions are skewed to our own limitations. Because the fairies are so small, an ordinary garden is like an entire world."

Lord Westhope looked baffled. Aunt Sophie looked amused. The young man reached out, took Amelia's unoffered gloved hand, bent over it in a perfunctory manner, and announced, "I am Frederick Simeon. Can I paint you?"

"Your niece's expression was beyond price. Then again, Freddie does have that effect on women." A genteel chuckle accompanied the words. "Have I mentioned it is delightful to see you?"

"I feel the same." Sophia eyed her hostess, a small smile twitching her lips. "As for Simeon . . . yes, I noticed Amelia was rendered quite speechless by his request to have her sit for a portrait. Is he as good as his grandfather?"

"Maybe even more brilliant, actually." Della Bosworth, tall, buxom, her dark hair just threaded with a little gray, laughed. "Lady Amelia is very beautiful in a youthful, fresh manner. He admires works of art, whether in the flesh or other sorts of representations, like mist-enshrouded mountains or pictorial sunsets over ancient ruins. Though I admit, he is more prone to nudes and figurative images."

"Figurative?"

"Goddesses and mythical creatures. His grandfather did some of those also. The neoclassical depictions were bread and butter, the portraits his true love, but his artistry is more adaptive to flights of imagination. In every picture he painted he included some fantastical element."

"It sounds like you knew him well." Sophia made the observation in a neutral voice while she slanted a glance around the crowded room.

"I knew Simeon."

"Della," Sophia said reproachfully.

"Depending on the definition of *knew*." Lady Bosworth adjusted the lace at her décolletage with a leisurely hand. "I refuse to say more about our relationship. It was all before I married Gordon."

In short, they had been lovers. Sophia wasn't surprised. Bella had always been a little unconventional, and a flamboyant artist would be just the kind of man she might pick for a dalliance.

"Doesn't it always depend on the definition?" Sophia asked delicately.

"Yes, darling, it does. So, your pretty niece? Definitely have her accept the offer of a sitting with Freddie. She'll be ravishing as Athena or one of the muses, or even an elusive Venus."

"I see you are caught up on the latest gossip."

"Indeed. Tell me she isn't in favor of Westhope. Nice enough, but too boring by half. Not a glimmer of intellect."

"No," Sophia admitted, watching the earl hover over Amelia. They looked attractive together, both of them with such fair coloring, his good looks setting off her beauty, but not—she had to admit—nearly as striking as her niece had looked in the arms of the devilishly dark Alexander St. James. "She's quite in love with someone else."

"Love? Excellent." Della didn't even inquire as to whom, but just surveyed the room. "Nice turnout, this. I hesitated to do it, you know. I've kept to myself these past years and solitude has grown to be my friend. But quite frankly, when I heard Freddie was going to show Simeon's work, I thought it was perhaps time to open the house again. This needed to be done right. Later the pieces will be displayed in a series of museums in various places from York to Bath, but this is the first venue. A nice splash, isn't it?"

"Very. You have everyone of consequence here . . . and a few not so consequential." The wine was excellent, not overly cloying and quite palatable. From the advantage of having the hostess in a corner all to herself, Sophia said, "You always did favor the bourgeois."

"I don't choose my friends for their stature, Sophia— you know that. In Italy I met the most delicious young gondolier." Her smile was mischievous. "You may have noticed I lingered there for a while."

"That sounds like a lovely reason." Sophia couldn't help the wistful inflection. Passion was not just for the young. She'd been thinking about Richard quite a lot lately, but what she felt for him was certainly nothing like the stormy desire she'd once shared with her William. Friendship was nice too, of course. He would make a delightful, thoughtful companion and a considerate lover, no doubt.

"It *was* lovely, but not in a lasting way." Della shrugged and made a languid gesture toward the room at large. "I belong here. Running away was nice for a while, I admit, but I wasn't going to find what I needed in Venice." A dimple appeared in one cheek. "Well, maybe what I needed for a short interim. How about you? Is there someone?"

"There might be," she admitted evasively. Until she was ready to acknowledge her interest in maybe deepening the relationship with Richard, it didn't seem fair to tell someone else first. "Amelia looks in need of some rescue. Shall we?"

Della wasn't fooled, but she did incline her head in good-natured agreement. "She and the earl are looking at one of my favorite paintings. It is called *The Seductress*. I think you'll find it interesting."

A few moments later, after politely making their way through the guests, Sophia found herself in front of a large canvas displayed on an easel to match the size of the work. The frame was rather plain, but the work of art itself, anything but ordinary.

"I think her sense of femininity is both subtle yet somehow overwhelming," Della observed, linking her arm through Sophia's as they joined Amelia and Lord Westhope. "It reminds me of Grecian statues, with the delicate drapery and emphasis on the female form."

His lordship's expression took on a peculiar look of embarrassment, as if the phrase female form was akin to uttering profanity out loud. Sophia studied the canvas to hide her amusement, because Amelia hardly seemed to notice the speech, her expression abstracted.

It was true: the central figure, a woman with long, sleek, dark hair, was in profile. Her body, illuminated by a distant light source not visible in the work, was reclining on a rock near the sea. She wore a filmy gown of some light material, the mermaid effect emphasized by a beautiful necklace of exquisite deep blue stones, a large diamond pendant nestled between her full breasts. Her graceful, slender form ended in the mythical fin peeking from the fabric of her gown, her arm resting across her stomach as if she were in a pose of deep thought.

It was, Sophia decided, a very moving painting. If Simeon's grandson was half as talented, she would like to see what he could do with Amelia as a subject.

"This has never been shown?" Her niece asked the question tentatively, half turning toward their hostess but not looking away from the painting.

"Never," Della confirmed with a nod.

"Then," Amelia murmured, "why do I feel like I've seen it before?"

Lord Westhope offered his arm, obviously anxious to move away and have her relatively alone—if one could feel so in such a crowded room—again. "Our minds do play tricks on us frequently, my dear."

Not his, at a guess, Amelia's expression said clearly, for such gymnastics of the brain were beyond Westhope.

"Just a moment," she insisted, ignoring his gesture to indicate they should move away. "This is familiar."

Della murmured, "As I said, I was told these works had never been displayed. His style is distinctive, though, so maybe you've seen another of his works."

Amelia stared up at the draped figure on rock, and her eyes narrowed. "The necklace."

Sophia peered up at the painting. It was a magnificent piece of jewelry, to be sure, but her niece's reaction seemed dramatic. "What about the necklace?"

Faintly, Amelia said, "I have seen it before. In a portrait in the gallery at Brookhaven. The subject is different, of course, but I could swear it is exactly the same diamond pendant with the gold filigree around it . . . and those blue stones . . . I am almost certain I am right."

"It is unique and striking. Perhaps Simeon had one of your family pose for him." Della looked intrigued. "I'll ask Freddie if his grandfather kept records on his models. I would assume he did, but he was a rather eccentric man, so one can never be sure."

The woman's glorious dark coloring didn't look like any Patton Sophia had ever met, but there was something about her . . .

"Oh, dear," she murmured, taking in the height of the cheekbones and lush fall of ebony hair. The necklace might be familiar to Amelia, but maybe something else also struck a chord. Earlier she'd seen Richard arrive, and now Sophia cast about the room, trying to locate him in the crowd. With as much calm as possible, she excused herself to Della just as Westhope insistently dragged Amelia off to the next painting.

It took some doing, but she finally found him, looking suave and polished in dark evening wear, his low laugh like a warm touch as he conversed with a small group of gentlemen, most of them his age, all of whom gave him a knowing smile as she edged through the crowd and unceremoniously grabbed his arm. "Good evening," she managed to say with what she hoped was reason-able aplomb. "Could I borrow Sir Richard for a few moments, please?"

Their expressions told her Richard's interest in her was not unnoticed by society, but it was the least of her worries at the moment. He followed willingly, but looked puzzled. "Is something wrong, my dear?"

She towed him toward the painting, doing her best to look bland. "I am not sure, but perhaps you can help. Have you looked at the entire exhibition yet?"

"I haven't looked at any of it, actually." He sounded perplexed. "It is terribly crowded and I just arrived. Why?"

"There's one you must see," she stated firmly, wondering if, while all the pieces weren't coming completely together, she was starting to gain a bit of understanding of the puzzle. Unless, of course, she was completely wrong . . .

It took some maneuvering, but she was able to edge her way back to *The Seductress* with a few apologetic smiles. She truly jostled only one irate woman in a hideous purple gown, who sent her a decidedly venomous look. By the time they had a clear view, Richard was chuckling audibly. "Not that I mind being abducted in front of witnesses by a beautiful lady, but whatever is so important?"

"That." She pointed with her fan at the painting. "Or more importantly, her."

He tensed. She could feel it in the stiffening of his muscles under her fingers, in the sudden fading of his affable smile. After a moment his head dipped just a fraction in acknowledgment. "That's Anna St. James."

Chapter Twenty

Lord Hathaway was in, Alex had been informed by the staid butler. But within moments the man returned to the elegant foyer, looking a little flustered, and handed him back his card. "I'm sorry, my lord. His lordship isn't receiving."

He'd known, of course, there was every chance the earl would decline to see him, but he'd hoped that either some modicum of courtesy or at least curiosity over the purpose of his visit might move in his favor. "Isn't receiving anyone," he asked wryly, "or just myself?"

"I couldn't say, sir." The elderly man seemed distinctly uncomfortable, so Alex guessed it was the latter and couched in very unflattering terms.

He presented the card again between two fingers. "Tell him I am my father's son, but I am not my father. He and I have no differences between us. To the contrary, we have one very important similarity. I merely wish to speak with him about Lady Amelia. Is she, by any chance, at home?"

"No, my lord. She is at the dressmaker's."

Just as well. If her father tossed him out on his ear, she would not be around to hear the shouting.

Reluctantly, the butler took the card and disappeared again down the polished hallway. Alex examined a fine marquetry table while he waited, not precisely nervous over the outcome of his visit, but cautious. He needed to play his hand close, for he didn't want to cause Amelia distress.

If he could give her a legitimate engagement, a formal wedding, and all of it with her father's approval, he would. The very least he could do was try. Her happiness was paramount, and the significance of how important it fell in his estimation was telling. He wanted her at all costs, but not on terms that caused echoes of friction in their future, if possible. There very well could be children—for all he knew there was one already to consider—and he tried to picture them being raised under the warring factions of the Patton and St. James families.

This needed to be resolved.

"I'm sorry, sir, but his lordship—"

Alex turned, his face settling into an emotionless mask. After all, he was the son of the Duke of Berkeley and he had seen icy hauteur since birth. No one could do the imperious lord like his father.

The servant correctly interpreted the look on his face and stepped aside. "I'm not sure—"

"I am." Alex knew perfectly well where his lordship's study was from his trip the night he'd first seen Amelia on her balcony. He walked past the butler, whose protestations died away, and counted the doors, arriving at the correct one when he saw Hathaway at his desk, his gaze focused on a piece of correspondence. Without looking up, Amelia's father said curtly, "I hope you are not here to present St. James's card again, Perkins."

"No."

At the sound of his voice, Hathaway glanced up, a scowl marring his features. "Get out."

Not an auspicious start, but Alex was still convinced this conversation at least needed to be attempted. "I need a few minutes of your time, my lord. For your daughter's sake, surely you can grant me that."

"For my daughter's sake?" His lordship stood, outrage in his reply, slamming his hand on the letter on his desk. "I expect an explanation for that assumption and this intrusion. And bloody close the damn door before you give it."

Being ordered about so summarily rankled, but Alex didn't want their discussion all over the servant's quarters either, so he turned and closed the door. "I didn't want to intrude. I called out of a sense of honor, because Amelia deserves this, and you, as her father deserve it also."

Surely that was fairly said.

Holding himself stiffly, his face rigid, the Earl of Hathaway did not look moved. "I am not even aware of how you might know Amelia."

"We move in the same circles." Alex was not about to go into his quest for the key. It was interwoven with their relationship, but hardly the issue at hand. "Of course I noticed her. She is the loveliest woman in England."

"It doesn't matter what you think of her looks. What matters is that—"

"*You* hate my father," Alex supplied, still standing because he hadn't been invited to sit. He hadn't been invited at all, and the hostile reception wasn't a surprise, but it was worse than he'd anticipated and not about to get better, from the man's baleful expression. "Do her feelings matter at all to you? It's an intellectual question from someone with a vested interest in the answer. I suppose, in essence, it is why I am here."

"Of course." The two words were said in a snarl. "But her well-being matters more. She's female and she's young. She's my child and my responsibility."

No expression of a genuine desire for her happiness, just dutiful parental obligation, Alex duly noted. It was rather like Amelia had intimated.

"Or mine. If you will just agree, sir."

The resulting silence was stone-cold. "You cannot be serious," Hathaway finally said, so emphatically Alex flinched. "Are you truly asking for my daughter's hand in marriage? Were I not so outraged, I would laugh myself into an apoplexy."

Now, there was an interesting solution to the dilemma. *This is going well.*

In the daylight, the earl's study was familiar and yet foreign, the desk Alex had searched spread with papers, an interesting painting of a sunlit seaside cove in a corner by one of the windows, the bookcases cluttered. The man standing behind the desk showed no such character, his face implacable and remote.

"Why?" Alex asked simply, his hands at his sides, resisting the urge to curl them into fists of frustration. "I am well aware you dislike my father and he dislikes you in measure. Explain to me why that animosity has anything to do with Amelia and me."

"I have no obligation to explain anything to you, St. James."

How much do I have to subjugate myself?

"I love your daughter."

Alex hadn't meant to be so forthcoming, especially since he hadn't even said it yet to Amelia, but it was the explanation for all this, simple as it was, and it was honest.

Hathaway bit out, "Once again, how the hell do you even *know* my daughter?"

Biblically.

At least he hadn't said it out loud. The man's antagonism was enough to test a saint. If he deserved it, that would be different. With studied self-control, Alex explained in staccato tones, "Lord Hathaway, I came here in all goodwill. I understand you have a past quarrel with my father. I'm guessing it results from what happened between your father and my grandfather's sister, but what I don't understand is why you measure me by something I was never involved in."

"Measuring you by what I've heard is enough." Hathaway's voice was like granite. "You are the heir apparent to the St. James legacy of vice and immorality. Do you imagine that is what I wish for my daughter? If so, think again."

Now was definitely not the time to tell the man he'd already seduced Amelia. The misty cool of Scotland appealed more than ever, but he'd gone this far. "Rumor is always such a reliable vehicle with which to judge a man's character," he said sardonically, the impudence in the remark brought about by the earl's lashing disdain. "I don't court innocent young ladies as a rule; even your most misinformed gossipmonger has never whispered *that* behind his hand."

"No, you prefer whorish opera singers and others of the same ilk."

He'd been in enough battles that Alex knew when to retreat and reform a battle plan. "My offer is an honorable one, done in good faith. Please keep it in mind. Good day, my lord."

Then he swung on his heel and left the room, simmering with both anger and frustration. A footman scrambled to open the door for him, and he stepped out into the gray afternoon, going down the steps rapidly.

The visit had been an ill-fated attempt at honor.

Amelia was at the dressmaker's. Which one? he wondered with a certain grim resolution. Maybe John was perfectly right. Maybe playing the gallant gentleman really was a waste of time.

"This was delivered for you, my lady."

Taking the missive, Amelia felt her spirits, previously in tune with the dreary day, lift. The dark scrawl on the envelope was her name in bold letters, and she knew instantly who had sent it.

"Thank you," she said demurely, barefoot and clad only her chemise, impatient anyway with the fitting.

The modiste's assistant who had brought the note did her best to not look curious, but didn't quite pull it off. The girl's eyes held a certain bright, inquisitive glimmer.

Alex had that effect on females. Amelia should know. Unable to resist, she tore open the envelope and quickly scanned the contents.

If he had been recognized delivering it, the word would be halfway across London by early afternoon, but she didn't even care.

Aunt Sophie, seated in a chair and perusing fashion plates, correctly gauged Amelia's expression. "I take it this appointment is over," she said dryly. "May I presume that note is from a certain gentleman we've been expecting to contact you?"

"You may. And I wasn't all that enthusiastic about this fitting in the first place," Amelia pointed out, stepping down off the small dais, the note carefully refolded in her hand. "I have enough gowns."

"A woman can never have enough gowns, darling."

"Mine are a bit more dull than yours," she pointed out truthfully. "The lack of variety means other than slight variations in color here and there, they are pretty much all the same."

"When you are married you'll have more latitude."

"In the interest of expediting that process, can we hurry?"

With an exaggerated sigh, Sophie snapped the pattern book shut, but her mouth twitched. "I suppose I shall have to forgo ordering that delicious Lyon fuchsia silk with the green stripes."

"It's just as well," Amelia informed her with a laugh. "I do not think even *you* can pull that one off, Aunt Sophie."

"No?" There was a wistful note in the question.

"No," Amelia said firmly, with a small shudder at the

mental image of her aunt sailing through a crowded room awash in vivid pink and lime green. "Let me change back into my gown and we'll be on our way."

She dressed quickly, slipping back into her pink muslin dress with the aid of one of the shopgirls, adjusting her hair by simply tucking back in a few errant curls. Sophie waited in a small room amid the bolts of fabric, having migrated naturally to some of the more brilliant Turkish brocades.

When they stepped outside, Amelia discovered her aunt wasn't the only one who'd waited for her.

There he is.

Alex stood by their carriage, talking casually to the driver as if the son of a duke normally conversed with servants. He glanced up when she emerged from the establishment, all conversation stopping.

Her heart stopped also when he smiled. The sun was obscured by lowering, sooty clouds, the street crowded with hawkers and pedestrians, but they might have been alone and the sun shining.

"My lady." He came forward and greeted her aunt, bending politely over her hand.

"Lord Alexander." The response was given in a modulated, amused tone. "How odd to run into you here. Do you frequently patronize this particular dressmaker?"

"No, I admit I do not." His gaze transferred back to Amelia. Very quietly, he said, "I blundered this afternoon. Perhaps not as badly as I might have, but a mistake just the same."

Obviously her heart hadn't ceased to beat altogether, for it began to pound. He was as gorgeous as ever, immaculately dressed in buff breeches that hugged his muscular thighs, polished boots, and a dark blue coat. That one dark, wicked curl that had caused such havoc during their lone waltz brushed his cheek again.

"You were idealistic to expect her father to agree in the first place," Sophie said, her tone serene. She motioned for the driver to open the door to the carriage.

"You know I went to see him?" Alex looked bemused.

"If you did, it would be a blunder, so it is an easy guess."

"Yes, well, now he knows the depth of my interest." There was regret in his tone. "It changes the game, so to speak."

He'd gone to her father, discussed their marriage, but not revealed it was necessary. She didn't need a translator to come to that conclusion. "I'm afraid," Amelia said quietly, conscious of the stream of people passing by, "you are guilty of excessive fits of conscience, my lord. I appreciate your trying to gain his permission."

His charming smile was rueful. "A highly unsuccessful endeavor, to be sure."

Perhaps it had been, but she was touched that he'd done it for her, and no doubt endured an unpleasant scene.

"May I suggest we finish this discussion with greater privacy than on a public street? Lord Alexander, can we offer you transportation to your next destination?" Aunt Sophie eyed two women who had stopped in front of the shop, not too far away, and were unabashedly watching and whispering. "That's Lady Drury and her daughter. This meeting will not go unremarked."

"If I am seen climbing into your carriage, Lady McCay, you would be implicated in what happens next. So no, thank you. Besides, I brought my own transportation."

Aunt Sophie gave him a searching look. "What happens next?"

"I am going to kidnap your niece."

What did he just say? Startled, Amelia simply stared at him.

A smug expression spread over her aunt's face. "A capital idea, Lord Alexander. How I wish I had thought of it myself. Wait a moment—I believe I did."

"Your wise advice was duly noted, my lady." He bowed slightly and turned to offer Amelia his hand. "What do you say, my dear? I could theatrically toss you over my shoulder, I suppose, but I have to admit I've always thought that position somewhat undignified for the female involved."

"You cannot kidnap someone who comes along willingly," Amelia pointed out, only barely resisting the urge to throw herself into his arms, the public venue and the avidly curious Lady Drury be damned. Instead she extended her hand to let him clasp her fingers.

"We'll be partners, then," he said softly, "in our duplicity."

"That sounds absolutely perfect." And despite the stream of pedestrians and Aunt Sophie's fascinated driver, she stepped close enough to reach up and tame that enticing dark curl again.

He smiled, but his midnight eyes were serious. "There will be no going back if you leave with me."

"How perfect," she whispered, and meant it with all her heart.

Chapter Twenty-one

Hand poised to knock, Sophia hesitated and murmured to her companion, "Have I mentioned yet I am glad you were available to accompany me?"

"Several times, my dear." Richard sounded his usual calm, composed self. He looked it too, fastidious as always in black breeches and a gray coat, his mustache and silver hair immaculately groomed. "I would naturally stand by your side during any trial or tribulation, including your brother-in-law's possible wrath."

"It isn't just possible," Sophia muttered darkly. "Unless you consider it only *possible* the sun will rise tomorrow morning. He is going to be furious with me."

"Then it is best to simply get it over with. Allow me." Richard knocked sharply, and a few moments later they were being shepherded toward Hathaway's study.

It was all well and good to play the kindly matchmaker, and she still had no regrets over letting Amelia go with St. James without a protest—oh, if she were honest, with the utmost encouragement—but she still dreaded telling Stephen Patton his daughter had gone off to marry against his wishes.

She was the chosen chaperone, and though the season had started off brilliantly, somehow she had managed to allow her charge to become enamored of the last man in London her father would approve of, be compromised by Alexander St. James, and then cheerfully run off with him.

Hathaway *might* have just cause to be angry with her.

But if given it all to do over again . . . she'd probably follow the same exact course. The moment when Amelia reached up to tenderly brush the curl from his cheek . . . that was enough. The look on her face, so glowingly happy, made Sophia square her shoulders and greet her brother-in-law with a resolute stance. "I hope we are not interrupting something important, Stephen."

Hathaway glanced up, registered Richard's presence, and frowned, setting aside his pen. "I am answering some correspondence, but suppose it can wait." His smile was thin. "This seems to be a day of interruptions."

The reference to St. James's visit was discomforting.

Sophia chose a chair comfortably faded by the sun, and folded her hands as Richard chose to stand next to her. Hathaway gazed at them expectantly, first one, then the other. "So?"

Perhaps it was better to just say it. "Amelia has eloped."

"*What?*"

She rushed on. "I felt it my duty to at least tell you before you started to worry over her absence."

"How kind." His voice was so icy she could imagine what she'd heard of the polar regions of the Americas. In fact, she rather wished she were there at the moment. Stephen sat back, his face rigid. "St. James, of course."

How could she deny it? Besides, only a complete idiot wouldn't link Alex's visit and her brother-in-law's consequent refusal of his proposal with the elopement. The young man had the right idea too, for this way Amelia hadn't yet been locked away or betrothed immediately to someone else.

But it left Sophia in a deuced awkward position, to be sure.

Hathaway scraped out, "I take it, since you know about this debacle, madam, you were part of the event?"

"I did not aid in it," she said stiffly, sitting up a little straighter. At her age, being scolded like a schoolgirl rankled.

"But you did nothing, evidently, to stop it."

"He was waiting for us outside the dressmaker's." Thanks to the observant Lady Drury, Hathaway would hear that part anyway, so best to just be frank about it.

"And you let him just persuade her to leave?"

"No persuasion was needed."

"Why didn't you stop it?" His voice had risen significantly to a near shout.

"Have you seen Alexander St. James, my lord?" She did her best to not let the sarcasm creep into her tone. "He's a tall, well-built young man. Explain to me how I was supposed to stop him."

"I didn't mean physically, madam, and you know it. Amelia, to my misfortune, it seems, listens to you. Unless he forced her—"

"He didn't force her. She is very much in love with him. I doubt anything I could say would change that."

The resulting silence could only be described as fuming.

After a few tense moments her brother-in-law broke it with scathing derision. "May I say now that all along I worried about you as a suitable influence on my daughter?"

That stung, but wasn't surprising. She was actually glad he'd said it. "May I mention now," she returned, lifting her chin, "that you are no influence at all?"

"What is *that* supposed to mean?"

"Do you know in the least what she wants?"

"As long as it isn't St. James, I am willing to let her choose."

"But if that is what she wants—"

"She can pick someone else. Ye gods, woman, what have you done?" Hathaway shoved himself to his feet, his face livid. "It is bad enough you wear absurd costumes and flaunt convention. I have overlooked it for the sake of my wife's memory. But to allow—no, *encourage*—such scandalous behavior in my daughter without any thought to her future—"

Sophia hadn't imagined this conversation to be an easy one, but she was not about to have her affection for Amelia questioned. She said tightly, "*I* adore her. She knows I do. Can you say the same?"

"How dare you?"

"I dare because I feel a certain latitude, since I know the answer to the question. She has no idea if you have any affection for her or not. You should be ashamed of—"

"Lady McCay has an impeccable reputation," Richard murmured, interrupting her growing tirade with a gentle hand on her shoulder. "I trust you will not blame this on her."

"I wouldn't be so confident." Stephen glared at her—there was no other way to describe it. "I entrusted my daughter's future to you! Look at what has happened."

"She fell in love," Sophia informed him, meeting his accusing gaze squarely. "Perhaps instead of censure I should receive some praise."

"Love," he scoffed, his cheeks ruddy from anger.

"Maybe you've heard of it. You were married once."

That got to him, and a muscle twitched in his cheek. "Amelia? With Berkeley's son? Perhaps you could whisk her down to Hades and introduce her to the devil's progeny. I am coming to the conclusion there is a conspiracy behind my back."

"For heaven's sake," Sophia said with exasperated candor, "it could have been right in front of your face, you pay so little attention."

"I know you dislike him, but Berkeley is a decent sort

in my experience." Richard's fingers tightened in unsaid comfort. "And Alex St. James should not be judged by his family lineage, though most would find it an asset rather than a detriment in a marriage."

"The scoundrel just ran off with my daughter."

"He loves your daughter and wants to make her his wife," Sophia said in staunch support of her niece's choice. "How different it sounds when put in that light. I understand he came here earlier to beg your permission."

"You are privy to details that complete your culpability. Where did they go?"

"I have no idea." At least she could say that honestly. A young man with St. James's connections could have taken her anywhere. No banns needed to be posted in Scotland, but there were ways to get around that in England as well.

"I am going to find them, and when I do—"

"Sarah would have wanted this for her."

Amelia's father flinched as if she'd slapped him, his face going ashen. "You are excusing your failure."

"No, I am explaining my success." Sophia rose, regardless of Richard's restraining hand, and took in a deep, deep breath. "Your problems with the duke and the past are just that—*your* problems. Now, if you will excuse us, I feel my duty is done here."

Had she not tripped over the edge of the rug when exiting the room, the regal departure would have been more effective. Richard caught her arm, steadied her, and they left the town house together.

"A fierce lioness could not have done better," he informed her as they went down the steps toward the waiting carriage. "Defending her cub's ultimate happiness."

The dreary weather had cleared a bit and there was a hint of clear sky and a peek of late-afternoon sunshine. With a resigned sigh, she asked, "Do I really flaunt convention and wear absurd clothes?"

"It is part of your charm," he said with unflappable

politesse. "Now, then, after all this excitement, would you care to join me for dinner?"

* * *

My darling Anna:

The day is gray, the garden dying as winter encroaches, leaves blowing in the chill wind and scattered on the wet lawn of the park. Perhaps the weather is the reason for my mood, but my melancholy introspection has done nothing but lower my spirits. I miss you.

How simple it sounds. How complex it feels.

I am trying to remember a time when I did not love you, but I cannot. There was no life before you and will be none after. . . .

This day had been gray also, but despite his less than satisfactory confrontation with Lord Hathaway, his spirits were buoyant. Alex recalled the beginning of the last letter he'd been sent and thought he could understand the sentiment. He unlocked the door to the simple cottage and stepped back to let Amelia enter first.

What if you loved someone you could never have? He didn't believe in infidelity, but maybe he understood a little of Samuel and Anna's story, though he was still convinced, even with the letters, that the whole truth was still just shadows.

"This is not," Amelia pointed out, glancing around the simple entryway, "a carriage rumbling northward. My impression was we were eloping."

"We are. But Scotland is rather a long way, and in this world, the friends you have can make all the difference," he said blithely and closed the door behind them. The place was spotlessly clean, the furniture simple but well made. An antique rocker by the stone hearth invited occupancy, the low beams in the ceiling above blackened from past warming fires, the rug plain but well woven in subtle shades of cream and tan. A small settee sat near the window of the main room. A polished hallway led to a staircase, presumably to the bedrooms upstairs. True to Michael's assertions and not far out of the city, it was private, with the river quietly flowing past it.

He expounded, "A special license, a certain bishop I know personally, and two reliable witnesses that won't speak a word about the wedding until we give them leave . . . well, if we can't have it the other way, this seems much better than haring off to Scotland. Besides, no one will know where we are. Your father might have sent someone chasing after us."

Stunning—because he always thought she was stunning—in a pale pink day gown, Amelia gazed at him, her azure eyes shimmering. "Glorious solitude. What a lovely gift."

He wanted—no, needed—to kiss her. Hold her.

"Thank the Marquess of Longhaven when you see him at our wedding tomorrow," he murmured, moving the one step necessary to be able to reach for her. "Michael is a particular friend of mine, especially at this moment."

Her hair was the deepest amber in the muted afternoon light coming in the deep-set windows facing the Thames. Her form melted into his embrace; her lips parted for his kiss. Amelia clutched his upper arms, and then with a whisper of a sigh, pressed her body against him.

Since he hadn't done much of anything but think about the night they'd spent together, the flicker of arousal flared into full flame.

That fast.

Tomorrow she would become his wife. For tonight, they were still just lovers, but he intended for the night before her wedding to be as memorable as the night after.

"I've been thinking too much about you," he confessed when he broke the kiss so they could both take a breath. "It has been driving me mad. Quite frankly, if someone had predicted I would feel this way even a month or so ago, I would have laughed in derision."

"You?" Amelia laughed, her long lashes half-lowered. "Being dragged to London and paraded before every eligible man my father deemed suitable was like being stuck in a scene in a bad play where I couldn't get up and walk out. Call me idealistic, but I dreamed of a solution to my entrapment, but never did I assume It would come in the form of a stranger on my balcony."

"Did I ever think fulfilling my grandmother's request would lead to you? To this?" He kissed her throat, his fingers easing along the neckline of her gown, tracing that luscious curve.

"Your grandmother?"

Alex paused, reflecting that such uninhibited passion was not a good catalyst to keeping secrets. "I misspoke."

"You can't tell me, you mean." Amelia ran her fingers through his hair. "Surely when I am your wife—"

"Tomorrow." He lifted her easily in his arms.

"Tomorrow." Her smile was faint and tremulous as she agreed. "Will you share with me why your grandmother sent you to retrieve the key you are looking for?"

"Does a new promise negate an old one?" He headed for the stairs, her skirts sweeping over his arm.

"What a study in ethics." Amelia laughed, the light sound floating out. "I don't know the answer, and quite frankly, at this moment, I don't care. In the morning, I warn you, I might feel differently."

He didn't blame her for her curiosity, but neither could he wax philosophical over whether breaking his word to his grandmother was less of an offense if the confidant was his wife. At least not now. "You feel perfect," he assured her, the ring of his boots loud on the wooden stairs.

Michael, he decided as he shouldered his way into the first bedroom, seeing the tester bed, the simple closed cabinet, the mellow view of the river and the meadowlands beyond, was nothing short of a genius.

Amelia touched his cheek with a light brush of her fingertips as he set her on her feet. "I think I am going to like being kidnapped."

"I promise you will." His grin was cheeky, his erection swelling, her evocative scent reminding him of heated desire and forbidden pleasure. "Have you always been so precocious?"

"Test me."

Take me.

He knew that look in a woman's eyes, understood the delicate game they played. Never had it gratified him so much, because it was no carefree flirtation, but would affect the rest of his life. "Oh, I will," he vowed with teasing—but complete—sincerity.

And this time, as he undressed her, she did the same for him, her slender fingers awkward but eager. Her dress went first, in a swish of soft material as it slid to the floor. His coat was shrugged carelessly off and discarded. The buttons were undone one by one on his shirt, and then her hands dropped to his breeches and he had to stifle a groan as she brushed his erection through the fine material. "Amelia."

Clad now only in her shift and stockings, she glanced up at the hoarse sound of his voice, struggling with the second fastening. "Yes?"

"You're killing me," he said honestly. "I can do it faster."

"You have more practice," she said, but dropped her hands.

"I undress myself every day," he agreed, smiling, not willing to discuss whether or not he'd ever let any other woman unbutton his breeches. He hadn't, actually, if he thought about it, but the truth of the matter was other women were incidental now. Quietly, he explained as if she'd actually asked, "I'm a private person. I read. I manage my father's estates. Visit my friends and debate politics. I attend some entertainments, but I choose carefully. Lately I rise at dawn to join a beautiful lady in a morning ride. That is my life, which now includes you. Forget whatever else you've heard."

"From now on, we can rise together." Her answering smile was like the sunrise itself, glorious and moving.

"From the same bed," he agreed, pushing his breeches down his hips. His cock was swollen and stiff, and he could not wait to have her beneath him, warm, wet, and receptive.

"We won't be a traditional *ton* couple, then, with separate bedchambers?" She laughed, in gorgeous dishabille, all flowing hair and supple limbs.

"We can be anything we want," he said on a low growl, and jerked her back into his arms.

The first time had been an adventure, slow and sensual, the journey of discovery an extension of those first two exploratory, forbidden kisses. This—*this*—was totally different.

Aunt Sophie had been a true jewel. Unconventional by nature, she hadn't blinked an eye, but let Amelia go off with Alex and assured them both she would handle her father. How that would be accomplished Amelia wasn't sure, but at the moment, she didn't care.

Late-afternoon sun slanted in the small window, illuminating the cozy, charming room. It was dominated by the bed, which seemed only apropos to the situation. She hadn't ever anticipated making love before it was fully dark out, but her lack of sophistication was balanced by a desperate need.

Did she know sexual desire could be like this?

Love goes toward love . . .

If Shakespeare was correct, count her the happiest woman on earth. Alex's hands slid up her arms and grasped her shoulders just before his mouth captured hers in a searing kiss. The brush of his tongue made her melt inwardly, and Amelia sank in joyful, intemperate surrender into his embrace.

Skin to skin, lips clinging, the strong circle of his arms a perfect cradle, she rested shamelessly against him, the evidence of his desire hot and hard through the material of her shift. That night in her bed had been a sweet, forbidden initiation, but this night there would be nothing but passion.

"I want you naked." Alex eased free the ribbon on her chemise, his breath warm in her ear. "In truth, I want you any way I can have you. Tonight is ours. I'd have it be perfect, if possible. How often have I said I think you are beautiful?"

Her laugh was spontaneous and soft. "More than once or twice, my lord."

"Good." His hands roamed downward, following the fall of her chemise to the floor. "I love the way you tremble when I kiss you." In demonstration, he pressed his lips to the hollow under her ear.

And on cue, she quivered in response. His chest was hard with muscle, a perfect foil for the resilience of her breasts, her nipples tight now. Amelia arched her neck, giving him access to the sensitive line of her throat. "I can't help it," she whispered.

"Perfect." She could feel the curve of his lips against her skin as he smiled. Alex licked a slow, tantalizing path downward. "Let's make sure it remains that way the rest of our lives, shall we?"

As if she could even voice agreement when his mouth closed over her nipple. The first gentle suckle no doubt wrung another shudder, for he tightened his arms and his tongue did something very wicked, sending a spiral of pleasure downward to her belly. "Alex."

He didn't respond to the sound of his name, but instead continued to tease her breast before moving to the other one, nuzzling, sucking, arousing her all-too-willing body.

Does it always feel so good to be shameless? Amelia wondered, trying to picture anyone else touching her in a similar fashion, and utterly failing. She stroked his hair, her pale fingers a striking contrast to the silky blackness.

"The bed," he said hoarsely, urging her backward. "This isn't enough."

Her bottom hit the high mattress, and then she found herself summarily lifted and deposited, with his rangy body following, dwarfing hers as he braced himself above her. The corner of his mouth lifted lazily, at odds with his erection throbbing along her thigh. "I'd wager I can truly shock you in the most pleasant way, Lady Amelia."

"I think I've lain with you before, am naked beneath you now, and I've just eloped against my father's carefully planned wishes," she retorted, reaching up to explore the tensile strength of his neck with her questing fingertips. "I doubt you can shock me more than that."

"Ah, don't test me, my lady." He nibbled briefly on her lower lip, long lashes lowered over his dark eyes. The moment simmered between them, and she wanted to drown in the depths of it.

Then his mouth moved a little lower. The hollow of her neck, the valley between her breasts, then tracing her ribcage and belly so her muscles tightened with each tender kiss, with every brush of his lips. When he exerted pressure on her inner thighs, spreading them, then lowering his head and gently pressing his mouth to her sex, she found he could absolutely shock her.

The jolt through her body was pure bliss, stifling her instinctive protest.

Was he really using his tongue between her legs?

Yes, he was. Her eyes drifted shut of their own accord and she arched into the next delicious lick. "Ooh."

It was infinitely too scandalous and so wicked she couldn't believe it.

And, she discovered seconds later, beyond anything

she'd ever experienced. It was both sublime pleasure and infinite torture.

It was heaven. It was splendor and showering sparks and a precipitous pinnacle of ecstasy.

And when she plummeted downward, he was there to catch her, holding her shaking body in his arms and saying the words she never remembered hearing in her life.

"I love you."

Chapter Twenty-two

He'd never before told a woman he loved her.

There was a reason, of course. He'd never experienced this particular emotion until now.

His family . . . yes, of course he loved them, but it wasn't like this consuming romantic love that stirred his very soul. Alex smoothed his hand down over Amelia's bare shoulder and essayed a smile, denying his hungry body as he gazed down at her. He repeated, "I love you. It must be love, for otherwise I would not have followed you up to your bedroom that night, gone to your father this morning with a fair idea already of my reception, and then haunted most of the notable dressmaking establishments in London this afternoon until I found you. All of it makes no sense whatsoever to me, and I have come to the conclusion it must be love."

"You don't sound very happy about it." Her smile was languid, satisfied, and her eyes held a surprising understanding.

"I hadn't planned on . . . this." He indicated their lover's position amid the tumbled bed linens. "On us."

"Is love ever planned?"

"I suppose not." Restive, aroused, out of his depth with this young woman who had changed his life, Alex circled her nipple with a fingertip in a deceptively lazy movement.

If he sounded disconcerted, it was because that was exactly how he felt. The light brush of her fingers across his chest, however, helped matters considerably. As did her siren's smile. She murmured, "You said it first. I was worried I would scare you with my naive declarations."

At that moment he realized his future wife was not just alluring as a woman; she was more than a match for him. Exactly what he wanted.

"When did you know?" He kissed her before he adjusted his position between her slender thighs.

"I've thought about nothing else since that singular moment you touched me on the balcony."

"Tell me," he commanded, conscious of his need to possess her completely, the desire unique in his life. The youthful, frustrated passion he'd once felt for Maggie had been *nothing* compared to this.

"I love you," she said shyly, her lush lashes lowering a fraction, the becoming pink of arousal tinting her smooth skin, the faint scent of roses drifting to him as her hands clasped his biceps.

He entered her with exacting slowness, savoring the wet, hot tightness of her passage. Hair the color of the finest amber spilled around her shoulders, and she sighed tellingly as he began his penetration.

If rapture had a definition, this was it.

The equation was very simple: a soft bed, the woman of your dreams, pleasure beyond your most outrageous imaginings . . .

And, apparently, love.

Sliding his hands beneath her bottom, he lifted her into his next thrust, gratified to hear a small, sensual moan. He moved with a control that cost him, because he wanted nothing more than to lose himself in incipient lust, but this was too important, too moving for him to rush any part of it. His rumored proficiency might not be as well earned as the whispers indicated, but he thoroughly understood the stages of erotic provocation. The heated cadence of her breathing as it deepened, the fluid motion of a woman's body in response to each penetration, the bite of her nails, just so, on his shoulders, told the tale of arousal.

"Alex," she gasped as he moved in a deep, fluid stroke.

In answer he slid his tongue over the luscious curve of her lower lip. "Hmm?"

"It feels . . . you feel . . . oh."

"I agree."

This is the ultimate, he decided in the next exquisite glide. The experience every man and woman should have at least once in a lifetime, rapture coupled with poignant emotion, the physical with the subliminal. His climax was imminent. The way his testicles tightened made a light sweat break out over his body, and he postponed it as best he could, hoping her already aroused body would get there first.

She did, the low cry and tightening of her inner muscles all he needed. When she shuddered, he went instantly rigid, gripped exquisitely by the contractions of her release, ejaculating with such force he was fairly certain he'd stopped breathing. The mesmerizing pleasure held him there, poised in erotic bliss, until finally the world came back into focus.

Homey room. Large bed. Whitewashed walls. The open window letting in cool evening air and the scent of the water outside . . .

Perfect.

Eventually he realized he was collapsed on top of Amelia's delectable body and probably crushing her. He rolled to the side, urging her to come with him. Breathless and damp, they lay there, intimately intertwined and silent. Outside somewhere a bird twittered, and another answered. His hand moved in slow swirls over the curve of her bare hip.

"It might be nice to stay here for . . . say, another hundred years," he murmured, content in the aftermath of such combustible pleasure. "Just exactly like this."

Amelia laughed, a muffled sound against his shoulder. "Like in an enchanted fairy tale."

"I haven't read any since I was in the schoolroom, but I suppose you are right. Exactly like that."

She playfully licked his collarbone. "I get to be the princess."

"And I ascertain that leaves me with the dubious role of the prince, though I don't recall any stories in which he seduced the princess before the honorable marriage."

"Then you don't remember them very well. It happened all the time."

"Did it, now?" He smoothed strands of her silky hair and lost himself in the azure depths of her eyes. "Tell me more about these stories I don't remember."

"Only one story interests me," she responded, warm and relaxed against him. "Ours. How is your family going to feel about this?"

It was a good question.

He shrugged. "First and foremost, it isn't their decision."

"How easy it must be to be male and have that prerogative."

She had a point. He said softly, "I'm not autocratic, Amelia."

"If I thought you were," she responded, "I wouldn't have fallen in love with you." Her expression changed, growing introspective. "You *talk* to me. It sounds simple enough, but it isn't."

Ignored by her father and little more than an object to be obtained by avid bachelors of the *ton* since her debut, she had understandable doubts about men.

He was no paragon, but he did feel confident that he could give her better. Alex ran his finger affectionately along the straight line of her nose. "My brother John knows already. He was the one who advised me to just abduct you and be done with it."

"He didn't mind?" She seemed endearingly concerned. "I'm a Patton."

"I'm a St. James." Alex lifted a brow. "In truth, he wasn't delighted when I told him your identity, but he does understand the power of romantic love. He thought a trip to Gretna Green would be an easy solution for all concerned."

"But you didn't follow his advice."

"I might be perceived to be like John, but I'm not really like-minded. My impractical approach was to go to your father, because it represented to me the proper course. Idealistic, maybe, but since we are now here, like this, I find it difficult to summon up regrets."

"I think *we* might be very much alike." She lifted her mouth a tantalizing fraction, all voluptuous womanhood, with her amber hair in disarray and her hands gliding down his arms.

"And yet so delightfully different." He accepted the invitation and kissed her, amazed to feel the returning surge of his erection so soon. Or maybe he shouldn't be. He already knew Miss Patton was exceptional.

It had begun to rain, and for once she didn't feel it was a gloomy sound of what the day would bring, relegating her to the house or the confines of parasol and carriage. It was instead cozy against the panes of the window. As Amelia lounged on the bed, she plucked a slice of cheese from the platter and took a nibble. "However did you plan this?"

His dark hair ruffled from her fingers, Alex was gorgeously male, sleek and powerful, clad only in his breeches and relaxed next to her after retrieving their makeshift meal from the kitchen. He handed her a ripe peach. "I sent a brief note. My father's steward seems to have taken me at my word. All I asked for was a simple dinner delivered while I went in search of you."

"Apparently the duke's son merits all due attention." The cheese was excellent, sharp and perfectly aged. It melted in her mouth, and she took a piece of freshly baked bread.

He grinned. "If his consequence earns me a dinner in bed with you, I will not argue it."

"It *is* rather decadent." She had slipped on her chemise, not yet brazen enough to eat dinner stark naked. "A certain part of me doesn't quite believe this. I am sharing a meal in a bedroom in a house I don't even know precisely where it is or who owns it, undressed and in bed with a man who is not my husband. Not to mention that back in London, I know my father is furious."

"Not *yet* your husband," Alex corrected her, his gaze intense. "That technicality will be rectified tomorrow. As for this cottage, a friend of mine owns it, but no one lives here at the moment."

The thought arrested her in the very act of biting into the luscious, fragrant peach. "How many people already know I've run off with you? My father, my aunt, your driver, my aunt's driver, Lady Drury and her daughter . . . and exponentially growing, I'm sure."

"Does it matter?"

The question sounded casual, but she knew it wasn't.

"No," she answered truthfully, setting down the fruit on a plate that bore the ducal crest in gilded silver along the edge. "If there is a scandal over this, I blame my father, quite frankly. It seems to me you attempted the honorable course."

"Amelia, I'd already ruined you. I am not sure honorable applies."

"Is that what happened to me?" she asked archly. "And here I felt more whole after that night. As if I'd discovered something special and wonderful. Ruined seems quite inappropriate. Perhaps they should change the term to enlightened."

His laugh was rich and mellow. "I agree, but I doubt we are going to set a trend the stiff-necked matrons of society will follow. Or, for that matter, the pompous lords who insist virginity as a prerequisite in a wife, while they frequent brothels and keep mistresses. Hypocrisy will live ever on, I'm afraid, my sweet."

He was undoubtedly right, and the scandal still loomed, but maybe it was all those years away from society in the countryside that made it seem trivial, especially now, with Alex, shirtless, propped up on one elbow next to her, the candlelight gilding his chest to bronze and adding shadows to his fine-boned face. "You have unfairly long eyelashes," she told him, picking the peach back up and taking a bite of the succulent flesh. It was sweet and perfectly ripe.

His downy brows went up a fraction. "I take it we have just changed the subject."

"Weren't we just discussing something we can't change? Why waste this"—her hand indicated the softly lit bedroom—"on what the dour matrons might or might not talk about?"

"What a very valid point."

"Tonight is just us." She extended the piece of fruit in her hand.

"Agreed." He accepted and took a bite, the heated look in his eyes telling her he meant it.

When a drop of juice ran down his chin, she impulsively leaned forward and licked it away.

"Amelia."

She liked the way he said her name, almost reverently. Sitting back, she smiled with deliberate provocation. "If we could only eat every dinner in bed, I think that would be perfect."

"I agree, if a bit messy. What about roast beef and gravy? Impossible, I fear, among fine linens." Alex poured more champagne into her glass, the bubbles gently fizzing against the rim. "But even if we have to use the dining room now and again, we can always utilize this option for less-dangerous meals. What else do you want of marriage? Tell me."

How many men—especially of their class—actually asked their prospective wives what they wanted? I am too lucky, she decided at that moment, though she'd known from the beginning there was something special about him that had nothing to do with his good looks or exalted bloodlines. "I don't know. To continue our sunrise rides, maybe. That would be nice. No one else seems to understand why I get up so early, but there is something special about the start of a new day."

"The air is fresher, which is important for you." His lean form was relaxed, and Alex regarded her with his head propped on one hand, the muscles in his arm impressively flexed and defined. "I've thought about a country house but never needed one, as so much of my business is in London and I have my own set of apartments at Berkeley Hall. All of that has changed now. Shall we purchase one?"

He'd read her mind. It came so easily, she almost didn't trust it. All along she'd worried that whatever husband she finally wound up with would insist on the city as his primary home, as her father always had. "Would you really do that for me?" The question was hushed, and her lashes were pricked by tears.

Of joy. The best kind.

"Of course." His smile was easy and oh, so charming. "Why wouldn't I?"

Because you don't have to. Because no one ever has before.

She couldn't even say it out loud.

"Where you are is where I'd prefer to be, naturally." Alex drank from his champagne glass as if the blithe declaration that her wishes mattered more than his was the normal standard for an English gentleman. "The countryside is better for your health, and you've told me you favor it for aesthetic reasons to the bustle and stench of the city. I'm thinking Berkshire, but if you have a preference, please tell me."

"Where you are is where I'd prefer to be," she repeated softly.

"And if I choose the country?"

"The downs of Berkshire are fine with me."

Anywhere. As long as you are there.

He carefully lifted the dishes aside, setting them on the tray he'd brought up from the kitchen, and rose, padding over in bare feet to set it on a simple table near the door. Then he turned, and the way he looked at her made her heartbeat quicken. His approach to the bed was reminiscent of the description she'd once read of a tiger hunting his prey, and he took the fluted glass from her hand with masculine insistence.

"We'll select it together." His lips brushed her knuckles as he lifted her hand to kiss it. "To celebrate our new life."

"New life. I like the sound of it." She reclined against the pillows, a small smile inviting him, sultry and yet somehow hesitant, as she was still learning.

And learning fast, under his expert tutelage.

He didn't miss it. "So do I," he muttered, just before his lips took hers.

Chapter Twenty-three

The note had been short and to the point, and never had so few words moved her more. It was not just indicative of consideration, but of trust also. No more than a time and an address, but Sophia was impressed. St. James had the faith she wouldn't betray them, and the sensitivity, it appeared, to know she wanted to attend her niece's wedding.

It apparently paid to have a cleric in the family, she noted when she alighted from the carriage, for how else could he secure a magnificent cathedral so quickly for such a small wedding? It must have cost him a small fortune to get a special license for a marriage to an earl's daughter without Hathaway's consent.

The ceremony was brief but moving. Amelia was radiant, wearing the same pale pink day dress she'd had on the day before, dressed up somewhat by a glorious pearl necklace that had to be a gift from her handsome bridegroom.

For such a small affair there was a rather illustrious, but not surprising, guest list. The Marquess of Longhaven, with his enigmatic smile and urbane good looks.

Viscount Altea, dressed in the height of fashion and enough to make any woman's heart flutter. Presiding over the proceedings was the bridegroom's own brother, who was very young to have received a bishopric and was a mirror image of their father, the duke.

"I am so glad you are here." Amelia hugged her, and Sophia returned the embrace with misty-eyed affection. The light from the stained glass windows shone in jeweled patterns off her niece's shining hair, and the vast space smelled of cool stone and candle wax.

"To be here is a dream of mine. I can now cross it off the list of events I wished to witness in my life." Sophia refused to be the only one in the room with tears in her eyes and blinked rapidly. "Now, then, what are your plans?"

"We have to tell his family." Amelia touched one of the blossoms in her simple bouquet—pink roses to match her dress, the furled petals as delicate as her beauty. "Alex doesn't seem overly worried about the outcome, but I am less assured. Though, I must say, his oldest brother already knows, and the other one just married us, so perhaps it won't be as daunting as it sounds." She paused and asked carefully, "How did my father take the news?"

"About as I expected."

"Can I venture a guess? Unhappy I didn't follow his wishes, but not truly concerned about me."

The resignation in her niece's tone made her heart ache, and if she could have denied it, she would have, but Sophia didn't believe in telling falsehoods. Besides, Amelia was now a married woman, and it seemed unlikely, unless Hathaway was willing to change his rigid ways, that their relationship was going to benefit from this change. "That's fairly accurate," she admitted.

Amelia's expression reflected a brief touch of sadness, which was inappropriate to the happy day.

"Lady McCay." Alex St. James walked up to slide his arm possessively around his bride's waist. He was dashing in a black superfine coat and an embroidered waist-coat in shades of gray and blue, dark breeches hugging his thighs. "I am very glad you could attend."

Amelia leaned back into him, the melancholy imme-diately banished. They were beautiful together, dark and light, male and female, virility and feminine allure, her pastel attire a foil for his masculine, stark elegance. The embrace was utterly natural also, as if they had known each other for years instead of mere weeks, and Sophia clearly recalled that same absurdly swift ease of inti-macy with William, as if at that first exchanged glance they'd just *known*.

Good God, Stephen was a fool to even think of deny-ing his daughter such happiness.

"I wouldn't have missed it. Thank you for inviting me," Sophia said in a slightly choked voice, her fingers tightening on her reticule, because such strong emotion was always difficult to handle. "Tell me, what are your plans now?"

St. James looked resigned. "I think we are obligated to go visit Berkeley Hall before my family hears of this marriage from someone else. My father left for the country estate a few days ago."

"Only I have a small wardrobe problem." Amelia's tone was wry. "What an odd notion to get married in the same dress I wore yesterday."

Though it was an imprudent promise, Sophia said immediately, "I'll arrange to have your clothing packed and delivered to you. Your father is unhappy about this defiance of his wishes, but he isn't entirely unreason-able, and what purpose could there be in keeping your belongings?"

At least she *hoped* Stephen wouldn't be unreason-able about it. He had just spent a small fortune on his daughter's wardrobe in the hope she would make a bril-liant splash with society and secure a prestigious mar-riage, not to elope with the son of his worst enemy.

Until he adjusted to the idea—if it ever happened—

he *might* just be unreasonable, and there was little doubt he was angry with both of them.

In light of that possible eventuality, Sophia hedged just a little. "But, just in case, perhaps the dressmaker could be persuaded to hurry the gowns you were measured for yesterday."

"I am more than capable of making sure you have anything you need, Amelia," her niece's husband said quietly. "Were haste not an issue today—"

She turned in his arms, her smile dazzling and happy. "I hardly care what I wear anyway. Ask Aunt Sophie. That isn't at all an issue. I don't expect you to spoil me."

"Don't deprive me of the pleasure." His dark eyes glimmered as he stared down at his bride, one long-fingered hand gracefully skimming her cheek.

Sophia knew they had both just forgotten her, lost in each other.

As it should be. If only love were *enough* . . .

But sometimes it wasn't. If Anna St. James was alive now to ask, what would she say?

Should I mention the painting and the necklace?

No, she decided. They were too happy and it was, after all, their wedding day. An old tragedy had no part in the festivities.

"I would like it noted I told Alex I thought he was in trouble," Michael said, doing his best not to sound smug as they walked along the street. "This impetuous marriage supports my observation."

Luke stepped aside to let a young woman pass, two children in tow and one clutched in her arms. His boots splashed a muddy puddle in the street. "Your intuitive observation on love is duly acknowledged," he said dryly. "I hope you won't be offended if I point out I hardly think you are the first person to realize the emotion can spell doom to the bachelor life."

"Maybe not." Michael was unfazed. "But I am not exactly an expert on the subject, and yet I told Alex he was being an idealistic fool if he thought he could control whether or not he was falling for the winsome Miss Patton."

"Now the winsome Mrs. St. James."

"Indeed. One of us three has fallen. I wasn't convinced I'd ever see it happen."

How true. As friends, Luke realized, they'd been brothers not just in war, but in other ways. In Spain, they'd been brought together by their dangerous roles for the British government: old friends and new comrades. He'd never pictured Alex succumbing enough to a romantic attachment to actually marry in haste and secret, and it brought back bittersweet memories and emotions he didn't care to reveal, not even to Michael.

The dreary drizzle of the day before had produced wet streets and more noxious smells than usual, but he philosophized that his boots were now sullied anyway from his step into the muddy thoroughfare, so it hardly mattered if he was careful where he walked. "This interesting business of the key has me curious. What is the key and why the devil was he looking for it? Has he ever elaborated?"

"No."

Michael could look bland like no one else.

"But there *is* another development." Luke might not be able to read anything into Michael's expression, but he knew his friend very well.

"There is an interesting catalyst for this unpopular romance, yes." Michael skirted an overhanging tree branch, the leaves still laden with crystalline droplets from the rain. "Someone is meddling."

"Meddling how?"

As they crossed the street toward his family's London home, he listened as Michael explained that someone had been sending old love letters anonymously to both Lady Amelia and Alex.

"It raises two questions: who and why?"

"Not to mention how," Michael added mildly. "It

took very little investigation for me to learn about the scandal that took place decades ago involving Amelia's grandfather, the then Earl of Hathaway, and the sister of the current Duke of Berkeley's father . . . Hathaway was married, as Alex told us, but that was hardly the problem; we both know marital vows are overlooked often enough. *She* was not, and my source says she was young, beautiful, and poised to make an advantageous match. Hence the duke's rage and his challenge when the lady died under suspicious circumstances. So he killed the earl in duel, which resulted in bad feelings all around."

Luke digested this, noting the damp air had formed a low-lying fog already on the street. "I suppose that explains the hatred between their families." Neither Amelia nor Alex had more than one family member at the wedding, and while they both looked happy and delighted in each other, it didn't really bode well for future serenity.

"Indeed," Michael agreed.

"It seems a natural assumption that the letters were between the two ill-fated lovers."

"It was the conclusion I came too as well."

"Who would send the letters?" Luke asked slowly. "And how the devil did they get them?"

"An interesting question. At first," Michael said, as if musing out loud as they went up the stone steps of the residence, "I assumed it was either Amelia's aunt or Alex's grandmother. After all, it seems rather the thing a woman would do to use an old romance to fuel a new one. But I really couldn't see how Lady McCay would have the letters at all. She is related to the Pattons only by marriage, and Amelia's mother has been gone a long time. The original feud involves Lord Hathaway's father, and if Hathaway had the letters, he'd hardly give them to his sister-in-law. Besides, if for whatever reason she did possess the letters and wanted Amelia to read them, wouldn't she just hand the whole bundle over?"

Luke opened the door to let them both inside, and a

footman hastened to come take their coats. The warm house felt good after the damp outside. A short while later, whiskey in hand and ensconced by the library fire, Michael went on. "For different reasons, I absolve the dowager duchess. The subtlety involved isn't at all in character, and I doubt seriously she would encourage an alliance in any way between their families."

"You are taking quite an interest in this drama." Luke was amused.

"It's Alex." Michael said it without discernable emotion, relaxing in his chair with his booted feet extended. "I am unlikely to forget regaining consciousness in that little hell of a French cell and finding him, his face black with gunpowder from the fight to take the armory, bending over me. I thought I was hallucinating from the pain."

"He was so sure you were there, but our informants said you'd been taken north. His conviction moved me to ask Wellington to give him permission to try to take it on the chance he was right." Luke still remembered how much persuasion he'd had to use, because they truthfully could not spare the men.

"I remember your part in it, believe me."

Luke said dryly, "The intelligence you provided from working behind enemy lines saved thousands of lives, including ours, probably more than once. No gratitude is necessary. Our motives weren't entirely altruistic. If we were going to win the bloody war, we needed you alive and working on our side."

He often wondered privately if Michael, so restlessly intellectual, so used to the games he'd played with the French, wasn't finding England a little dull. The war was over—or at least Bonaparte was exiled to St. Helena and the continent was licking its wounds—and all three of them, he and Alex included, had to make an adjustment to coming home.

Of them all, Luke guessed, it was most difficult for Michael. Alex had proved an able commander and soldier, but he had no difficulty in leaving the conflict behind, confident and pleased with their success, ready to take on the management of some of his father's estates. Luke had his responsibilities as head of the family, and with Elizabeth's coming-out, the role as her guardian to fulfill.

With the sudden death of Michael's older brother while he was still in Spain, he'd been moved to the position of ducal heir, which Luke knew he hadn't coveted at all.

His vivid hazel eyes reflective, Michael mused, "The war aside, our meddler has a purpose. My intuition—and the facts—tell me the timing of all this has something to do with it."

"Your legendary intuition is rarely wrong."

"It has failed me once or twice, my capture by the French a case in point, but I do listen to my gut." Michael idly swirled the amber liquid in his glass. "This situation has all the melodramatic elements of a classical theme: star-crossed lovers, an old secret, and, of course, our mysterious interferer."

"You wish to pit wits with this shadowy foe. Is that it?"

"Foe? Hmm, I'm not sure he—or she—is a foe at all. I am starting to see the purpose of sending the letters in a new light. I wonder if it isn't so much to facilitate the romance as it is to tell the true story."

"I don't see the purpose of that. After all, it happened years ago. If the young woman was seduced and ruined, the old earl should have been held accountable. It's one matter to indulge in a casual affair, but one doesn't dally with the unmarried sister of a duke."

"Or the unmarried young daughter of an earl?" Michael said with wry humor.

"True enough, but Lady Amelia and Alex are hardly the first couple to marry against the wishes of their families." Luke took a thoughtful sip from his glass. "I am not sure what I would do if Elizabeth became enamored of someone I disliked. I guess I hadn't considered it before now."

Michael's chuckle was irritating, but, Luke supposed, understandable. He wasn't all that comfortable in his supervisory role over a nineteen-year-old woman either. "I doubt you would be as unbending as Hathaway, but one never knows—does one?—until the situation is forced upon you."

"I suppose not. Let's hope I never experience the dilemma." Luke cocked a brow. "What about the infamous key? In your little investigation, did you learn anything about it?"

"No," Michael said with perfect quiet and believable confidence, "but I will."

Chapter Twenty-four

"How is your breathing?" Alex watched his wife with concern. She'd shifted position several times and her hands were visibly clenched in her lap. "Are you in distress?"

"I'm fine," she assured him as they turned into the long drive. "It isn't that at all. I'm just a little nervous now that we are here."

She would not be the first person to be awed by the seat of the Dukes of Berkeley.

The approach to the house had changed little over the centuries and was still designed to impress and maybe even intimidate. Set back amidst level upon level of greenery, rising stone steps, and long rectangular pools, the manor had been modified time and again, the magnificence of the front partly the sheer size of it, and partly the elegance of design and form.

Berkeley Hall was much like other baronial homes of its age: splendid in its proportions, the front facade rising three stories, domineering and vast. Though Alex had affection for it as the place where he spent his boyhood, the modest country estate he and Amelia had discussed held a much greater appeal.

"It's immense."

"Now you see," he remarked, as his wife gazed out the window at his childhood home, "why I'm not interested in ostentatious residences. I believe I've had my fill."

"My father's country estate is a bit more modest." Amelia's smile was not quite steady, and she sat on the opposite seat with intense rigidity. Either her father had conceded or Aunt Sophie had liberally bribed the seamstress, for that morning a trunk had been delivered to his town house. He'd refrained from asking if the gowns were new, or if some of her wardrobe had been sent, and she hadn't elaborated. Especially now that because of him her relationship with her father was strained to the breaking point, Alex didn't want to make her unhappy by discussing it. At the moment she was elegant and lovely in a blue georgette traveling costume, her dark gold hair knotted at her nape, but the tension in her slender shoulders and those tightly clasped hands contradicted her serene expression.

As the gravel of the drive crunched under the wheels of the carriage, he reached over, pried her gloved hands apart, and clasped one in his. His gaze was steady, and, he hoped, reassuring. "My family will adore you. Relax. Even if in some absurd, infinite stubbornness they didn't, it wouldn't matter. We're married. See there? Problem solved."

"I doubt it will be quite that simple, Alex. My father's reaction to your proposal being a case in point," she murmured with infallible honesty. Her fingers tightened around his and he was reminded that she was still so very young and inexperienced, and had given her well-being—her very life—into his care because she trusted him.

A humbling experience, to be sure. Especially since the term whirlwind romance absolutely applied to their clandestine relationship.

"Men are different." His shoulders lifted prosaically. It was the truth. "He's protective of you, and I asked to take you away from him. That sounds simplistic, but—"

"I'm not anyone's possession." The interruption was said with impressive calm and dignity. "Nor am I representative of what happened between Anna and my grandfather. Most of this is very unfair to us."

"Exactly, my sweet. Just keep it in mind as you face the lions."

She smiled then, but it was tremulous. "Any idea of how ferocious they will be?"

The way the sunlight coming through the window lit her hair distracted him enough that he processed the question a moment later than he should have. Just that morning he'd buried his face in that silken gold mass as he climaxed inside her in pure, rapturous pleasure, and she shivered in his arms in her own sexual release. There was something infinitely different about making love to your *wife*. Why had he never realized it would be that way?

"Alex?"

He recovered, doing his best to dismiss the erotic memory. She was understandably nervous, and if he could, he wanted to assuage her anxiety as much as possible. "My father seems stern, but underneath I think he is a great deal like your father. Not unfeeling, but just unapproachable in many ways."

She let out a small laugh. "I doubt they'd like very much being called alike."

"I'm eight-and-twenty," he told her, as if it explained everything. "I've traveled, fought in bloody battles, and even survived the infinitely more trying viciousness of the *ton*. I have my own fortune, and even if I didn't, I would find a way to provide for us." His boots brushed her skirts as he adjusted his position. "I think what I am trying to say, my sweet, is that worrying about what comes next isn't necessary. We aren't dependent on their cheer and goodwill."

He didn't say he *wanted* his family's acceptance for her, since other than her aunt, she'd never had it. In all other circumstances, he was certain his father and grandmother would support him, but in this one . . . he wasn't as sure.

Damnation.

Promises were impossible.

The carriage rolled to a halt by a circular fountain, the musical ripple of the water as it flowed down three immense tiers a pleasant, familiar sound. Alex alighted and then lifted Amelia from the carriage, glad at least that John would not be shocked by his arrival, a bride in tow. His hand at the small of her back, he escorted her up the series of steps to the front entrance, the magnificent door carved with the family coat of arms: an upright sword flanked by a wild boar on one side and a rampant lion on the other.

"Dare Not Cross," Amelia murmured.

He glanced at her, surprised at the translation. "You read Latin?"

"Also enough Greek to make my way through some of the classics that weren't translated in my father's library."

Alex tipped up her chin and smiled. "Have I mentioned I am enamored by intellectual young ladies with singularly blue eyes?"

"Have I mentioned I am surprisingly attracted to rakish burglars?"

"How nice for both of us, then." He lowered his head.

Her lips were soft and smooth and warm, and the kiss quite satisfying until he realized someone had opened the door. When he glanced up, he saw that Oates, the butler, stood there. Of an indeterminate age, with all the proper bearing expected for his position as head of the household of an august duke, he had a slightly pained look on his thin face; whether it was for interrupting a tender moment or at the indiscreet embrace right on the doorstep, Alex couldn't be sure.

The older man cleared his throat. "Good afternoon, Lord Alexander."

"Good afternoon, Oates."

"I was unaware we were expecting you." There was just a hint of disapproval in his tone, reminiscent of his childhood.

Needless to say, Oates was always aware of everything in regard to Berkeley Hall.

"It is an unannounced visit," Alex said, straightening in amusement. Amelia's cheeks were decidedly pink from either the kiss or because they been caught in the middle of it. "May I introduce my wife, Lady Amelia."

Even Oates's legendary impassiveness faltered for a moment. His jaw dropped so he might actually have gaped, which would be a severe blow to his dignity, but he stalwartly regained his poise and bowed. "A pleasure, my lady. Welcome to Berkeley."

"Thank you."

"Her ladyship will need a maid." Alex took her arm and led Amelia into the foyer, all marble floors and soaring ceilings, the gold leaf mosaic above the columns done by a Florentine master two centuries before, the same intricate design in parts of the Vatican. "And I believe we would like to change and refresh ourselves before we see the rest of the family."

"That can be arranged, of course, my lord."

Oates strode off with impressive speed, and Alex grinned. "I was a scapegrace as a child. I didn't think I could ever shock him again, but I believe I just succeeded."

"Popular opinion has it that you are still a rogue," his wife reminded him primly, gazing at a priceless, brilliant scarlet-and-white vase full of hothouse flowers, the black lacquer chest it sat on also imported from the Orient. Then her interest strayed to the magnificence of the elaborate chandelier overhead. She seemed resigned, but to his relief, not quite as intimidated as maybe one would expect from a sheltered ingenue.

I like her in my home, he thought, dressed in vivid blue to match her exquisite eyes.

She was even more spectacular undressed.

Had he ever imagined this? Arriving with his *wife* at Berkeley?

"True enough." He thought about the upcoming evening and murmured with dark, sensual promise, "I will show you how much of a rogue later when we are alone."

At least she was out of her bath when the knock came at the door. Amelia wasn't sure whether or not to answer it clad only in her dressing gown, but when the gentle rap came again, at her nod, the maid, a quiet, young girl with a lilting Welsh accent, crossed the room, opened the door, and immediately dropped into a quick curtsy.

The woman who stood there was, at a guess, in her late twenties, brunet and pretty in a wholesome fashion, dressed in an elegant but modest gray gown with Belgian lace around the neckline. "I'm Diana."

The simple introduction left Amelia at a loss for a moment.

"Marchioness of Busham," the woman elaborated, "and currently married to the formerly infamous John St. James, your husband's older brother. Forgive the intrusion, but may I come in?"

The warmth of her smile precluded a refusal, and besides, this was apparently her sister-in-law. Amelia stammered, "Of . . . of course. Please."

"I thought you might need a little friendly company before dinner." Diana glided in, graceful in a swirl of silver skirts. She had a heart-shaped face and soft brown eyes, and her expression was openly curious. "Actually, let me be truthful. I'm being madly inquisitive and couldn't wait to meet you, but let me assure you, in the most benign of ways. I adore Alex."

The quiet maid crept out of the room and discreetly shut the door without being asked.

There couldn't be a better way to proverbially break the ice. Amelia tightened the belt on her dressing gown a little self-consciously, but she replied, in perfect truth, "I adore him too."

The Empire bed required a footstool to reach it, so her sister-in-law sat in a chartreuse silk-upholstered chair. All of the room reflected the same taste and elegance, with pale green silk walls, priceless Aubusson rugs underfoot, and heavy, carved rosewood furniture. Alex had casually mentioned that if she wished she could redecorate their apartments, and though her own father was a wealthy man, she'd readjusted her estimation of her new husband's fortune.

Diana St. James regarded her from her repose. "I hope so, if you married him. Without affection, I promise you we would throttle the male of our species if tied to them for a lifetime. Now, then, tell me how you met. John was infuriatingly vague about the details, because he is a typically obtuse man."

Hearing the future Duke of Berkeley referred to in such a way rendered Amelia momentarily speechless, as did the casual irreverence of her guest when referring to the ducal heir.

The marchioness looked at her expectantly, but there was a sympathetic gleam in her eyes.

It would be very nice to have a female friend when in the enemy camp, Amelia thought wryly, but Diana's question was a devil of one to answer. Amelia's new husband seemed adamant about keeping his mysterious promise, and she didn't know if it included his foray into breaking and entering.

She settled for the truth without elaboration. "It was quite romantic, actually. I sometimes have difficulties breathing. It's a childhood affliction I have not yet outgrown completely, and maybe never will, I suppose. I stepped outside for some fresh air one evening and he was nearby, and, well . . . he saw my distress and quite gallantly lifted me in his arms."

"And you fell in love."

"Then and there, I think." Amelia could still vividly recall the first, tantalizing feel of his mouth touching hers and her willing participation in that fateful kiss.

"It must be true from your blush." Diana smiled.

"We'd never even been introduced." Amelia stifled a laugh. "Come to think of it, we *still* haven't been formally introduced."

"I have a feeling *that* formality is no longer necessary," the marchioness said, her gaze speculative and amused. "You are very beautiful, of course, but what else drew Alex to you?"

"Pardon?" Amelia was a trifle taken aback.

"I'm unremittingly frank, you'll find." Diana St. James moved a hand in a languid, careless gesture that was all aristocratic dismissal, but her hovering smile was friendly. "One of my faults, or so John will tell you. I don't dissemble well. Let me rephrase my question. What makes you different from all the other *ton* beauties so anxious to capture my handsome brother-in-law's attention?"

After a moment, Amelia said with the warmth of memory of their conversation just before their arrival, "He claims he is enamored of intellectual young ladies with blue eyes."

"I see." The two words were said softly.

"I think I am also more provincial than most of the ladies of his acquaintance," Amelia elaborated, not ashamed she lacked the brittle sophistication of the beau monde. "I spent my entire youth in the country. Before my bow, I'd never been to London."

"Yet I understand you were dubbed this season's Incomparable. I still read the gossip sheets, though they are a few days old when they arrive here. Elusive Venus, am I right?"

"For my generous dowry, and how I look. It's a superficial measure of a person, don't you think?" Amelia looked at her new sister-in-law squarely.

"I couldn't agree more, actually. I am hardly one of the dazzling beauties John always had on his arm"—her mouth quirked—"or, let's be frank since you are now a married lady, in his bed. His reputation was beyond the pale. My parents were vehemently opposed to our marriage, despite the prominent exclusiveness of his position as a marquess and a ducal heir."

Such candor was startling, but Amelia preferred it to the innuendos and sidestepping of society. And she also disagreed about her self-description. Diana St. James had a different sort of beauty—an inner glow that was hard to define. Her skin was pale and flawless, her figure a bit voluptuous, undoubtedly from recent childbirth, but still lovely, and she exuded an intangible charm of honesty and lack of affectation. Amelia blurted out, "Alex tried to talk to my father even though he knew it was futile."

"That sounds like Alex. Under that jaded exterior, he is actually quite a sensitive man. Where do think he is right now?" Diana raised a brow, her expression indulgent.

After the arrival of the maid to unpack Amelia's trunk and help her undress so she could bathe, Alex had disappeared into the adjoining room of their suite. Amelia assumed he was still there.

"Men take somewhat of a shorter time to dress for dinner. He didn't see the need to rush you either, or at least that was his excuse for having a few moments to go up to the nursery. I am unfashionably not using a wet nurse and had just finished feeding Marcus. Alex insisted on holding him, though I did warn him to take off his dinner jacket first and that he might need a new shirt and cravat before all was said and done, but he was unfazed. That is how I knew you would be alone to talk for a few moments."

Amelia sank down on the padded velvet seat of the bench at her elegant dressing table. She confessed, "I am trying to picture him holding a baby."

"There is something indescribably moving about seeing your husband holding your child." The marchioness had a soft light in her brown eyes. "A tall, strong man with such a tiny being in his arms. If John is representative of his gender, he has an endearing helplessness when it comes to babies, despite being so confident about everything else. Someday you will know exactly what I mean when you and Alex are blessed with children."

"It seems early to be thinking of a family," Amelia murmured. "We have a few obstacles to hurdle before complicating the situation further."

"That's why I decided to come here like a proper interfering sister-in-law. The dowager duchess and the duke can be a little intimidating, but it is nothing insurmountable." Diana rose gracefully and walked over to the armoire, her smooth brow knitted. "Shall we choose together what you should wear?"

The evening suddenly wasn't quite as daunting with such staunch support from an unexpected source. "Yes, thank you." Her voice was hushed.

"We're family now, my dear."

Speaking the truth, she admitted, "Other than Aunt Sophie, who is wonderful in every way, I've never had a family."

"That," Diana informed her mischievously, fingering a rose gown with an edging of silver lace, "has all changed. You are a St. James now. What about this one? It will look glorious with your fair coloring."

Chapter Twenty-five

*M*y joking remark back in the carriage might not
have been so facetious after all, Alex thought,
poised at the entrance to the private drawing room in
the family wing. The traditional glass of sherry before
dinner gathered his family together in a formality he'd
known all his life, but he'd never before considered how
formidable they might all look when occupying the
same room. His father and John, both tall and dark, conversing by one of the fireplaces with his uncle Edward,
his grandmother seated on a silk-covered settee with his
aunt Leticia next to her, Diana in a chair nearby, chatting with Joel, also up from London after the wedding.
Which meant the details of both the marriage and the
identity of his bride were now common knowledge.

A pride of lions indeed, for at his entrance with Amelia on his arm, all conversation stopped abruptly and
heads lifted as if, in a figurative sense, they caught scent
of their prey.

He didn't miss Amelia's sharply caught breath or the
tremble of her slender fingers on his arm. "Steady, love,"

he murmured. "Always face opposing forces with the stern resolve that the battle will go your way."

"You aren't worried?" She asked it under her breath, so quietly he had to lean closer, which was not exactly a hardship. The floral scent drifting from her hair was beguiling, as was the excellent view he had of her décolletage, the graceful, enticing upper curves of her breasts displayed by her fashionable gown, silver lace and rose against ivory skin. The long-lashed beauty of her eyes as she gazed at him in uncertainty also made him want to simply skip dinner and whisk her right back upstairs, where in his bed, he could demonstrate most thoroughly that, no, he wasn't worried.

"There's no need to be," he assured her, and hoped sincerely that the good manners bred into the lineage of the Dukes of Berkeley asserted themselves this evening. Later, he was sure his father would have something to say on the subject of his marriage to Hathaway's daughter, but he counted on it being in private, just the two of them.

Silence.

At least it didn't feel like a hostile silence, but more an expectant one, and he was the one who had married someone none of them had ever met, so perhaps it was up to him to break it. "Good evening. My apologies for our late arrival." He turned and took Amelia's hand where it rested on his sleeve and raised it to his lips. "I'd like you all to meet my wife, Amelia."

Diana, his brother John's wife, rose graciously, her warm smile encouraging as she came over, and instead of simply extending a hand and a greeting, hugged Amelia. "We are all so delighted Alex has married!"

God bless my generous sister-in-law, Alex thought with both amusement and gratitude.

As much as he wanted to reassure his wife she would be easily accepted, he was aware—especially after his brief, unpleasant conversation with the earl—of the depth of the enmity between his father and Hathaway. As usual, the Duke of Berkeley's cool impassivity gave away very little of what he might be feeling, watching his enemy's daughter—now his daughter-in-law—approach. John, on the other hand, produced his infamous smile, a slow, appreciative curve of his lips. Naturally, Alex thought with a twinge of irritated possessiveness, my brother would admire Amelia's undeniable beauty. "My father, the Duke of Berkeley, and my brother John, Marquess of Busham." His met his father's gaze steadily. "My wife, Amelia St. James."

To his credit, his father didn't hesitate, but took Amelia's hand and bent over it with exquisite politesse. "Forgive our surprise. Welcome to Berkeley."

Not exactly gushing cordiality, but his father didn't gush in the best of circumstances. Amelia looked relieved and murmured something back, actually letting out a small, nervous laugh when John winked irreverently and kissed her hand with a great deal more enthusiasm. "Enchanted," his older brother said as if he meant it.

"Not too enchanted, I hope," Alex muttered dryly, and drew her away for the rest of the introductions, pleased that even his grandmother seemed able to not sound too icy. Though she did shoot him an accusing look that said she well remembered that moment at the opera when she had pointed out Amelia's beauty, and he had wholeheartedly agreed but declined to mention they knew each other.

When the courtesies were done, Diana came and linked her arm through Amelia's and whispered conspiratorially, "That went very well, in my estimation. I'm sure Alex would like a drink. Come sit with me."

John pressed a glass into Alex's hand when he got to the small, elaborately carved Persian table where decanters and glasses were set out. His brother said with a slight grin, "No one here is going to bite your beautiful bride, brother, or rest assured Diana will bite them back. She has a new, protective mothering instinct since Marcus was born, and she is inordinately fond of you."

"I promised Amelia this wouldn't be an ordeal." Alex

took a bracing sip of sherry and wished it was something stronger. It was odd, but his family's acceptance apparently meant more to him than he realized, and Diana wasn't the only one with a new, protective instinct.

"If she were anyone else, it wouldn't be." John, elegant in stark black and crisp white, sounded philosophical. "But keep in mind Diana's parents were adamantly—and I emphasize that word—opposed to me for their beloved daughter. Their Methodist tendencies made my fortune and title negligible assets in their estimation, and my reputation for vice an affront to their pious ways. I've been in your lovely wife's position, believe me."

Alex had been in Spain at the time, so the details of his brother's courtship were vague at best. "Yet they finally agreed."

John watched with an assessing gaze as his wife guided Amelia toward a settee by the window, Diana chatting the entire time. "I give due credit to my wife's power of persuasion. I still have no idea why I perversely had to become enamored of the only eligible female in England who at the time wasn't angling for my title and fortune, but I am damn glad I did."

"I believe I can understand that sentiment."

Practical as ever, John murmured, "Your choice is controversial on both sides. My father-in-law and I have now become civil at least. I don't know if you will ever be able to say the same."

Alex had his own doubts. "I am not going to take odds on Hathaway's benevolence. I don't know if he'll even ever be cordial to Amelia again."

"His loss," John murmured.

"I couldn't agree more."

"She's stunning, little brother. You are fortunate I have completely abandoned my licentious ways and am a happily married man."

Alex said quietly, "We have that in common, then."

*　　*　　*

"My bed or yours?"

Amelia hadn't heard the door between their bedrooms open. Hairbrush in hand, she turned around and saw Alex with one shoulder against the doorjamb, a dark blue dressing gown carelessly cinched at his waist, the faint smile on his mouth teasingly erotic.

"I was just wondering," he said, not moving but letting his heated gaze wander over her, "if you might be interested in a wild night of passion to celebrate surviving your introduction to the St. James family?"

"Is celebrate the correct word?" She carefully set aside the ornate silver brush on the polished surface of the dressing tale, not certain her smile held steady. "Other than our brief introduction when both your father and grandmother were excruciatingly polite, they never spoke to me again the entire evening."

"It's hard to discourse when sitting at a table roughly the size of the Patagonian plateau. One is obligated to talk only to those in close proximity or raise one's voice to an undignified shout, and neither my father nor my grandmother is ever undignified."

He had a point, but she wondered if by the duke's decree they'd been seated at the other end of the table to allow him and the dowager duchess to avoid conversing with her. "I suppose in my naïveté I hoped it would not be as bad as anticipated." Even to her own ears, her voice sounded small.

"Rather like my highly unsatisfying visit to your father. See how similar we are?"

"I rather doubt anyone would think you naive."

Quite the contrary, he was the epitome of seduction, with his glossy dark hair in disarray and quixotic smile.

"I rather doubt anyone would think I would form a romantic attachment to an innocent young woman either.... Though I must admit, I fulfilled everyone's expectations, and you were not nearly as innocent once I did form that attachment." There was a slight rueful quirk to his mouth.

"As much my fault, I believe, as yours." She would always remember that night in her bedroom in Cambridgeshire. *She'd* brazenly suggested her bedroom, not him.

And what had happened next ...

One of his dark brows rose, his negligent pose not belying the powerful width of his shoulders. She could see the gleam of his bare chest through the V in his robe, and despite the grueling evening, her pulse quickened. Alex asked reasonably, "As for my father and grandmother, did you expect them to simply toss aside the prejudice of two generations so quickly? I didn't, though I was happy to see my faith in their rigid good manners won out. And I anticipate their doubts will thaw as they come to realize your beauty is as much inherently part of your personality as the exquisite exterior. I'm sure they believe I married just a beautiful woman. When they realize I married a beautiful *person*, their attitudes will adjust."

"What a lovely compliment." Her voice was hushed.

"What a lovely truth. How lucky am I?"

He was too self-assured, too handsome, too intoxicatingly close. Amelia felt her breasts tighten; a physical reaction to what she knew was to come. His sentiment was touching. She'd just hoped for more universal acceptance, though both his brothers and Diana had been wonderful.

Enough. She wasn't going to let it ruin the entire evening. "I don't believe I've ever been called exquisite before."

He straightened with a lazy, mesmerizing smile at the changed, soft tone of her voice. "All those poems you received rhapsodizing over the color of your eyes and comparing your hair to the darkest honey, deepest amber, or whatever nonsense they came up with that doesn't do it justice, and no one ever managed to include the word exquisite? I am ashamed of British gentlemen everywhere."

The laughter was welcome, the strain of the stilted dinner melting away. "*You* have never written me a poem," she mentioned archly, watching as he came toward her with predatory intent.

"I've never written a poem at all." Ebony brows lifted a fraction.

"I'd like one," she teased. "From the scandalous Lord Alexander St. James. What a coup."

"I don't think my bent is literary composition." Alex caught her hands and abruptly pulled her to her feet and against him. "But I'm willing to give it a try, I suppose."

The hardness of his tall body embodied strength and safety, and even more, a virility she was coming to very much appreciate. The rigid evidence of his arousal was easily felt through his robe, and his warm breath against her ear made her body tingle. "How shall I begin? What about, your hair invites me like the sun on a garden rose, sweet and as soft as the most delicate petal."

"A nice start," she teased, leaning into him.

His fingers drifted through her loose hair in a lingering caress. He continued in the same husky whisper, "Your skin is like smooth, warm satin."

"Unoriginal, but pleasant."

One hand parted her dressing gown and slid upward slowly, over the rounded curve of her hip, across her stomach, making the muscles there tighten, over her ribcage to cup her breast, his thumb making a tantalizing circle around the nipple. "Your breasts are perfectly made just to fulfill my fantasies. Full, firm, and so female."

"I confess I've never heard that before." Amelia stretched on tiptoe and kissed his throat, tasting the salty essence of his skin. She was warm, especially between her legs, but his temperature was still several degrees above hers. She ran her fingertips along his chest, closing her eyes as he lightly squeezed her captive breast.

"How am I doing?" Alex kissed her temple. "Enough poetic comparisons yet?"

"Your bed," she murmured breathlessly, answering his initial question. Would it be too sentimental to point out they'd used her bed that first night and now she wanted to lie with him in *his* bed? Maybe, but it didn't matter, because she was beyond explanation as he obligingly picked her up in an easy upsweep and grinned.

"I'm out of descriptive words anyway," he told her as he shouldered his way through the door. "Demonstration is more my forte."

His room was the antithesis of hers; no pale colors or elaborately carved roses decorating the fireplace mantel, but instead cut-velvet hangings in dark green on the large bed, a lacquer armoire in one corner, and a businesslike desk by one of the windows, stacked with books. She caught all this in just a flash of impressions, because Alex laid her on the bed and shrugged out of his dressing gown. It fell to the floor in a sinuous ripple of silk, and his dark eyes gleamed. Magnificently aroused, his erect cock was beaded already with the evidence of his desire, the tip glistening.

He never doused the lights like she imagined a lover or a husband would. She'd overheard enough twitters from Aunt Sophie's friends to understand most men did—or maybe most wives asked them to keep lovemaking in the subdued dark.

She preferred it this way, languid with desire, pulling open the sash on her dressing gown. So she could see the play of light over the hard contours of Alex's defined musculature, the ripple each movement caused, the glory of his sensual smile.

Her lashes lowered provocatively. After all, he was a very good teacher.

The bed dipped as he joined her, large, male, and totally nude and confident. "I like you like this, half-naked and for me alone. . . . Did you know I've been jealous of every man you danced with since we met?"

"I think I became cognizant of it the night you practically dragged me off the dance floor in front of most of the beau monde."

"Which incited a riot of gossip. I'm sorry."

"Don't be. I think I'll adjust to the constant scandal following us." Amelia traced the line of his jaw playfully. "Besides I think I was the one to truly get everyone's attention when I dragged you back for our waltz, which looking back on it, was entirely my idea."

"I'm older. I should have—"

She pressed her fingertips to his lips. "What that has to do with it escapes me right now, because I am uninterested in assigning fault and quite interested in something else."

He touched her cheek, his eyes full of amusement and unconcealed heat. "May I offer making love as an alternative to our current discussion?"

"That sounds like an excellent substitute," she whispered, and pulled him down into her kiss.

It was amazing a woman so grass-green in bed could inflame him to such an undisciplined degree. Alex rolled on top of his wife's soft, supple body, never breaking their kiss. She was impatient. He knew it because of the subtle but imploring lift of her hips against his erection, because of the intoxicating clutch of her fingers on his shoulders, because of the veil of half-lowered lashes shielding her eyes. . . .

"Alex."

"I need to make sure you're ready, love." His fingers slid through the small triangle of curls at the apex of her thighs, and he was gratified to find she was wet and receptive as he slid one finger deep inside her and she made an inarticulate sound in response. "Hot satin, so tight and yet yielding."

"That's nice," she said with a small sigh as he did it again. "But I know you can do better."

His new, inexperienced wife was abandoned and uninhibited in bed, he was discovering, and nothing could make him happier. He slid his fingers out and adjusted position, the exhale of her breath against his throat causing his already rigid erection to surge.

The cradle of her opened thighs held him naturally, and he entered her slowly, watching the flush deepen on her cheeks, feeling the heave of her bare breasts against his chest. Inch by inch with excruciating care and control, because this wasn't about quick, lustful satisfaction but a joining, and not just of their bodies.

When he was fully inside her, Alex kissed her softly. Their lips clung and she moaned into his mouth as he rocked just enough to put pressure in exactly the right spot. "Hmm, you like that."

"Very much. Do it again." Her neck arched backward as he complied. "Yes."

"More?"

"Stop teasing me. Yes, more."

"Maybe you'd rather be in charge." He propped his weight on his elbows, entranced by the look on her face.

Her lacy lashes lifted and she looked at him in confusion.

"Like this." In one smooth movement he rolled over, holding her hips to keep his cock deeply inside her, so she straddled his hips, her long hair spilling down her back and brushing his fingers where he clasped her waist in a delicate, arousing touch.

As if he needed to be more aroused. He was battling the urge to ejaculate as it was, and the sight of her, gloriously nude, her opulent, bare breasts limned by the low lamplight, her small hands braced on his chest, might just take the day. His testicles tightened, he took in a shuddering breath, and by some miracle will won out over tempestuous desire.

"Ride me." He splayed his fingers over her slim hips and lifted her, then eased her back down. "Like this."

"Oh."

There was one advantage—well, more than that, actually, but the only one he cared about at the moment was sexual—in having a bedmate who had been sheltered enough she hadn't been poisoned by the idea that sexual enjoyment was for men alone. Amelia began to move experimentally, lifting until his cock almost slid free of her delectable heat, and then sinking back down at first in an awkward rhythm, but then catching on quickly and angling her body to give herself the most pleasure. He helped with subtle movements, letting her set the pace, gritting his teeth in an effort to make sure she found satisfaction before he did.

It happened much faster than he expected, her low, keening cry and the tightening of her inner muscles around his throbbing erection enough to tear a groan from deep in his chest. Rapture cascaded through him like a spill of scalding water, molten, unruly, immeasurably brilliant, and he poured himself into her still-contracting passage as she climaxed.

She collapsed on his chest, which was a rather nice bonus to the breathless aftermath, and Alex took a different kind of satisfaction by stroking the graceful line of her spine, the tactile sensation of delicate bone and damp skin delightful.

"I think," she eventually murmured against his neck, obviously sleepy, "we need to find out what happened. Maybe it will help . . . everything."

Sated, replete, half-asleep himself, Alex lifted his brows, not following her statement at all. "What happened?" Hazy moonlight lit the curtains, which were ruffled by a small night breeze. He was immensely satisfied, his wife in his arms. . . .

Amelia lifted her head and her expression was poignantly sincere. "Between Anna and my grandfather. Why my father hates yours and the feeling is reciprocated. Who sent us those letters. Whatever you are looking for, we need to find it."

"You're thinking about this *now*?" He couldn't decide whether to be amused or insulted. "I thought I'd sufficiently distracted you from anything to do with either of our families."

Lush, nude, with the evidence of his discharge iridescent on her thighs, Amelia resembled every man's vision of Venus, in his opinion, albeit not an elusive one. "This seems the perfect time to think about it," she said simply. "What of our children? Do we want to raise them between two warring families?"

A valid point, he had to admit. He looked into his wife's beautiful eyes. "We've relinquished the autonomy of independent action, haven't we?"

"I never had it." She traced the line of his brow with one slender finger. "Therefore I understand more thoroughly than you do how important it is that your family not only accept you, but love you."

He wanted to repudiate the idea that his father would disdain his grandchildren for any reason, but he found he couldn't. Instead, he said quietly, "I think you are right."

Chapter Twenty-six

The sun was warm on the rich Flemish rug, a myriad of delicious smells stirring her out of a sound sleep, and Amelia rolled over and opened her eyes. A huge silver tray sat on the polished walnut table by the bed. At a glance there were warm pastries, a bowl of glistening fruit, bacon, sausages, shirred eggs in delicate porcelain cups. The luscious scent of coffee filled the air. Sleepily, she murmured, "Good heavens."

"I ordered up breakfast." Alex sat on the edge of the bed, fully dressed and pulling on his boots, his expression indulgent. "I am not sure how many people the chef thought would be eating it with us, but he apparently does not want you to go hungry."

"Yes, I get that impression."

The second boot slid on and Alex stood in one lithe movement. He wore doeskin breeches and a fine white linen shirt, open at the neck, his ebony hair brushing the collar a stark contrast in the morning light coming in through the tall windows. "I assumed you'd rather not make polite small talk with my grandmother this first morning."

I am still nude, Amelia realized with a small twinge of chagrin when she sat up and the sheet slid downward, baring her breasts. Her husband's appreciative grin as she snatched the sheet back up didn't help. "You assumed correctly," she told him, aware of her blush. "Thank you for the consideration, but where are you going?"

"I've a meeting with my father. The royal decree arrived with the tray, properly sealed with the ducal crest and nestled strategically next to the pot of coffee. One does not dare ignore it." His smile was full of roguish charm. "I expected no less."

"To talk about me." She wasn't sure how to feel, but it was a statement rather than a question.

Alex bent over, the mattress giving as he braced an arm on either side of her body, and kissed her. "To talk about the estates. To talk about various other forms of business, as I just met with Hawthorne last week, who is my father's main solicitor. To talk about the health of the king, Liverpool's latest policy changes, and yes, no doubt, to eventually touch upon the subject of my abrupt marriage."

He was so calm, so *certain.*

A part of her adored him for it, because his demeanor spoke of an indifference if his family disapproved of his choice in a wife, and part of her was jealous of how blasé he could be about the consequences of their sudden marriage. It was obvious Alex was sure of familial support even if his choice wasn't one they wanted, and she had no such safeguard. For all she knew, her father had disowned her.

Yet, she thought in the rosy morning glow, with her husband smiling at her, *if I had to do it again, I most absolutely would make the same choice.* His arms, his touch, his kiss . . .

And it wasn't that alone. It was his solicitude . . . and, quite astonishingly, their actual growing friendship. Sexual attraction was a powerful force and she was still a novice at love in so many ways, but the practical side of her knew time spent in bed was only part of a relationship. She hadn't been interested in any other of the myriad gentlemen her father had paraded before her, but this one man—*the* man—had caught her interest and held it in a devastating way, and it wasn't just his good looks or charm.

"I hope he will accept me for your sake, but in my mind, we found each other," she whispered, "and that is all that is important."

He held her gaze, suddenly very still. "Now, that, Mrs. St. James, is exactly right. If you had asked me just a short time ago, I would have called such sentimentality ridiculous, but I have changed my mind. If you will excuse me, I am going to keep my appointment with the duke, and then we'll have a ride so I can show you Berkeley's grounds and some of the countryside. It's a beautiful morning."

Amelia sank back against the softness of the pillows, shoulders bare, her nervousness about his family in abeyance under the generous warmth of his smile. "That sounds lovely."

After he'd gone, she searched around until she found her discarded dressing gown. It was in a telltale heap of blue satin on the floor near the end of the bed, flung there in the heat of the moment the night before, and whoever had delivered the tray must have seen it. The idea of that was mortifying, but quite frankly, she reminded herself with firm logic, she was a married woman now—a woman married to the infamous Alex St. James, no less. The distraction of the food made all embarrassment fade into the background. She'd eaten virtually nothing at dinner the evening before, too nervous to do justice to the seven sumptuous, elaborate courses.

Pouring steaming coffee into her Sevres cup, Amelia contemplated what of the vast offering she should have, finally deciding on a biscuit dusted with caramelized sugar, two of the perfectly cooked eggs, and some fruit. She ate slowly, pondering how quickly life could change.

The discreet knock on the door brought her out of her reverie and she looked up, startled. "Come in."

The maid who entered was not the quiet girl who had helped with her toilette the evening before, but an older woman. She curtsied quickly and handed over a thick cream envelope. "This is for you, madam."

Madam? At nineteen, that would take some adjustment. Amelia accepted the note. "Thank you."

Curious, she broke the seal and read the spidery handwriting.

It seemed Alex wasn't the only one with a request for a regal audience. Clearing her throat, she said to the waiting servant, "Could I have some hot water sent up, please?"

They'd walked the perimeter of the stables, discussing the possibility of adding new bloodstock, before the subject of Amelia was introduced. Just after they rounded a corner of the impressive brick structure, his boots crunching the clean white gravel, his father said in a neutral tone, "Can you please tell me how *this* happened?"

Alex considered pretending he didn't know exactly what the subject of the abrupt switch in conversation might be, but instead said, "I suppose you can blame the old scandal. In my quest to help Grandmother, I encountered Amelia. That was enough."

A groom went by, leading one of the new foals, his gaze lowered deferentially as he bowed his head and the young horse skipped sideways in skittish revolt against the lead. His father looked as distant as usual, but he said grudgingly, "She's lovely. She looks very much like her mother."

"You knew her mother?"

"Don't look so surprised. Of course I did. For all his faults, Hathaway is an earl and we do move in the same company."

"I don't think his daughter would disagree with you

about his faults." Alex watched a bird of prey, probably a hawk from its graceful flight, land on the branch of a tree. The sky was almost a painful blue without a wisp of white cloud. "He's alternated between virtually ignoring her existence to regulating her life. In case you haven't already guessed this, I was most definitely denied his permission to marry her."

"At least he was asked."

The asperity rankled. "I'm almost thirty. Did you expect I *would* ask you?"

His father hesitated and then shrugged with a sigh, walking next to him up the path from the outbuildings toward the gardens. "I suppose you have a valid point, much as I hate to admit it. I am so used to making decisions for everyone. At times I might just think I am entitled when I am not."

An interesting concession from a man who rarely made concessions of any kind. His father's aristocratic profile was predictably remote. Alex kept pace with him, their long strides matching. "Your aversion for Hathaway is separate from my relationship with Amelia, or at least I hope it can be. She is quite apprehensive, for understandable reasons, that you will dislike her just for who she is. I have tried to reassure her you are more fair-minded than that."

"Have you?" His father looked faintly amused for a moment, a rarity. "Using flattery to induce my congenial behavior, I see."

"If it would work, gladly. Her happiness is important to me."

"So it should be." The words were crisp but also telling. During the recitation his father seemed completely calm. But when they reached the outskirts of the gardens, to Alex's surprise, his father stopped abruptly and turned in the pouring sunlight of the warm morning. "Hathaway may be vindictive."

Alex halted also. "So he might be. I married his

daughter against his express wishes. I'll refrain from the hypocrisy of expecting him to smile and shake my hand next time we meet."

"You don't understand."

The normally impassive duke might be right. His face showed a certain strain that Alex had never seen before. Slowly, he responded, "No, I apparently don't, sir. Care to enlighten me?"

"He may tell her the truth, or at least the truth as he sees it."

That would be refreshing. Alex somehow managed to refrain from saying it out loud. Instead he asked, "What truth?"

There was an ornate stone bench next to a small bush tinted pink with tiny blossoms near a statue of cupid—ironic, that. His father gestured at the seat and said heavily, "Perhaps we should sit down."

"I *need* to sit for this?" Alex didn't wait for an answer but took his seat, stretching out his legs and staring at his obviously discomforted parent.

"We are descended from royal bloodlines." His father settled next to him, upright and stiff, his face taut. "The blood of William the Conqueror is part of your lineage, and—"

"Pardon me, but what has that to do with any of this?" Alex interrupted—a cardinal sin, but he was starting to truly feel in the murky quagmire of ignorance that he was missing something crucial, as he had all along. "If you are about to claim Amelia is not good enough for me, don't bother."

"No." In the morning light, his father's face had taken on an almost human vulnerability. Even in country clothes he was elegant, reserved, and though usually unapproachable, he exuded an unusual quietude even for him. "I'm pointing out that our heritage includes some of the noblest men in English history, and yet, even in the most privileged of aristocratic families, there are dark secrets."

"I'm getting that impression, yes," Alex said grimly. "Care to enlighten me about the St. James secret that obviously exists?"

The lines around his father's mouth deepened. "You already know part of the story of Anna St. James and Samuel Patton, the third Earl of Hathaway."

"I know a great deal, actually, as I have read some of their private correspondence. Someone has taken to mailing both Amelia and me their love letters, one at a time."

That brought a severe frown. "Someone? You don't know the identity of the sender?"

"No." The slight breeze was pleasant, ruffling Alex's hair and reminding him of the morning ride he'd promised Amelia. "Though I am wondering if Grandmother might be able to take an educated guess, given she is the one who started this entire drama. I am not arguing with the outcome so far, naturally, but it is like a puzzle with bits and pieces scattered everywhere."

"She won't guess for you. Trust me."

"I believe that," Alex muttered. "It's like coming up against Hadrian's Wall. Old and yet stubbornly still in place."

"The letters I can't explain, but I can pull together part of it for you." His spine very straight, his father stared out unseeingly over the vast, sculpted gardens, brilliant now with spring flowers. "You wish your wife's happiness, and that is laudable. Unfortunately, there is a somewhat formidable obstacle you face when you explain to her—for I think it should be *you*, not her father—that your grandfather killed her grandfather."

"I know about the duel," Alex admitted, "but have not yet told her. Still, I think, given the circumstances and that she never knew him, she will—"

"Understand? I'm not sure even *I* understand."

Sunlight, incongruous to that untenable declaration, the floral-scented air, the vast green of the park around them, lent a surreal background to that dismaying information. *What the hell does that mean?*

In the same reasonable voice, his father went on speaking in unemotional explanation. "According to my father, it was an informal duel. According to the Pattons, it was murder. As I pointed out, our family has a legacy of honor that goes back eight centuries. It is inconceivable that my father unfairly shot Hathaway in a rage over his sister's seduction, but there were no witnesses, only his word on it. Your grandmother says my aunt's untimely death at such a young age set all the events in motion. Apparently, at one time my father and Hathaway were friends. That's how the earl met Anna."

It was difficult, but Alex found his voice. "There were no seconds?"

"None. I was too young to remember any of it, nor would I have been told anyway. My father's influence kept the scandal of his sister's disgraceful relationship with Hathaway quiet, and Lady Hathaway hardly wanted it public knowledge, so it was all hushed up as much as possible. That is really all I know to this day."

Assimilating all the various repercussions from the deceit perpetrated by both families took a moment, but Alex had a feeling his father was correct and explaining to Amelia their respective grandfathers had a deadly encounter was not going to be pleasant, which was probably why he hadn't told her yet.

The star-crossed lovers theme was getting tiresome.

And where the hell did the key fit into all this?

He said slowly, "The source of enmity between you and my wife's father somehow becomes very clear. Your father killed his father not under fair circumstances, like I originally believed, but in a manner that leaves questions. How many men could possibly still like each other after such an event?"

"His father took advantage of my father's young, innocent sister. Tell me how he deserved anything except retaliation for his iniquitous behavior."

Alex would agree wholeheartedly if he stood on the outside of this, but he was firmly planted in the middle. "I've read the letters. They were in love."

"They had no business being in love," his father countered crisply. "She was a debutante and he was a married man."

"You think you can order love?" Alex unconsciously quoted Michael. "It isn't how it works—take my word on it. If so I wouldn't have chosen someone who would gain me inevitable family disapproval."

After a brief pause, his father said neutrally, "It's true I wish she were someone else's daughter ... anyone else's daughter, to be honest. But I am more personally involved than the rest of the family. Your brothers both seem charmed. Diana also has an adoptive sister-in-law air that is unmistakable. Her beauty aside, your young bride must be likable."

This could possibly be the most personal conversation they had ever shared. If nothing else, at least that good came out of the situation.

"She is ... different." Alex smiled. "Genuine is the best word I have. At first I was angry on her behalf when I realized how Hathaway kept her secluded in the countryside, out of his sphere. Now I'm grateful. She has no affectations. She's cognizant that all the attention she garners is because of her looks, position, and dowry, and yet also intelligent enough to know that none of those attributes portray the real woman inside."

"Spoken like a man truly infatuated."

Infatuated, yes; guilty as accused. Completely out of stride with what the realities of the situation required, no. "I'm lucky," he said quietly, "and not willing to give up happiness because of an old disagreement between two families who have, it seems, an undeclared war going on."

"Undeclared? There you are wrong, son." His father rose, his scrutiny intense, his face once again holding a patrician sort of distance that was familiar. "Battle lines were clearly drawn years ago."

*   *   *

Amelia thanked the footman who guided her to the door to the duchess's private sitting room. She squared her shoulders and stepped inside, hearing the soft sound as the door shut behind her.

She certainly hoped this wasn't going to be a session of verbal riposte and the requisite dance backward, for she'd had enough experience in her brief time with society to recognize the signs, but not enough to be proficient to spar with a dowager duchess.

The exquisite room was awash with sunlight, the draperies a plush, light blue velvet, the carpet patterned in lemon yellow and cream and the same shade of blue, the furniture dainty and feminine. An enormous pier mirror above the carved Italian marble mantel reflected the light, making the spacious room even brighter. On one wall hung a striking portrait of a young woman, her blond hair becomingly upswept, one hand resting gracefully on the shoulder of a young, dark-haired boy as they stood on a small rise framed by leafy trees.

"Myself and your new father-in-law." The cool voice spoke from the other doorway into the room, presumably into the duchess's bedchamber. "Quite obviously painted many, many years ago, but always one of my favorites."

Amelia turned and dropped into a formal curtsy as the older woman came into the room. "Good morning, Your Grace."

"As you are apparently now my granddaughter, there is no need to be so formal, Lady Amelia. Take a seat, please."

The crisp words weren't actually reassuring, but Amelia straightened and chose a floral settee opposite where the dowager duchess took a chair that seemed to be her normal seat, she went to it so naturally. There was a small table, the top inlaid with mother-of-pearl, between them, and a maid came at once into the room and deposited a small tray with demitasse cups and a porcelain pot.

"I have an affection for chocolate in the morning," the duchess said.

"So do I, Your Grace."

"Is that so? I suppose we have that in common, then. Will you pour?"

"Of course." Amelia hastened to comply. Though her hands were not entirely steady, she still managed a passable job and passed over the cup and saucer.

Dressed immaculately in gray silk, Alex's grandmother accepted the cup with thin, blue-veined hands, her gaze speculative. "You are a beautiful child, aren't you?"

Not a child any longer, she wanted to point out, but she merely murmured, "Thank you."

"I can see why my grandson is so enamored."

The evening he'd spoken with Lady Fontaine came to mind, as did his resistance to the woman's not-so-subtle overtures. Gabriella was considered to be one of the beauteous darlings of society. Amelia said firmly, "It's hardly my looks. He isn't that shallow. Give him due credit. He would not marry someone just because he found them attractive. The *ton* has a plethora of beautiful women eager enough for his attention."

"You defend him and not yourself." The older woman's thin brows rose. "That's well-done and promising, I suppose."

I suppose. In light of their circumstances, it was not surprising that easy acceptance was withheld, but Amelia knew Alex regarded his grandmother with genuine affection. "I think love is always promising, Your Grace."

"But then again, you are young enough you would." The duchess took a genteel sip of her chocolate, a vague sadness in her pale blue eyes. "Some love affairs have only tragic consequences."

"Like Anna and my grandfather." Amelia didn't see the point in dissembling, since everyone—probably even including the servants by now—knew it was the point of contention between their families.

"I see you don't wish to tiptoe around the subject."

"Is there any reason we should?"

Was there a glimmer of approval in the older woman's eyes? "All right, then. Yes, exactly like Anna and your grandfather." The duchess set down the cup with exaggerated care on the tiny table. "In their case, they should have disregarded their scandalous impulses. It caused nothing but distress for everyone."

"They couldn't. She loved him too much."

"I am not surprised you take a romantic view of it, given your age."

Amelia didn't think impetuous love was reserved for the young alone, or she certainly hoped not. It was her fervent wish that the simmering passion between her and her new husband lasted a lifetime. "You were there. . . . She was your sister-in-law. I've read her letters, but they don't detail how they initially met."

"Letters?" The momentary thaw turned back into glacial ice. "How would you get my sister-in-law's letters?"

"Someone sent them to me."

"Who?" Centuries of command went into that imperious demand.

"I don't know," Amelia said with complete honesty. "I wondered if maybe you would."

"Well, I don't." The response was clipped, but the shortness wasn't personal, Amelia decided. The other woman's expression suddenly became abstracted. The duchess gazed at the same portrait that had drawn Amelia's attention earlier, her cooling chocolate ignored. Her posture was rigid, her hands folded now in her lap.

"Seems an odd joke to play on us. Alex has gotten letters as well."

"He has?" Millicent St. James quivered. Just a small movement, but discernable just the same, and she suddenly looked pale.

Alarmed over the older woman's pallor, Amelia

asked, "Do you want me to ring for your maid, Your Grace?"

"No . . . no." Immediately she straightened again. "I just remembered . . . well, it was a trying time and I thought I'd put it safely behind me."

Safely behind her? An odd statement, to be sure. Amelia said carefully, "But someone knows."

"Yes." The agreement carried a fatalistic note. "Apparently, if you're getting their letters, someone knows."

It was odd, but in that moment, in the brightly lit, elegant room, she felt, instead of intimidated and disliked because of the past, that she and Alex's grandmother shared a strange sort of kinship. "Tell me about her."

Alex's grandmother stared at her for a moment, and then picked her chocolate back up and took an absent sip from her cup. "You wish to know about Anna?"

"In my place, wouldn't you?"

"Perhaps. Very well." A pause. "My sister-in-law was very young, very beautiful, and far too free-spirited. Rather like you, I imagine."

"Thank you, Your Grace."

"Don't thank me, child. This conversation is not going at all in the direction I imagined." A prim sniff accompanied the words. "I'd thought to instruct you on what it means to be a St. James. Though I loved her, Anna is not an admirable example."

For the first time, Amelia laughed, a small, muffled sound. "Nor how I imagined it either, Your Grace. And you needn't tell me I am lucky to have Alex."

"Not precisely what I was going to say"—his grandmother's voice was dry—"but I am not certain admonishments of decorum to a young woman married to my somewhat impetuous scapegrace grandson wouldn't be wasted anyway. His marriage to anyone would set tongues wagging, and his marriage to you in particular will set off a torrent of whispers and the expectations of an eighth-month child. I hope you are prepared."

Such a blunt statement made warmth suffuse her

cheeks, but Amelia had to concede the duchess was probably right. "Whether or not there is gossip doesn't matter. I wouldn't change my decision."

"Excellent. Perhaps you will make an admirable St. James after all. We are simply going to ignore the scandal." There was an arrogant tilt to the duchess's chin.

How nice to have the stately assurance of pretending something never happened. Amelia couldn't help but let her gaze drift to the portrait again of the present duke and his mother. If she and Alex had a son, would he have his father's glossy dark hair or her fairness?

Her eyes narrowed a fraction, and she realized why she'd been so struck by the painting in the first place. Upon closer inspection, the background wasn't ordinary; instead of what appeared to be woods, there was the hint of faces on the trees, and the shadows of the figures threw fantastical shadows on the smooth lawn.

The unique style was strikingly familiar. "Your Grace . . . can I ask you who painted that portrait?"

The abrupt change in subject made the duchess go surprisingly very still, the delicate cup poised in her blue-veined hand.

Or *was* it a change in subject?

The dark-haired mermaid . . . the beautiful necklace . . .

Amelia set aside her chocolate. "It is a Simeon, isn't it?"

The older woman inclined her head half a fraction.

"Did he ever paint Anna?"

"I suppose it wouldn't do any good to deny it," the dowager duchess said heavily.

Chapter Twenty-seven

"What is all this?" Sophia gazed around the drawing room in utter confusion, the heavy floral fragrance in the air almost intoxicating. Vases of roses sat on every flat surface, a few even on the floor. All colors, from the deepest crimson to a pure ivory. She sat down on a chair next to a bouquet of magnificent pink blossoms, a bit overwhelmed by the display.

"Flowers, my lady."

She shot her butler a disgruntled look. "I realize they are flowers, Hastings, but where did they come from?"

"There are no cards or I would have collected them for you, naturally. However, you do have a gentleman caller."

Richard. She didn't need to be told, though truthfully, he'd never sent her flowers before. Richard knew her favorite flowers were roses, just as Alex St. James had discovered Amelia's penchant for lilies.

When gentlemen exerted themselves, they *could* be very charming.

"Show Sir Richard in, please." She suddenly wished she wasn't wearing her demure sprigged muslin, but the brilliant burnt orange gown she had just ordered from the modiste. It was a bit bright for daytime, but went rather well with the color of her hair.

"I see the florist took me at my word." Richard strolled into the room and wrinkled his nose with comical exaggeration. "It will be impossible to visit my club without bathing after this call. I refuse to enter the sanctified confines of masculine refuge smelling like an overblown rose garden. Good afternoon, my dear."

"I knew they were from you, but I am not sure why you sent them."

"It worked so well for St. James, I couldn't resist. I was delighted to get your note telling me of their marriage."

Sophia gazed at him. He looked the same; the neatly brushed hair, trimmed mustache, fashionable clothing . . . but yet he was different also. It was perhaps the gleam in his eyes, so removed from his usual benevolent twinkle. Slowly she said, "I suppose it did work for Lord Alexander, though it took more than a roomful of flowers to win Amelia."

"I didn't expect you to fall at my feet over an emptied conservatory, my dear." His chuckle was familiar. "But since I am courting you, I wanted to make a bold statement. I think I succeeded."

Since I am courting you . . .

"Indeed you did." She was touched, but she was also an experienced widow. With a sweep of her hand she indicated the crowded room. "But this excess isn't necessary."

"It might be. May I sit?"

"Of course." That was an interesting comment. She watched him choose a chair—coincidentally, the chair William had always favored. It was a bit faded, but she didn't have the heart to have it replaced. "Why would it be necessary?"

"I have a confession to make. My conscience deems it necessary, though I will admit I debated my need for honesty. The roses are not just a token of my sincere interest, but a bribe so you'll forgive me."

"Richard, you are confusing me."

"I was the one who sent St. James and Amelia those love letters."

Sophia had to admit that whatever she anticipated hearing, it wasn't that. Her mouth parted. "You?"

He hastened on. "I suppose it could be construed as matchmaking of a sort, but once you imparted to me their interest in each other, I decided fate had stepped in." Under his tailored jacket his shoulders lifted negligently, but his gaze was direct. "You approved of their romance, and I was in a position to help it along. I am not sure how much of a role the letters might have played, but quite obviously everything has turned out satisfactorily."

To say she was struck speechless was an understatement. After a moment she sputtered, "In a position ... how?"

"I had the letters exchanged between Anna St. James and Lord Hathaway," he explained patiently, like he was talking to a child.

"How?" she repeated like a parrot.

"Anna gave them to me. She had the ones he wrote her, naturally, but he also usually sent back her letters when he responded. Because of his wife. He didn't want them destroyed."

That statement took confusion to new heights. Maybe it was the heady scent of all the roses, but she was a little light-headed all of a sudden. "Are you telling me you knew Anna St. James?"

"Indeed. I was supposed to marry her." His smile faded and he looked away briefly. For a moment his face was remote.

She was ... stupefied. There was no other term for it. Richard and Anna? She protested, "It happened too long ago."

"Not at all. She was fifteen years younger than her older brother, the duke at that time."

Sophia did the mental calculation and decided he could be right, for Richard was about the same age as William. Her husband had been almost two decades her senior, and . . .

It *was* possible. More than possible, because Richard would never lie.

Now was as good a time as any for him to learn of one of her questionable habits, if he was serious about this courtship. Sophia shoved herself to her feet and went to the drinks table in the corner, trying to find glasses and the decanter behind a spray of bloodred roses. "Brandy?"

"No, thank you. It's still a little early for me." There was a hint of humor in his voice.

"Do you mind if I do? I think a little libation is appropriate to the moment."

"You don't need to ask my permission, my dear."

That answer was better than bushels of flowers. One of her reasons for resisting the idea of remarriage was how the rigid strictures against her sex confined so many women. William had never censured her in any way, and he indulged her wayward sense of style. The joy of their relationship would be hard to duplicate.

But maybe *not* impossible.

She dashed brandy into her glass and went to sink back down. "Start at the beginning."

His smile was thin. "I don't remember the beginning. Our fathers were friends. We were betrothed at our births. I was only a couple of months older than Anna. We grew up knowing each other. It was an exalted match for me, but then again, Berkeley had six children, and she was the youngest of four girls. I'm the youngest son of a viscount."

It was confounding to think Richard was a part of the St. James and Patton drama. Sophia murmured, "Rather like St. James with Amelia. She could have made a more prestigious marriage, but a love match is always preferable."

"I think so." All three words were weighted with meaning, as was how he looked at her.

Sophia actually blushed, or perhaps it was the first gulp of brandy that warmed her. Still, this story was fascinating. "Go on."

"It's been decades, so I can look at it with impartiality now. I loved Anna," Richard said in a pragmatic tone. "When she developed such a passion for Hathaway, I was unaware of it at first."

"Is that why you never married?" She couldn't resist the question. She'd always wondered.

"Because of Anna?" He seemed to consider it for the first time, his forehead wrinkling. "Maybe so. I hadn't considered it. I think I was just waiting for you."

As a declaration of intent, a woman could ask for little more. Moved, it took her a moment to respond. "No one should be denied true love at least once in this life." Sophia meant every word.

And maybe even twice, if they are extremely lucky.

"I admire your romantic heart." Richard lifted his brows.

"I," she said with asperity, "am not the one who sent old letters to two young lovers."

"Excellent point. I'll concede we both have romantic hearts. See how well we match each other?"

She was coming to the same conclusion.

"You've yet to explain much, Richard."

"At my age, you do not rush into anything." His smile was the usual easy, charming curve of his lips.

"Do not use age as an excuse, and you aren't that damned old."

"I'm glad you think so." Her profane speech—outré for a lady, most certainly—made his eyes light in amusement.

"How did you find out?"

"About Anna and Hathaway?"

"Yes, about them."

"She sent me the letters."

"Why?"

"I think it was to explain why I was being jilted."

"I . . . see." This was important, but the explanation no doubt intruded on his old pain, and Sophia was at a loss. "I'm sorry."

"The letters arrived, and then I was told she was dead."

It was all making less and less sense. "If she didn't know she was going to die, then . . . oh." Sophia stopped, assailed by an inevitable conclusion. "Oh, dear. She did away with herself."

"Not precisely," he said in his calm, unruffled way.

"Not precisely? What the devil does that mean? Either she did or she didn't. There's no middle ground I can think of."

"That's just it." His expression was actually devilish, which no one would ever normally say about the reserved Sir Richard Havers. "Anna is very much alive."

"My lord, you have a caller."

If the infinitely dignified Oates came out of the house himself instead of sending a footman, the caller held some measure of importance.

The butler intoned, "The Marquess of Longhaven is on the back terrace, as his lordship said he preferred to sit outside until your return."

Michael was here? That was interesting.

"We'll be right in." Alex slid off his horse, tossed the reins to a waiting groom, and went to lift his wife from the saddle. They had ridden out every day in the morning since their arrival at Berkeley Hall and today was no exception, the gracious weather adding to the balmy bliss of newly married life. The blue skies wouldn't last forever, and they planned on returning to London soon anyway. But for now the sun was shining, his family was more accepting of his bride than he expected—even his father had unbent a little—and he considered himself blessed.

Amelia looked at him, her crystal blue eyes questioning. "You weren't expecting him?"

"No." He caught her hand, entwining their fingers intimately as they started to walk up the steps to the house. "But as he never does anything without a good reason, I expect this impromptu visit has a purpose. Why don't you go upstairs and change? I admit I am curious to see why he is here."

More than curious, he thought as he watched his wife go down the polished hallway, unable to resist admiring the gentle sway of her hips as she walked before he headed for the back terrace.

Michael was there, lounging in a chair overlooking the gardens, a teacup next to his elbow on a small table. As always, his pose was nonchalant, booted feet crossed at the ankle, his face serene.

Glancing up at Alex's approach, he gave his version of a smile—one that denied the recipient any notion of his true emotions—and reached into his pocket to extract a small oblong box. "I hope you don't mind me calling without notice. After all, this is your honeymoon. Though if you don't mind the observation, I would not spend mine with my family."

"I didn't have time to plan a proper wedding trip, and circumstances dictated I try to settle matters with my father as soon as possible." Alex sat down and curiously eyed the offered box before taking it. "What's this?"

"Your precious key."

He took it, touched the gold filigree clasp, and saw that indeed, nestled against red velvet was a tarnished silver key. "Where did you find it?"

"Let's say I find the earl to be unimaginative and leave it at that, shall we? Upon a few discreet inquiries I learned he kept his father's effects all together and the key was among them." Hazel eyes regarded Alex with a hint of humor. "As this mystery started to unravel, I be-

came more and more interested in finding it. If nothing
else, war honed my deductive powers. It didn't prove,
after all, that hard to locate."

"*I* looked for it." There was a testy note to Alex's
response.

"The hard way. You need to learn to utilize a wilier
approach. Besides, I rather think you were preoccupied
with Lady Amelia."

Now, *that* was true. But at least he had the damned
thing. Alex carefully shut the case. "What mystery
started to unravel?"

"Anna and Lord Hathaway, and then Lord Hathaway
and your grandfather."

"You learned about the duel, I take it." Alex said it as
a statement, not a question. The sunshine slanted across
the flagstones in warm blocks, and Michael said nothing
as a maid arrived with a tray containing another cup and
a fresh pot of tea next to a plate of small pastries.

"Thank you," Alex said to her abstractly, watching
his friend's face. There was more to this visit than that
damned elusive key, obviously, and what Michael was
going to say next he didn't want overheard.

"You are welcome, my lord." She hurried away, Oates
no doubt an exacting taskmaster.

"The duel. Hmm." Michael looked noncommittal
once they were alone again.

That made Alex go still, the steaming cup of tea
inches from his mouth. "I know that tone and when you
look *that* bland. It usually means something. What do
you know, Michael?"

"What did *you* hear?"

"A question to a question. That's never good. It isn't
like you to hedge."

"On the contrary, I hedge very well indeed. Just tell
me what you know, and I'll tell you what I uncovered."

"Fair enough. I owe you for that key and for any
other trouble you've gone through. My father told me

a rather fascinating—and unfortunate—truth the other day, but I'm still far too much in the dark."

"May I venture a guess?" The breeze ruffled Michael's chestnut hair and he carelessly brushed it back from his brow. "He said that Lady Anna drowned herself in the river that borders this estate because she was with child, though everyone was told it was an accident. Stricken with grief and outrage, her brother—your grandfather— challenged her lover to a duel, shot and killed the Earl of Hathaway with no witnesses, and your two families have been locked into a cycle of hatred and accusations ever since because both deaths were covered up as best as possible. Am I right?"

"It is very close to accurate," Alex muttered in consternation. "How did you learn all that?"

"The first rule one learns working as a spy is it is virtually impossible to keep anything a total secret." Michael's brows lifted a fraction. "It might be a jaded point of view, but it is an educated one. For instance, servants know just about everything. When you owe your livelihood to one person such as the Duke of Berkeley, for instance, his problems are of great interest to you. Your grandfather's gamekeeper is an old man now, but he lives in the village. For a tankard—or, shall I say, many tankards—of ale, he was amiable to discussing the incident years ago."

Birds twittered in the trees, lending a cheery note to the less than ebullient conversation. Alex studied his friend with amusement, taking in the tailored superfine coat, chamois breeches, and polished Hessians. "I'm trying to picture the well-dressed, urbane Marquess of Longhaven swilling tepid ale in a village tavern with an old gamekeeper."

"I've consorted with much less well-bred individuals, believe me."

"Actually, I do. I recently recall a tawdry inn where I was certain most of the patrons would gladly slit our throats for the sport of it. So, tell me, what did you learn?"

"The real story . . . or most of it. I admit some is conjecture."

"I'd like to hear it."

Michael's face was expressionless. "Let me outline what I think happened, if you will."

"I'd be in your debt." Alex restively shifted in his chair and tapped the case holding the key. "But I already am. My grandmother will be happy to have this."

"My pleasure." Michael's gaze was speculative. "How would you react if I told you there was no duel, Anna St. James never drowned, and there is a small fortune in sapphires in her coffin, but no corpse?"

Alex choked on a mouthful of tea.

"That's about how I thought you'd take that revelation," Michael murmured with a small smile. "Let me fill you in on the rest."

Chapter Twenty-eight

"Perhaps," the duke said in a frigid voice, "we could go at midnight to search the crypt, carrying torches and chanting incantations."

Alex was unmoved by the sarcasm, his voice carrying a singular insouciance, his nonchalant pose by the fireplace giving the impression the outcome of the conversation didn't matter all that much to him.

Yet Amelia knew it did.

Her husband drawled casually, "Michael is rarely wrong. Besides, he looked. I'm just suggesting maybe we should all look too. I have it on good authority the coffin was never sealed."

His grandmother, Amelia noted, was remarkably quiet. Since she'd seen the fortune in sapphires herself around Anna's neck in the portrait Simeon had dubbed *The Seductress*, she was starting to have a glimmer of what might have happened all those years ago.

Alex said evenly, "Think about it. No good could have come from Anna and Samuel's illicit romance." He glanced at where Amelia sat on the edge of a velvet chair, her sherry clutched in her fingers. "I take that back," he said in a softened tone, his eyes holding a light that made her heart melt. "Something very wonderful came from it, but my point is, I think Michael is right. Anna's death was faked and Grandfather sent her abroad."

Their gazes locked and she wondered with a quiver in the pit of her stomach if they would always look at each other in this special communication, as if the rest of the world didn't exist. . . .

"That's preposterous," the duke said in scathing denial.

"Actually," his mother said coldly, "it's not all that outlandish, Marcus."

"What?" The duke, normally so impassive, stared at her, clearly shaken.

"She was unreasonably infatuated, like only a young woman can be." The duchess sat very upright, like her spine was infused with steel. "As news of the affair began to surface, I talked to her, tried to reason with her, but she would have no part of it."

It was just the four of them in an informal parlor, the windows open to the pleasant afternoon air. Amelia said softly, "Pardon me, Your Grace, but from the tone of her letters, she understood quite well they couldn't be together, nor did she enjoy ruining his marriage."

"What a very young, very foolish woman might understand, and what she chooses to do can often be two different things, my dear child." The duchess lifted her brows. "I believe you are an example. Didn't you recently marry my grandson against your father's express wishes?"

It was impossible to not blush a little over the truth of that statement.

Alex stepped in. "*I* wasn't already married. I believe what Amelia means is that in the tone of their letters they both express a certain despair over their untenable position. If Grandfather saw a way to save his sister from the folly and give her a new life, I think that is a reasonable solution to an unreasonable situation myself.

After all, she had no hope for a future with a man who could not offer her marriage."

"I always think of him as older just because he was my grandfather," Amelia murmured, "but truthfully, he was about Alex's age when this all happened."

"A veritable relic," Alex said sardonically, but his smile was ironic, and she loved him all the more for his attempt to reconcile the situation, especially under the glowering disapproval of his father and grandmother.

"Why not," he said with gentle remonstrance, "just tell us what happened?"

If possible, the duchess sat up even straighter, her regard chilly. "Longhaven alleges this?"

"Longhaven never alleges. It isn't in his nature. If it wasn't true, he wouldn't have brought it to my attention." Alex was reassuringly calm, one shoulder braced against the fireplace mantel. "If he says the jewels are in the coffin and nothing else, I am certain it is true. How he knew the key was to the family crypt, I'm not sure, but he was certain enough that he went to look."

"I wish you'd just found the key and brought it to me, and all of this could have been avoided."

"All of what, Mother?" the duke said irritably. "I find I am in agreement with Alex and his wife. At this point, just explain."

His wife. Well, it wasn't a warm welcome, but it was an acknowledgment of her presence. Amelia said quietly, "The painting being shown in London now. It is of Anna, isn't it? In it, she's wearing a necklace that is a Patton family heirloom. I recognized it at the Simeon showing. My grandfather must have given it to her."

"It was very fashionable at the time to sit for him." The duchess spoke stiffly.

That agreement was a confirmation.

"This is Michael's theory, and in my experience—the Crown will bear me out—he isn't wrong often. Care to hear it?" Alex straightened away from the wall, his expression intent.

"No."

"Yes."

The words spoken simultaneously, the duke and dowager duchess glaring at each other in frosty disagreement.

"Mother, don't be difficult." Amelia's father-in-law transferred his gaze to his youngest son with austere authority. "Please continue. I am tired of this drama haunting my life."

Alex smiled as only he could, with that intriguing curve of his mouth. "I'll start from the beginning. Lady Anna and Lord Hathaway met and fell into undeniable love, and the ensuing scandal threatened both their families. As a result, despite her unconventional approach to life, Anna really had little choice. Her lover wasn't going to leave his wife, and she wasn't going to be his official mistress, but as Grandmother just said, word had already leaked out and rumors were spreading. So she agreed to the pretended drowning. Apparently at some point, she sent her lover the key to the family vault. I was puzzled at first as to why she didn't simply return the necklace, but I suppose what she wanted was for him to discover the truth about her death."

The dowager duchess sat in stony silence.

"For whatever reason, he didn't understand the message." Alex added quietly, "And I believe, Grandmother, you can fill in the considerable gaps in what we know. After all, you are the one who suddenly wanted that key so badly."

For a moment Amelia thought his grandmother would still disdain to provide the missing details, but then the older woman sighed, her shoulders slumping slightly. The lines around her mouth were pronounced. "I should think it is obvious. I wanted to have the necklace for when Hathaway saw the portrait of Anna wearing it, for in his place, I would assume the St. James family had it and demand it back. No one"—she gifted Alex with censorious glare—"was supposed to look in the tomb. That was precisely what I wished to avoid."

"Longhaven can be unpredictable. But don't worry. He won't tell anyone." Alex didn't seem repentant. "Had you just told me the truth, I would have picked the lock and retrieved the necklace, and we could all have been spared the drama, Grandmother."

"I don't have your dubious skills that I won't inquire about, and I hardly wished for you to look in her coffin either. I wanted the key so I could get the necklace myself."

Amelia was starting to understand. Softly, she said, "You didn't want anyone to know she hadn't drowned, even Alex."

"Or your son." The duke's voice was subdued. "Why not, Mother? It isn't as if we would tell anyone . . . far from it."

"Your father made me promise." Her tone was curt. "No matter that he and Samuel were at odds over Anna, he didn't want his family to know he'd murdered his friend."

Murdered? Amelia felt clammy all of a sudden, her palms damp. "He *murdered* him?"

"Not literally, of course."

"Then perhaps you should elaborate." Alex had an unrelenting glint in his eye and he crossed his arms over his chest.

"Fine." His grandmother pressed her lips together and then spoke in a brittle voice. "Here is what happened"—her steely glance touched on them all—"and I expect it to stay in this room. Anna and Samuel first met when the earl visited here, at Berkeley Hall. They apparently formed a misalliance, and unfortunately, unbeknownst to us, it continued. When she miscarried his child, there was no choice; I had to tell Charles." She looked at the duke, her thin hands clenched together in her lap. "You remember your father. Needless to say, he was displeased, betrayed, furious, and yet sorrowful."

"I can only imagine." The duke had regained his formidable composure. "Go on, please."

"Staging her death seemed a logical step. With the pregnancy and loss of the child, Anna realized it wasn't all a romantic tangle any longer, and there were consequences to their actions. She was ruined, Samuel was an adulterer, and it couldn't go on. She agreed to the plan of a false drowning." The duchess paused. "Until a few weeks ago I didn't know the painting by Simeon existed or that she had sent Samuel the key to the crypt."

"How did you find out?" Alex was deferential yet quietly demanding.

Disconcertingly, the duchess turned to look toward her. Amelia stiffened and returned the perusal.

"Anna wrote to me, warning me the portrait existed and that in it she is wearing the necklace. That's when she explained about the key. She'd heard somehow that Samuel's granddaughter was a young woman now, and wanted to make sure the necklace was returned."

Alex was fairly sure he might prefer having his fingernails extracted one by one than attempting to pry information from his grandmother. Gritting his teeth, he said as pleasantly as possible, "You've been in communication with your sister-in-law all this time?"

"Yes."

His father said an undecipherable word and then muttered, "Italy. Sorrento. The estate included a special provision for funds paid there and wouldn't specify why. When I inquired after I inherited, the solicitors refused to disclose the identity of the recipient of the funds. I wondered all along if there was a mistress or an illegitimate child. . . . Why the devil didn't Father just *tell* me?"

The duchess blinked rapidly and swallowed. "He felt horribly guilty, naturally. Marcus, please put yourself in his place. First of all, he fails in his duty to keep his sister's future secure. Then he is forced to face she's fallen from grace, not to mention that she mourns the loss of the child she carried. Her compromised state is no secret, for a midwife had to be called in and servants know everything. Anna was heartbroken twice over, but she was young and the young are resilient. Charles wanted a new life for her and did what he thought best. In England she was irrevocably ruined, but abroad she could begin again."

Amelia's voice was thin and high, but the tilt of her chin resolute. "I am not defending his choices, but explain to me how killing my grandfather would solve anything, especially if he believed her dead."

"Charles didn't kill him. There was no duel."

The resulting silence was profound. Amelia sat with her soft mouth parted, her startled expression a reflection of the general consternation.

"Samuel committed suicide," Alex heard his grandmother say, stunned enough at this latest revelation that he had no comment. "He shot himself by the river, at the spot where he thought she'd drowned. And for the rest of his life, Charles bore the guilt. He'd orchestrated what he thought to be the perfect solution, and he never thought the man he once considered his friend might take his own life once he heard Anna was dead."

"So he lied and said they'd challenged each other to protect Hathaway's family?" Alex asked hoarsely.

"To protect Anna," his grandmother said with impressive dignity. "To protect a man he once considered a friend. And yes, to protect the Patton family also, because he hadn't anticipated the tragic outcome of what he'd thought was a feasible course of action."

"And how did Anna know the painting was going to be displayed?" Alex asked, conscious of his father's continued silence and Amelia's stricken expression.

"I don't know," his grandmother answered with convincing sincerity. "Before her letter arrived, I had no idea of anything about the portrait or the necklace. I knew, naturally, she'd posed for Simeon years ago, but quite frankly, with everything else, I never asked myself what became of the painting. All I wished was to be able to obtain the key and enter the vault so that when Hathaway demanded to know what became of the jewels, I could simply hand them over. If I claimed to not have it, he would wonder what became of the necklace—it is worth a small fortune, as I understand it. He might even demand to know if she was buried with it.... I am not sure how a magistrate would feel about it, but I did not want to risk anyone looking in her coffin."

"Why not simply purchase the painting?" the duke asked darkly. "Once you knew it existed, Mother, why not buy it from young Simeon? He could name his price."

"The infuriating young rascal won't sell it," she snapped back. "The necklace aside, I'd very much like to have it for sentimental reasons, but he won't budge. His bourgeoisie inclinations annoy me. He claims money is an unnecessary evil."

"A painting, Grandmama, would have been far easier to locate than a key," Alex said with a lifted brow.

"I am a St. James. I didn't ask you to steal, Alex. I asked you to recover something that rightfully belongs to our family."

"The key is back in our possession, but that really solves very little." His father had been sitting in an emerald brocade wing chair, and Alex watched as he stood abruptly and paced over to the window, staring outside. "You are right, Mother. We need to face that even if Hathaway doesn't have the key any longer, there is every chance he'll see the painting and demand to know where the necklace is. To be fair, in his place, I would do the same."

"Exactly what I hoped to avoid." Alex's grandmother nodded in terse approval.

"Then, I suppose," Alex said in resignation, "we should go raid a tomb."

*   *   *

It might not have been midnight, but the family crypt was still not exactly a cheery spot, even in the warm late-afternoon sunshine. The small bank of white blooming flowers at the base of the structure did not lighten stones worn with time to a fine gray patina, and lichen had grown along the gothic arched roof. The family coat of arms had faded into an almost indecipherable tracing of forms and words just above the door.

"You do not need to go in," Alex told Amelia, looking not all that eager to do so himself. "Visiting crypts is not on my list of favorite pastimes and certainly both of us don't have to endure it."

"I *would* rather wait here," she agreed, her gaze on where his father now fitted the key in the lock, her smile just a bit wan.

The door creaked open on protesting hinges, the musty smell inside a contrast to the pleasant, waning afternoon. Good sense told her that since the last St. James had been interred a good twenty years ago, the odor was just from the dank, shuttered interior, but still she stifled an involuntary sense of squeamishness.

It was impossible to not take a glimpse at least. The coffins lined the walls, laid neatly in their spots, and the floor was dusty . . . and unmarked.

Her father-in-law muttered, "I thought Longhaven entered the crypt."

"He did." Alex coughed out a laugh, the sound incongruous to the surroundings. "Don't ask me how he didn't leave footprints. Let's just get this over with, please."

When they emerged what felt like an eternity later— but was probably only a few minutes—they were both visibly relieved to leave the confines of the place where no living person ever sought to enter.

It wasn't Alex who approached Amelia but the duke, his face grave, his dark eyes somber. "Here," he said in a remarkably gentle voice for such a distant man. "I think this belongs, in fact, to you, Lady Amelia."

The sparkling jewels caught the light as he handed her the necklace. It was magnificent, but then again, she wasn't sure she was the appropriate custodian either.

The duke seemed to sense her hesitation, for he said quietly, "You were a Patton and now are a St. James. I think that gives you a certain unique right. I think both Anna and your grandfather would want you to have this."

Epilogue

London, one month later

The room was scented with the earthy odor of love-making, and the muscular shoulder Amelia currently used as a pillow flexed as her husband moved. Supine and relaxed, Alex murmured, "That was ... let me search for the word. Exhilarating? No, too tame. Ethereal? That's a bit more appropriate."

Sated and languid in his arms, Amelia stretched and turned. "Considering the events of the day, I can't believe either of us had the energy to do anything but fall into bed."

"Never underestimate my desire for you, and bed is a delightful place to demonstrate it."

Her laugh was smothered against his bare chest. "In public it might cause a splendid scandal, my lord."

"That would hardly be unique to either of our families."

"Aunt Sophie's wedding to Sir Richard did come without much warning," she admitted, brushing her tumbled hair from her face. "It is hardly a scandal, but it is a sensation."

"It might not have been if it wasn't right on the heels of our unconventional marriage." He lightly squeezed one bare buttock.

And he had a point.

"I am still stunned that not only was Sir Richard the one sending us the letters, but he was once engaged to Anna."

"It is an ironic twist." Alex circled one arm behind his head.

"Let's not forget your great-aunt's empty casket."

"It wasn't empty."

"My father was more gracious than I expected, I admit, when he learned that the duke returned the necklace." She rose on one elbow and propped her chin in her hand. "It is odd to think of Anna not as that bold, love-stricken young woman, but old and content in some Italian villa overlooking the bay, married to an Italian gentleman with several children of her own."

"And grandchildren," Alex added, nude and gorgeous, resting against the pillows, his dark hair rumpled. A smile curved his lips. "Not at all the outcome I expected of this interesting series of events."

"I suppose it explains why she never came back."

"Yes, it does, though the story still holds some elements of a Shakespearian tragedy."

Playfully, Amelia trailed a finger down his damp chest. "Not ours. Other than our one balcony scene."

"Your father still doesn't approve of our marriage." He caught her hand and brought it to his lips, tenderly kissing the pad of each finger in a way that made her entire body tingle, despite their recent exertions.

"But he *is* trying. Lord Altea told me the other evening that the two of you had a drink together at your club."

"I see you have spies everywhere."

She laughed as he tumbled her to her back. He nuzzled the sensitive hollow beneath her ear and said, "I have a few questions of my own, you know."

The tips of her breasts hardened as a spiral of anticipation coiled with in her. "Such as?"

"How did you get Simeon's grandson to agree to give my grandmother the mermaid painting?"

Amelia slid her fingers through the silk of his hair. "He wants to paint me nude."

Her husband went very still, his growing erection hot and hard against her thigh. "I beg your pardon?"

"Have I just shocked the scandalous Lord Alexander St. James?"

"I think perhaps you have. Tell me you didn't agree to pose for him naked, Amelia."

Dark eyes stared into hers, and she ran her fingertips lightly along his jaw and then across his mouth.

He had such a lovely, seductive mouth.

"Would you mind?"

"Answer the question, my lady."

"Actually, I agreed we would *both* pose for him naked. He wants to call the painting *The Lovers*."

"You must be joking." Her notorious husband actually seemed aghast.

Fancy that. She really had managed to shock him.

Amelia laughed, wondering if all newly married women felt such joy in the arms of the man they knew they were meant to be with forever. "Actually, I am," she said with a mischievous smile. "The original idea was Venus, like Titian's famous painting, but I convinced him I would be better as Athena, goddess of the hunt, complete with some sort of archery equipment and a gossamer gown. It did not seem like much of a price to pay to gain your grandmother Anna's painting."

"Minx." He kissed the tip of her nose and laughed softly.

"Before you, definitely not. I was standoffish and odd, remember?" She slid her arms around his neck and stretched luxuriously. "Is love always like this?"

"Like what?" He brushed her temple with his mouth.

"Pure happiness."

"Ours is," he said, and took her lips in a convincing, scalding kiss.

And a few moments later, she was convinced even more.

Read on for a preview of Emma Wildes's
next enthralling historical romance

Our Wicked Mistake

Second in the Notorious Bachelors series

Coming in October 2010 from Signet Eclipse

He wasn't often rendered speechless, but Luke had to admit, as he gazed across the elegant, civilized drawing room at the beautiful woman he thought about far too often, he couldn't think of a single thing to say.

Ghostly pale, Madeline sat only a few paces away, her slender shoulders visibly trembling. No simpering ingenue, at twenty-six she was a mature widow with her own fortune, a reputation for wit and impeccable taste, and a darling of society, much sought after by any hostess of consequence.

Sought after by quite a few gentlemen also, himself included. As far as he knew, he was the only one who had ever succeeded coaxing the delectable Lady Brewer into his bed, that one night indelibly preserved in his memory.

For her to be shaken out of her normal serene self-possession told him even more than her words had. Normally she was all poise and sophistication.

Except, an errant voice in his head reminded him, *when she was trembling and breathless in my arms.*

Luke finally found his voice. "I'd stake my life you aren't capable of deliberate malice, so maybe you'd better just start at the beginning and explain what happened. Please include where the incident happened. Who, why, and how might also be useful."

Midnight blue eyes, with a shimmer of hovering tears, gazed at him. "I am not even sure why I sent you that note."

"You know perfectly well why you sent it." It wasn't the easiest task on earth to keep his tone even and reasonable. "Because you realize, despite our differences, that I will help you. So just tell me."

"It was Lord Fitch."

This just got worse. Fitch was a prominent figure in British politics, with influence and money, and he was an earl in the bargain. Luke never liked the swaggering bastard, but that was neither here nor there. His lordship's demise was unlikely to go unnoticed. If the man was dead, there would be inquiries. "He's annoyed me once or twice, but never enough for me to murder him. What happened?"

"I didn't *murder* him," Madeline shot back. He was happy to see her square her shaking shoulders and some color come back into her face, even if it was due to outrage. "I accidentally killed him and it is quite different, thank you."

"I stand corrected." He felt a flash of amusement over her reaction despite the grim revelation she'd just made. "But keep in mind you have yet to tell me the sequence of events."

Her knuckles whitened as her hands clasped together tighter in her lap. "He's been making improper suggestions for quite some time. It has gone well beyond the stage where it is an annoyance and into downright harassment. I loathe the very sight of him."

The blackguard. Luke wished with savage intensity the man weren't dead so he could strangle him himself. "I am not a female and have never been subject to that sort of persecution, but I don't blame you for your aversion to his lordship. In fact, I wish you'd come to me sooner."

"I didn't want to ask for *your* help even in my current circumstances."

The trembling of her shapely body made him want to rise, go to her and take her in his arms, cradle her close, and promise all would be well. But he knew she wouldn't appreciate it, so he stayed where he was, though it took some effort. "Very well, perhaps I deserve that, but let's get back to the matter at hand. Fitch was lascivious and inappropriate. Go on."

"I've tried to avoid him." Her lower lip, so lush and full, quivered. "At every function, in public venues . . . *everywhere*."

"Madge, I am sure you have."

"It didn't work. He deliberately put himself in my path as often as possible."

Luke silently waited for her to continue, stifling futile fury at a man who was already dead.

"He . . ." She trailed off, looking forlorn and very young suddenly, with her pure, averted profile and tendrils of hair escaping from her chignon and caressing her neck. "He has something of Colin's."

Of her deceased husband's? Luke wasn't sure how that was possible when Lord Brewer had died at least five years ago . . . perhaps even six.

With a tremor in her voice, she went on. "I very much want it back and endeavored to bargain with his lordship, but there is one price I am not willing to pay."

Price? His jaw locked. The use of her luscious body. She didn't even have to say it out loud. Luke felt the angry beat of his pulse in his temple and actually flexed his hands to keep from reaching for her when the crystalline line of a tear streaked down her smooth cheek. Even his jaded sophistication was no match for her genuine distress. "He's been blackmailing you?"

"No." She stared at the patterned rug. "Not precisely."

Not precisely. What in the hell did that mean? The gravity of the moment precluded him from muttering *women*, but he had to acknowledge a rising sense of frustration from the lack of a clear explanation. "I don't understand. It seems to me a person is being blackmailed or they are not."

She made a small, hopeless gesture with her hand. "He . . . he knew things. And would mention them at inappropriate times. I began to suspect . . ."

By nature he wasn't a patient man anyway. And when she trailed off again, Luke prompted curtly, "Suspect what? Devil take it, my dear, perhaps I am obtuse, but right now I have little more idea what has happened than when I walked through the door. Just explain it to me so we can deal with this."

"It's mortifying."

"Good God, woman, you just told me you killed a man. If it is mortifying, so be it, but get to the point. With my reputation, I am unlikely to judge you."

For a moment, she just stared at him, her beautiful eyes wide, as if seeing him for the first time. Then she nodded, just the barest tilt of her head.

"Colin kept a journal." She took a deep, shuddering breath but went on. "He was always scribbling something in it. Apparently, he wrote down everything, even details about our . . . our married life. Lord Fitch got a hold of it, though I can't really imagine how. After enough lewd, but accurate, comments and suggestions, I began to realize the odious man *must* have the journal. They weren't friends, and Colin would never tell him anything so private. I can't imagine he'd tell *anyone*. It was the only explanation. *I* hadn't even read it because it seemed like too much of an invasion of Colin's privacy, so I'd locked it away. Sure enough, it is missing."

And, it went without saying, it was certainly an invasion of Madeline's privacy as well. Luke knew she'd loved her husband with all the depth of a woman's first passion, and his death had been a devastating blow to her. He could only imagine the sense of violation she felt over his personal notes and thoughts being read by a stranger.

"I almost had him buried with it." Her voice was choked. "But I suppose I thought one day I might want to read it for comfort."

Instead a heartless toad like Fitch had made a travesty of the intimate writings of the man she loved. If the earl hadn't already met his untimely end, Luke could have killed the worthless scoundrel himself. He said with forced coolness, "Whatever happened to his lordship, it sounds to me like he quite deserved it. Where is he now?"

"In Colin's study." The answer was said in such a low whisper he almost didn't catch it. Madeline looked blindly at the wall, her expression so remote it worried him. One slender hand plucked restively at her skirt.

"Here?" Luke asked.

She nodded, the movement jerky. "I requested a meeting to discuss the journal. It seemed prudent and more to my advantage to conduct business in a way a man would do so, and Colin's study was a logical location. I had Lord Fitch escorted there when he called in response to my note."

At least they were getting somewhere. Luke rose. "Take me there and we'll sort this out."

As if one could sort out having a dead lord in a man's study, but he was willing to do his best. For her. Because, though he didn't wish to admit it, even to himself, Luke had an admiration for Lady Brewer that extended quite beyond her matchless passion and undeniable beauty. Since defining it meant examining his own feelings, he'd avoided too much introspection on the matter, but he certainly had come running when she asked.

That was telling. Knight in shining armor was normally a role he disdained.

Woodenly, with the movements of a person who had suffered quite a shock, she got up and without speaking walked out of the drawing room and led the way down the hall.

Her hope that it had all been some sort of bizarre dream was dashed when, unfortunately, Lord Fitch still lay on the floor in the same lax sprawl, in a pool of his own blood. It was a pity, Madeline thought, because she'd always rather liked that rug, even if it was faded on one side from the sunlight that streamed in through the window in the late afternoons. Since Colin's death she often came in and sat at his desk, the aroma of his tobacco in the jar on the desk familiar and poignant, his pipe just where he left it the day he first complained about the headache that eventually blossomed into a fever, aches, chills, and, within two days, death. The room, with its paneled walls and worn books was a comfort. Or it had been until now.

"I take it the fireplace poker was the method of dispatching his lordship to where even now, I imagine, he is shaking Satan's hand." Luke gazed dispassionately at the dead man, his tone cool and calm. "Not an original choice, but perhaps it is so popular because it is so effective."

"Yes." Lord Fitch had been taunting her ... enjoying it. She could still hear his oily voice. *So, Lady Brewer, is it true you once, at the opera, behind a curtain, you let your husband lift your skirts and ...*

It had been impossible to reason with the gloating old goat and certainly appealing to his nonexistent sense of honor hadn't been effective.

"When a request for him to return the journal didn't work, I offered him money for it. He merely laughed at me and said it was far too entertaining and wasn't for sale." Her voice was low and dull, but the awfulness of the evening had begun to take its toll. "I pointed out that it was mine in the first place and returning it was the least any gentleman would do. He refused and continued to make the most disgusting, insulting suggestions you can think of."

"My imagination is excellent," Luke said in a tone that was pleasant, yet it sent a shiver up her spine. "For instance, I would have chosen a much more painful manner of execution for this piece of refuse right now soiling a perfectly good rug. Finish the story."

"He threatened to publish it."

Damn it all. Another tear ran down her cheek and she swiped it away with the back of her hand, like a child might, but while the last thing she wanted to do was weep in front of Luke Daudet of all people, in the light of this current disaster, she didn't care all that much.

"So you conked him with a poker. Excellent decision."

"I didn't 'conk him with a poker,' as you put it," Madeline said defensively, "just because of that, though I was appalled. Men settle things with violence. Women are more civilized."

With irritating logic, he pointed out, "Ah, perhaps, but I am not the one with a dead man in my study."

Ignoring that comment, she explained haltingly, "I—I had by then realized any further discussion was useless and disliked the way he looked at me, so I got up to go fetch Hubert to escort the man out. When I came around the desk, Lord Fitch— he, well, grabbed me and whispered an extremely repulsive suggestion. He'd obviously been drinking, for his breath reeked. I was close to the fireplace and as I struggled to get away, I must have grabbed the poker for next I knew he was lying on the floor."

"Clearly self-defense." Luke reached into the pocket of his perfectly tailored jacket and took out a snowy handkerchief embroidered with his initials in one corner and handed it to her.

"Thank you." She wiped away another wayward tear.

Luke knelt by the body and took up one limp arm. "He's still warm, so I take it you sent for me immediately. Where's his carriage?"

"That's the one blessing in all this. He must have walked, as he lives only a block or so away."

"What did you tell your staff? Obviously everyone is in bed."

"That his lordship dropped off due to too much drink and that I sent for you to see him home."

"Good thinking." He frowned, his handsome face in profile showing the first true expression of chagrin of the evening. "Only we have one enormous problem, my dear."

One? She'd just killed an earl in her husband's study. She had countless troubles ahead as far as she could tell.

"The bastard is still alive."

"What? There's so much blood!" Madeline stared, not sure if she even believed him, crumpling the fine piece of linen in her hand. "He wasn't breathing—I'd swear it. I checked."

"You were understandably distraught. I am going to suspect, but I can feel a pulse. I'm no physician, but as irksome as it might be, it seems quite strong and steady. Head wounds, also, bleed with notorious profusion. I saw my fair share during the war."

She experienced a wash of relief so acute her knees nearly buckled. "Thank God. While I am not an admirer of Lord Fitch, I did not wish to be the cause of his death."

"You are kinder than I am, obviously. I'd gladly meet him on the field. And if he survives, I just might call him out. However, I can't countenance killing an unconscious man, no matter how much he deserves it, so I suppose our first order of business is getting him home and some medical attention. If you'll just open the door for me, we'll be on our way."

Call him out? Madeline was startled by the lethal vehemence of Luke's tone, not to mention the grim expression on his fine-boned face, but too upset to address it.

Though Fitch was portly, he was much shorter, and Luke heaved his lordship's body over his shoulder with what seemed like little exertion.

"He's bleeding on your jacket," Madeline whispered, leaning limply against the desk.

"I have more clothing."

"I . . ."

Lifting Lord Fitch's plump posterior in the air, Luke looked at her, his brows elevated in sardonic question. "Just help me get this horse's arse out of here, then have a glass of wine and forget it all happened."

How easy he made it all sound.

"Luke," she started in protest. For truly, though she wanted his help, she hadn't counted on him shouldering the entire problem.

"Open the door. I'm going to take care of everything. You needn't give it another thought." His voice was full of quiet, purposeful promise and completely unlike his usual flippant tone.

She moved to comply, preceding him through the quiet town house, helping with opening doors, and when he slipped out the servant's exit, she watched his shrouded figure disappear into the darkened alley, only to hear the rattle of wheels a few moments later.

If locking the door was effective, she didn't know— not as effortlessly as Viscount Altea had accessed her house—but she did it anyway. Then she wandered back to Colin's study. The ghastly stain on the rug wasn't going to be easily dealt with, and she supposed the whole thing would have to be discarded.

And how to explain it . . .

Nosebleed, she pondered, wandering over to stare at the horrible spot, wishing she'd wake up and find it all a nightmare. Could she claim Lord Fitch had a dreadful nosebleed and had ruined the carpet?

Maybe. Until the selfsame lord told the true story. While she was glad she hadn't actually killed him, she wasn't all that delighted he was still going to be able to torment her. Madeline stood there, trying to imagine the rumors that would surface if Fitch spread the word she'd invited him to come to her home, and twisted the reason why. He'd been smart enough to not actually blackmail her, so no real crime had been committed except some repugnant comments. All he had to do was deny he had the journal and accuse her of attacking him without cause.

The facts were the facts. If he'd been spiteful and sly before, he'd be tenfold worse now if he recovered.

If.

She took in a shuddering breath, clenching her hands into fists at her sides. Luke had sworn he'd take care of it.

That was another matter entirely.

Of all people, she'd called on Luke Daudet, the notorious and sinful Viscount Altea, sending her footman haring first to his club, and then apparently to one of the most shameful gaming halls in England.

Which was worse? Being held captive by Lord Fitch's malicious amusement or being beholden to Luke?

She wasn't sure, but certainly counted *this* as one of the worst evenings of her life.

Read on for a preview of Emma Wildes's
next enthralling historical romance

His Sinful Secret

Third in the Notorious Bachelors series

Coming in November 2010 from Signet Eclipse

"This should have been stitched together." Fitzhugh tossed aside the crusty bandage and sent him a level glare of disapproval "I say you should damn the questions and summon a physician to look at it, sir. It's a right nasty one."

Michael returned the look with a small smile, though the injury was sore as hell and the removal of the wrapping had caused a light sweat to sheen his skin. "I am uninterested in having a physician perhaps reveal to someone he treated the Marquess of Longhaven for a knife wound. I've been hurt worse and you've seen to it. Stop fussing and just get on with it."

The older man shook his head but obeyed, cleaning the wound and placing clean linen on it before wrapping strips of cloth to keep the pad in place. Thin, weathered, and trustworthy, he played valet with as much efficiency as he'd performed his duties when they served together under Wellington's command. A few moments later Michael eased into his shirt and surveyed his appearance in the mirror. Clean-shaven and dressed, he looked perfectly normal, except maybe for the faint shadows under his eyes. He hadn't slept well, partly due to the wound itself, and partly due to its cause.

Two murder attempts, a volatile matter to handle for his superiors, and now a problematic wedding night.

No wonder he hadn't managed more than a half doze for a few hours.

His former sergeant had an uncanny ability to read his mind. "What are you going to tell her, if I might ask, my lord?" The form of address still came awkwardly. Fitzhugh was used to calling him *Colonel* and frequently lapsed out of sheer habit.

"I'm not sure." He finished tying his cravat and turned around. "I thought of saying I fell from my horse, but I fear even to an inexperienced eye, it looks like what it is—a knife wound. Eventually the bandage will come off and the scar will prove me a liar. Not an auspicious way to start a marriage."

There was a small, inelegant snort. "The lovely young lady had better get used to half-truths with the business you dabble your toes in."

He ignored the comment. "I have to come up with something else."

Fitzhugh picked up his discarded robe and bustled off to the dressing room to hang it up. It was a warm morning and brilliant sunshine lit the bedroom with golden light. Michael hadn't taken Harry's suite of rooms—it felt like the worst kind of betrayal to take any of his brother's things, and taking any more was beyond what he could stomach. The furnishings were a bit austere, the same as before he left for Spain. Plain dark blue hangings on the carved bed, a simple cream rug on the polished floor, matching curtains at the long windows. He'd been twenty-one when he'd boarded the ship to sail away to war, and decorating was hardly a top priority in his life at that time. Maybe Julianne would care to redo their portion of the Mayfair mansion, but then again, maybe she wouldn't. He knew very little about her really.

It doesn't matter what she might be like, he reminded

himself. He was going to marry her regardless, for his parents mourned his brother with acute grief.

He'd been startled and off guard when they had asked him to please honor the arranged marriage and take Harry's place. Though he wasn't at all sure if years of war and intrigue hadn't hardened him to a frightening degree, there still must be some vestige of sentiment left, for he hadn't been able to refuse. He'd come home, assumed his brother's position, inherited his title and fortune, and now was going to appropriate the young woman destined to be his wife.

It would make him feel much less guilty if Harry hadn't been so infatuated with her and looking forward to the union.

The dutiful letters from home at first only hinted of it. His older brother had mentioned how beautiful she was becoming as she matured, how intelligent and good-humored, how charming and gracious. The final letter, which hadn't reached Michael until Harry was gone and in his grave, had explained how fortunate he was to be pledged to a woman who would not only grace his arm in public and his bed in private, but also enrich his life.

Did Michael feel undeserving?

A resounding affirmative to that question, he thought as he sighed and ran his hand through his neatly combed hair, ruffling the thick strands. He was nothing like Harry. There wasn't an easygoing bone in his body, and his mind worked in circles, rather than straight lines. He'd seen enough horror that he'd come to understand it, and that was frightening of itself, and all the scars he bore were not just skin deep. "My marriage will be a matter of convenience."

"Yours or hers?" Fitzhugh was as blunt as always. "You conveniently go about your business and she conveniently doesn't notice stab wounds, long absences, and late-night comings and goings. Is that how it will work?"

"How the devil do I know how it will work? I have never been married before, but most aristocratic unions—especially those arranged by parents, involve a certain level of detachment. Besides, she's very young. Not even twenty."

"What does that have to do with it?" Fitzhugh furrowed his brow. "She's got eyes, hasn't she? A very pretty pair of them, at that. Now, I say you'd better come up with a good excuse for your current state of incapacitation, Colonel, or there will be all hell to pay from the beginning. I'm guessing from the looks of that wicked gash you're not going to be in top form tomorrow night to claim your husbandly rights. Young or not, that bonny lass will wonder why you didn't enjoy taking her or, worse yet, why *she* didn't enjoy it."

"I can't imagine she'd know the difference between a good performance or a poor one," he said dryly. "And thanks for your confidence in my masculine prowess."

A flicker of humor washed over the other man's broad face. "I imagine you'll get the job done."

"Thank you. Ah, at last, some indication of faith."

"My faith is in her allure doing the trick, Colonel." Fitzhugh grinned. "There's no denying she's a beautiful girl. It wouldn't be like you not to notice."

"I've noticed." Michael turned and restlessly moved across the room.

Yes, he had. The unusual rich color of her glossy hair, like mahogany silk, warm and soft, framed a face that was fine boned and elegant. Her figure was slender but yet nicely shaped in the strategic places, and Fitzhugh was right—the long-lashed beauty of her dark blue eyes was striking. Julianne was a little quiet for his tastes, but then again, he hadn't really ever attempted much conversation with her either.

In his mind, she still belonged to Harry. Unfortunately, he got the sense he also held the same preconception.

It seemed like the worst treachery to ever contemplate bedding the woman his brother had wanted for himself. On the other side of the coin, his parents had set aside their acute grief in celebration of this marriage. His mother, especially, had thrown herself into the preparations for the wedding with almost frantic joy, and it was hardly a secret that in her opinion the sooner a grandchild arrived, the better.

Michael was in one devil of a dilemma because of the murderous assault, and that was discounting the mystery of just who had bloodthirsty designs on his person.

"I suppose I could just tell her the truth. That on my way home from an appointment, someone attacked me. I have no idea why or who he was, but I managed to defend myself, and he ran off. I kept it secret so as not to put a damper on the celebration or worry my mother in her current state of happiness. What do you think?"

"The truth usually isn't your first choice." Fitzhugh looked both dubious and amused.

"It usually isn't an option at all," Michael pointed out with cynical humor. "As for my mother, that is true enough. She has had little joy since my brother's death. Julianne might understand my motivation in keeping such an event from her. I'm sure she still mourns Harry also."

" 'Tis natural. So you do mourn him, sir, or you wouldn't be marrying the girl."

Did he? Maybe. He'd never given himself time to think about it. Sometimes Fitzhugh was too damned insightful for comfort.

Michael gave a philosophical shrug, and then grimaced as pain shot through his side. "I would have to marry someday, so why not her? It's expected."

"Not what *you* expected, sir."

That was true. He said neutrally, "She's lovely and seems even-tempered and not as spoiled as some of the petulant young society ladies I've had the misfortune to meet. At least now I won't be besieged by eager mamas parading their daughters in front of me at every event. All my good friends have married."

For love. Both Alex St. James and Luke Daudet, his comrades and brothers in arms, had found the women who completed them—the women they had to have despite family and social obstacles.

Not everyone was so lucky.

He added succinctly, "It's time, and there's freedom in being a married man."

His valet chuckled, the sound rumbling out into the sunny room. "Freedom? Let me know if you still feel that way in a few months, Colonel."